THE
STORY OF EVIL

Volume IV: The Cursed King

Tony Johnson

Map of Element

Drawn by Tony Johnson

Legend:

△	Mountains
▲	Forests
⚐	Woods
Tϊ	Tropical/Rainforests
S	Swamplands/Bogs
〜	Canyons
⌒	Grasslands
∴	Desert

Dedication

The Cursed King is dedicated to Becca's and my newborn daughter, Ellie, and to any children we may be blessed with in the future. I hope we're good parents that raise you up the right way and that you'll have a positive impact on this world. Always know that you are loved.

Chapter 108

Snowflakes fell from the overcast sky, piling onto the dense white blanket that already covered the ground and coated the trees. Hours earlier, the Frostlands Forest had been a serene location, its landscape marked only by the paw prints of forest critters. Now, the snowy terrain was a violent battlefield.

Crimson Singe cut through the flurries, exhaling an inferno of fire onto a section of the enemy army below. Wheeling around in the air, he struck again, melting another group of monsters with the extreme heat of his flames. The red dragon shrugged off arrows and elemental attacks that harmlessly bounced off his fiery scales. With all the aerial monsters in Silas's army killed in Casanovia, none remained to give him a formidable challenge as he, Alazar's five elect, and their Misengard allies attacked the Python's half of the army; the half Silas had sent ahead to Bogmire to more quickly gain control of the north.

In red armor, the same color as the dragon above him, Steve used the Aurelian Sword to fight through the horde of monsters before him. Twelve weeks had passed since the Battle for Casanovia, and his broken leg had healed, albeit improperly. The Celestial warrior was glad he could help finish off the remnants of the army that had failed to take Bogmire, but a noticeable limp marked every stride he took. It was a disability he'd have for as long as he lived, given to him by his twin brother, Silas Zoran.

"It's six to seven now," Steve called to Ty, pulling his bloodied, golden blade out of the back of a female orc who nearly killed the Elf. "Just because you can control lightning doesn't mean you still don't need me to save you!"

"Streaks are made to be broken!" Ty added to the playful banter, referring to Steve's second consecutive point in their ongoing tally. In the midst of such chaos and danger, they'd made a habit of finding any semblance of light-heartedness.

Moving away from Steve, Ty scanned the battlefield, searching for Shana. He intended to keep his girlfriend nearby to ensure her safety, but the chaotic first phase of the battle had separated them.

Please protect her, Alazar, Ty said a quick prayer, not able to spot her with so much carnage all around. Instead, Ty noticed Misengard warriors, clad in the city's colors of dark and light purple struggling against a group of orcs.

Electrically-charging the blades of his swords, Ty fired two blasts of lightning at the unsuspecting enemies. He ran forward to kill those that weren't knocked down by the attack, smiling as he fought in close-quarters combat, dodging and countering every enemy who turned their attention towards him.

He's letting them close in on him on purpose, Kari could tell as she kept her own enemies at bay near where Ty battled. *He's getting too cocky with his powers.*

"Killing isn't a sport!" she yelled at him, but her voice was lost among the clanging of weapons and warcries.

2

I wish he knew that it doesn't matter if it's a monster, person, or animal; it's wrong to take joy in the death of a life.

Seeing more orcs converge on the twenty-two-year old Elf so that he was vastly outnumbered, Kari moved closer to Ty so she could use her element of water to raise the temperature of the snow in the Elf's vicinity. Steam rose in the air, leaving Ty and the orcs surrounding him in a deep puddle. Knowing he'd be unaffected because of the lightning element employed on his yellow armor, Ty stuck his swords down into the ice-cold water and increased their voltage, electrocuting all the monsters surrounding him.

"I could've handled them," he made his way over to the Halfling archer, shaking his head at the fact he didn't get the glory of defeating them to himself.

On the far side of the sprawling battlefield, Shana held her own against the enemies she faced. Whereas in the Battle for Casanovia she simply blocked with her shield and jabbed with her spear, now, with over three months of training, she employed her improved arsenal of attacks.

When a minotaur sized her up and discharged a plume of flames at her from its weapon, Shana sent a burst of wind from her spear to blow the fire away and avoid being burned. Pointing her metal shield directly at the monster, she fired off a powerful pulse, knocking the enemy backwards into a tree trunk. Before it could get up, she covered her armor in her element, allowing her to sprint forward at a rate of speed unattainable to anyone without the element. Within seconds, she closed the distance between them and plunged her speartip through the minotaur and deep into the bark behind it.

"Keep pressing forward!" she heard Misengard's Captain Emmett Ortega call out. "Victory is within reach!"

Turning to an orc mounted atop a direwolf charging at her, Shana grabbed three throwing daggers on her belt and flung them at the Anthropomorphic Monster's neck. Only one of the three tiny daggers landed, but it was enough to cause the orc to fall off its mount and spasm to death.

The direwolf, however, didn't stop its charge. Shana attempted to use wind from her spear to slow it, but she was too late. With no time to defend herself, the monster pounced on her, knocking her down and sending her spear clattering out of reach. Lying on her back, with her shield being the only thing between her and the Animal Monster's vicious bites, Shana called out to Ryland Artisan, the sentry warrior she'd just seen nearby, but the thin-framed Dwarf was too busy with his own enemy to help.

Forced to wrestle the beast atop her, Shana didn't quit until she got on top of it. Then, using her shield like before, she sent out a pulse of wind, slamming the direwolf through the deep snow and against the frozen ground. Calling the wind to push her spear towards her, she snatched the pole-weapon and plunged its tip into the beast, pushing and twisting it deeper and deeper until the direfox no longer moved and the light in its eyes faded.

Advancing forward, ahead of Shana, Grizz fought more viciously than anyone. The Dwarf dominated the battlefield, using his dual-headed, rock-encased weapon to cleave and crush enemy after enemy. When an ogre attempted to take the Halfman head on, Grizz raised Skullcrusher over his head and powerfully threw it end-

4

over-end into the body of the brute. Then, palming the heads of two nearby goblins in each hand, he lifted them up and smashed their skulls against each other. Since he kept his focus on the elementally-empowered weapon after it left his hand, he recalled it back to himself from where it landed. Once its leather-wrapped handle struck his palm, he closed his fingers around it and sliced the cleaver side of the anvil-headed weapon into the ogre to finish it off.

There it is! Grizz said to himself, spotting the Python in the distance; the target he wanted to kill more than any other. Its sewer pipe-thick body created a ring of protection around itself. Stretched out fully, the rare Animal Monster lay over a hundred feet long. But here, coiled up, it stood ten feet tall, easily killing the Misengard warriors who attempted to engage it in combat.

It's been one-hundred-and-eleven days since this Python killed my wife and son. This is my chance for revenge, he thought as he cut through a horde of goblins on his way to the monster.

Also seeking the death of the beast, Grizz's blacksmithing apprentice, Dart, made his way to his master. "Let me help you!"

"No, it's too dangerous."

"I can help!" the sixteen-year-old was adamant.

"You can help by staying out of the way. Willis!" Grizz gained the attention of the Serendale warrior and pointed to Dart, "Keep him back. I'm going to finish this."

"Kill it for us," Willis called out before Grizz ran out of earshot. Then, taking Dart with him, the red-haired Elf headed to where Commander Krause faced off against a trio of orcs with his glaive. The long, pole-based weapon with a blade attached to the end was perfect for the warrior leader, who, despite his position, was inexperienced in battle and preferred to fight from a distance.

With Dart, Willis, and Krause busy battling monsters, Grizz approached the Python as the sole representative of Serendale. The Halfman watched the giant monster kill more warriors, blasting its lightning element into a group of them. Too blinded by rage to act rationally or strategically, Grizz covered himself in his armor and charged headfirst at the beast.

The Python hissed and spit a stream of venom at the tattoo-headed, black-bearded Dwarf rushing at it. The translucent liquid bounced off Grizz's plate of rock armor, but some of it splashed on the Dwarf's cheek.

Grizz ignored the immediate blistering of his skin. No pain could prevent him from carrying out his mission. In mid-sprint, he picked up a fallen warrior's shield and coated the metal in rock. *I can use this to block more attacks,* he planned, knowing the Python, like all Animal Monsters, had enhanced features of the animal counterparts Zebulon based them off of. *Its venom is dangerous and vastly exceeds the potency of normal pythons.*

Reaching the beast, Grizz swung Skullcleaver into the Python's side, but did little damage. *With a body this thick, it'll take hundreds of strikes to kill it,* he hacked away three more times to no avail.

He jumped out of the way to avoid the Python's lightning and wind attacks, causing him to stumble, which the Python used as an opportunity to encircle the Halfman, barricading him from his surroundings. Unable to climb or jump out of his predicament, Grizz summoned the circle of ground beneath him to rise up so he could escape, but the Python tightened its grasp, tightly coiling around Grizz and crushing him in its clutches.

Grimacing, despite still being protected by his rock-covered armor, Grizz cried out in pain when the Python electrified its entire body. Had Grizz been like any ordinary man, he would've been killed, but his element absorbed the powerful current. However, the Python didn't stop in its attack.

He's going to keep me ensnared like this, pulsing me with lighting until I no longer have the energy to employ my element and am electrocuted. I have to do something.

Looking to the surrounding forest, Grizz focused on the many severed tree trunks, branches, and stones displaced from the fighting. Closing his eyes to focus on as many objects as his powers allowed, he pulled them all towards himself with the greatest speed he could manage. All the debris hit or impaled the Python while Grizz remained safely protected by its body.

Releasing its grip with a pained cry, the Python uncoiled itself and stood before the Dwarf. With its attention lost in its fury, it didn't notice an orange-furred direfox sprint up from behind. Copper sunk his teeth into the beast's head, pulling it down to the ground.

That'a boy! Grizz thought, thankful for the aid Copper supplied in leveling the monster so that the front half of its body was outstretched on the ground. Wasting no time, he used his earth element again by summoning all the surrounding tree roots under where the Python lay to rise and break through the ground's surface. With a simple mental command, they all wrapped around the Python's body, holding the monster parallel to the ground.

At first, the Python violently jerked back and forth, trying to break free, but Grizz subdued its thrashing by using more roots to prevent its escape. Unable to move or blast its elements since its head was forced down, all the monster could do was stick out its forked tongue and hiss incessantly.

Grizz climbed onto the monster and raised Skullcleaver, cursing the beast while slamming it deep into the Python's neck.

The first chop didn't go through. Neither did the second. But the third severed the Python's head from the rest of its body.

Following the death of the army's leader, the morale of the enemy faltered. Some surrendered, but a few of the stronger monsters retreated and regrouped farther back in the forest, refusing to give up.

With his voice as booming as a Giant's despite being a Dwarf, Captain Ortega ordered anyone inexperienced in battle to stay behind while Alazar's Elect and the Misengard Warriors headed to battle the dangerous final enemies. He and his men had years of extensive training, Alazar's elect had their elements to aid them, but others hadn't yet developed the skills needed to be effective against stronger monsters. People like Captain Jarek and his pirates, who Steve had hired to increase the number of their army, as well as the Andonia crew, stayed behind while the others continued the battle.

After a decisive victory, Steve, Ortega, Ryland, and everyone who went after the regrouping enemy returned to find Captain Jarek and his men killing monsters who'd laid down their weapons and gave up fighting. Although Kyoko, Haruto, and Min-ye pleaded with the raiders to end the brutality, they refused.

"Stop this at once!" Steve shouted, coming into the clearing as they gleefully carried out kill after kill. "These monsters have surrendered. Their lives are to be spared!"

"I don't care if they've surrendered. I'm preventing them from killing others in the future!" Jarek slit the throat of a goblin he held in front of him, all while keeping unwavering eye contact with Steve.

This is a direct act of insubordination to me as the future king, Steve knew. *Jarek is trying to show he's under no one's authority and can do whatever he desires.*

"You were commanded to stop!" Willis yelled, reiterating Steve's order.

"What are you going to do about it, Ginger?" Jarek spat at the red-head, daring the Serendale warrior to make a move. Then, looking back to Steve, the former naval captain argued, "You hired my men and I to help fight and ensure victory would be achieved. I'm doing what you paid me too!"

As Jarek moved to grab the next goblin kneeling before him, and knowing he couldn't prevent it in time, Steve called out, "Crimson!"

The red dragon, having observed the altercation from above, swooped down, and breathed flames between the pirate leader's men and those who'd surrendered. Fanning the flames with his wings, Crimson set a strip of trees on fire, creating a wall to separate Jarek from the monsters, allowing them to scamper off into the Frostlands.

Moving to stand over the murdered bodies, Steve gestured down to the corpses. With the hundred-foot cedar trees a crackling wall of flames at his back, he shouted not only to out-voice their intensity, but to ensure everyone why he was so bothered despite their success against the Python's army.

9

"This is not our way! If war takes our honor, then even in victory we won't win. This is not our way!" he drove home the point by repeating it. In a softer tone, he turned to Captain Ortega while pointing to Jarek and those who stood with the ex-warrior. "Have some of your men lead these pirates back to the city. They've disgraced this battlefield and I don't want them here while we take care of our dead and wounded."

Chapter 109

The hearths burned hot, the drinks flowed steadily, and there was more than enough food for everyone to have their fill many times over. Along with the celebrating Misengard warriors, the close-knit group of companions forgot about the state of the kingdom and sat together, laughing, telling stories, and listening to Grizz and Ty's raucous banter. It was only Steve who couldn't bring himself to be in a celebratory mood no matter how hard he tried. Leaving behind the delicious smells and loud noise, the heir to King Zoran's throne quietly exited Misengard's Great Hall. Heading up to the battlements to be alone, he found a secluded spot that offered a scenic, nighttime view of one of the kingdom's oldest cities.

Whereas Celestial was tent-shaped with buildings that grew from shorter outside to taller towards the center, Misengard's design was more sporadic. While it featured ancient architecture and historical landmarks, renovations and additions after decades of tumultuous events had led to a labyrinth-like layout.

In the winter night's chilly breeze, Steve surveyed the landscape from his tall vantage point on the city's wall. Various lights populated everything he overlooked, casting a pale glow on the snow-covered rooftops of many buildings. In the distance, the icy Darien Sea shimmered under the bright green moonlight.

I miss home. I want to go back to Celestial, but the sooner I do, the sooner the words on this sword will come to fruition. Taking the Aurelian Sword out of its sheath at his side, Steve ran his fingers over the tiny words imprinted down the length of the golden blade.

> *Victory will come for either darkness or light*
> *Through one of two siblings, born the same night*
> *To the same father these twins are born,*
> *Sons of evil, to which their father is sworn.*
> *After the death of one of the twin brothers,*
> *The second will sacrifice his life to save many others.*
> *In his death the kingdom will start anew*
> *At the cost of him buried under the city he overthrew.*

"Reading it again, huh?" a voice came from behind, catching him off guard. Steve knew it was Kari before he turned. Even though he'd come to the battlements to be alone, he was happy to have the company of the woman he loved.

"Sorry, I noticed you weren't enjoying yourself and left the celebration early, so I followed you to make sure everything was okay. What are you doing up here in the cold?"

"It's just these words again. I can't get them out of my head," Steve admitted, sheathing the sword. "They're always in the back of my mind. Don't get me wrong, I'm happy we found victory this morning, especially with so few casualties, but I feel like every step closer to reclaiming Celestial is one step closer to these words being fulfilled."

"I know it's bothering you since you told us elect about it back in Casanovia, but you have to remember it's ambiguous. It might not be you it's referring to as the one to fulfill the prophecy."

Seeing Steve's eyes glazed over and that her words offered no encouragement, Kari gently grabbed his face and turned it towards her, forcing him to focus on what she was saying. "Don't get so consumed by death that you miss out on life." Her voice grew softer and sadder as she shared, "Our relationship started off so strongly, but ever since this prophecy I feel like you've been drifting away from me. I want to get back to where we were."

Immediately struck with a pang of guilt, Steve apologized and took Kari's hand. "I know. I want that too. I haven't been distant because I don't love you, it's because I love you so much. I don't want to allow myself to get closer to you just for me to die. I'd never put you through that type of pain." He slammed his fist onto the stone parapet he leaned against. "Sometimes I wish I never got this sword, that I never learned about who I am."

Kari stepped in close to Steve, using her body to block a sudden gust of stiff wind and snow flurries from hitting him. Seeing him shiver despite her interference, she covered her armor in water. While raising the temperature of it to heat the area between them, she said, "Let me ask you something. Take the prophecy out of the equation. Do you want to be king?"

Steve thought for a moment, considering the question. "I don't know. My goal as a warrior has always been to honor Alazar through serving and helping people. Becoming the king will allow me to do that on a grander scale. I want nothing more than to give the kingdom back to the people it's been taken from and try to build upon the great foundation King Zoran started, but the pressure and responsibility of the position seems overwhelming."

"The fact that those things are what you're anxious about shows why you're going to make a great ruler," Kari commended him, and then thought to herself, *Good, by answering my question he's shown he's considered what his life will be like if the kingdom is reclaimed, despite the prophecy. However small it may be, there's a part of him holding onto the hope that he'll survive this war despite what the prophecy says.*

Trying to guide Steve to a more positive outlook, the Halfling encouraged him, "Good news is that people are starting to see you have the qualities a king needs. I heard Captain Ortega has been impressed with you, especially after seeing you carry out the plans to defend Misengard."

"Not everyone supports me though. There were people in Casanovia after I killed Silas who didn't kneel when they found out about my lineage. I don't blame them," Steve was quick to add. "King Zoran dies, then some stranger comes into their city and says, 'I saw a vision that showed me I'm the son of Princess Kyra.'" He shrugged his shoulders. "Anyone could say that and claim the throne. Until there's definitive proof, I won't be able to convince the skeptics. Meanwhile, we'll have more instances like what happened today, with Jarek and his men challenging my orders."

"Well, you won't have to worry about him and his pirates anymore," Kari shared. "I saw Jarek using Sharksbane's metal-plated hull to break through the ice so he and all his ships could sail out of the harbor."

I'm sure he's off to find something more lucrative than what I promised to pay him to fight in our army, Steve thought. *Either that or he left because what happened in the Frostlands made him decide he couldn't stand being under my command.*

Thinking similarly to Steve, Kari added, "You and him never saw eye-to-eye. There'll always be people like that who don't respect you, who don't submit to authority, but the more people see your perseverance, loyalty, and courage, the more it'll be hard for them not to follow you." Kari smiled, showing her confidence in Steve as if she could picture what she was about to say in her head. "By the time you're standing before everyone, giving some epic speech with the Hooded Phantom's entire army on the other side of the battlefield, any qualms they have will be gone. There won't be a single person who doesn't look up to you. And as far as proof of your lineage, maybe when you get your vision we'll figure it out."

"Yeah, when's that going to be?" Steve scoffed at the idea. "It's been over three months since we saw your vision. I'm trying to be patient, but mine is taking longer than all the rest combined."

"It'll come," Kari spoke with assurance. "You're Alazar's elect, too. Otherwise, you wouldn't have seen the visions. However long it takes, it'll be worth the wait. We'll have all five elements and be able to defeat the Hooded Phantom and take back what's rightfully ours."

She's right, Steve nodded, glancing down to his sheathed sword. *I've been thinking so much about the prophecy, I lost sight of the fact our purpose is to free the people of Celestial from Malorek's tyranny.* Convicted of his attitude, he apologized, his second time in the conversation.

"I'm sorry, Kari. I've been so pessimistic and selfish lately, but you've been so patient with me. You always help me stay positive. I don't know how I could do this without you."

The Halfling pulled her boyfriend in for a hug, appreciative of his comments. "You and I are a team. I'll be there for your ups and downs because I know you'll be there for mine. I know it's been difficult for you lately with everything you're dealing with; finding out about your real family, learning the prophecy, and wondering about the people suffering in Celestial. I'm sure you couldn't stop thinking about it all while you sat cooped up, waiting for your leg to heal. But just know, whatever trials you go through, you'll always have my support because I love you. I loved you yesterday, I love you today, and I'll love you tomorrow."

"I love you, too," Steve said, pulling her in for a kiss. After they separated, he exclaimed, "Hey! That phrase you just said was the exact same thing I told you back in Casanovia!"

"I know," Kari smiled. "And I liked when you said it. I was thinking if Serendale has their motto of, 'Strength, Speed, and Safety,' so why can't we have our own?

I loved you yesterday, I love you today, and I'll love you tomorrow, Steve thought. "I like it," he shared Kari's smile. He took her hand in his and led her back down to the city. "Come on, I should've never left earlier. We should be celebrating what we accomplished today. The entire army Silas set out with from Celestial has been defeated. Let's go eat, dance, and enjoy our time with everyone."

As Kari followed along, she caught a glimpse of the Aurelian Sword at Steve's side. Losing her smile, she couldn't help but think what was inscribed on it. Although she'd tried to convince Steve, and even herself, that it wasn't him who the prophecy spoke of, deep down Kari

16

couldn't deny Steve was the only person that fit the criteria. She squeezed the hand of the kingdom's cursed heir in a bittersweet embrace, knowing the prophecy's fulfillment meant taking back Celestial would result in the death of the man she'd grown to love.

Chapter 110

"Kari, Shana, time to wake up," Grizz pounded on the door outside the room the two women had been staying together in since they'd arrived in Misengard.

Groggily awakening and pulling themselves out of bed, the Human and Halfling women both groaned, sore from the battle against the Python's Army two days prior. Farther down the hallway they heard the Dwarf's booming voice say, "Steve, Ty, get up. Captain Ortega wants us all at the barracks in fifteen minutes. He's received word from Celestial."

"Here," Steve tossed one of his neatly-folded tunics across the room to where Ty frantically searched through messy piles, trying to find which articles of clothing didn't smell the worst. The Elf slid into the oversized shirt, combed his fingers through his blonde hair, and followed his brother out into the hallway.

Kari emerged from her room the moment Steve approached it, less concerned about her appearance than Shana, who took longer to make it look as if she hadn't just been sleeping. After she and Steve headed off to the barracks, Shana called out to Ty. "Come talk to me while I get ready."

Relishing every opportunity he had alone with his girlfriend, Ty smiled at the invitation, entered the room and closed the door behind him. Although Shana's back was to him, his eyes connected with hers in the mirror she looked into as she braided her newly-dyed pink hair.

"What do you think?"

"I like it!" Ty exclaimed, knowing she'd been planning to make a switch from her lavender shade to another of the neon colors based on her love for Fluorite Crystals.

"Kari helped me with it. I had to walk her through every step though since she'd never dyed her hair before, let alone anyone else's. I wanted to show you last night, but I thought it'd be a nice surprise for today."

"You should've. I missed you," Ty said, hugging Shana from behind and planting three soft kisses on the side of her neck. She giggled at the tenderness of each peck.

"I still can't believe we're dating," Ty continued holding her, considering himself lucky to be in her company, as he did every day since he'd asked Shana's mom, Leiana, for permission to date her daughter.

"Same here," Shana replied to her boyfriend of six weeks. "It's hard to imagine how bored I would've been being holed up here in Misengard for the winter if I didn't have you to spend it with."

Shana's heartfelt answer earned her more kisses from Ty, who let her go and headed to the door as he said, "We should get going. Grizz said Captain Ortega wanted to see us all in fifteen minutes."

"Fifteen minutes? So we have time to spare?" Shana asked in a flirtatious voice, grabbing Ty's arm and pulling him back towards herself. The two held each other tightly and kissed, first slowly, then more deeply with each successive one. Neither cared to quell the intense passion between them, especially in this early and exciting phase of their relationship.

Twenty-three minutes later, hand-in-hand, and with flushed faces, Alazar's lightning and wind elect entered the commander's council room in the barracks, the last two to arrive.

Although Ortega shot the Elf and Human a look of annoyance at their tardiness, he immediately began his address once they arrived. Looking over the room to the group that included his top Misengard captains, Alazar's Elect, Commander Krause, Ryland, and Willis, he shared, "I gathered you all here this morning because I wanted you to be the first to hear the message we received from a raven that came in from Celestial last night."

A carrier raven is black and black always means bad news, Steve knew. *If Celestial was sending good news, they would've attached their message to a white dove.* Exchanging a nervous glance with Kari, Steve and everyone else eagerly listened to Captain Ortega as he pulled a piece of parchment from his pocket, unrolled it, and read its words.

"An attack on Celestial has left the city destroyed and its people in captivity. Lend us your aide! Many of us have escaped through a secret passage. In uniting, we can take back our capital. Rally your warriors and come to our location. If we don't do this now, their army will grow stronger. Assembling an army of our own is our only hope of saving the kingdom.

"It was signed with the initials, D.C.," Ortega finished.

"D.C. That's Darren!" Ty turned to Steve, bursting with excitement. Explaining the significance to everyone else in the room he shared, "Those are the initials of our brother, Darren Canard."

20

"How do you know?" Ryland asked. "There must be hundreds of people from the capital whose first name and last names start with those letters."

"It's him." Ty didn't qualify the Dwarf's question with an answer because he was confident the raven had been sent by his older brother.

"Why'd he only put his initials down?" Steve asked.

"Maybe he hasn't gotten Cassandra and Lucan free," Kari suggested. "Putting his name down would jeopardize their lives if that message fell into the wrong hands."

"That's the same reason he didn't list the location they escaped to in the letter," Krause added. "If the monsters who attacked Celestial knew where they were, they'd put them all to death before more could join them."

"He told us where he was though," Willis piped up, "Captain, may I see that letter?"

Once Ortega handed it to the red-haired Elf, Willis scanned it and pumped his fist in excitement. With his suspicions confirmed, he gave the letter back to the Misengard leader and instructed, "Read the first letter in each sentence."

"A-L-M-I-R-I-A," Ortega announced each letter individually. "That must be where the group escaped to. Whatever secret passage they used, maybe we can enter Celestial through it. This could give us a tremendous advantage in taking back the city."

"It will, but only if we go about this strategically," Shana stressed. "I'm assuming Darren sent that message to all the Primary Cities he could. Plus, when we were in Casanovia, we sent ravens to every political, warrior, and cleric leader to ensure they all knew what occurred. At his point, every province should know of the ongoing war and the threat to the kingdom."

"Why don't we send out another letter and ask them all to meet us in Almiria?" Ortega gave his input. "We've known for months now that recruiting help from throughout the kingdom will be the next goal in our efforts to take back Celestial. Winter should end in a couple of weeks. Large groups of people will finally be able to travel. They can start heading to Almiria."

Willis supported the captain's idea. "People will be more likely to join our cause if we bring them up to speed and tell them Alazar's new elect have joined together and that the newly-revealed grandson of King Zoran is leading the rebellion."

"We'll do that, but I don't know if it'll be enough," Krause spoke up. Since he was the highest-ranking warrior in the room, because of Misengard's Commander not being present, he felt it was important to share what little expertise he'd acquired from his time in Serendale. "From my experience, the best way to recruit is to ask in person. A letter doesn't carry the same weight as it would for them to hear of the horrors we've experienced first-hand."

Ortega nodded, deferring to Krause. Although the Dwarf was nearly forty, near in age to Krause, Ortega only held the rank of captain. For eighteen years, the moniker preceded his surname. Misengard's lazy and manipulative commander knew Emmett didn't want a family and cared only about his service, so he got him to do all the hard and dangerous work, teasing his promotion like a carrot put in front of a donkey; in sight, but always out of reach.

In his fully-colored armored suit of purple pieces, Ortega surmised, "The last thing I want is to only have a few cities take this lightly and we end up like the warriors in the Second Great Battle who didn't summon enough of an army to fight Draviakhan. People had to survive under that monster's regime after that failure. We can't allow that to happen again. That's why I think it'd be good for leaders in the Primary Cities to see your elemental abilities. They'll known you aren't making up your story."

"Do you have any idea how long it will take to complete a kingdom-wide, face-to-face recruit?" Ryland asked, his tone suggesting it wasn't worth the time.

"We can't rush back to Celestial," Steve spoke up. "I know people there are hurting, but we need to take our time and build our army. We only get one shot to take back the capital. Ortega's right. To fail will set us back years, maybe even decades. This is the most important battle of our lifetimes. That being said, I think if we split up it'll speed up the recruiting process."

"It's the most efficient option," Captain Ortega agreed, scanning the room to see if anyone had a better alternative.

"Is it the wisest move though?" Willis posed the question and looked from where Steve, Kari, and Grizz sat and then over to Ty and Shana. "You five are the elemental elect and our greatest hope in this war. That means you each have a target on your back. Being separated from each other will make it easier to be picked off one by one."

Steve nodded, knowing the Elf always looked out for them. "There's no doubt there's strength in numbers, but I'm willing to sacrifice safety to grow our army. Long-term, this is our best option. And I don't expect us to go individually. Traveling in pairs would be wisest. Are you guys all good with this?" Steve asked his companions.

With no objections, Ortega wheeled a giant globe of Element from the corner of the room to the center. With everyone able to see it, he said, "We should visit any

Primary City that hasn't seen the monsters under the Hooded Phantom's control."

"That would be all except Celestial, Serendale, Almiria, and Casanovia," Kari listed them off. "How should we split up?"

"I don't need another elect with me," Grizz offered. "I know you two like each other," Grizz pointed from Kari to Steve, "and you two can't keep your hands off each other," he pointed from Ty to Shana, "so you should travel in pairs."

The four smiled, finding it funny the Dwarf considered the group's relationships.

"I can take Willis, Copper, my apprentice, and my son with me."

"I'd like to come to," Krause spoke up, looking anxiously at Grizz. "With me along you'd have everyone from Serendale working together."

Grizz hesitated, uneasy with allowing the commander to accompany them. Although he no longer sought Krause's death for the commander's abandonment of Serendale, he still wasn't at the point where he was ready to forgive the Human.

Knowing their tumultuous history and that traveling together could provide an opportunity for reconciliation, Steve pushed for Krause's inclusion. "How about it Grizz? Having a commander with you would help add a level of legitimacy when you're recruiting."

Grizz crossed his arms. *Krause isn't my favorite person, but he's apologized to me and despite his past tendencies to shy away from battle, he overcame his fears and fought alongside us in the Battles for Casanovia and Misengard.* "I suppose having one more in our party can't hurt," Grizz turned to the warrior leader and spoke about him instead of addressing him directly, "but he's lost his right to give orders. I'm in command."

Krause held his hands up. "I'm fine with those terms. I just want to help in whatever way I can."

Willis piped up, not as agreeable. "With all due respect to you, Grizz, I'm a warrior, so I take orders from no one but my commander. Regardless of if we're in Serendale or not, I can't follow anyone but Krause."

"My orders are that you follow the blacksmith," the mustached-commander made his will known, eliminating any potential controversy.

"What cities do you want to go to?" Ortega asked Grizz, moving the conversation along.

"I spent a few years of my life in Twin Peaks. I know its layout and leaders. That's where I want to go. Plus, I want Nash to see where his ancestors came from."

"Are you sure taking your eight-year-old along is a good idea?" Ryland asked. "It'll be dangerous in the wilderness. I'm sure there's someone in this city who would look after him."

"He's coming with me. That's not up for debate," Grizz objected to the fellow Dwarf that in physical appearance differed from him in every aspect. "Nash is safest when he's in my care."

"You know what's best for him," Ryland shrugged his shoulders in a passive-aggressive way that showed he didn't really agree with Grizz.

Standing and moving to the globe, Steve traced his finger from Twin Peaks to a couple other cities, trying to determine the best path for Grizz and the Serendale team to take. "Do you think you could travel to Bogmire after that and then take all the troops you've collected and head to Almiria?"

"Sure, I don't see any issue with that. We could even stop by Casanovia at some point and check in with Captain Nereus."

"And Ishaan Artazair," Shana took the liberty to make a note about her hometown. "Almiria's naval commander stayed in Casanovia to watch over his city's people. You should connect with his as well."

Steve nodded, confirming the plans for Grizz's team, and then turned to his brother. "Ty, I know you don't like sailing, but we have Jun-Lei here with us in Misengard. I'm sure she'd sail you and Shana to Elmwood. It's not far from here. After that you can head to Oceanside, covering both Seacoast cities."

"As long as she's got enough ginger root to quell my seasickness, it won't be a problem."

"Ryland, you can go with them," Ortega determined.

"I thought I'd go with Steve and Kari," he countered and turned to the red-armored nineteen-year-old. "If anyone should have added protection, it's you, Brightflame."

"I'd accept your offer, but Kari and I are left with heading to the two desert cities of Al Kabar and Stonegate. We'll never make it through Deletion on foot, so I was thinking we'll have Crimson Singe fly us. Three people would be too much for him in covering that distance."

"That's alright," Ryland waved it off. "I have no problems going with Ty and Shana on Andonia."

With two-thirds of the parties finalized, Kari turned to Steve and said, "There's a place I was thinking we could make a stop before Al Kabar and Stonegate. What do you think about Holders Keep on Mount Anomaly? We could offer freedom to anyone who volunteered to fight for our cause."

"Releasing hundreds of the worst criminals back into the kingdom is a bad idea," Ryland critiqued the notion.

Kari cut the pale-skinned Dwarf a look. For so many people in the room, many of whom ranked higher than Ryland's sentry warrior status, the middle-aged Halfman seemed to be adamant about countering every proposal made. Ryland, oblivious to the many disapproving glares in his direction, continued without pause, "Those prisoners were put there in the middle of nowhere for a reason, because their crimes were so heinous we wanted to get them out of society forever. To unleash them would be an injustice to the warriors who worked so hard to put them there."

"People deserve second chances, Ryland," Shana stated, siding with her Halfling roommate.

Again, the warrior opened his mouth to speak, but Steve interrupted him, settling the issue. "I'm okay with their release. We need all the help we can get, especially after losing Jarek and his pirates. And we could easily make that detour work," he traced his finger from Misengard to Holders Keep, and then from Holders Keep to their two other destinations in Deletion. "After we're done in the desert, we can head to Triland. Ty and Shana, that's close to where you'll be, so we can rendezvous with you there and set out for Almiria together."

"I can have doves sent to all the cities, letting them know they'll soon be visited by one or more of Alazar's elect, and, if they want, anyone interested in fighting can be sent in advance to Almiria," Ortega proposed.

"Let's keep the detail about Almiria being where our army is stationed out of the letters," Steve interjected. "That should be kept top-secret so it doesn't get out and the enemy attacks the people there. Instead, let's simply collect the volunteers in each city and tell whoever's

27

leading them to head to Almiria. There, they can forge weapons, armor, and other battle structures. We can also start training anyone sixteen and older in the basics of battle, just like we did in Casanovia. Ty's been doing that with Jun-Lei's crew and he was training Jarek's men before they deserted. After we feel like everyone's prepared, we'll determine our plans on how to best confront the army and take back Celestial."

As everyone stood up, now that the plans were finalized, Willis told the group, "I've heard people talking about the state of the kingdom and what's to come. They're already referring to this time as the Third Great War and the Battle for Celestial will determine the victor."

"It's ironic then," Steve shared his observation. "King Zoran built Celestial over the location where so many of our people died in the Second Great War. Now, there's going to be another battle on the same lands and the outcome will forever change the course of history."

"Let's hope we're victorious, this time."

"We will be," Steve replied with brazen determination.

Chapter 111

Twelve days after their plans were made, the three groups of travelers met at Misengard's docks. Although the snow was melting, the weather was still cold, forcing everyone to wear long-sleeve tunics or cloaks over their armor to combat the shiver-inducing chills.

"We won't be seeing each other for a while. Take care of yourselves," Steve hugged his brother and half-sister.

"I'm glad I'm headed to Elmwood and not Holders Keep like you," Shana told Steve. "I'll take sailing on a ship over riding a dragon any day," she glanced nervously at Crimson Singe. Although she'd fought in two battles where the aerial monster wreaked havoc on all the enemies he encountered, her heart beat faster every time she was close to the giant red dragon.

Next to his green-armored, pink-haired girlfriend, Ty bent down to Nash. "You take care of your dad, okay?" he made the boy promise, instilling a sense of purpose in the eight-year-old Dwarf. After Nash, Ty said goodbye to Grizz and the rest of the Serendale crew. He ended with Copper, who everyone loved as much as a household pet, before following Shana and Ryland up the gangway and onto Andonia.

"We all have our assignments," Steve announced. He called up to Ty, Shana, and Ryland, where they looked

29

down on him from the ship's main deck. "Kari and I will meet you in Triland. The rest of you, we'll rejoin each other's company in Almiria. Until then, may Alazar protect all of us in our travels."

Everyone waved goodbye to those on Andonia as Jun-Lei steered her ship out of the harbor and towards Elmwood. The three patchy sails of the old vessel grew smaller and smaller as the shipmaster settled into a wind current and allowed it to propel her ship forward.

"I hope they brought enough ginger root for Ty," Grizz joked, playfully bouncing Nash on his shoulders to mimic the rise and falls of Andonia over the choppy waters. "I can't believe he chose to set foot on that ship after how seasick he got."

"If it wasn't for Shana, it'd be one of us in his place," Kari said. "But he's so head over heels for her, he'll do anything to stay by her side."

While everyone smiled, thinking about the over-the-top affection Ty and Shana had been constantly showing each other, Grizz announced, "I guess it's time for us to head out as well."

Kari caught a look of sadness pass over the Dwarf's face. *Maybe he's seeing Steve and me in love, as well as Shana and Ty and it's making him miss what he had with his wife.* She felt sorry for the twenty-eight-year-old Halfman, but then noticed Grizz once again started bouncing his son up and down. *He's sad, but he's reminding himself of what he has,* she could tell, glad Grizz had found a positive outlook, rather than drowning himself in his sorrows.

The father and son headed over to where four horses stood. Grizz mounted one of the steeds, setting Nash securely in front of him. Krause, Willis, and Dart each planted their foot in the stirrups of their own horses to vault themselves up into their saddles. As Kari said goodbye to the three men, Grizz and Steve shared their own farewell. What was once an arduous rapport between the Dwarf and Human had grown into a friendship of mutual respect.

Speaking to Steve from atop his horse, Grizz told his Human friend, "You stay safe out there. You're our king and our leader. We'll need you in Almiria. Maybe when I see you there, you'll finally have your element," he teased. "We can train against each other."

"Let's hope I do better than our scuffle in Casanovia," Steve smiled at his self-deprecating reference.

Grizz belted out a hearty laugh as the rest of his party trotted over to join him. He moved his mouth to the side, clicked his tongue three times, and lashed his horse's reins to gallop away.

"Speed, strength, and safety to you two," Willis followed after Grizz, but briefly stopped to quote Serendale's warrior motto to Steve and Kari.

"And the same to you," Kari nodded, putting her arm around Steve as they watched the group take off towards Twin Peaks.

The men soon rounded a corner, leaving behind only a trail of horses' hoofprints, intermixed with the indentations made by Copper's massive paws.

"Now's our time to say goodbye to Misengard," Steve stated, taking Kari's hand and walking towards where Crimson waited for them.

"Shana wasn't the only one nervous," Kari admitted as they approached the dragon. "I've never flown before."

"I felt the same way my first time," Steve tried to quell her fears as the giant, red-scaled monster lowered himself to the ground so the Human and the Halfling could mount him. "Every warrior trainee test-rides a flying monster when deciding if they want to serve their career as a land, naval, or aerial warrior. Once you get up there though, it can be fun, even relaxing if you allow it to be."

"I'll start off nice and slow," Crimson promised, sensing Kari's apprehension. "If it's too scary, or you feel sick and need to land, just shout out to me. I'll hear you over the wind."

Everything's going to be fine. All I'm doing is mounting a really large horse with wings, Kari told herself as she grabbed one of Crimson's spikes and pulled herself up onto his back. Plopping down in the saddle Crimson had been fitted with, she strapped herself into the leather harnesses and took a deep breath.

Steve checked that their bundles were securely tied down, climbed up into the saddle in front of Kari, and fastened the buckles of his own straps. Before he forgot, he took a pair of blacksmithing goggles from around his neck, placed them over his eyes, and handed an extra pair to Kari. "Here, Ty got us these and said they're helpful in protecting your eyes from drying out."

Once Kari put them on, Steve patted the scales on Crimson's neck. "We're ready!"

Extending his wings outwards, showcasing a wingspan twice his body length, Crimson powerfully flapped them up and down as Kari closed her eyes and wrapped her arms around Steve's midsection. The dragon's massive body quickly rose into the air, where he caught a strong breeze that he used to ascend even higher in the blue sky. The wind increased dramatically the more they climbed, as did the chilling cold.

"Here comes the worst part," Steve warned Kari, "Your ears are going to pop from the elevation." Once they did, and Crimson found a comfortable pace to fly forward at, Steve excitedly told Kari, "Alright! Open your eyes!"

The moment she dared to peek, they flew through a giant, white cloud, so nothing was visible. But when they broke through it, Kari gasped.

For a moment, the sight was dizzying, but the temporary effect of nausea quickly subsided and was replaced by an awe for the beauty of the landscape beneath them. Misengard sat encompassed by the Valpyrio Mountain Range. The sprawling city featured tiny roads snaking back and forth in disorganized fashion.

There's their arena! And there's the giant library with its glass-dome ceiling, Kari enjoyed spotting the various landmarks she and Steve had explored together during their time in the city.

To the north of Misengard, dozens of ships floated on the Darien Sea. *They look like flakes of pepper on a giant tapestry of swirling blue. Ty and Shana are among them,* Kari knew, although she was too high to make out the details that'd allow her to distinguish Andonia from the rest.

"What do you think?" Steve asked, turning in his saddle to see Kari behind him.

"Flying's not so bad!" she smiled, continuing to look around, taking in the sights. She even dared to release her death grip around Steve's stomach and outstretch her arms to feel the cold wind through her fingertips.

For the next several hours, they flew east over the Frostlands. Everywhere else on Element the snow melted away, but the Frostlands remained blanketed year-round. Many small villages populated the serene landscape, some of which Steve and Kari asked Crimson to stop at when they needed to eat or use the lavatory. Anytime they did, they brought the locals up to speed on the war and asked for volunteers willing to head to the nearest city of Casanovia where they could join others headed to Almiria.

When night drew near, Crimson made one last push to cover as much of their route as possible before eventually setting down on a beach near the northwest point of Lake Azure.

"We're outside the borders of the nearest province," he warned his riders. "There's a higher chance of encountering monsters now that we're outside the boundaries of the kingdom, but I think we'll be safe here. You don't even need to stay up and keep watch. I'll encircle you with my body, so anything that might want to harm you has to go through me."

Having eaten supper only hours prior, all that was needed for preparations for the night was collecting firewood from the nearby woods, which, once set in a pyre, Crimson set aflame with his element. The friendly dragon, exhausted from the day's travels, promptly collapsed in the sand and fell asleep. The flickering firelight bounced off his scales, making them glimmer as Steve and Kari unclasped their bundles and set their makeshift beds next to each other.

"So flying's not as bad as you thought, huh?" Steve asked.

"Not at all," Kari smiled, realizing she had worked herself up to the point that she made it more intimidating than she needed to.

Sitting in the sand in the reverse position of their riding formation, Steve massaged his girlfriend's shoulders while gazing into the shifting fire. Along with Kari, he listened to the peaceful sound of crickets chirping in the woods mixed with the rescinding high-tide waves.

"Look at the sky," Steve gestured, pointing out the millions of stars, each sparkling individually.

"It's beautiful. You can't see the heavens from cities. Remember the first time we were out in the wilderness like this under the stars?" Kari asked Steve even though she wasn't facing him.

The Evergreen Forest. "That was over four months ago," Steve recalled, reflecting on how much they'd been through and how close they'd grown in their relationship together. "It makes me wonder where we'll be four months from today."

"Well," Kari theorized, "we'll have already collected warriors and volunteers from all the Primary Cities and have attempted to take back Celestial. The kingdom will be reclaimed or the monsters will have achieved victory against us, and I refuse to believe the latter."

Steve nodded. "I hope we're successful. And despite what the prophecy says, I hope I'll still be alive when it's all said and done. More than anything, I want you and me to be together once this war is over."

"I want that too," Kari reached up to her shoulder and caught Steve's hand in her own. Not releasing her grip, she stood up, moved to sit behind him, and began working out the many knots in his back caused by constant stress. "I also want to have found the answers about my father. I hope we'll learn what happened to him through your vision."

"I can't believe Malorek set him up as the murderer of all those warriors, but at least we know he survived. I'm trying not to set my hopes too high that he's still alive, but if he is, I'd want you to meet him. I think you'd both get along. I don't have very many memories of him, but what I do remember is that he was always looking out for me. He cared for me and he cared about being a warrior and serving the kingdom. You're just like him."

Having gotten out the knots, Kari patted Steve's back to signal she was done. They shared a sweet, tender kiss and slid into the warmth of their bedrolls.

"If you get too cold, wake me up and you can have my blanket," Steve offered.

"I'll be okay, I don't want you to be cold and get sick."

"Maybe Alazar would bless me for my chivalry and give me the fire element. Then I could just lay here in my armor on a low-warm setting."

"I'm sure if you got your element you'd be running all over this beach with your sword, testing out what you're capable of!"

"Yeah, you're right!" Steve laughed, knowing it was true. "Alright, sleep well, Kari. I love you."

"I love you too," Kari said, before closing her eyes and drifting off to sleep amidst the crackling fire and crashing waves.

Steve woke in a panic, inhaling a breath that pushed his lungs to their capacity. In his sleep, he'd rolled out of his bedroll and lay in the sand next to it. Jumping up, he reached for where Aurelia sat propped against his bundle.

Where am I? he questioned, wiping the sweat from his brow. His heart raced until he found Kari peacefully sleeping next to the orange embers of the dying fire. *Another nightmare*, he shook his head in disgust. *That makes the fourth one this week.*

"Bad dream?" Crimson asked Steve in a hushed voice, careful not to wake Kari. Even in his attempt to be quiet, his voice boomed across the beach, but the Halfling merely turned over, muttering in her sleep.

36

"Sorry to wake you," Steve got up and stretched, planning to pace around until his heart-rate settled down.

"Don't worry, you didn't," Crimson made it known he'd already been up. "I used to love when Oliver would tell me his dreams. Do you want to tell me yours?"

"It's a reoccurring one that won't seem to go away. Instead of me killing Silas, it was him who killed me. He lived out my life of being adopted, becoming a warrior, and surviving the attack on Celestial and I was the twin who grew up in the castle, betrayed my grandfather, and led part of the Phantom's army only to be killed in Casanovia. I guess it stems from how lately I've been wondering if we switched spots if I would've turned out like him."

"Like Silas?" Crimson pondered. "I don't think you would have. With Alazar's creations, everyone is different, even twins. Who a person becomes depends on their personality, their choices, their environment, and the events of their life. Even if you and Silas grew up together and did everything exactly the same, you still would've turned out unique from one another."

"I'm sure you're right, but I just wonder how different things might be if minor aspects of the past were altered."

I wonder who I would be now if Thatcher wasn't the one who adopted me, or if I didn't decide to follow in his footsteps and become a warrior? What if things had gone differently? Steve's mind trailed off before returning to his conversation with the giant, red dragon. "I'm not saying I wish I could change my life," he clarified, "but it makes you think about what could have been."

Crimson nodded, understanding why Steve was so bothered. "It's interesting, isn't it? This entire war stems from the life of Malorek. Had it gone different for him, I don't think we'd be here right now."

Like Steve, the dragon had no answers in response to their ruminations, but he tried encouraging the warrior by saying, "Just remember that soon, how the kingdom fell and how events have played out won't matter. Celestial will be ours and you'll be able to rest peacefully."

Steve chuckled to himself, realizing the morbid irony of the dragon's words, considering what the prophecy on the sword in his hand said. Moving the focus of the conversation away from his stressors, he asked Crimson, "Why were you awake?"

"You're not the only one with a lot on your mind. I've been reflecting on the past few weeks living in Misengard and getting to be among people. Getting to see the glow on the faces of everyone in the villages we visited today was wonderful. It's what I've always wanted: to be part of the kingdom I helped Oliver claim. But we knew Nightstrike was after me for killing his father and if I didn't live in isolation, I'd be bringing unwelcomed danger to any city I was in."

"We'll have to kill Nightstrike when we take back Celestial so after he's gone you can live there and experience that kind of happiness every day."

With sharp white teeth glistening in the moonlight, Steve noticed Crimson Singe smile at the idea. For a moment, he wanted nothing more than to march to Celestial and help the dragon attain what he desired. *He deserves to get whatever he wants, considering he risked his life for our kingdom and defeated the evil of his generation.*

"I know what we'll be up against," Crimson acknowledged the tough challenge awaiting them, but remained undeterred in playing a part in helping overcome them. "This sense of dread and unease surrounding this war reminds me of how things were back during Draviakhan's reign. We were all stressed and worried about what was to come. It affected our daily life, even our minds at night," Crimson referenced the reason he and Steve were awake. "But despite the darkness, we found glimmers of hope. I used to find mine in Oliver's and my friendship."

Crimson remained talking, but looked up to the red moon, not allowing Steve to see the twitch in his face as he shared, "Traveling with you today reminded me of the old times. When you climbed up onto me, it took me back to when Oliver used to do the same. Today was the first day anyone's flown on me since he did."

"I can tell you miss him," Steve noticed the dragon's forlornness. "I know he was your friend."

"He was, and more than that, he helped make me into who I am and what I stand for. What I wouldn't give to have one last moment with him, just the two of us. It's not like we didn't have a proper goodbye after we defeated Draviakhan, but one more moment together would've been nice."

That's exactly the same thing I wish I could have with Thatcher, Steve thought.

"I would've loved the chance to talk to my grandfather more," Steve echoed Crimson's desire. "All we had was a brief conversation in the King's Tower. It would've been nice to get to know him better."

"I'm sure he'd be proud of you and what you've accomplished."

"I haven't done much yet," Steve admitted. "And our accomplishments mean nothing if we fail to take back Celestial. Even if we reclaim the capital, I might not even be alive to be king," Steve sighed, once again bothered by the prophecy, despite his talk with Kari.

The red dragon took a long, strange pause before he responded, "I know there's a lot on your mind, but sometimes allowing yourself to have a break so you're not over-analyzing everything can help relieve the stress of the weight on your shoulders."

Kari encouraging me to celebrate in Misengard helped me to do that, Steve remembered.

"Don't let these things overwhelm you, especially the prophecy." Crimson looked like he wanted to say something important, but he only replied, "There are things you don't know yet. Someday soon you'll be able to step back and see the bigger picture and it won't seem so intimidating."

"You know something, don't you?"

Crimson didn't answer one way or another. He simply said, "The only advice I can give is the same thing Oliver used to tell me. Hold to your faith and do what is in accordance with it and you should always be on the right track."

"I'll keep that in mind," Steve promised. He began to walk back to the campsite, but stopped and turned back to the dragon, unable to shake the feeling that Crimson was awake for more than the reason he'd mentioned. "Is there anything else you want to talk about?"

Crimson sighed, a heavy breath from deep within. "Everything's fine," he replied, despite an expression of consternation on his face. "Goodnight, Stephen. Sleep well."

Steve nodded, knowing if Crimson Singe wanted to talk, he would have, but the dragon kept his burdens to himself.

Chapter 112

It took nearly twenty-four laborious hours to navigate through the Darien Sea where ice build-ups had not yet melted before Jun-Lei was far enough away from the coast to sail swiftly. Now, on their second day of travel, Elmwood was only two more days away, but attempting to recruit the city's warriors to Andonia was the last thing on Ty's mind.

"How is she?" Jun-Lei and Haruto came into the forecastle cabin, where the blonde-haired Elf sat on a chest next to Shana's bunk, changing out a cold compress for a new one. She moaned as he dabbed her sweat and gently placed it across her forehead.

"She's not any better," Ty shook his head. "She's been throwing up and has barely said a word. I don't understand what's wrong with her."

"That's what Haruto and I came to talk to you about," Jun-Lei revealed. Turning to her nephew, she beckoned him to explain what he'd found.

"I searched through my medical books to find what these purple rashes are that are covering her body, and it's pretty clear she's contracted the Henshura Virus. It's a potentially fatal illness someone can get through ingesting a specific concoction of berries."

"She was poisoned?" Ty came to the conclusion Haruto was leading to.

"Yes," the Elven warrior confirmed while lifting Shana's pant leg to examine her sores. "The symptoms usually present themselves two to three days after contraction. Do you remember her complaining about a bitterness in anything she ate or drank back in Misengard?"

Before he could answer, Shana grabbed the bucket at her side and heaved into it. Ty hurried to grab a towel and wipe the vomit dripping off her chin.

"I don't remember anything like that. And I don't know anyone who would want to harm her," he said as he drew on her arm to comfort her. "Maybe she was a target because she's one of Alazar's elect, but why am I not suffering from the same symptoms?"

"We thought about that too," Jun-Lei mentioned, "But since you are fine, maybe whoever did this only had a certain amount of poison, or maybe they were interrupted before they could carry out their mission to hurt you and the rest of your friends."

Pulling a vial out of his vest, Haruto explained, "The good news is, I created a concoction to counteract the toxins and purge her system more quickly. She needs to drink as much water as possible and continue resting, but she'll be back on her feet soon enough," he added, tilting her head so she'd drink the antidote since her lack of energy prevented her from doing it herself. Pulling out another vial, he explained, "I'm also giving her this herbal tea to help her fall asleep."

"You saved her," Ty stood and shook Haruto's hand. "Once again, the Andonia crew has come through for us."

"Just be thankful my father was interested in herbology and left me with the books he collected before he died," Haruto played down Ty's appreciation. "Otherwise, I don't know what we would've done."

Over the course of the next day, Shana's sores faded and color returned to her face. In that time, Ty sat by her side, racking his brain, trying to figure out who had poisoned his girlfriend.

Once she was alert enough that Ty could explain what happened, Shana too, struggled to think of who could have poisoned her. "The night before we left, it was you, Grizz, Nash, and I together eating at the same table. There were three pitchers of water, each with fresh fruit in them. I drank some of them all."

"Did anyone else drink them?" Ty asked aloud, trying to play back the moment in his mind.

"I think I was the only one who had the water with cucumbers in the pitcher. It could've been meant for any of us."

She shook her head, frustrated with the insufficient evidence and the idea that the poisoner was out there, still unidentified.

"So, all we have to go on is that it was someone in Misengard," Ty sighed. "That leaves dozens, maybe even hundreds of potential people we interacted with."

Working through the list of people they knew, the couple created theories about who had the motive and opportunity to poison her, but they stopped after realizing how jaded they were becoming, assuming the worst intentions about everyone.

"I think I can hear Ryland training the crew," Ty focused on something more positive. "I asked him to take over for me while I stayed with you. He's got them training day and night, except for Jun-Lei. I think after Casanovia she realized she didn't have the youth and

43

vigor that battle requires, and she said she didn't want to be a liability, so she's committing herself to help in other ways. Do you want to go up and watch? Some fresh air might do you some good."

Eagerly agreeing to the idea, wanting to get out of the forecastle cabin she'd been laying in for nearly three days, Shana slowly stood on unsteady legs and took Ty's arm to lead her out onto the main deck.

"Look who's up!" Min-Ye and Kyoko were overjoyed at Shana's recovery. They set their katanas down and ran over to greet her while Haruto hurried over as well, noticing Shana faltering. Taking her under the arm opposite Ty, the two Elves led the nineteen-year-old Human to a crate she could sit on.

"Come on, let's get back to work," Ryland smiled to Shana so he didn't come across as an uncaring jerk, but let his trainees know how annoyed he felt that they dropped their weapons to greet her. "What we do in practice mirrors what happens on the battlefield. You're not going to abandon your katanas in a fight, so don't do it during training."

"Sorry," the crew apologized to their mentor. They each held a high respect for the small-framed Dwarf as he took the time to teach them fighting techniques. Since they had a similar slender build to the Halfman, Ryland's quick, controlled, and precise attacks with his halfswords fit their style perfectly.

"Now," the sentry warrior continued, once the three were back in a fighting stance in front of him. "Let's continue to go through how to defend and attack against monsters with different elements. Any Anthropomorphic Monster that controls earth doesn't have a ranged attack. Up close, they are incredibly dangerous, so the best way to defeat them is from far away." He toggled the halfbow and quiver across his back. "If you can weaken them with ranged weapons until their energy is depleted, they are ineffective.

"Ty, come help me," he beckoned the blonde-haired Elf sitting with his arm around Shana to step forward. When he did, Ryland handed the fellow warrior a spare set of spaulders and a steel plate since Ty's yellow suit of armor was in the forecastle cabin. While Ty put on the protective gear, Ryland explained, "Now, for enemies with the element of lightning, it's best to slash at any openings in their armor."

"Well, that's not technically true," Ty argued. Instead of letting Ryland use him as an example, he stepped forward, and touched the Dwarf's armor, covering the metal in a low voltage so Ryland could serve as the illustration.

"First things first is don't let a monster come in contact with your armor. Otherwise, they can manifest their element on your armor, just like I'm doing to Ryland," Ty explained. "The only way our Dwarven friend isn't being electrocuted is because I'm not allowing the lightning to hurt him. A monster in my position won't be so merciful, so don't give them the chance to get close and control any metal on your person.

"And now, to refute Ryland's point," the Elf took Ryland's halfsword from him and carried out a slow-motion slash, pretending to stab Ryland's electrified armor. "What's the difference between these two attacks?" he asked the three trainees.

"When you slash, more surface area of your blade will connect with his armor. You're a conduit for more voltage," Kyoko answered, but bit her lip, unsure of herself.

"That's right!" Ty encouraged her. "In most cases, it wouldn't be enough to instantly paralyze you, but you'd still feel some paralysis. That's why it's better to jab or stab in any openings they may have." To demonstrate, he again thrust his sword tip towards the uncovered sections between Ryland's armor pieces.

"I guess veterans like me still have techniques to learn," Ryland shrugged. He clapped his hands together and announced, "Last thing for today! I want to cover shields. Ty, keep my sword and move to the far side of the deck."

Ryland picked up a metal shield, and instructed, "Shields are not only great for blocking arrows and bolts. They can also protect you against elements. Alright, Ty," the Dwarven warrior shouted across the thirty-foot gap between them. "Charge up and fire a blast at me."

Doing as he was told, Ty coursed electricity through his blade, pointed it at Ryland's shield, and sent out a bolt of lightning across Andonia's deck.

Ryland crouched, and although he gritted his teeth and grimaced, fully defended the attack with his shield.

Turning to the young Elven trio, the Halfman explained, "Nearly every shield is designed with leather straps to help prevent the electrical current from affecting you. It's your choice if you want to carry one or not. Personally, I don't because they're cumbersome and my style relies on stealth and speed."

Ty returned to the group and added one caveat to Ryland's advice about shields. "The shield works well in protecting you from elemental attacks, but it won't work if there's a storm and a monster calls a blast of lightning down on you. Nature's lightning is far more powerful than what an element can produce."

After spending an hour sparring and practicing some techniques they'd learned during their sunset session, Ryland ended their time together.

As per usual, Min-Ye, Haruto, and Kyoko, each dripping with sweat, limped back to the sterncastle cabin to collapse in exhaustion.

"We'll practice more at first light," Ryland announced, laughing as the trainees groaned at the news.

Ty came up behind the Dwarf, chuckling as well. "Little do they realize Warriors' Boot Camp is ten times harder than what they're going through."

The two men walked over to Shana, who also found the trainees' exhaustion amusing.

"What are you laughing at?" Ryland teased her. "As soon as you're healthy, you're going to be right alongside them."

Looking to her boyfriend for him to exempt her from the tiresome training, Ty merely shrugged and sided with Ryland. "Being Alazar's elect gives you more reason to learn how to fight."

Playing along with the teasing, Shana got up and began walking back to the cabin at the front of the ship. "I better get my rest then. I'll be using the full force of my wind on you, Ryland. After all, if you're such a skilled teacher, you should be able to show us all how to defend against it!"

Throwing his hands up in the air, the clean-shaven Dwarf joked, "I retire then! Ty, you can have your teaching spot back now that Shana's healed. I'd be a fool to take on Alazar's elect head-on!"

As Shana laughed, she faltered in her step and stumbled. Both Ryland and Ty, warriors who relied on speed and quick reactions, caught her before she fell.

"You're looking a little pale," Ty noticed, checking her over. "Maybe you need more rest than we realize. Here, I'll help you back to the cabin."

"I'm fine," Shana argued. "I can stay out here."

"You're sounding like your half-brother," Ty tightened his grip on her arm as she nearly lost her balance again. "I can't tell you how many times Steve has told me he's fine when he's not."

Following a minute where Ty and Shana bickered while Ryland felt like an awkward bystander, Shana agreed to let Ty accompany her back to her cot.

"You don't have to stay by my side," she said after half an hour of him asking if she needed anything every five minutes. "Why don't you go hang out with Ryland for a while? You've been sitting next to me all day as I slept, you must not be tired."

"I'd rather stay with you and make sure you're okay."

"Please, I insist. Plus, I'm sure he could use the company."

"Okay," Ty took her up on her suggestion, "As long as you're sure you'll be fine."

"I will be," she declared, sitting up to kiss him goodnight.

On the main deck, Ty found Ryland, still in his armor, sitting on a crate with a canvas sheet and an assortment of pastels in a metal bin at his side. The Dwarf worked away, occasionally gazing at the sunset on the horizon, taking in the details he wanted to incorporate into his drawing. When a pod of dolphins swam past, jumping along the water's surface, he quickly grabbed a gray pastel to sketch the image.

"Sometimes nature is too magnificent not to draw," Ryland remarked, feeling Ty looking over his shoulder.

"Some of these sights aren't going to last forever, so they need to be captured while they still exist."

Ty was so amazed at the artwork, he didn't question Ryland's melancholy statement. He simply replied, "I forgot how talented you were."

"It's odd to hear praise from the public, let alone from a fellow warrior, like you," Ryland harrumphed. "It's an unfortunate reality that more people would rather see violence with a sword than beauty with a pastel."

I guess that's true, Ty considered the Halfman's opinion. *Thousands don't flock to Celestial each year to watch warriors competing in art contests, they come to see jousts, the Battle Royale, one-on-one combat, and tons of other Tournaments.*

Realizing he knew little about the warrior who'd left Casanovia to accompany Alazar's elect, Ty somewhat convictedly thought, *I've spent so much time with Shana, this is my first time alone with Ryland.* He leaned on the ship's rail next to where Ryland sat, observing the tranquil sea and fiery sunset, looking forward to getting to know the Dwarf better.

"Thanks for taking over for me training the crew while Shana was sick. You seem to know your stuff," Ty tried to be polite even though he thought the sentry warrior could have taught the basics better. "You said you grew up in Celestial. Who was in charge of Boot Camp when you were there?"

"Captain Ostravaski," Ryland answered, "Although, he was promoted to one of the watchtower commander positions after I graduated from Warrior Training. He continued training, though, even when he was a commander because he loved bossing people around so much."

"That he does! He's the one who trained me in Boot Camp, too," Ty confirmed, impressed at Ostravaski's longevity, especially considering Ty had celebrated twenty-two namedays to Ryland's forty-one. The Elf bowed his head as he thought about the Giant who'd dedicated his life to training up future generations of warriors, reminded that Commander Ostravaski was likely among the many who died in the capital.

"I overheard the others talking about the visions you all had," Ryland inquired. "Your father was a Celestial warrior too, huh?"

"Yeah, he was an aerial warrior like me, but he was killed on duty. Right before I received my element, it was revealed the Hooded Phantom murdered him." Ty shook his head, still unsettled by the lasting images from the vision.

"I'm sorry to hear it. My father was killed in the line of duty too," Ryland revealed, taking a break from his sketch to stretch, as if he was preparing himself for the uncomfortable topic. "It was soon after I became a warrior. One night on patrol, I was talking to my brother, who was coming off his shift, and a warrior who'd taken arrows to his shoulder and foot staggered up to us. He said he'd been on a special assignment to track down a warrior archer, but when his team found the man, the archer attacked and killed everyone except him."

This is what happened following Kari's vision! Ty recognized the details of the story. *Ryland and his brother must've been the warriors Malorek came up to when he was setting up Quintis as the murderer!*

Letting Ryland continue, Ty intently listened as the Halfman explained, "The warrior said he'd trapped the archer, so I ran to find more help while my brother went into the house which was on fire. There, he found the warriors who'd been killed, one of whom was our father."

Ryland stopped speaking and took a moment to compose himself, setting down the pastels in his shaking hand.

"My brother later told me how he came upon the warrior responsible for the deaths. He was pinned under two bodies."

"What happened to the archer?" Ty was too impatient not to interrupt. *I need to know what happened to Kari's dad!*

"I don't know," Ryland admitted. "When I got back, my brother prevented me from being near the man because he knew I was so angry, I would've killed him if I got my hands on him. All he said was he took care of the archer, but he never explained what he meant, no matter how many times I asked. I'm still angry that guy killed our dad. I don't know what my brother did with him, but if I knew where he was, I'd march right up to him and kill him this very instant."

"Ryland," Ty broke the news to the Halfman, "that archer's name was Quintis Quinn; Kari's father. He wasn't the one who murdered your dad. It was Malorek, the man we now know as the Hooded Phantom. He's the warrior who came up to you and your brother."

"What?" The Dwarf's face went paler than his already pale skin.

"Malorek set up Quintis because he planned to kill Zoran, Queen Evalyn, and Princess Kyra so he could become king. He needed a scapegoat so he could take the throne and not have people question his involvement in the murders. Kari's vision showed us five elect everything that happened that night. I'm sorry to say it, but I watched Malorek kill your father and the other warriors sent out to capture him."

"I don't believe this," Ryland ran his fingers through his hair. In the minute he took to collect his thoughts, Ty could see the forty-one-year-old replaying the moments of the eighteen-year-old event in his mind. In a burst of anger, Ryland swiped the back of his hand at the tin of pastels, scattering them across the main deck. "I should've questioned Malorek instead of believing him at face value!" he gritted his teeth and groaned.

"You didn't know. You can't beat yourself up about this."

"I can," Ryland argued, "You don't know the anger I've carried with me my whole life at the person who murdered my father."

I understand more than you know, Ty wanted to counter, but gave Ryland the space he sought as the Dwarf returned to his art. Although it was an unamicable ending to their time together, Ty felt connected to Ryland more than ever before.

He's just like the rest of us, Ty thought of Alazar's four other elect. *Malorek tragically influenced our lives and none of us knew. I'm sure if there was a sixth element, Ryland would be the one to wield it.*

Chapter 113

The apprehension in Grizz's voice was evident when he announced to the men riding alongside him, "The mountain should be visible just around this corner." Once they rounded the bend, he gulped at the two jagged silhouettes on the horizon whose precipices appeared to pierce the setting sun. "There it is. Twin Peaks."

The very sight of this place brings back such painful memories for me, but I know I can't hide from them forever.

"There's a good place to camp," Willis pointed to a flat, secluded area just off the snowy mountain pass they traveled on. "It's got a good vantage point so we can see anything coming our way, but we're not so high up we'll freeze to death at night."

Agreeing to the proposal, Krause and Dart tied up and fed the four horses, Willis searched the surrounding area with Copper, and Grizz and Nash started a campfire. The group shared a simple meal under the quickly darkening sky during which Nash slumped over, falling asleep against his dad's side.

"Looks like someone's tired from a long day of travel," Grizz whispered to the group, gently picking up his son and carrying him over to the side of the campsite where everyone's bedrolls had been laid out. He tucked Nash in, brushed the boy's hair to the side, and kissed him on the forehead.

Copper came over and curled up next to the child and looked at Grizz with his big, blue eyes, as if to say, *I'll watch over him while he sleeps.*

Grizz pet the direfox, thankful for the beast's companionship. Before returning to the group of men sitting around the campfire, he took a minute to watch Nash peacefully sleeping.

Thinking to himself as if his son could hear, Grizz reflected, *Even back in Serendale, your mother and I would watch you and Liam sleeping, warm and safe in your beds. Every person has certain moments that fill their heart with joy, and for me, this is it.*

"So we'll reach Twin Peaks tomorrow?" Dart asked his master once Grizz sat back down.

"Yes, barring any setbacks."

"Is it true you grew up here until your mother was killed?" Willis asked, broaching the subject he knew Grizz rarely talked about.

"I did, but then I was sent to live with my uncle in a Celestial orphanage."

"It must feel strange to come back here after so many years."

"It hasn't been as long as you might think," Grizz turned to look back at his son. Upon confirming that Nash was still asleep and wouldn't hear the story that'd ruin the image his eight-year-old had of him, he told the group about his last visit to Twin Peaks.

"I didn't stay long in Celestial after Malorek killed my uncle. I headed back here because the only thing that fueled me was killing the man that murdered my mother. Malorek inspired me in that orphanage to seek the justice I wanted, especially against those who hurt my family,"

Grizz explained. Across from him, through the fire, he noticed Krause break eye contact and stare down at the ground.

"I was a kid and had no one taking care of me, so I squired for blacksmiths to provide for myself until I was sixteen and could officially begin my formal training under them. Meanwhile, I was always looking for the man. One day, I saw him. I had a dagger on me, and the next thing I know it was plunged deep into his chest. It was in the middle of a public market, but I was so bloodthirsty, I pulled it out and stabbed again." Grizz shifted in his seat, uncomfortably recalling the event which played such an influential role in the path his life took.

"Even after he died, I didn't let up. A warrior came up to stop me, a Giant nearly twice my size, but my rage hadn't ended. I turned and stabbed him until he died, too. It happened to be the general's son. That's what the Warrior Commander is called here," Grizz paused for a moment to note the nuance.

"General Graynor was his name. When I was sentenced, he requested I only be given four years in prison for murdering my mother's killer. He didn't want his son's death counted at all, which could've and should've gotten me the death penalty or sent me to Holders Keep. He came to my cell and told me that although it was difficult, he forgave me for what I did."

Grizz finished by adding, "Graynor said his son's life was unfairly taken, but mine didn't need to be ruined by rotting in a cell. The man gave me an opportunity. The reason I wanted to come here was to thank him for the mercy he showed me and to show him I made the most of the chance he gave me."

"I bet you telling him you are the earth-wielder, one of Alazar's Elect, will give him further peace about sparing you," Willis encouraged Grizz in his mission.

"I hope I get the opportunity," Grizz stated. "I never did before because after I was released from prison, it wasn't safe for me in Twin Peaks. While Graynor had forgiven me, other warriors had not. They had put a hit out on me and almost succeeded in taking me out. Sometime I'll have to show you the scar they gave me," Grizz shook his head at the memory of the attack as he patted the side of his brown plate of armor, near his ribs.

"Because I was targeted, I knew I had to start fresh somewhere else. I'm glad I chose Serendale because that's where I met Juliana." Grizz grimaced at the thought of his dead wife, a look highlighted by the shifting flames of the campfire, but then he smiled and said, "Even though she's gone now, I don't think I'd change a thing about my past, because it led me to her."

"Here's to new starts," Krause held up a wineskin of mead and took a swig. "Sometimes it's not until you hit rock bottom that you can take your broken pieces and rebuild them better than before."

Krause passed the wineskin to Willis. The Elf took a drink and tossed it to Dart. The container finally made its way to Grizz, who shared his own toast and nodded to Krause before taking a sip. "Everyone makes mistakes, but we do our best to learn from them and become better."

Krause acknowledged the Dwarf's remark, and could tell the blacksmith was not only attempting to show his forgiveness, but was also expressing regret for throwing him off Andonia in an attempt to kill him.

"Well, I don't have anything to top Grizz's story, so I'm turning in for the night," Willis said, standing up and stretching. Following suit, Grizz, Dart, and Krause got up and headed over to their bedrolls to sleep for the night.

As they approached, Nash closed his eyes as tightly as he could, pretending to be asleep. He'd heard the entirety of his dad's story and was proud to be the son of someone who overcame struggles in their youth and changed their life for the better.

Once he knew the men's eyes were closed and everyone had fallen asleep, Nash looked up to the stars and prayed to Alazar, "Please, let me become a great Dwarf like my father is." Then, the eight-year-old fell asleep with a smile on his face.

Chapter 114

Flying over the desert on their way to Holders Keep, the sun baked Steve and Kari atop Crimson Singe. For a while, Kari activated her element and rested her hand on Steve's plate, turning both of their armor into ice to cool them down. But now, time had passed, and her exhaustion and lack of energy made it difficult to continuously summon her power.

Uncomfortable from their long flight, the Human and the Halfling wiped the sweat dripping from their brows, unaided by the air which lacked any semblance of a breeze. The conditions of travel exhausted Crimson as well. With no air currents to drift on, he was forced to constantly flap his wings to continue flying.

The vast Deletion Desert had few towns and villages, especially on the route to their destination. *Nowhere to land means nowhere to rest,* Steve told himself. *But at least we have water.* Drinking the last drops of his canteen, he handed it to Kari, who easily used her element to refill the metal container.

Blue above us, tan below us, Kari thought, shifting her goggles to the top of her head while looking in all directions. *Nothing but a cloudless sky and boring, empty desert.* The only difference she noted was far off in the east, there appeared to be a mile-high cloud stretching across the horizon and moving their way.

Crimson also observed the spectacle. "It's a sandstorm," he called back to the two riders on his back. "They happen a lot in this part of the world."

"That's not our biggest concern!" Steve shouted to Crimson with a sudden panic in his voice. Unlike Kari and the dragon, whose eyes were affixed to the wall of billowing clouds in the east, Steve stared intently at a dark, black object zipping towards them from the west.

"Is that Nightstrike?" Kari asked. From far off, the hauntingly massive, spiked dragon quickly grew larger with every passing second.

"It is," Crimson could tell. "I knew after I revealed I was alive, it was only a matter of time before he found out and came to kill me."

"How'd he know exactly where we are, though?" Steve wanted to know. "Somehow he learned we were heading to Holders Keep and intercepted us on the way."

"Someone must have sent word to Celestial?" Kari guessed. "The only people that knew the destinations we were each heading to were those in the council room back in Misengard. You know what that means, don't you?"

Steve nodded as Kari answered her own question. "We've been betrayed."

The feeling of knowing that someone in their inner circle of trusted confidants was actively plotting against them made the two companions sick to their stomach. They each tried to recall every person who had the opportunity and reason to conspire against them.

I hate not knowing, Steve thought, frustrated he couldn't reach a conclusion. *Whoever this traitor is, I bet they're the twelfth warrior that was working for Silas. It can't be happenstance he selected eleven Celestial warriors who would serve as his personal Guardian Knights when Zoran had twelve. Ever since Casanovia, we've known the twelfth is out there. Now there's good reason to believe that person's infiltrated our ranks.*

"Nightstrike's already caught up more than half the distance to us!" Kari noticed, knowing she needed to focus on the problem at hand, rather than try to figure out who betrayed them. "Don't forget he has the wind element," she thought back to the dragon attacking her, Steve, and Ty as they hid under an uprooted tree in Whitebark Woods. He'll catch up to us within minutes."

"I may have been able to defeat him before with the help of Oliver, but one-on-one, he has four elements while I only have fire. The only way we survive this is if we lose him."

We can use the same strategy we employed when Jarek chased Andonia and Jun-Lei sailed us into the storm, Steve thought, shouting, "Crimson, head for those sand clouds!"

"Can't Nightstrike control the storm with his elements of earth and wind?" Kari picked up on the plan. "He'll be able to use it to his advantage."

"To an extent, but not that much," Crimson answered, flapping his wings as powerfully as he could to pick up speed, "All elemental abilities have their limitations: range, output, and duration. Nightstrike can only control so much of a storm of this magnitude. It's the same reason you can't freeze all the water in the ocean according to your will."

With Crimson approaching the giant wall of billowing clouds before them, Kari put her goggles back on. Almost immediately, grains of sand from the storm pelted her skin.

In front of her, Steve removed the sash from around his waist. "Here, take this!" he shouted back, handing it to Kari to use as a bandana to cover her nose and mouth. Reaching under his shoulder spaulder, he ripped off the sleeve of his tunic to create his own piece of protective fabric.

Before he tightened the leather straps and gripped the horn of his saddle, Steve reached behind once more and squeezed Kari's thigh, encouraging her that everything would be fine, despite heading straight towards the ominous sandstorm.

Crimson had brought them to within a quarter-mile of the storm's edge. Nightstrike was the same distance behind and closing fast.

"There's no going back now!" Crimson roared, concentrating on his stability against the increasing winds. "Hold on!"

Punching a hole through the wall of the billowing sand cloud was like being swallowed into a new world. Within seconds, the sweltering desert sun was blotted out and nearly all visibility was lost. Lightning bolts illuminated the darkness, only to reveal multiple tornados within the sandstorm.

Bursting through one of the spiraling cyclones of sand at their side, Nightstrike roared in anger. Out of his open mouth, he fired an ice beam at Crimson. The red dragon dodged the element, looped around, and breathed fire at his enemy. His flames were met by another one of Nightstrike's chilling frost attacks. The two elements collided in the air as both dragons maintained their elemental attack as long as possible, battling against each other in a test of stamina. Nightstrike gained the upper hand when Crimson's energy ran out and the ice blast hit him.

Shaking the blow off, Crimson had no time to collect himself before Nightstrike tackled him. As their bodies became entangled and the two dizzily spun out of control, the dark dragon used his talons to slice open Crimson's underbelly. Roaring in pain, the red dragon moved to retaliate, but the inside of Nightstrike's mouth turned green, and he sent a burst of wind into his sworn enemy, purposefully sending Crimson backwards into an approaching tornado.

Hit by the intense barrage of wind and sand, Steve and Kari held on as tightly as they could. The onslaught of attacks and being jerked back and forth was uncomfortable and disorienting. They, like Crimson, tried to collect their bearings, but Nightstrike was relentless. The dragon harnessed the storm's lightning and sent multiple bolts at Crimson.

A few of the strikes landed, slamming into Crimson's neck and tail. Another directly impacted his side, sending enough voltage through his body that Steve and Kari felt it in their saddles. It was enough to send Crimson crashing down into the desert in a violent impact that was damaging in its own right.

"I'm outmatched," Crimson breathed so hard he could barely get the words out. "If you stay near me, he'll kill you too."

Unstrapping themselves, Steve and Kari tumbled out of their saddles, down Crimson's side, and fell face-first into the sand.

Far off in the darkness above, lightning illuminated the silhouette of the dark dragon's hovering body. Once the brightness of the flash dissipated, a glowing blue light appeared where the dragon's maw had been.

He's going to use another ice attack! This one will kill Crimson, Kari could tell. She reached for the bow slung across her back, but stopped, knowing her arrows would make no difference. *I wish there was something I could do!*

At the very moment Nightstrike swooped down and unleashed his ice beam on them, Kari closed her eyes and threw her hand up into the air. Daring to look, she saw that she'd stopped the attack. It was as if the ice beam struck an invisible force-field and was deflected to the sides where it evaporated.

Just as Nightstrike tested his elemental stamina against Crimson, he did the same with Kari. Taking a deep breath, filling his lungs as he sat hovering in the air above them, he blasted another ice beam down at them, this one even more powerful. This time Kari, used two hands and focused completely on the beam of ice. *I understand a part of my power I didn't before,* she thought as she easily held off the attack until Nightstrike no longer had the energy to deploy it. *If a monster uses a ranged attack with an element you wield, you can mentally control the half of it that's closer to you and deflect it away.*

"He's going to switch to an element you can't stop," Crimson told them, slowly picking himself up out of the sand. "Get as far away from here as you can!"

Not a second later, Nightstrike careened down from the sky with all his scales turned to stone. His body, weighing over fifty times heavier than it had before he covered himself with his element, crashed into Crimson. The red dragon reeled in pain, his back nearly broken from Nightstrike's high-speed tackle.

"Come on!" Kari muffled through her makeshift bandana, grabbing Steve's hand and leading him away from where the dragons wrestled on the ground.

Now that his riders were off him, Crimson covered himself with his own element, bursting to life with orange fire. Nightstrike compensated by changing his scales from stone to ice, but was still forced to back off when Crimson increased the heat of his flames, making it unbearable to be near him. Using the space to maneuver, the fire-covered dragon shot up into the sky, trying to lead Nightstrike as far away as possible from Steve and Kari.

From the ground, the couple stopped running and stared up at the silhouettes of the dragons battling in the storm. It was an equally magnificent and terrifying sight to behold the foes battle amidst the tornados, lightning, and sand as they fired elements back and forth.

The storm was even stronger than before when they were near its eye. High winds whipped the desert sands around so swiftly, each grain that hit their skin felt like a bee sting. The constantly changing gusts made it difficult to stand up straight, let alone continue to create distance from the dangerous monsters battling to the death.

"Kari! Brace yourself!" Steve yelled, turning to see a small tornado barreling directly towards them. He gripped her hand tighter in his own, but it wasn't enough to withstand the power of the weather. Their grasp was severed. The gale tossed Steve, sending him bouncing up and down along the desert surface more than Kari, who coated her armor in as much ice as possible to weigh herself down.

"Steve!" she called out from where he was, unable to see where he'd been thrown because of the lack of light. Running throughout the eerie darkness in the direction she assumed was correct, she kept the ice covering her armor. Her element allowed her to carry the additional weight with no extra burden as she searched the area, but Steve was nowhere to be found. *I couldn't even hear him if I wanted to,* Kari panicked, her senses dulled by the violent storm.

"Kari, where are you?" Steve called out. Since he'd lost the shred of tunic he'd been holding over the bottom half of his face, enough sand filled his mouth that he gagged on it and couldn't spit out his four-word question a second time.

Above him, the dragons continued battling until the light of Crimson's fire, barely visible through the sands, disappeared altogether. *Either he purposely stopped employing it or he was just killed,* Steve nearly cried, terrified at the idea of the latter and what it'd mean to lose not only a friend, but the most powerful asset in their army.

Losing his footing and falling down a sand dune, Steve hunkered down at its base, hoping, one: that Nightstrike would not come after him, and two: that lying down where he was would help protect him against the ceaseless winds.

Finding Kari would be like finding a needle in a haystack in this storm. It's safest for me to stay where I am, he believed, curling up in the fetal position and covering his head with his arms.

Unlike Steve, Kari continued wandering in search of her companion, but had no luck. Forty-five minutes later, after the storm had passed and the sky cleared, she hiked up the tallest dune near her, but in surveying the landscape she found no sign of Steve, Crimson, or Nightstrike.

"Steve!" she called out a dozen times in all directions, waiting for a response that never came. Moving to another sand dune a mile away, she shouted for him again, but still heard nothing back.

I don't know what to do, her heart raced. *I may have nearly an unlimited water supply through my element and canteen, but I can't stay here in the desert waiting for*

him. At least he and I both know how to navigate from
our position based on the sun's placement in the sky. We
know we're heading to Holders Keep, so no matter where
he ended up, we'll both be heading in the same direction.

Taking a swig of water, already feeling the unbearable heat now that the storm wasn't blocking the scorching sun, Kari tied Steve's sash around her head as a turban and set off to the east.

Chapter 115

After leaving Ryland to himself on the main deck, Ty realized everyone was in bed, except for Jun-Lei at the helm of the ship. Heading to accompany the shipmaster, he met the fellow Elf on the stern deck.

"It looks like Shana's doing better," the fifty-five-year-old said, "I saw her come out to watch the training."

"Yeah, I'm glad she got some fresh air. Haruto really came through with his antidote."

"He always rises to the occasion. Plus, I know he cares for you guys." Jun-Lei shook her head and let out a chuckle. "Sometimes I can't believe it's us who have the honor of transporting Alazar's elect around the world."

"We're the lucky ones. I don't think we would've made it this far with anyone else."

Accepting the compliment with grace, Jun-Lei told Ty with a smile, "Thanks, and thank you for taking the time to train my crew. They should be able to hold their own in a fight. At the very least, they've learned how to properly defend themselves. I just don't want them thinking they can take on a dozen monsters and survive. I've already seen Kyoko growing far too confident.

"I've noticed that too," Ty admitted. "She's talented, but talent rarely beats experience. She'll learn that soon enough, hopefully in practice rather than battle."

"I hope so," Jun-Lei grimaced at the idea of her daughter getting hurt. "Power, riches, fame, knowledge, skill: I've seen how each of those can change a person if they acquire it unexpectedly. Some aren't affected by it, but others are. Those things can exemplify your worst traits, so you always have to be on guard."

For a moment, Ty was taken aback, wondering if Jun-Lei was categorizing him with Kyoko, especially after Kari and Shana had both called him out for his overconfidence and unnecessary risk-taking in battle. Feeling an uncomfortable pit of conviction in his stomach, he turned the focus of the conversation off himself and asked Jun-Lei, "Did you give up the gold we gave you for sailing us from Port Meris to Casanovia because you feared it'd change you?"

"It was more because I knew gold was Jarek's weakness, and by offering it to him, I could ensure his aid in helping Casanovia. Would it have changed me though?" the shipmaster speculated aloud, "I don't know. I'd like to think it wouldn't have because I try to be content with what I already have. Some people think it's a blessing to receive power, money, or popularity, but I think it can be just as much of a blessing not to have them."

"It's ironic, because people like you who don't want those things are the ones who deserve them most of all."

Jun-Lei shrugged in response to Ty's heartfelt sentiment, too humble to acknowledge it. Similarly to Ty, she quickly changed the topic of conversation by looking up at the sky, charting the stars, and telling the warrior, "We should arrive in Elmwood tomorrow morning. Ever been there?"

Ty shook his head. "We're already farther south than I've ever traveled."

Jun-Lei smiled. "I'm interested to see what you think, not only of Elmwood, but of Oceanside. The seacoast provinces have quite a different culture than what you experienced growing up in Celestial. Different attire; architecture; even art and statues are more of an impressionist style than the realism approach you're used to from the capital. More than anything, it's quiet and relaxed here. Everything moves at a slower pace.

"I was born in a small village twenty miles northeast of Elmwood," Jun-Lei explained, knowing Ty wondered how she knew so much about the two cities on opposite sides of the Darien Sea. That's why my name is hyphenated. Most people that live in the Seacoast provinces have a hyphenated name."

"How did you end up in Port Meris?" Ty asked, interested in learning why they'd found the Elven shipmaster in the rundown fishing village north of Serendale.

Jun-Lei chose not to elaborate. She simply answered, "The place where I grew up carries dark memories for me. I chose to leave, and I have no interest in setting foot on these lands again. That's why I won't be coming with you into Elmwood. That doesn't mean I can't give you advice though. Elmwood is one of the few cities that allows both male and female warriors. Last I heard, the commander is a woman who hates hearing about women in other cities who desire to serve but aren't allowed to. You might use that to your advantage."

"That's a helpful tip," Ty thanked the shipmaster. "So you're going to stay on Andonia when we arrive tomorrow?"

"Yeah, once again, I've got repairs to make," she stomped on a loose board under her foot which kept springing up. "Always seems like when one thing is fixed another thing breaks. Min-Ye can stay here with me since I'll need someone to help with the repairs, but you should take Ryland, Haruto, and Kyoko along with you. It won't hurt to have extra eyes watching your back, especially after Shana's poisoning. If there's one person out there intent on harming Alazar's elect, who's to say there isn't more?"

"I'll talk to them about accompanying us. I never want to see Shana that close to death again. I was so scared I was going to lose her."

Jun-Lei nodded, as if she knew exactly the emotion Ty was expressing. She turned the spokes of Andonia's wheel to better handle the waves of the Darien Sea and shared, "The last time you were on this ship, you were single. Now, you're in love with someone you didn't even know existed. Isn't it funny how life works? Sometimes the blessings and happiness we desire for so long are right around the corner waiting where we can't see them."

Ty smiled at the idea and began laughing as sea mist unexpectedly sprayed him. "Do you need anything before I turn in for the night?"

"No thanks, Kyoko will take over in a couple hours. I'll be fine until then."

"How'd it go?" Jun-Lei stopped making repairs to the ship as Ty, Shana, and the rest of the crew returned to Andonia only three hours after they had docked in Elmwood's port. Min-Ye stopped working as well and came over, eager to hear the results of the meeting with the commander.

"It was way easier than expected, Ty grinned uncontrollably. "The commander is sending a third of those in her service to Almiria, and she's going to have her captains speak to men and women throughout the province to see if she can't get more to join. She's offering to pay five gold pieces to every civilian who travels with her warriors and the councilor of the city offered to match that."

"That's great!" Jun-Lei was surprised at the offer, but immediately skeptical of the too-good-to-be-true news. "Commanders and councilors are notorious for holding on to their assets to protect their own city. How did you get them to contribute so much?"

"Well," Ty's smile turned mischievous, "I can't deny their willingness to serve the kingdom, but I may have prodded them by bending the truth a little."

"A little!?" Shana blurted out, then set the record straight. "You lied and said Misengard women who volunteered were told they could do so, as long as they knew their place and stayed in the kitchens and cooked."

Shrugging his shoulders, Ty began laughing. "The commander started cursing under her breath, mumbling words like patriarchal and antiquated. Then she said, 'If the fate of the kingdom is at stake, the gender of the person plunging their sword into these monsters shouldn't matter.'"

"They're planning to lead all their warriors and any volunteers to Almiria three days from now," Shana noted. "That'll give them more than enough time to put plans in place to keep Elmwood secure and continue recruiting as many people as possible."

"So we're good to continue on to Oceanside then?"

"Yep!" Ty was pleased with the results of their journey thus far. "We were welcomed to stick around, but there's not much left to be done here."

"We're almost set making repairs," Jun-Lei drove the final nail into a loose board she'd been hammering back into place. "It'll be a three-day ride."

"Perfect," Ty held up a crate he carried under his armpit, "we stopped and bought so much ginger root, I could sail this world ten times over!"

At his exaggerated declaration, Jun-Lei, Kyoko, Haruto, and Min-Ye laughed at Ty's confidence in the anti-seasickness concoction he'd been drinking. Kyoko nudged her mom with her elbow, and whispered through her laughter, "Little does he know we're about to sail through some of the most treacherous waters on Element! That ginger root tea is barely going to help him."

"What's so funny?" Ty asked, wanting in on the joke.

"Oh, nothing," Kyoko stated. "But you better start drinking as much tea as you can." With that, she walked away laughing, disappearing off into another section of the ship along with the rest of the crew.

"What does that mean!? How much do I need?" Ty called out after them.

Haruto was the only one to answer by calling out, "That entire crate is a start!"

"Only a start? This is more than enough ginger root to make ten weeks of tea!" Ty stated, still confused.

Instead of any explanation, all he heard was the continued laughter of the Andonia crew.

"Just know that I love you and I'll take care of you, but it sounds like in a few hours you're going to experience a bout of seasickness," Shana clasped Ty's shoulder with both a smirk and a grimace. "We've all known about the waters we'll be heading through, but no one had the heart to tell you, even when you were buying all that ginger root!"

Shana and Ryland headed off as well, leaving Ty standing alone on the main deck, regretting his decision to ever volunteer to set foot on Andonia.

Chapter 116

Nearing Twin Peaks in the late morning, the Serendale crew stood amazed at the immense size of the two snow-capped summits. Colorful houses dotted the faces of both precipices. Sprawling tracks of metal and wood connected the clusters of homes before disappearing into tunnels in the mountainside, leading to the subterranean city inside. From far off, Twin Peaks looked like a giant piece of inhabitable swiss cheese.

Sitting in the saddle in front of Grizz, Nash excitedly pointed out people in wooden carts riding on one of the tracks spanning the chasm between the two summits.

"Those are called The Rails," Grizz explained, beaming at his son's admiration. "They're on the inside of the mountain too. You can ride them all over Twin Peaks to get to where you need to go. Thus," Grizz's voice grew louder so that he was speaking to the men around him rather than just Nash, "we don't need our horses anymore."

Reaching into his coinpouch, Grizz rode up to a stablemaster outside the city's main entrance and paid a couple silver pieces for four stalls. "Nash, you can ride on Copper," he lifted the boy and put him on the direfox's back.

Grizz didn't want to say it, but he knew despite the transportation the Rails provided, the amount of walking they'd be doing was far too much for his son. *Even with his crutches, he seems to only be able to support himself for a short way before his legs give out. Juliana had mentioned Nash managed to walk the two miles to and from school, but he must've had a setback because he's not able to make it more than half a mile.*

Grizz ruffled his son's hair as Nash held onto the fur between the shoulder blades of the orange-furred beast.

I hope him riding Copper won't be a problem here. People in Casanovia were fine with us having a strange direfox with us since he was always at our side, but you never know how someone might react to seeing a monster.

Walking alongside Copper with Krause, Willis, and Dart following along, the group passed under a giant stone archway erected in front of where the two summits connected.

No sooner did Grizz introduce his friends by saying, "Welcome to the Twin Peaks," a warrior came out from under the threshold of the city entrance and stopped the group from entering. "What business do you have here?" he asked, crossing his arms.

Great, Grizz rolled his eyes. *This is exactly what we don't need: some warrior so bored with his job, he has nothing better to do than harass every person seeking to enter.*

"We're looking for the general," Grizz answered in a tone reflective of his annoyance. "He should be expecting us."

"Do you have proof of your claim?"

"We don't, but I'm the Commander of Serendale," Krause announced, stepping forward to convince the captain of their credibility.

"If you were Serendale's commander, you'd have the colors of your city on your armor and you'd be sporting your badge. You have neither."

"This is a new suit of armor," Krause shot back, not caring to explain that his typical light and dark green suit lay somewhere in the ashes of Serendale. "There are bigger things at hand than me worrying about painting my armor."

The Twin Peaks warrior shrugged, not accepting the excuse. "And where are you from?" he turned back to Grizz while glancing at the Dwarf's brown and black armor, which belonged to none of the Primary Cities.

I remember this guy, Grizz suddenly realized as he glared at the man. He shook his head, finding it unbelievable that the first warrior they encountered was one who was part of a group who assaulted him after his prison stint. *He doesn't recognize me though. He's too focused on giving me a hard time because he thinks only warriors are worthy of wearing armor, not civilians. He hates the idea my custom armor is painted and he has yet to finish his.*

Unafraid of answering the question honestly, Grizz responded, "I'm from here, same as you. That is, until a bunch of warriors assaulted me and left me for dead. You don't know where I could find any of them, do you?"

To add to the intimidation of his cutting question, he gripped the handle of Skullcrusher and turned his weapon to stone as it laid sheathed across his back.

"I don't know," the warrior stuttered and lied in the same sentence.

Smiling nefariously, Grizz retorted, "Then how about you stop analyzing every nuance of our armor and tell us where we can find the general."

The warrior stuttered between his words even more than before. "He's down at the base, dealing with the troll infestation. There's an entire colony of them living underground, deep below the mountain. If you take the red-line rail, it'll get you to where you need to go," he pointed with a shaking finger. "It's just to the left, beyond the entrance."

"You were mean to him, dad," Nash spoke up from atop Copper once they were out of earshot.

"Sometimes you need to be assertive with people to get what you want," Grizz explained. "There's nothing wrong with that."

"So that was one of the warriors who gave you a hard time after you were released?" Dart asked.

Grizz cut his apprentice a sharp look for being too inquisitive and nearly revealing too much about his past with Nash present. Nonetheless, he answered, "Yes," but chose not to elaborate on the unhappy memory.

Together, the men entered the mountain, leaving behind the snowy, cold weather they'd trudged through for days. Even though they stood under countless tons of rock and stone, there was little change in the amount of light. Between the sunlight that came through holes in the mountainside and the amount of Fluorite Crystals embedded into the walls, the cavern didn't lack illumination.

Finding the line of tracks painted red, Grizz opened a cart door for Copper and Nash and climbed in with them. With no room left, Willis, Krause, and Dart piled into the wooden cart behind them.

After picking Nash up and off Copper and setting him on the floor for safety, Grizz pulled a lever, unlocking the brakes underneath them. The sudden jerk forward almost forced Nash to lose his balance, so Grizz gestured to the handles for his son to hold onto while also resting his hand against Nash's back to serve as a brace.

I forgot how fun the transportation is here, Grizz felt the wind whip his beard around as they picked up speed and headed down an incline. Thinking back on childhood memories of riding The Rails for fun with his mother, he looked down to see if Nash was enjoying the ride, but the boy stood with his eyes squinted closed and a death-grip on the cart's handle. Although Copper was licking Nash's hand, trying to calm him, the eight-year-old's unease remained.

Grizz picked up his son and held him close against his shoulder. He broadened his stance, bracing for the sudden jerks and bumps in the uneven rail system. The wheels screeched with every turn, creating a loud, unsettling sound for those unfamiliar with it.

"I know it's dark and scary, but you're safe. I've got you. Nothing can hurt you when I'm around. Here, I want you to see something," Grizz told Nash, who dared to open his eyes after hearing his father's caring voice. "Coming up is one of my favorite..."

Before he could even finish his sentence, they came around a bend, revealing a huge cavern which held the bulk of Twin Peaks' population. Below them in the giant, hollow section of the mountain lied temples, houses, markets, streets, and people. Above it all, a collection of Fluorite Crystals featuring hundreds of shades of sparkling colors hung down from the cavern ceiling like a giant chandelier.

"Wow! It's awesome!" the majestic sight of the bustling city enthralled Nash. Rather than taking in the view for himself, Grizz watched the face of his beaming son, which he found just as precious as overlooking the grandiose metropolis.

"Twin Peaks is the most technologically advanced city in the kingdom," Grizz was proud to explain its history as Nash gazed upon it. "It was officially established and named by Dwarves who settled here during the Race Wars centuries ago. Not only did they build this rail system, they forged many new weapons and armor styles. Plus, they invented gunpowder, which gave us scorcher bombs, trip mines, and other useful items in battle."

"If Dwarves live here, then why was that warrior we spoke to a Human?" Nash asked.

Grizz understood the eight-year-old's confusion. "Nowadays, Giants, Elves, and Humans all live here, but Dwarves are still the prominent race. You'll often find that parts of the kingdom heavily feature a certain race or people of a certain skin color because of events marked by hatred and prejudice in the past."

Not wanting to further delve into the less-than-savory parts of Element's past during the magical moment, Grizz ended the conversation by setting Nash back down. Now enjoying the ride, the boy promptly threw his hands up to feel the breeze as they picked up speed and went in a downward corkscrew around and around the mountain's interior into the city below.

Instead of diverting to a track where carts stopped and they could enter the city, the Serendale men continued riding downward, heading underneath Twin Peaks.

"My ears popped!" Nash exclaimed, looking to his father for advice.

"Open your mouth as wide as you can and swallow," Grizz said, showing his son by doing it himself.

Soon, the natural skylight that illuminated their tunnel disappeared, only to be replaced by Fluorite Crystals in sconces evenly placed along the walls.

Nash excitedly called out each of the colors as they passed. Since the crystals were organized in no particular order, he repeated some colors more than once.

"Pink, green, pink, purple, yellow!"

"Good try, but that last one was called Amber," Grizz corrected him, explaining to Nash the names of shades the eight-year-old hadn't yet learned. "And this upcoming one looks blue, but it's actually turquoise."

"Amber. Turquoise," Nash announced, to which Grizz nodded in affirmation.

One of the greatest joys in life is watching your child expand their knowledge of the world, Grizz thought, smiling as he relished in the privilege of getting to teach his son things he'd always carry with him.

As Nash continued to call out the colors and Copper yipped alongside him, catching on to the game of announcing each of the crystal-bound lights as they passed them, Grizz got a sinking feeling about the distance they'd traveled.

How far down have we come? This is miles below the lowest point in Twin Peaks from how I remember it.

He got his answer only a minute later when the pitch of their cart leveled out and they slowed to nearly a complete stop at the end of the rail.

Together with Nash, who climbed up onto Copper, and the three men in the cart behind them, the Serendale crew stepped out onto a platform that led into a large tunnel. Its dimensions were much larger than the short and tight one they'd just come down through on the last leg of their rail ride.

"They're quarrying," Grizz said aloud, seeing barrels of gunpowder ready to be transported to parts of the underground cavern where they'd be used to blast through rock.

"For minerals and gemstones, apparently," Willis added, picking up a log off a pile of crates and flipping through the pages. "It looks like they've completed a bunch of orders to clients throughout the north over the past several weeks and now they're working on collecting for deliveries to Triland and Stonegate."

So it's not an infestation of trolls, Grizz pieced together the bits of information he had. *I bet miners stumbled across a bedrock they figured could earn them a fortune, but as they dug deeper, they encountered an underground colony of trolls and asked the warriors to help hold them off.*

"Hey, put that down!" a warrior captain yelled at Willis, coming from around a corner further down the large tunnel. Accompanying him were two miners, one of whom pushed along a wheelbarrow full of expensive rubies and topazes. "What are you doing down here? This section is off-limits," the captain approached the Serendale group, reaching for his axe when he spotted the direfox.

"What are *you* doing here?" Grizz returned the question, unhappy with what had been unfolding deep underneath Twin Peaks. "Why have you continued quarrying instead of sealing off this area? Is it worth risking a war with trolls just to get rich?"

"All the profits are going to the betterment of Twin Peaks," the captain nodded to the two miners who pushed their wheelbarrow onto a shaft system that pulled them up into the city above. "Why do you think us warriors are giving our lives every day to hold off the troll attacks so the miners can collect as much as possible? It's what's best for this city!"

"Hold them off?" Grizz spat, annoyed at the warriors justifying their actions. "You're destroying their home and murdering them for the sake of gluttony and greed."

Stepping in-between the Dwarf and the Twin Peaks captain, who appeared ready to arrest Grizz on the spot, Krause supported Grizz's argument of abandoning the mining.

"Riches should be the least of your concerns at the moment. The kingdom is under threat. Your general should have received a letter announcing our arrival. We've traveled all the way from Misengard. The sooner we speak with him, the sooner we can seek food and rest."

"You're part of the group that set out from Misengard?" the captain cocked his head at the unique party in front of him. "We were briefed on your arrival and the need for volunteers, but I don't think we can help you with how busy we are trying to mine – erm – protect the city," the man corrected himself.

"I'm sure the general would like to know you're here, though, so follow me," he shrugged his shoulders and sighed, annoyed at the inconvenience of having to head back the way he came. "I'll take you to see the general, but he's going to tell you the same thing I did."

As the Serendale crew were led by the captain down the winding tunnel, Grizz thought about what the warriors were up against. Trolls were short, broad-shouldered monsters with short legs and long arms. At creation, Zebulon formed two types of trolls, Dusk Trolls, which were like drow in that being out in sunlight too long would kill them, and Dawn Trolls, who didn't have such restrictions.

Since we're underground, these warriors are likely battling Dusk Trolls, Grizz knew. *Instead of their counterpart Dawn Trolls, these ones have adapted to their environment by forming scales on their back and various parts of their bodies, making it crucial to attack them where a blade can slice through.*

Nash proved Grizz wasn't the only one with the Anthropomorphic Monsters on his mind, when he asked his dad aloud, "What's a troll?"

Answering before his master could, Dart explained the monsters in a much more terrifying way than how Grizz would have. "Dusk trolls live in colonies in tunnels and caves. Imagine them all, with their scaly hunchbacks crawling around underneath us right now. At any moment, one can reach up through the dirt and grab your leg!"

"Dart! He's only eight. There's no need to frighten my kid!" Grizz shook his head in annoyance and turned to assure his son, "They can't do that, Nash. They're not like skeletons."

"Even if they could grab me, I'm not scared!" Nash piped up. Then, glaring at the teenager eleven years older than him, he told Dart, "I don't care how evil trolls are. My dad can protect this entire city from them."

I don't know about that, Grizz thought. *Even without them having elemental abilities, they cannot be taken lightly. These monsters have plagued this area for centuries. Back in the early 600's, a battle caused part of the mountain to crumble, killing thousands of people.*

The captain soon led the group to a gate where two warriors restricted entrance. After a brief word with the guards in which Grizz heard one of the two men complaining about not trusting civilians since some had been sneaking down and taking gemstones for themselves, the captain used his position of authority to gain access. Beyond the gate, the tunnel quickly expanded into a large cavern. It wasn't nearly as enormous as Twin Peak's main cavern miles above where they stood, but it was large enough to serve as a hub for six different mining tunnels leading out from its central location.

Tents of various sizes filled nearly the entire cavern, from wall to wall. The captain navigated through the maze, a third of which seemed to belong to warriors and another third to miners. The last section of tents belonged to clerics. Many held warriors, whose gruesome injuries were being tended to. "Don't look in there," Grizz told Nash as they passed by one where a warrior cried out in pain from his leg being amputated.

It looks like from this location General Graynor has collected most of Twin Peak's warriors, miners, and clerics, and is having them all work together to fight back the Dusk Trolls and seize everything profitable. Something's not right, though. This is all disorganized, unplanned, and greedy. Graynor was the exact opposite of this. He was punctual and orderly, and never needlessly put his men in harm's way.

"The general is inside here," their guide stopped outside the largest tent in the cavern. "Don't go in until one of his aides comes out to receive you. He doesn't like unannounced visits."

Taking a spot in line behind a veteran warrior waiting to go in, the colorful-armored man was brought in by an aide. In less than a minute, the group heard the captain being screamed at. Although most of what was said was

84

muffled, Grizz could make out the words, "failure, demoted, and embarrassment." After the man came out, his face beet red, the aide told the Serendale crew, "it'll only be another minute or two."

Why am I so nervous? Grizz thought to himself, catching himself tapping his foot incessantly. *I'm about to confront the man who begged for my life to be spared when he had no obligation to. I don't know if he'll recognize me, or if seeing me will bring back too much pain for him. I don't want to cause him that.*

"Krause, maybe you can explain why we're here," Grizz asked in a shaking voice. "Being that you're the commander of Serendale and all, it'll give us more credibility."

"Sure thing," Krause accepted Grizz temporarily handing over leadership of the group. Behind him, Willis and Dart looked at each other in surprise. Grizz's bald head shined with an unusual amount of sweat. Underneath the Dwarf's armor, they noticed the collar of his tunic was drenched. It was easy to tell that after twelve years, the Dwarf was nervous to confront the general whose son he killed.

The longer they waited, the more Grizz talked, the opposite of his normal, reserved demeanor. It was a practice common for people either very excited or very anxious about an upcoming meeting.

Once the aide came back out to usher them in, Grizz began gulping repeatedly, trying to clear his throat and quench his nervousness. Along with the others, he entered the tent expecting to see General Graynor, but was surprised that instead of finding a light-skinned Giant, the man who awaited them was a fellow Dwarf with skin the same dark shade as Grizz's. Unlike Grizz, the man had a full head of hair, parted into intricate braids.

"I'm the Commander of Serendale," Krause extended his hand to introduce himself. "Are you the general here?"

"I'm wearing the badge, aren't I?" the Dwarf answered as his eyes scanned the group disapprovingly.

He expected more when he received word Alazar's elect was coming to pay him a visit, Grizz could tell, wanting to slap the skeptical look off the face of the Dwarf. In less than a minute, Grizz could already tell he hated the Halfman they stood before. "Where's General Graynor?"

"He retired from his position a few years ago. I took over his spot. I'm General Dvorak."

"Retired? He still had at least a decade left to serve." *Graynor took great pride in his position. There's no way he willingly retired. And there's no way this guy, who can't be any older than me, has earned color for all his armor pieces,* Grizz thought as he noticed Dvorak decked out in Twin Peak's black and gray hues.

"Sometimes changes need to be made. Us warriors took a vote. The majority thought I would do a better job. Graynor's retirement was more of a collaborative decision than a personal choice."

"So instead of working hard for the position you desired, you got impatient and stole it through a popularity contest rather than credentials. Tell me, Dvorak," Grizz dared to ask. "Graynor didn't have this troll problem when he was in command, did he?"

Krause cut his companion a sharp glance and shook his head, as if to say, "We're not going to get the help we need if you say stuff like that!"

"I don't have time for this," the general crossed his arms. Then, looking not to Grizz, who insulted him, but to the two men armored as warriors, Dvorak asked Willis and Krause, "Do one of you guys want to tell me what you're here for?"

Krause used his pointer finger and thumb to smooth out his mustache before he spoke up. "We're recruiting warriors and anyone who wants to fight alongside us for Celestial. I'm sure you've received the letters."

"We have, but I cannot spare any men at this time."

"We need volunteers from every city. Is there nothing you can do?" Willis asked.

"No," Dvorak stated flatly. "I need to worry about the safety of my people before anyone else's."

"If you don't help us, the trolls will be the least of your problems," Grizz scoffed.

"Is that a threat?" Dvorak took a step forward.

Grizz realized how he spoke came across unintentionally aggressive, but he didn't apologize. He simply replied, "Whatever enemies you are dealing with, they are pesky houseflies compared to the invasion that's coming if we fail to stop the army seeking to take over the kingdom. It'll be only a matter of time before they're at your door, threatening your city."

"Well then, you better not fail."

"Is there anyone willing?" Krause asked, trying his best to reason with the general since he seemed offended by everything Grizz said.

"All the warriors here follow my lead," Dvorak gestured to everyone outside of his tent. "If I tell them to stay, they'll stay."

"What if we help you defeat the trolls?" Willis tried to compromise.

"What, the four of you and the crippled kid on the direfox?" Dvorak noted the lack of muscle in Nash's legs. Grizz growled and stepped forward, forcing Krause to hold him back.

"We handle our own problems here in Twin Peaks. We don't need your help. Now, please, if I haven't made myself clear already, I don't know what else I can say. There's no help to be had here."

"But we have someone who can change the tide in this battle you're in!" Dart stepped forward to speak. "This man is one of Alazar's Elect!" he grabbed his master's shoulder spaulder. "He can control earth. I've seen him take on ten monsters and defeat them all without a scratch."

"Is it true you're one of Alazar's new element-wielders?" Dvorak raised a scarred eyebrow at the tattoo-headed Dwarf.

Before Grizz could answer, a captain ran into the tent, speaking breathlessly, "General! The enemy is advancing in three different tunnels! They're attacking all at once. We don't have enough men to cover them all!"

"This is the attack we feared!" Dvorak slammed his fists on his desk. He turned to Krause as if looking for help from a fellow commander. "They've dwindled down our numbers over the past month and now they're launching a full-scale assault from multiple sides because they know we can't stop them." He turned back to his captain. "You were stationed to guard the northwest. Why wasn't the alarm horn blown?"

"All the men there were killed! I couldn't get to the horn, so I ran here as fast as I could," the warrior's voice shook with his next revelation. "All I could do was lock the gate and sprint here. They'll get through it in minutes, though. Two dozen trolls are coming up the tunnel straight for here! We'll be overrun!"

"Calm yourself!" Dvorak barked in frustration at his anxiety-riddled captain, whose dramatic worrying did nothing to help solve their problem.

"General, would you like me to have men sent to the northwest tunnel?" one of Dvorak's aides asked.

"What men!? We don't have any reinforcements left!"

Suddenly, the deep bellowing of a horn sounded from far away, deep in the tunnels of the mountain base.

"That alarm came from the southeast," another aide announced. "They must not be able to withstand the charge."

Dvorak craned his neck upwards and let out a sigh of frustration. There was no way they could hold off the enemy.

"Grizz," Willis proposed, "what if you allowed the trolls to advance up the southeast tunnels as far as possible? Even if some of them had control over earth, you could overpower them and collapse the tunnels on top of them. Their backs might save them from being crushed, but they'll run out of oxygen before they can dig themselves free."

"If you do that, it'll allow the rest of us to help defend the other tunnels," Dvorak's face lit up at the possibility of achieving a decisive victory.

Excitedly unclipping the hilt of his axe from where it was fastened to his belt, Dvorak headed to run out of the tent, "Captain, lead this Dwarf to where the charge was coming from. The rest of you, come with me to aid the northwest."

Willis drew his sword and was about to run and help, but Grizz caught his arm and told the warrior, "Stay put."

Seeing the group refusing to follow, Dvorak turned back, only to find that Grizz hadn't moved a muscle. "What are you doing? Come on! There's no time to waste!"

Grizz remained where he stood and crossed his arms to further accentuate his non-compliance. He looked

Dvorak dead in the eye and slowly asked, "How many men will you give us?"

"Are you kidding me? Now is not the time to negotiate. Can you collapse the tunnel for us or not?"

"I can, but not until you promise me you'll send men to Almiria to join our cause."

"Fine," the general knew every second counted, and their only chance of preventing the enemy from overrunning them was the elemental Dwarf's help. "Seventy-five warriors. If we defeat these trolls today, I can spare that many."

Grizz continued to stand in the same spot with his arms still crossed. His unblinking eyes never wavered from those of Dvorak's.

"One-hundred-and-fifty. That's the daily amount who serve in these mountains. That's the best I can do."

"It's not," Grizz declined. "You have warriors covering the rest of your province. It extends out farther than just Twin Peaks."

At the sound of a second warning horn, again requesting back up, General Dvorak panicked and doubled his last offer. "Three-hundred."

"That plus whatever civilians decide to join us, there's a possibility we're looking at around 500-700 total," Willis told Grizz, beginning to feel impatient himself.

"It's only a deal if you join us in Almiria as well," Grizz countered, not rushing his urgency in the slightest. "If these men respect you as much as you say, nothing will inspire them more than seeing you lead Twin Peaks in the fight for Celestial."

"Fine, it's a deal."

"Good," Grizz agreed, grabbing Skullcrusher from its sheath across his back and turning it into stone. "Let's go kill some trolls!"

Chapter 117

Covered in sand from where he'd laid down to ride the storm out, Steve stood up and brushed himself off. Annoyed by the gritty particles that'd gotten under his armor and tunic, he stripped everything off his torso and shook out all the sand before putting it all back on.

Just as Kari couldn't find Steve, Steve couldn't find the Halfling in the clearing after the sandstorm. Using the same strategy she had, he climbed to the top of a dune, but couldn't spot anything other than desert.

"Kari!" he called out over and over again until his voice was hoarse. Giving up, he prayed, *Please protect her, Alazar. She's my best friend. If anything bad happens, I'd rather it be me who suffers instead of her.*

With no signs of life, Steve sighed. *I don't see Kari, Crimson, or Nightstrike,* he thought, half-expecting to find that one of the dragons had been killed in the violent duel. *I wish Crimson were here. We didn't have time to get our bedrolls or packs off of him. He has all the food and my shield, not to mention King Zoran's crown. That is such an iconic fixture. I hope it's not lost.*

Steve looked down at his body and knew he'd have to survive on what he carried. *All I have is my armor, Aurelia, and this canteen,* he unclasped the metal container from his belt only to find it was already halfway empty.

I need to savor this as much as possible. I don't know when I'll find water again. Nightstrike attacked us in the middle of nowhere. It would take me days to return to the last village we saw from atop Crimson. There's no way I'd survive that walk. My only option is to press forward towards Holders Keep.

Knowing he was in for a lengthy trek, Steve ripped the other sleeve off his tunic and wore it as a head-covering to help protect from the extreme heat of the desert. Setting off at a brisk pace, the blistering sun beat down upon him. With the bright yellow ball of fire at his zenith, there was nowhere to hide to escape its scorching rays.

Hours of hiking provided no change in scenery. Every time Steve walked up a sand dune only to find nothing but endless, empty desert before him, his countenance sank.

The monotonous travel grew worse as his eyes burned from constant sweat that he couldn't wipe away. Every so often, he'd take off his makeshift bandana and wring out the collected perspiration that evaporated before reaching the hot sand. Thirsty, exhausted, and depleted, he finished every drop in his canteen by the fifth hour of his journey.

Rather than the heat or lack of fluids, Steve's right leg concerned him most. His limp returned, as it often did when he went too long without resting. *I'm not going to survive if I can't move faster than this,* Steve was annoyed at his limitations. *I'm half as slow as my regular walking speed. Taking twice as long to travel means it will be double the time it takes until I have food, water, rest, and shade. Even if I was going at a normal pace I'm not sure I could make it.*

Finding the will to climb another dune, he squinted and shielded his eyes from the sun glistening off the surface of the sea of sand before him.

"Crimson!" Steve croaked out of his parched throat. In the distance, he saw the motionless, red-scaled dragon laying in a pool of water. "Crimson," he yelled again, but this one was hoarser than his last utterance. Futilely trying to gulp down saliva to cure his sandpaper tongue, Steve realized no moisture remained in his dry mouth.

Ignoring the tremendous throbbing in his femur, he picked up his walk into a run and headed as fast as he could towards the injured monster. But as he closed in, what he believed to be his aerial friend turned out to be another sand dune. Likewise, the pool of water was only an optical illusion caused by the intense heat of the sunrays.

It was just a mirage, Steve collapsed to his knees as soon as he understood his hallucination.

Forcing himself to continue on, every minute drained and dehydrated him more than the last. Soon, the sun began disappearing below the horizon. At first, Steve welcomed the drop in temperature, but the desert quickly became unbearably cold. "Now would be a good time for my element!" he shouted to the heavens as he crossed his arms and held them in front of his body, shivering in the frigid night.

It wasn't long before the increase in cold brought along strong winds, forcing Steve to hunker down to avoid another sandstorm. Once it was over, instead of getting up, he felt much more comfortable laying where he was. *I'm too tired to get up,* he told himself, *I'll just close my eyes for a few minutes and then I'll keep going.*

Waking up in a panic, hours later, Steve tried to stand, but his body was so stiff and sore it took him multiple attempts before he found success. For the second time in less than a day, he brushed sand out of his locks of black hair and shook it out of his armor and clothes.

I have to keep going, not only to get my blood flowing, but because I'm in a race against time before dehydration renders me physically and mentally incognizant. My life is slowly being depleted out of me.

Traveling through the early morning hours, Steve watched the sun rise and again felt the dramatic shift in temperature as the cold gave way to unbearable heat.

Please let me see something from the top of this dune, Steve prayed, trekking up another sandy hill.

Once again, only the vast, barren desert stretched out before him. Nothing was visible in any direction for endless miles.

I have to keep going, he repeatedly told himself as he plodded forward. But despite his best intentions, his body quickly broke down. Each footfall became heavier than the last until the point he felt like he was trudging through molasses. Eventually, he collapsed, passing out in the desert sands where the sun beat down on his already sunburned face.

Chapter 118

Instead of a three-day journey from Elmwood to Oceanside as Jun-Lei had expected, favorable winds propelled Andonia across the Darien Sea in two-and-a-half days. Everything went splendidly, except for the five-hour trek through a choppy section of the Darien Sea's waters known as the Black Depths. It took Ty an additional five hours before he stopped heaving over the side of the ship.

The rest of the trip flew by once Ty recovered from his bout of seasickness. He and Shana enjoyed time to themselves during the day. At night, they hung out with the crew and played them all in a tournament of Kings when Jun-Lei shouted down to everyone on the main deck, "Get up here, now!"

Since her voice went unheard because of the ocean's waves and steady winds, she pulled the bell line, signaling an emergency.

"Look!" the shipmaster pointed to the horizon once everyone ran up to meet her on the sterncastle deck. Even though it was dark out, the green moon and bright stars outlined Oceanside's skyline on the horizon. The iconic four-tiered pagodas were a sight to behold, as they were exclusive to both Oceanside and Elmwood as the only seacoast cities. The tall structures stood in direct contrast to the one-story, single-floor homes that populated the tropical forest that'd been demolished to build the city.

It was before all this, in the harbor in front of the city, that Jun-Lei brought everyone's attention to. Flashes of cannons illuminated the silhouettes of massive ships. Andonia was so far away, the boom of each blast reached them far after the lead ball exploded out of the bore it'd been stuffed down inside.

"A battle?" Shana couldn't believe the amount of flashes.

"Seems like it. Here, look through this," Jun-Lei handed her magnifying tube to Shana. "Tell me if you see what I see."

Staring through the small glass hole that showed far-away distances up close, the nineteen-year-old squinted to make out the distant objects. "Those are Captain Jarek's ships! His symbol is on the sails!" She moved her sights to see what Sharksbane and the other vessels were firing at, only to find that they were the ships of Oceanside's naval warriors.

"Jarek's pirates aren't the only problem," Ty took the magnifier to see for himself and looked to the sky beyond the ships, where a bunch of tiny dots zipped around. Many of them were made of bones or decaying carcasses. Bright red, blue, green, and yellow colors emitted from their mouths.

I see the same bright colors below them, disappearing and reappearing on the shore of the city. They are the flashes of elemental attacks being summoned, Ty figured before telling the group, "The Accursed are on the beach fighting Oceanside's warriors and it looks like skeletal monsters are in the air battling aerial warriors. I bet the

Hooded Phantom sent them here from Celestial and Captain Jarek is working with them."

"I think you're right," Jun-Lei confirmed. "We heard rumors that the Hooded Phantom was gathering pirates and raiders from across the kingdom to join his army. He promised them power and gold in return. Jarek occupying the Oceanside naval warriors while the skeletons attack on shore is likely his initiation to test his loyalty."

"If the Accursed are victorious, we won't be recruiting the people of Oceanside, we'll be fighting against them," Haruto noted.

"That's why our priority is to stop them," Ty suggested, to which Kyoko breathed an audible sigh of relief, knowing they weren't going after Jarek and his men.

"Shouldn't we go after those that betrayed us?" Ryland pointed not to the shore, but to Jarek and his pirates. "They deserve to die for defecting!"

"Their time will come," Ty argued, "but not today. Every skeleton we kill is one less we'll have to face in Celestial. The sooner we can get to the beach to help the warriors, the better." Ty gazed off into the distance, tapping his foot.

Sensing her boyfriend's impatience, Shana headed down to the main deck, used her element to focus on all the wind around the ship, and concentrated on having it blow into the largest sail. Andonia's speed steadily increased, and within minutes they were skipping across the harbor's deep blue waters.

"We haven't gone over how to battle skeletons yet," Min-Ye shuffled her feet, nervous for the looming battle as Jun-Lei sailed to the beach, avoiding the ongoing naval battle.

"You have to be careful. Metal is the tool Anthropomorphic Monsters and Alazar's Elect can use to harness elemental powers, but it has an additional property for anyone who's Accursed. Any living creature stabbed through the heart by a skeleton-wielded blade becomes one of the undead."

Sharing a positive note, Ty added, "The more skeletons they kill, the more powerful their army grows, but their weakness is the memories of their previous life are gone and their bodies are weak. One hefty blow can crumple them."

"If they're so weak, why haven't they all been destroyed?" Haruto wanted to know.

"Because the powers of the Skeleton King always transfer to someone new," Ryland answered before Ty could. "If the leader of the Accursed is killed, whatever skeleton has added the most to their army through their killings takes over. The leader of their army can mentally command any nearby skeletons. Otherwise, the mindless, default mode of the Accursed is to kill whatever living things they can."

"Zebulon designed it perfectly then," Kyoko posited. "We could kill all the skeletons here, but even if we did, the leadership would jump to wherever the skeleton is in the world with the most kills. Even if the leader was a skeleton locked up in a cell, they could order any nearby Accursed to come and rescue them. It's nearly impossible to wipe out the army completely."

"That's why for centuries, they've been providing us warriors with problems," Ty interjected. "Sometimes, we hold them off for years, but there are always outbreaks, and they always come back."

"You should all get ready," Jun-Lei suggested. "There's a pier I can bring Andonia right up to it so you can join the fray."

Everyone ran off in different directions, heading to get their armor and weapons.

"Come on, Shana, let's get your spear and shield," Ty grabbed her hand, breaking her concentration on using the wind to propel the ship. "You've already helped speed us up enough, and you can't use all your energy up before the battle."

In the forecastle cabin, Ty stood behind Shana and helped fasten the straps on her green plate, spaulders, gauntlets, and everything she wore below the waist. "There's something you should know about who we may be fighting," he divulged, his voice cracking as he spoke. "The Skelton King, the one who leads the Accursed, is my great-grandfather."

Although he couldn't see her reaction since her back was to him, he knew she was confused based on her body language.

"What? How is that possible?"

"His name was Jackson Canard. He was with Oliver Zoran before Celestial was built. They came under attack by the Accursed and my great-grandfather gave his life to save Oliver. Eventually, Jackson gained the most kills and became the leader of the army. I was told about it when I was a teenager."

"Ty, I'm sorry," Shana wasn't sure of what she could say that would comfort him.

"It's fine," Ty played it down, then pounded her shoulder spaulder twice with a closed fist, testing its durability and signifying she was fully armored for battle. "Malorek somehow got him to fight for his army. I may not have ever known my great-grandfather, but he is my family, so I want to defeat him and give him the rest he deserves."

Heading out to the main deck, the Elf and Human joined Ryland, Kyoko, Haruto, and Min-Ye, and noticed their proximity to Oceanside's shore now allowed them to make out more details of the attack without the aid of the magnifying tube.

Half the city seems to be floating on the sea, made up of houseboats on a maze of piers that stretches out from the coast, Shana noticed. Despite the dark night, she could see citizens piling into small vessels and heading out of the harbor, away from danger. Andonia passed one sailboat full of people heading in the opposite direction. Like Jun-Lei, the person steering the ship also avoided the area where the pirates and raiders battled the warriors.

Meanwhile, warriors engaged in an all-out brawl on the beach, battling the skeletons. Some tried preventing the Accursed from accessing the half of the city on the water, while others prevented them from heading further inland to the pagodas and other buildings bordering the lush, tropical wilderness. *Teams are forming to work together strategically,* Shana took in the chaotic scene before her, *but for the most part, it's a free-for-all where the only goal of both sides is to kill as many enemies as possible. This is what the Battle Royale in the Warriors' Tournaments looks like. No matter what, we have to keep the Accursed contained to the beach.*

"Get ready!" Jun-Lei shouted down to the group of six as they neared the shore. She came in at a high speed, but her control over her ship allowed her to accurately parallel herself to the pier so everyone could jump onto it.

"Only monsters who had elemental powers in their previous life have them in death as well," Ty told the group as they ran forward, trying to think of any and every tip he could that would help Andonia's three inexperienced Elves. "Any member of the Accused who is a Human, Elf, Giant, or Dwarf doesn't have powers."

"Remember your training and you'll be fine," Ryland added, "but if it becomes too much for you, head back to the ship and leave the fighting to me, Ty, and Shana."

It didn't take long to reach the end of the pier and join in on the chaotic fight. The waves crashing over the beach were just as noisy as the war-cries of warriors fighting in Oceanside's blue and orange armor.

Ryland drew his half bow and shot at skeletons from afar while Kyoko, Haruto, and Min-ye headed off to fight the enemy, never allowing more than a few feet of separation between them. Shana followed Ty further down the beach, where the bulk of the Accursed appeared to be. She blasted wind from her spear at a skeletal horse charging her, but otherwise didn't get to take on any for herself. Ty selfishly hogged the fighting, sending lightning from his sword at any and every skeleton in range.

"Ty! You're going too fast!" Shana called out ahead, unable to keep up with his pace since she he was much more physically fit.

"I won't slow down!" he yelled back, leaving Shana behind so he could continue forward towards where he spotted dozens and dozens of armed skeletons clustered together. Accursed minotaurs, orcs, ogres, and other monsters stood in a circle or ranks three rows deep. They formed a phalanx with large shields and spears, a wall Oceanside warriors found impossible to penetrate. Behind the lines of defense, more of the skeletal

Anthropomorphic Monsters sat atop Accursed beasts in a smaller circle. Their riders each wore expensive weapons and armor they emitted their elemental powers through. At the center of them all, a skeleton with intricate black armor sat atop a horse.

That's him! That's my great grandfather, Ty could tell. *He's wearing the armor I've seen in paintings of him from before he was killed. He's keeping the strongest of his army around him to defend himself with. And he must be adept in battle, too, if he had their army's most kills. Without elements, no less!*

Before he could make it closer to aid the Oceanside warriors attempting to break through the defenses and kill the leader who controlled all the nearby Accursed, a skeleton gryphon and its lance-wielding rider careened down from high above crashed in front of Ty. The impact kicked up sand, temporarily blinding him. Upon wiping the gritty particles out of his eyes, Ty saw the dozens and dozens of bones broken apart around him. What he didn't see was the Accursed Elf that charged him from behind on a decaying horse.

The rancid smell of the dead stallion was the only thing that alerted Ty in time to roll out of the way and avoid being impaled by the Elf's sword. As Ty's assailant wheeled around to attack again, Ty noticed the horse had only recently been converted to the Skeleton King's army. Decaying flesh hung from its bones, exposing its ribs and other parts of its skeletal structure. Hundreds of maggots gnawed on the muscles and tendons on the horse's legs and other various parts where the skin had rotted away.

In his yellow armor, Ty stood still, baiting his enemy until the last moment when he leaned out of the way from an attack and swung his lightning swords through the front and rear legs closest to him. His weapons severed the two limbs, collapsing the horse and allowing Ty to stride forward and kill the Elf and its mount.

More and more skeletons converged upon Ty, who purposely allowed them to close in on him. He sheathed his swords behind his back and picked up the lance of the dead gryphon's rider from among the monster's bones. Accursed riders used the long pole weapon so they could plunge the speared tip into the hearts of warriors' mounts, thereby converting them to their army.

Ty expertly fought with his new elemental weapon, parrying, counterattacking, and disarming his enemies, but not without several close calls.

What's he doing? Shana caught a glimpse of her boyfriend's reckless maneuvers from where she fought herself. *He's fighting arrogantly with a weapon he's not familiar with. It's the opposite of what he's been teaching the Andonia crew. He's purposely taking on more skeletons than he should just to see if he can overcome the odds.*

After summoning wind from her shield to deflect fire sent from an enemy gryphon dive-bombing her, she watched a skeletal dawn troll slam its mallet into a warrior's chest, crumpling his armor like paper. The monster then squared up to Shana, who'd never seen a troll before, but could tell what it was based on its long arms, short legs, and tusks. Its spine was straight, not hunched like dusk trolls that could only live in caves and underground.

Not wanting to let the dangerous enemy anywhere near her, Shana sent a gust of her element out from her spear tip, which she used to propel the monster into the sky. Once the dawn troll was high enough and out of her range, she relinquished her control over the wind and watched the Accursed monster plummet to the ground. Every bone broke apart upon impact.

All around her, the chaotic battle continued with no rhyme or reason as to where to go or what to do. Both sides seemed to pick an enemy out, head straight for them, and try to kill them before finding their next target.

Before Shana could do the same, the warrior the dawn troll had defeated called out from where he writhed in the sand.

With no threats in her immediate vicinity, Shana knew she'd be safe to run to the man's side and comfort him since he wouldn't last more than an hour after taking such a brutal blow to the chest.

He's around the same age as me, she gulped as she came upon the young, clean-shaven warrior. The green moonlight glistened off his silver plate of armor, highlighted the concave dent in it. *He's only served for a few years, just like Steve, Ty, and Willis.*

"Please kill me!" the man cried upon seeing the pink-haired Human. Each word he spoke deeply pained him, but he was adamant about making his intentions known. "I'm already going to die, just don't let me become one of them!"

No sooner did he finish speaking, the warrior's eyes rolled into the back of his head and he passed out from the pain of his injury.

Reluctant to carry out the man's request, Shana remained crouching awkwardly next to the warrior, knowing he wanted her to end his life before a skeleton could impale him.

"Finish him, Shana!" Ryland startled the nineteen-year-old, coming up behind her, having witnessed the encounter. He coaxed her in a slow, demanding tone that she would've thought was fitting of a villain if she didn't already know and trust the Dwarf as a friend. "He's in no shape to defend himself if the enemy finds him here."

"I can't!" Shana was nearly in tears, unable to bring herself to deliver the fatal blow to the gravely injured Elf.

"He's going to die anyway, so why not?" Ryland argued. He struck down two skeletons nearby that came towards them and continued, "I watched you kill a monster in the Frostlands in this same position. You didn't hesitate then! And you tortured Krater, the minotaur the other sentries and I found outside Casanovia. Unlike them, this warrior actually desires death, so I ask again, why not? Why kill monsters but not him?"

"I don't know!" Shana cried out.

"You do know!" Ryland spat, killing another two skeletons, then answering his own question for her. "With monsters, you're so conditioned to believe they are evil you don't think or care about them." He paused to let his words sink in while he pulled out an arrow, notched it in his halfbow, and added, "Anyone who poses a danger to innocent life needs to be removed before their influence spreads and more are threatened by their existence."

Ryland drew back his bowstring and aimed it at Shana's chest. Her heart jumped into her throat and she froze, thinking he was going to shoot her, but he moved his aim to the head of the warrior instead. "Sometimes doing the right thing is the hardest thing," he declared as he released his arrow into the unconscious man's skull.

Over the next several minutes, the tide of the battle heavily shifted in favor of Oceanside's warriors, on land, in sea, and in air. The warriors on the beach prevented the enemy from advancing into the city or out onto the docks, the aerial warriors defeated their foes, and the naval ships held off Jarek and his raiders.

The ex-warrior, Captain Jarek retreated first, turning his fleet to sail away, followed by the Skeleton King and his unbreachable lines of defense, who rode back to Celestial. The few skeletons that survived joined his group retreating to the capital.

"I didn't get to kill my great-grandfather!" Ty lamented once he reconnected with Shana. His blonde hair was matted with sweat, flat and messy from fighting so aggressively.

"You'll get another chance," Shana assured him.

"Ty, Shana! Glad to know you're safe!" Kyoko came up to the two with her cousins. The Elf and Human were just as thrilled to see the Andonia crew unscathed.

"We overheard one of the Oceanside captains saying they were going to work through the night, checking the bodies of warriors, horses, and aerial monsters to find which ones were pierced and will become Accursed," Min-ye explained.

"How long does it take to turn?" Shana asked and immediately followed it up with a second question. "Can they be prevented from turning?"

"It's unknown," Ty shared what he knew. "It might be two hours, or it might be twenty. It's always different how long it takes before they rise from the dead, but we can make sure they don't by destroying any bodies. Usually, they're collected together and burned."

"We're going to aid them with the sorting," Kyoko glanced over to where Ryland stood with other warriors who'd already started the process.

"We'll join you," Shana looked to Ty, who nodded in agreement that he was just as willing to help. "It's the least we can do for those who gave their lives to prevent the Accursed from advancing into the city."

Chapter 119

What happened here? Kari wondered to herself, coming upon a giant boneyard about thirty miles east of where Crimson Singe had battled Nightstrike. *The desert here is littered by the skeletal remains of no less than a hundred aerial monsters. There must've been a great battle many years ago,* she thought, making her way down into the valley and walking through the fully-decayed carcasses, all of which rested half-sunken in the sands.

Exhausted from her long walk in the scorching heat, the Halfling passed through the skeletal ribcage of a dragon and slumped against its open-mouthed skull. Even though the shadow it cast was no more than five feet wide, the drop in temperature between the shade and the sun provided instant relief.

I'm tired and dehydrated, Kari thought, filling her canteen with her element and drinking it in its entirety for the umpteenth time. *I hope I cross paths with Steve soon. I don't know how he'll survive without water. He can't be too far away if we're both headed in the same direction.*

She set her bow in her lap and removed the head covering Steve had given her. What had once been used as a jousting cape, then a sash, then a turban, was now a scarf as she allowed it to rest around her neck. She ran her hands through her long, dark hair, but gave up on the third time after her fingers got stuck in the matted, knotted mess. She rested the back of her head against the skull behind her and closed her eyes. *Just for a minute I'll relax and then continue on.*

Kari awoke, startled, not meaning to have fallen asleep. Throwing up a hand to block the sun beating down on her face, she realized it'd been at least an hour since she'd found refuge in the skull's shadow.

Knowing the day was winding down and the sharp drop in temperature meant she'd be forced to endure the desert's dangerously cold conditions, Kari jogged out of the valley of bones.

Now that it's getting colder, I'll raise the temperature of the water covering my armor to keep myself warm, but I can only employ it for so long before I run out of stamina. I need to find some form of shelter, anything that can help me survive the night, she panicked, looking around and seeing nothing but sand.

After walking ten more miles, her worries soon ceased and her anxiety turned to joy upon climbing to the crest of the tallest sand dune. *I can't believe this,* she thought, seeing what lied on the horizon. *Mount Anomaly*. The singular mountain rose out of the desert, an uncharacteristic feature compared to its desert surroundings.

Holders Keep is housed there. Steve, Crimson Singe, and I would already be at the prison if it hadn't been for Nightstrike's attack.

Staring at the precipice's sinister silhouette, Kari remembered its history from her childhood education. *Mount Anomaly used to be a volcano that erupted, leaving a giant crater in the mountain. Since the lava created a fertile landscape, it was decreed a wall be built to fully-enclose the crater so it could serve as a self-sustaining prison. I can make it there before it gets too late,* she picked up her pace.

Upon reaching Anomaly nearly an hour later, Kari ascended a set of steep, hand-carved steps in the mountain face, each one more crudely made than the last. Craning her neck upwards, she couldn't see where they ended because of the staircase's height and the fact they wrapped around the side of the mountain.

I hope this climb ends soon because my legs feel like wet noodles, she rubbed her thighs which ached from the unending climb.

Eventually, the exhausted Halfling came up to a landing and the end of the winding stone staircase.

This reminds me of the stone platform in Celestial's courtyard, she noticed an iron-wrought portcullis blocking a set of giant wooden doors. *But instead of barring the entrance to a magnificent castle, beyond this gate is the base of the crater atop Anomaly. It's the dumping ground for the kingdom's worst criminals; those who were convicted of lifelong sentences, but came from a province where capital punishment wasn't supported.*

I can't believe I'm at Holders Keep, she told herself, finding it hard to believe she was looking at the ominous entrance to a place she had nightmares of after hearing about it as a child. It was surreal to look up and see the mountain. Its sharp, steep sides continued on for miles above, enveloping nearly the entire prison.

Perched high on the crater's rim, unnoticed by Kari until it spread its gigantic wings, a blue-scaled dragon flew down to the tiny speck it'd seen moving across the flat landing.

At first, Kari reached for her bow, but remembered the monster was friendly. Two aerial monsters were stationed at the keep to accept transports of new prisoners. Other than that, and preventing inmates from natural disasters, they had no interaction with what happened inside the mountain.

Although the dragon gracefully glided down towards Kari, the simple act of its massive body landing on the stone landing created what felt like an earthquake.

It's a female, Kari felt drawn to the horned beast whose element was the same as her own. She stood in awe of the dragon's smooth blue scales shimmering and shining as they reflected the final sunrays of the day. *She's equal parts beautiful and frightening.*

"It's rare that we have visitors come to our gate," the dragon spoke eloquently, intrigued that someone was actually standing before her. "How did you get here?"

"I flew most of the way," Kari began to answer, but had to restart once she noticed the monster craning its neck to hear her better. Even at the base of the crater, only halfway up the mountainside, the strong desert winds were overpoweringly loud. Stretching her arms out to her sides, showing she meant no harm, Kari moved closer to the dragon and shouted up to it, "I came here on a dragon named Crimson Singe, but we were attacked."

"Crimson? That can't be," the dragon reeled backwards, as if the name was a dagger driven through her heart. "He died nearly fifty years ago."

"That's what he and Oliver Zoran wanted everyone to believe, but it's not true," Kari explained. "Crimson lived in isolation because he knew anyone associated with him would be in danger. One of Draviakhan's sons desired to

111

find Crimson and kill him to avenge the death of his father.

"Nightstrike," the dragon mumbled to herself, familiar with the events of the Second Great War. Still doubting the Halfling's story, the dragon squinted, trying to detect any signs of dishonesty. Her look of skepticism quickly faded when she realized Kari wasn't lying.

"What's your name?" Kari asked, attempting to establish a cordial friendship with the beast she knew was a sworn protector of Holders Keep.

"Glaciara," the dragon announced. Like many aerial monsters, the elements she controlled were alluded to in her name. Not only did Glaciara control water, she could also manifest and manipulate the wind.

"Glaciara," Kari put her palms together as if she was praying, pleading for the dragon to understand. "Crimson's resurgence is part of the reason I'm here. Celestial has fallen and he, I, King Zoran's heir, and many others are gathering anyone willing to help in the fight to restore the capital to its rightful ownership."

"And you want to add the prisoners here to your army," Glaciara nodded, but immediately shook her head. "I'm afraid we can't let anyone leave. Myself and the other dragon here with me took an oath to that effect as part of our year-long assignment here." She looked up to where the other dragon could be seen, its silhouette dark against the sunset. "The only way we can free these prisoners is by official decree of the king."

That doesn't make sense, Kari saw the futility of the situation. "The heir won't be crowned king until we take back Celestial but we can't take back Celestial without the help of the prisoners here. It's a paradox."

"I don't know what to tell you," Glaciara stated. "The men and women beyond this gate are here to stay."

Following a moment of silence in which Kari considered what options remained, she realized there was only one. "I want to enter."

"I highly advise against that. You can willingly enter, but you can't willingly leave. Once you're in the keep, you're a prisoner for life. And it won't be easy. The lifespans of those inside are short. Very short," she emphasized.

"I can protect myself. I have the same element you do," Kari declared, although she was too exhausted to showcase her abilities. She ignored the monster's caution and continued to rationalize her spur-of-the-moment decision. *Everyone knows Steve and I were heading here. It won't be too long before someone comes to rescue me. In the meantime, I can bring the prisoners up to speed and tell them their sentences will be expunged if they join our cause.*

"Please reconsider this," the dragon pleaded. For not knowing the Halfling woman, she earnestly cared for Kari's best interests. Continuing to dissuade her, Glaciara looked up to the other dragon in the sky and explained, "Boulderdash and I have no jurisdiction inside. Warriors don't either. There's no law in there. Whoever takes command makes the rules."

As she continued to caution Kari, the second dragon guarding Holders Keep swooped down, controlling the wind to increase his speed. As a male with many spikes accompanying its brown scales, its appearance intimidated Kari. *Other than Nightstrike, I've never seen a dragon with more horns on its head and spikes on its back.*

"She wants to enter," Glaciara informed Boulderdash of her discussion with the half-Human, half-Elf.

Not caring to discourage her intentions, the earth dragon explained the rules to the Halfling in a gruff voice, matching the hoarse, dry nature of the desert. Unlike his female counterpart, he skipped words and had faulty syntax as he spoke to Kari. *His lack of a strong command of vocabulary likely meant he grew up alone during his formative years,* Kari assumed as she listened to him growl, "Whatever you carry, you can enter with. Gold or food, weapons or armor." Boulderdash added the last two items after noticing Kari's bow, quiver, and her matching blue set of plate, gauntlets, and spaulders.

"That's the only perk of entering as volunteer instead of convict," Glaciara mentioned, and then continued to persuade Kari to rethink her plan. "There's two conditions you should know of that need to be met upon entering. The first you are exempt from. Since this prison is for both sexes, all men that enter are castrated to limit assaults. Since you're female, that doesn't apply, so you have to fulfill the only remaining requirement."

Boulderdash interrupted Glaciara by turning his head towards the gate and breathing flames on a bucket containing a bunch of three-foot metal poles.

Kari stepped back from the intense heat, and realized that even though at first glance Boulderdash only appeared to have the elements of earth and wind, dragons sometimes had additional elements that were not telegraphed by the color of their scales or their names.

His attack lasted only a few seconds, but when the fire disappeared, all the poles glowed bright orange as if they were fresh out of the forge.

"If enter, you have to brand yourself with mark of prisoner," he explained, gesturing for the Halfling to step forward, take a pole, and press its red-hot, crater-shaped emblem against her skin.

This is a small price to pay if it means bettering our odds of winning back our home and saving the kingdom, Kari told herself, preparing for the pain she knew was to come.

Rolling up the sleeve of her left arm, she took Steve's sash off from around her neck and stuck it into her mouth. The taste of salt from the soaked-in sweat made her almost spit out the fabric, but she knew she needed it to help muffle her scream.

If I prolong the branding, there'll be more of a chance I talk myself out of it, Kari knew. She quickly grabbed one of the poles, froze its handle so she didn't burn her palm, and jabbed the metal emblem into the muscle of her shoulder. Her skin sizzled like a fresh steak thrown on the grate of a firepit. Kari screamed as loud as one can through gritted teeth, drowning out the hissing and searing caused by pressing the emblem into her flesh as hard as she could.

The second it was done, Kari dropped the pole and kicked it in anger, sending it clattering across the landing. She opened her mouth, letting the sash fall out, and took a knee to steady herself. Immediately, she pulled out a dagger, covered its blade in ice and held its broadside against the burn.

"You weren't kidding, you do have control of the water element," Glaciara's deep blue eyes widened in surprise.

"Yes, and I'm also not kidding when I say I will walk out of here with the prisoners accompanying me." Kari's tone had a savage and unnecessary bite to it because of the pain she was in, but even knowing the reasoning, she felt sorry it came out as it did. *Glaciara's been nothing but kind to me and has only tried encouraging me to do what she thinks is right.*

"I wouldn't show off your abilities in there," the blue-scaled dragon thought speaking of something other than the branding on the Halfling's arm would help the Halfling take her mind off the pain. "In a place like Holders Keep, it's best to lie low and not draw attention to yourself. Follow me," she beckoned, walking on all four towards the gate. "The only way in or out is having two dragons pull on the chains to raise the gate."

After the blue and brown aerial monsters raised the portcullis, it took all of Kari's strength to push open one of the wooden doors nearly five times her height.

When the door closed behind her, it and the fifteen-thousand-foot-tall crater wall encompassing the prison became her permanent backdrop. As the only intact remnant of the former volcano, the height of the unscalable wall of slate rock made it impossible to see out into the desert from any direction.

My heart is racing, Kari could tell as she gazed upon Holders Keep for the first time. Whenever she embarked into a new place, not knowing what to expect made her anxious. But her first glance at the prison was not what she had in mind. In the shadows of the mountain walls, Holders Keep looked like any other city, but on a smaller scale. Designated sections made the layout easy to understand. Near her was a section of fields where prisoners tilled the fertile dirt and harvested crops. Elsewhere, a group slaughtered and skinned domesticated animals for the night's food. Behind the fields and livestock pens sat five groups of buildings.

Before she could take in any more of the layout, let alone explore the actual grounds, two uniformed guards abandoned their post overlooking the fields and came straight towards the newest prisoner. The laborers they'd been observing seemed to ease up, an invisible weight lifted from their shoulders.

Even if the opening of the giant door didn't signal my presence, I surely wouldn't have made it far without being noticed, Kari thought, uncomfortably aware of how she looked among the prisoners garbed in either green, gray, or red tunics.

The only ones in different attire were the male and female guards approaching Kari. Each wore sky-blue cloaks and silver armor plates.

These two are outfitted like warriors, but I know they can't be. Glaciara said warriors have no jurisdiction here. Plus, they're not physically fit like warriors usually are. Both look like they haven't missed a meal in quite some time.

"It's still a couple weeks before the monthly transport comes in," the female guard came up to Holders Keep's newest prisoner and looked her over. She positioned herself close enough to attack Kari before the Halfling had the chance to draw an arrow, but stayed far enough away that she was safe from a melee strike. "What city brought you here, Halfbreed?"

"None. I came of my own volition."

"Your own volition?" the male guard laughed, deriding her decision. His belly jiggled up and down underneath his plate of armor. "What a stupid thing to do. What should we do with her, Dejana?"

The woman continued to eye Kari up and down, making special note of the Halfling's bow and quiver. "First, we'll teach her us Skycloaks are in charge here. Then she'll be treated like everyone else who crosses through those doors," Dejana spoke about Kari as if she wasn't even there. She held up four fingers and put down

117

each one individually as she listed off four groups. "Farming, forging, fighting, and food. She'll either grow, build, serve, or entertain in one of our four essential components of society. It's our job to determine what she's best suited for."

Finally looking Kari in the eyes, Dejana spoke directly to her and said, "Usually we choose where you go, but if you give me that bow you carry, I'll let you pick where you're stationed."

Kari removed her bow from her shoulder, but had no intention of giving it up. "This bow is mine to keep," she declared, positioning herself to defend against the attack she knew was coming from declining the offer. All the while, she thought about Glaciara's advice. *I don't want to reveal I have elemental powers. Not yet, at least.*

The male guard shook his head and laughed again, knowing Dejana wouldn't like the Halfling's refusal. As Dejana lunged forward and grabbed the bow, initiating a tug-of-war, the male guard repeatedly punched Kari right on the freshly-branded shoulder she'd been clutching when she entered the keep.

Even after they'd ripped the bow from her, the two guards continued assaulting the Halfling, wrestling her to the ground. Kari stood no chance since each of the guards had at least fifty pounds on her. Each of them kicked her over and over again. Most of the blows Kari softened by blocking them with her gauntlets, but a couple, one of which was to the back of her head, couldn't be avoided.

"Our pretty new Halfbreed seems like a fighter. What do you think, E'liad?" Dejana asked her male companion. "How about the pit for her?"

E'liad grabbed a handful of Kari's hair and jerked her head back so he could get a close look at her face. "Sounds like the right place to me, although I hate to waste someone so beautiful," he answered before savagely kicking her in the ribs.

"How about a fifth group?" Kari suggested after taking a moment to pick herself up and wipe a trickle of blood from her mouth. "If you had clerics, they could not only help heal those you Skycloaks assault, they could teach you morals, like that it's wrong to hit a woman," Kari glared specifically at the male guard during her last few words.

Instead of E'liad responding, Dejana did. "Morals? Alazar? Honey, neither of those things can be found here in Holders Keep. This is a lawless, godless society. You fend for yourself and you don't trust anyone." She put Kari's bow over her shoulder and turned to her partner. "Come on, let's bind her and get her to the pit."

After forcing the Halfling's wrists into chains, they led Kari deeper into the keep. Ignoring the throbbing pain in her shoulder, a rapidly swelling eye, and other bruises from the assault, Kari tried to memorize the layout of the prison.

Each cluster of buildings seems designated for one of the prison's essential groups. It's like how Celestial is divided by its districts, Kari realized, *I just don't understand why I'm counting five sections, when Dejana only mentioned four.*

Set apart from the others was a gated set of buildings which featured hot springs, greenery, and multi-level structures, a stark contrast to everywhere else. *I wonder if Skycloaks claim this area as their own.*

Kari was led past the compound, to the least-lavished spot in the keep. Here, the only other multi-level structure stood, a circular building taller than any other.

It's a coliseum, Kari realized as they entered. *This must be the fighters' section of Holders Keep, the source of the prisoners' entertainment.*

Inside, the many rows of the enclosed amphitheater reached to the sky, although not nearly as high as the crater walls surrounding the prison.

I get why Dejana and E'liad called this place The Pit. Those who watch events from the stands must feel like they're staring down into a deep chasm. *Instead of being a wide oval like Celestial's arena, this one is a perfect, tight circle.*

It wasn't hard for Kari to imagine what occurred within the coliseum. A section of the curved wall had giant metal spikes jutting out from it. Blood-stained sand covered as much of the coliseum's floor as unblemished sand. Strewn about lied the bones of both people and monsters. Kari even spotted partially-decomposed bodies, their corpses attacked by flies and maggots.

This place smells terrible, she thought, wishing her hands weren't bound so she could plug her nose.

"You wouldn't be here if you would've just given me your bow," Dejana happily reminded Kari, patting the weapon on her shoulder. "Once you see your living quarters, you're going to realize what a terrible mistake you made."

E'liad explained what was in store for the Halfling. "Pit fighters live underground in 'the cells.' Some people prefer to fight in the coliseum just to end their torture. Don't worry though," he grabbed Kari's butt and squeezed. "You're plump enough. If you don't want to be killed up here, you can let the rats eat you alive down there."

As Kari's face grew red and her body froze up from the unwanted touch she couldn't fight back against, the two guards brought her to a gate at the side of the coliseum which was manned by another cape-wearing Skycloak. He was a light-skinned Human who looked to be in his early forties. Dark shadows underlined his weary eyes, and his balding head was just as patchy as his thin beard.

Dejana threw Kari down at the feet of the man and told him, "We've got a fresh one for you, Quintis."

Chapter 120

Grizz awoke from a long sleep, exhausted from using his powers to collapse multiple tunnels onto hordes of drow in a battle that lasted many hours.

"I spoke with General Dvorak earlier this morning," Willis told him over a late breakfast. "He's lending us three dogsleds and the teams to go with them so we can head to Bogmire."

"Good," Grizz smiled. "I'll take dogsleds any day over horses. It'll be the fastest way down this mountain and across the Frostlands."

Before they headed out, Grizz took Nash atop Copper and gave him a tour around the city. Although much had changed in the years since he'd last walked the dirt streets under the giant Fluorite Crystal chandelier, Grizz still had time to show Nash his childhood home and some of his favorite spots around Twin Peaks.

Meanwhile, Krause, Willis, and Dart collected food and supplies, later rendezvousing with the father, son, and direfox on a snowy, mountainside field where three dogsled teams of six tethered huskies awaited them. The eighteen animals lounged around, some licking themselves, some sleeping in the snow, and the rest fighting over a rawhide bone, which was a quickly-decided battle after Copper ran over and took it for himself. With the biggest of the huskies barely a fourth of the direfox's size, none of the dogs attempted to take it back. Even so, Copper snarled and bared his teeth, threatening them all not to interrupt him as he feasted on the treat.

Outfitted in multiple layers, topped with a warm wool coat, Grizz gathered his similarly dressed companions around the dogs to explain the basics of sled travel. "Those are called runners," he pointed to the two pieces of wood coming out from the bottom of the sled. "You stand on them and yell 'Mush' or 'Hike' for your dogs to start running and 'Woah' to stop. There's an emergency brake handle if you feel you're going too fast, but you won't need to use it. The dogs are smart."

"Seems like it'll be fun," Willis grinned, excited to try a new form of transportation. "I can lead the way. Dvorak told me about a route they built last year that'll be the fastest in getting us to the bottom of this mountain. It begins just on the other side of this training yard. Dart, there's enough room for you to sit in my cargo hold since we don't have enough sleds."

As everyone double-checked that their bundles were tightly fastened, Grizz caught Nash taking in the spectacle of the two majestic mountain peaks, the bright blue sky, and the field of snow before them glistening in the sunlight. Watching his eight-year-old propped on his crutches, enjoying the scenic view forced Grizz to stop and admire it as well.

Sometimes we're so focused on what's next, we forget to stop and appreciate where we are and what we've accomplished, Grizz thought, convicted of rushing to head to their next destination.

The Dwarf considered both the joyous and tragic moments of his life in the city beneath the layers of rock and stone. Grizz gulped down a lump in his throat as he reflected on the past he so often suppressed. *I thought I'd be able to hold in these emotions. Why is it all hitting me now, at the end of our time here?*

Positioning himself away from the men in the group, so they wouldn't see his eyes welling up, Grizz prayed to the god he forsook after his mother's death and only reconnected with due to his wife's encouragement.

Alazar, I never wanted my sons to go through what I went through as a child, but Nash has seen his mother die, just like I did when I was young. Help him not to blame you for her loss. Help him not to waste years of his life fueled by anger, hatred, and revenge. Please let him follow you. I know it's the best way to find purpose and know peace.

Finishing his prayer, Grizz reached down to where Nash stood propped up on his crutches and ruffled the boy's messy mop of brown hair. "I'm sad to say goodbye already," he told his son, speaking open-heartedly. "There's so much more I wanted to show you here. Maybe once our adventure's all done, we can come back and I'll show you more from my childhood."

Returning to tying down the final bundles of provisions he'd brought with him, Grizz secured the last of the boxes when a voice called out from behind them.

"Grindstone!"

Because of the use of his surname, Grizz would've thought it was Dart calling for him if it hadn't been for a distinct inflection in the man's voice. Even though it'd been twelve years since he'd heard it, he instantly knew who was coming out from under the mountain's archway and calling for him.

General Graynor.

"You guys go along. We'll catch up," Grizz choked out the words, angry at himself for no longer being able to hide his emotions from the men he constantly strove to act so strong in front of.

Watching Willis and Dart's dogsled take off with Krause following behind, Grizz and Nash were left alone with their six huskies, Copper, and the former Twin Peaks general standing before them. The Giant held a small chest under his arm which he awkwardly repositioned to hold better.

"I'm sorry, sir," Grizz immediately apologized for his sentimental state.

"Don't worry about it," Graynor's calming voice set Grizz's heartbeat to a resting pace. The man's full-gray beard, twice as long as Grizz's, muffled his voice. "I was told you wanted to see me. I'm glad I could catch you before you left."

"You're just in time," Nash felt comfortable enough to speak to Graynor even though he was a stranger. Despite dark bags under them, there was a certain kindness in the former general's eyes.

Using his son's interjection to collect himself, Grizz took a breath and said, "I wanted to thank you for the mercy you showed me many years ago. I didn't deserve it. I want you to know how sorry I am for how my actions hurt you and your wife. I've tried my best to live a life that honors the memory of your son."

Although the Giant knew he was coming out to see his son's murderer, Graynor's jaw clenched at the mention of the tragedy and his face became a mixture of sadness and discomfort. Grizz bowed his head, unable to look upon Graynor, knowing the man's pain resulted from his actions.

Nonetheless, the Giant said, "Thank you, Grizz. I'm sure you have. I see you have a son of your own now."

Grizz nodded. "He means everything to me."

With a twinkle in his eye and in the softest of voices, Graynor muttered to himself more than anyone else. "I know." Clearing his throat, he asked the elder of the two Dwarves before him, "Is it true you're one of Alazar's Elect?"

"I am," Grizz proved his ability by changing his armor into stone. "I don't know why I was chosen," he turned his element off, embarrassed by his past. "People like you deserve these powers. Not people like me."

"Don't be so quick to discount yourself. Sometimes it's the people who think they're undeserving who are most deserving of all."

After a moment of letting his words sink in, the Giant stated, "I remember at your trial you were asked what you wanted to accomplish in your life, and you mentioned perfecting your craft by forging a golden weapon. Have you taken advantage of your freedom and fulfilled that dream of yours?"

"I tried, but I failed," Grizz admitted, casting his head down. *I feel as if I've let him down by not achieving what I set out for. The fact that I had aspirations was probably one of the reasons he didn't want me to be imprisoned for too long.*

Graynor wasn't disappointed in the slightest. "Keep working at it," he encouraged, stepping forward and handing the Dwarf the chest he carried under his arm.

"There's a golden ingot in there. Maybe you can melt it down and craft something to help you in the battle for the capital."

Grizz couldn't believe the generosity of the Giant. The value and rarity of a gold ingot was so high, Grizz knew he'd only ever be able to afford a few of them throughout his lifetime. As he expressed his appreciation, Nash saw the admiration in his father's eyes and wanted to know if they could look forward to seeing the Giant in Almiria. "Sir, are you going to help us take back Celestial?"

"I'm on my way to get my belongings packed," Graynor nodded. "General Dvorak is leading a large group that's heading out in a couple of days, so I'm going to make sure I'm ready. I heard you guys are headed to Bogmire first, though."

When Nash confirmed their destination, Graynor turned to Grizz and warned, "Be careful on your way through the Frostlands. There are bandits outside the city limits and tribes of barbarians farther out in the wilderness. Watch out for the barbarians, especially. They're men and women who believe in a god other than Alazar. Because of that, they don't subscribe to the rules and regulations of the kingdom so they live outside its boundaries."

"Thanks for the warning. We'll do our best to avoid them. See you in Almiria," Grizz stepped forward to shake Graynor's hand.

In turn, Graynor shook the Dwarf's hand, followed by Nash's. "Don't let your dad go too fast, okay?" he made the boy promise to keep the dogsled under control, before nervously reaching out to pet Copper.

"Can I stand with you on the runners?" Nash pleadingly asked after Graynor headed back into the mountain.

I can see the excitement in his eyes. How can I say no? Grizz's choice was non-contestable. "Not for too long, though. Let me know when your legs get too tired and I'll stop so you can sit in the sled's cargo."

Securing Nash's crutches down with the rest of the load, Grizz set the eight-year-old in front of him and found a spot for his feet on the runners behind his son's.

"Do you remember what to say to go?"

"Mush, mush, mush!" Nash's high-pitched voice yelled as loud as it could. It was enough to alert the huskies. All six dogs jolted to attention, their metal harnesses jingling as they shook off the snow they'd been laying in.

The first couple seconds, the sled moved slowly, but it quickly picked up speed once the dogs found their footing. Grizz watched Nash in front of him and saw the boy's wide-grinning smile as they swiftly skidded across the snowy field and down the path that twisted and turned down the mountainside. Copper ran alongside them, playfully challenging the pack of dogs to match his speed.

After catching up to Krause and Willis, who eventually let Dart take over as the sled driver, the Serendale crew took three hours to make their way to the Frostlands Forest. Once there, they spent two hours drifting across the landscape, following the trails west.

"Woah, woah!" Krause called out after a while, slowing his team to a stop. Following behind him, Dart and Grizz stopped as well. Before them, the forest gave way to a three mile-wide, ice-covered lake.

"Let's rest here for a few minutes before we cross," Grizz suggested. "Our dogs could use a break, and I'm sure we're all starving."

Together, the four men pillaged through their bundles, pulling out snacks and their canteens for quick replenishment. Grizz handed some cornbread to Nash, then tossed Copper a slab of goat meat he'd purchased in Twin Peaks that hadn't spoiled since the cold weather preserved it.

"Was that the general you were telling us about who came out before we left the city?" Dart asked his master in between handfuls of trail mix.

"Yes, General Graynor. I'm glad I got to see him. I owe my freedom to him. I wouldn't be here right now if it wasn't for his mercy."

"I always wanted to be a warrior like that," Dart shared. "Men like Graynor are what a warrior should be; someone who's not in it for their own position and power, but to protect people, serve them, and lead by example."

"So the exact opposite of General Dvorak?" Willis chuckled to himself, deriding the Twin Peak's leader.

Krause ignored Willis's comment and instead pressed Dart, returning to the teenager's brief anecdote. "You wanted to be a warrior?"

Shifting where he sat, Dart answered, "Yeah, I took the Entrance Exam, but I didn't score high enough, so I had to take an apprenticeship with Mr. Grindstone," he glanced over to Grizz. "It's okay, though. My dad used to tell me and my brother when life doesn't work out how we want, if we stay positive and make the best of our circumstances, good things will come. Looking back, I realize if it wasn't for my fallback plan of being a blacksmith, I would've never been in position to get to Almiria and warn them of the coming attack."

"Do you still want to be a warrior?" Krause asked, following up his previous question. Seeing Dart nod, the Serendale commander replied, "You know those admittance tests, they're not always perfect. They test you physically, mentally, and emotionally, but they can't measure the heart of a man. I've seen warrior material in you. More than just helping us fight the drow, you've shown you're always willing to do whatever it takes to help the team.

"After this war is over I plan to head back to Serendale. I may have failed to defend our city, but I intend to be the one to lead the rebuilding of it and I want good men to work alongside. Dart, your experience as both a blacksmith and a warrior would be invaluable.

"What do you think, Willis?" Krause turned to the Elf, "Should we let Dart join our ranks?"

Chipping in with his own support, Willis answered Krause by speaking directly to Dart, "Even when we didn't let you fight in Casanovia because you didn't have training, you took your role to heart when you were sent to guard the women, children, and elderly in the dungeons. I'd trust you to have my back, and that's the most important trait in being part of the warrior brotherhood."

"Well, that sounds good enough for me," Krause turned to the sixteen-year-old. "What do you say? Are you interested?"

Smiling ear-to-ear, Dart nodded. "In memory of the family and friends I lost, nothing would make me prouder than helping bring Serendale back to its former glory."

"Good! Once we get back home, you can say your oath. For now, keep working with Willis and I, and we'll try to teach you everything you need to know."

"Dad!" Nash cried out, pointing a shaking finger into the deep recesses of the Forest. "Something moved out there!"

Before the words had even left his mouth, Copper took off sprinting through the brush and trees. A boy of no more than twelve or thirteen namedays, dressed in a white wool cloak, drew his bow and fired an arrow, but the shot missed, allowing Copper to pounce on him and tackle him into a drift of snow.

From roughly a hundred feet away, where the Serendale men stood on the bank of the frozen lake, they watched the teen pull a dagger out and struggle with the direfox.

"Dart, stay here and guard Nash!" Grizz yelled, taking off with Willis and Krause. All three men were intent on aiding their monster friend. No one wanted to see Copper killed, let alone hurt.

Closer to the scuffle, the three realized the orange direfox didn't need their help. Copper chomped down on the boy's arm and viciously tossed him about. He released his jaws after two distinct cracks, sending the boy crawling backwards, clutching his shredded arm and crying out in pain. Unfortunately, Copper only dismembered one of the boy's limbs. He used his working arm to reach to his belt, grab a ram's horn and blow into it, sounding off a deep echo that reverberated deep into the confines of the forest.

The loud noise disturbed Copper, who promptly lunged and tore out the boy's throat. It was only then that Grizz, Willis, and Krause arrived at the direfox's side.

"He's dead," Willis confirmed, checking on the body of the boy whose white wool coat was soaked in blood.

"He's a barbarian. I can tell by his garb. And there's going to be a lot of them coming our way since he sounded his horn before Copper killed him. They're not going to be happy one of their own is dead, especially one so young."

"I thought they tended not to interfere with travelers as long as we stayed on the paths between cities," Krause said at the same time a return horn could be heard from somewhere off in the distance.

"Copper killing him changes all that," Grizz argued. "Let's get out of here."

"They know these parts better than us. We can't outrun them," Krause wanted to try a different approach. "Let's reason with them."

Willis took his commander's side, "If Steve and Kari are getting prisoners to help fight, why can't we recruit these people?"

Grizz glared at the commander and warrior, angry that they disagreed with him instead of following his orders. "This isn't Holders Keep," he countered hastily. "We have nothing to offer barbarians. They don't want freedom, money, or power. But they will want our heads."

While Krause had made his opinion known and refused to speak further on the subject, Willis couldn't bring himself to follow the strategy of a blacksmith over a high-ranking warrior official. "Running makes us look guilty. Copper was defending himself! This is a mistake, Grizz!" The warrior stretched out his arms in a sign of peace and turned towards the direction he knew the barbarians would soon come from.

"I am the leader of this group, and I'm deciding we're leaving!" Grizz barked, roughly grabbing Willis and pulling him back. "Stop sabotaging our escape!"

With a sharp look at Willis, Krause let the young warrior know it was no longer time to argue, but to uphold their word and let the Dwarf lead.

Back with the sled dogs, after hearing a second call from deeper in the Frostlands and seeing the Dwarf, Human, Elf, and direfox sprinting back towards them, Dart quickly picked up Nash, set him in Grizz's sled, and headed for his and Willis's. The huskies jumped up, sensing the excitement, so all three teams were ready to go when their handlers set foot on their sleds and yelled, "Mush, mush, mush!"

"Out onto the ice!" Grizz pointed to the expanse of the wide lake before them. "We have to lose them on the other side!"

Through the trees behind them, a group of barbarians, similarly cloaked in white fur as the boy, came charging through the snow. Three were on sleds with dog teams of their own, two rode on a pair of direwolves, and five more were on foot.

"For All-Mother!" the barbarians yelled, calling out to the female god of nature they believed in instead of Alazar and Zebulon.

"Fan out! The ice is getting thinner!" Grizz shouted, trying to keep the weight of their three sleds evenly distributed instead of centralized all in one area.

As he and Nash continued straight, Willis headed left while Krause turned right. All three of their teams lost some distance between them and their pursuers, who were much faster than they were.

Like the men they were after, the barbarians fanned out. Some headed to attack the red-headed Elven warrior and the Human teenager in his cargo hold, while the rest went after Krause. Once their riders were within range, the barbarians threw spears and fired arrows, two of which hit Grizz's dogs, while three hit Willis'. With a whimper, they tumbled and crashed, but were still harnessed and dragged along by the rest of the huskies. The immediate change in the synchronicity of the sled teams disrupted their pace. Grizz's dogs slowed dramatically. Willis's stopped altogether.

Instead of using ranged attacks on Krause's canines, the barbarian sled teams came alongside him, altering his course to send him towards Grizz.

It's as if they're sheepdogs and Krause is the sheep they're herding, Grizz realized as the Serendale Commander was forced towards him. *There's nothing I can do! I wish I had Kari's element. With only my thoughts and focus, I could use this ice to our advantage.*

Unable to move out of the way, Grizz yelled to Nash, "Hold on!" as Krause's sled team was steered into his own.

The dog teams yipped in pain, colliding with each other in the unavoidable impact. Even trying to stop did nothing, since the slippery ice made it impossible. Grizz tried holding onto his handlebars as tightly as possible, but lost his grip when his sled tipped over and spilled him out onto the ice. The momentum of the two entangled dog teams carried them far away from him, where Nash remained in the sled. In the center of the river, the weight of Krause, Nash, the dogs, sleds, and all their bundles proved too much for the thin ice. With a great cracking sound, the ice fractured underneath them.

From where he watched, too far away to help, Grizz heard Nash scream in terror, a bone-chilling shriek that was every parent's worst nightmare. With his foot caught in the leather straps of the cargo, preventing him from climbing out, his sled capsized upside down in the water. The dogs harnessed to the sled were pulled down after him, disappearing into the frigid waters where Nash's screams were cut off.

No! Grizz stood petrified, knowing even if his son could free himself, he wouldn't be able to swim because of his disability.

He's going to drown! There's no way I'll make it to him in time!

Unlike Nash's sled, which went underwater first, followed by the dogs, Krause's dogs fell first while he remained on his sled. It teetered on the unbroken ice on the edge of the gaping hole. In a quick-thinking move, Krause drew his glaive and cut the tether, preventing two dogs and his sled from being pulled into the water.

Looking back to Grizz, the commander yelled, "I'll save your son, they need you!" He pointed behind the Dwarf to where Willis, Dart, and Copper battled a group of the barbarians. Their chances were about to grow even slimmer since the barbarians that forced Krause and Grizz to crash were heading back towards them. They'd realized the commander and boy posed no threat and neither did the Dwarf who stood stranded alone. They wanted to aide their fellow barbarians in the fight against the most dangerous enemies.

It only took a quick glance for Grizz to see he was much closer to Willis, Dart, and Copper than he was to Krause and Nash.

Noticing the Dwarf's hesitancy at leaving the saving of his son in his hands, especially after he had failed to protect Grizz's family the last time they needed him, Krause repeated with more certainty than before, "I'll save him. Get to the others!"

Putting his trust in the commander, Grizz sprinted to his apprentice, the Serendale warrior, and the direfox. He first reached Copper, who fought against two black direwolves gnashing and clawing him to death. Red blood leaked from the direfox's wounds and matted his orange fur as Copper fought back as best he could.

Covering Skullcrusher and the armor beneath his wool cloak in stone, Grizz heard the ice beneath him cracking from the added weight. *I have to fight these beasts without my powers,* he knew. He swung the axe-side of his weapon deep into one of the unsuspecting direwolf, nearly severing its head. Now that Copper only had one enemy to defeat and quickly gained the upper hand, Grizz moved on to Willis, where the Elf tirelessly fended off four barbarians.

Together, the blacksmith and the warrior defeated their enemies, one of which wore a necklace distinguishing him as the shaman of the tribe, second in power only to the chieftain. Grizz and Willis turned to help Dart, who was ganged up on by four barbarians of his own, but they were too late.

After Dart aggressively swung at a man in front of him, one of the female barbarians snuck up behind him and impaled him through the back with her spear.

Grizz and Willis cried out in dismay for the Serendale teenager as the barbarian woman pulled her spear out and Dart fell to the ground, dead.

Chapter 121

Since Kari's left eye was swollen shut from getting kicked by E'liad, it was only her right eye that widened and filled with tears as she remained on her hands and knees at the feet of the man she was thrown in front of. Paralyzed by her emotions, she knew, from the briefest of moments in which she'd glimpsed his face, that the man above her was her father. Even though she'd only been four when she last saw him and couldn't remember what he looked like, somehow, she could tell she was in the presence of her long-lost dad.

Just as Kari recognized Quintis, Quintis knew the woman brought before him was his daughter. It wasn't hard to make the connection between the light-skinned, half-Human, half-Elf with dark hair similar to his own. That, and the fact that the Skycloak accompanying her carried the unique, sapphire-embedded bow Quintis had used as a warrior in Celestial made the identity of the bound, bruised, and beaten twenty-three-year-old unmistakable.

Above her, Kari heard her father audibly gasp, which he quickly covered up by pretending to clear his throat. Overcompensating for his shock, he roughly grabbed Kari's arm and pulled her up. The moment Kari winced, however, Quintis slyly changed his grip, realizing his fingers were pressing into the spot where she'd been branded.

Now that she was up, the former warrior archer stared into the face of his daughter for the first time in nineteen years. He took in her almond-shaped blue eyes that looked so much like his own, and the pointed ears she'd acquired from her mother's Elvish visage.

Masking his emotions as much as he could, Quintis discretely advised his daughter by telling the two guards, "She better make allies, because there's an event planned for the coliseum tomorrow." Although Quintis's voice cracked as he spoke, the other two Skycloaks didn't give it a second thought.

"Hope it's a better fight than last time."

"Don't worry. Kexian's got something big planned," Quintis revealed. Then, through speaking to Dejana and E'liad, he again gave his daughter advice by saying, "If I were a pit fighter, I'd do whatever it took not to be selected to fight."

Quintis stood, fumbled with a ring of keys on his belt, and opened the door he was guarding. The door stood as part of a fifty-foot iron-barred fence at the base of the lower bowl of the coliseum. It led into a weapon's room where fighters could grab whatever they wanted before heading out into the arena.

There's every type of weapon and armor imaginable in here! Kari looked around as she was pushed through the door into the armory. An assortment of weapons aligned the walls and rested on various tables around her.

Swords, knives, axes, flails, morningstars, spears, bows, crossbows, shields, helms, body armor; there's even less conventional weapons, she noticed, finding a corner where a pitchfork, slingshot, spiked club, and whip rested. *They're all bronze or wooden weapons of the cheapest quality so the pit fighters will stand little chance if they revolt against the Skycloaks with their high-quality armor and swords.*

At the far end of the weapons room stood a rusty iron gate with a staircase that led down into a dungeon where all pit fighters were kept. On the other side, a deranged man repeatedly bashed his head into the bars. Blood poured from multiple lacerations, covering his face in a crimson mask.

"He's at it again, huh?" Dejana ambled up to the man, shaking her head in disbelief. She picked up a nearby staff and jabbed it into the man's stomach, crumpling him to the stone floor. The pit fighter got up and slammed his head into the bars again, this time harder than before.

Dejana turned to her two fellow Skycloaks. "If I ever become as mentally unhinged as he is, just put me out of my misery," she laughed as she continued to toy with the man. "I can't tell if he's trying to break through the gate or if he's trying to use it to kill himself."

"Believe it or not, he's far from the craziest one down in the cells. You can never trust what any of them are willing to do to free themselves," Quintis remarked.

Another message, Kari knew. *He wants me to play it safe and distrust everyone. I'll have to keep my relation to him a secret.*

"Face the wall!" Quintis barked at Kari. She could tell it hurt him to have to raise his voice to her. "You can keep your armor, but no weapons are allowed down in the cells."

He patted down Holders Keep's newest pit fighter, checking for any contraband. When Quintis's hand hit Kari's hidden dagger on her waist, he pretended not to notice and called out, "Clear!" to Dejana and E'liad standing nearby.

While rubbing her chaffed wrists that E'liad came forward and cut the binds off of, Kari heard a primal shout and turned to watch the deranged pit fighter ram his head into one of the iron bars so hard he knocked himself unconscious.

Dejana swore, angry the prisoner couldn't last longer so she could continue to torture him. She took the staff in her hand and poked it into Kari's back, prodding Kari through the inner gate that Quintis unlocked.

"I'll come find you down there," Quintis whispered as Kari walked past, careful not to be heard by Dejana and E'liad.

Once he locked the gate behind her, E'liad called out to Kari, who'd bent down to check on the non-responsive pit fighter.

"I can't wait to see your pretty little self out in the coliseum, Halfling," he jerked his thumb over his shoulder, pointing back to the arena. "Try not to get killed too early on so I can have the pleasure of watching you." Even though he found Kari attractive, he spit at her and the other pit fighter through an opening in the iron bars, making clear the value of pit fighters compared to Skycloaks.

"Time to go, E'liad," Quintis coaxed the young guard and Dejana out of the weapons room. "Stop fawning over that Halfling nobody. My relief will be here soon and I want to get some sleep before my next shift in the morning."

As the three left, Kari shivered in disgust and used Steve's sash to wipe the spit out of where it landed in her hair. She watched her father until he was out of sight, before heading down the winding staircase to the cells.

I can barely walk, Kari thought, not knowing if her legs felt unstable from the bruises swelling after her beating or if they couldn't support her under the weight of the revelation her father was alive. *He's been in Holders Keep all this time. I don't understand though. How'd he get here?*

As questions flooded her mind during the dizzying descent, Kari finally reached the bottom of the spiral staircase and entered a windowless dungeon. The only light came from sconces spaced along the stone walls, half of which were burned out and needed to be relit. Dirty, disheveled people sat along the walls or in overcrowded cells connected to the long, narrow hallway. None of the cells had gates. They were just a bunch of tight, confined rooms, each one identical to the last.

Rather than the pit fighters being men and women physically fit from the action they faced in the coliseum, Kari noticed the people she walked past were malnourished. *These people are the complete opposite of the guards in power. They're emaciated and gaunt,* she observed, unable to look away from their ribs protruding out of their sunken-in stomachs. The smell of the dungeon was just as rancid as the decaying corpses in the coliseum above, with many of the fighters sitting in unsanitary conditions. A few Kari passed writhed in pain and were in obvious need of medical attention.

No one should live under this kind of oppression! I thought they'd all be eyeing me up and down, viewing me as their competition in case they were pitted against me, but I don't think my presence affects them at all. I'm their last worry when they're as close to death and defeat as one can be.

She walked to the far back of the dungeon and found that no exit existed except through the two gates at the top of the spiral staircase.

*These people are prisoners within their own
prison,* Kari couldn't believe. *They live like some of the
homeless people I used to see back in Celestial. They have
absolutely nothing.*

Heading back to one of the cells she'd seen with only
four people when the rest had six or more, Kari
wordlessly entered and sat on the hard, stone floor. No
one bothered her as one slept, one rocked back and
forth, mumbling to himself, and one was coughing so
much, he couldn't make conversation. Kari pulled her
knees to her chest, hugged them with her arms, and
bowed her head.

So much weighed on her mind. She couldn't stop
thinking about her father being alive or how he and the
rest of the Skycloaks could allow such inhumane
treatment of pit fighters. Considering the reason she was
even at Holders Keep, she questioned, *How are any of
these people going to help us take back Celestial? They
barely look like they'll survive the week. Sure, there are
the Skycloaks and the other groups of people who all play
a part in everyone's survival here, but how can I recruit
them if I'm stuck down in this dungeon? This is the worst
place to be in and I don't even know how long it will take
for the others to come and rescue me.*

As Kari debated if coming to Mount Anomaly was
worth her time and energy, the footsteps of two people
entered her cell. Although she felt on edge, not trusting
any of the strangers she was surrounded by, she kept her
head down, too tired to lift it after her trek across the
desert and taking a beating from Dejana and E'liad.

"If you're wearing armor, it can only mean one thing,"
a woman's voice spoke from the doorless arch of her cell,
"You voluntarily came here."

When Kari declined to confirm the stranger's suspicions or even acknowledge her presence, the woman asked, "Why did you come here?"

Again, no response came from the Halfling.

"I'm talking to you, sweetie. Come on, I already have one mute. I don't need another. And unlike him, I'm guessing you still have your tongue."

Finally looking up, Kari was surprised to find an Elven woman and a yellow-skinned ogre staring down at her.

The woman was as scrawny as everyone else in the dungeon, but the ogre was so big, Kari stifled a gasp. Nearly twice the size of Kari, both in height and width, it was large for its kind and had to duck awkwardly just to fit inside the cell.

"This is Gladiator," the Elf introduced the monster before herself. "That's the name given to the most dominating pit fighter. Down here, we call him by his real name, Torgore."

Noticing Kari staring in awe at the monster, especially his biceps and shoulder, which looked like they'd burst if they gain one more ounce of muscle, the Elf added, "The Gamemaster always forces him to eat a lot of meat and exercise rigorously. He establishes Torgore as a fan-favorite among the prisoners by making him overpowered compared to everyone else."

"And my name's Seraiah, by the way," the Elf reached into her back pocket, grabbed a piece of bread, and tossed it to Kari.

Kari took the slice and flipped it over in her hand. *Even though this is hard as a rock, I desperately want to eat it because I'm starving. I have eaten nothing for over a day now. Maybe two. I can't even remember,* she struggled to think, adversely affected by prolonged exposure to the sweltering heat.

Forgoing her innate desires, Kari tossed the piece back to Seraiah and stated, "I'm sure anything you give me isn't done without conditions. If I take something from you, you're going to expect a favor in return. But I don't live my life owing anyone anything. I make my own way."

"Did Dejana and E'liad tell you not to trust anyone?" Seraiah asked. "They're always playing mindgames like that. And it looks like they tagged you pretty good," she pointed to Kari's black eye with a grin, exposing a mouth where half of her teeth were missing. Kari didn't know if they'd been lost because of substance abuse or an injury in the coliseum. "Here," Seraiah tossed the bread back. "I can tell you're hungry. How about that bread for your story? It's got to be interesting because it's rare that someone willingly comes to the Keep."

Kari's stomach growled and she knew she couldn't resist eating any longer. "I'm here to offer freedom to anyone who wants it," she explained, succumbing to her desires and biting into the stale bread. "There'll be people coming to rescue me soon and when they do, anyone willing to join us in the fight to take back Celestial will be freed from this prison."

"Take back Celestial? It's fallen?"

Torgore grunted, also surprised at the news.

"You haven't heard?"

"No, Holders Keep only hears what's happening in the kingdom once transports are brought in. And us pit fighters are lucky if any of that information makes its way down here. Is it really true?"

"Yes, and there's a team of us trying to gather as many people as possible."

"It must be bad if you're stooping to the worst of the worst criminals," Seraiah surmised. "I wouldn't be so quick to assume people will rally to you, though. You can come here, get branded, and offer them freedom, but these are the type of people that won't follow you until you earn their respect."

"Any tips on how I can do that? Free tips," Kari clarified with a smile, again making it clear she still didn't want to be indebted to anyone.

"I don't know, it'd take time, and that's the opposite of what you've got. You're a pit fighter now, and we fight to the death. No one here has lasted more than a year or two. Torgore included," she elbowed the Gladiator. "We're the keep's method for population control. When there's too many people or not enough food, they throw prisoners down here to die. So if you want to survive, you best be praying your friends come quick. There are rumors of an event scheduled for tomorrow."

"I heard that too. What type of fighting happens in the coliseum?"

"We never know until the day of," Seraiah explained. "Sometimes it's a Battle Royale, where the last fighter standing wins. Sometimes it's one-on-one combat, where people fight to the death. It's like the Warriors' Tournaments, but instead of blunted weapons, we use real ones. The Gamemaster always keeps things fresh and exciting. He and the Skycloaks under his command come down here, stroll through the cells, and pick out who will fight. Nearly everyone in Holders Keep comes to the coliseum to watch. In this world, it's the only thing they have to look forward to."

"The dragon guarding the keep told me, 'Whoever takes command makes the rules.' Why don't you all ban together and overthrow the Skycloaks and end this brutality?" Kari asked.

"Trust me, it's been tried. How do you think Torgore here lost his tongue?" she nodded to the silent, emotionless ogre who stood with his back to the wall, arms crossed. "We were planning an uprising, but someone told the Skycloaks about it. Their leader, Councilor Kexian had prisoners tortured trying to find out more. They could tell Torgore knew something, but he didn't reveal it, so Kexian said, 'If you're not going to talk, there's no point in having a tongue.' Then she had a bunch of Skycloaks hold him down and cut it out."

Competent enough to follow along with the story, despite not being able to tell his rendition of it, the giant yellow ogre pretended to hold a knife, jabbed the imaginary blade into his open mouth and began sawing.

Along with Kari, Seraiah watched Torgore's reenactment and explained what happened next. "After that, someone eventually ratted and revealed our plans. Kexian told the Gamemaster to host an event that would cut the prisoners in the cells in half. Somehow, Torgore and I survived, but we learned to keep quiet about discussing plans involving escaping, revolting, or freedom. Threatening Kexian's authority has only ever brought disaster."

"What else can you tell me about him, this Kexian fellow?" Kari asked.

"Him? It's she, not him," Seraiah clarified. "Alexis Kexian. But, like I said, she likes to be called Councilor, just like how some Primary Cities give that esteemed title to their elected political leader. No one knows what deception she employed or people she crossed to achieve her position, but whatever you can imagine has been discussed as a theory. From what we know of her down here in the cells, she chases after anything that gives her power or pleasure and she doesn't care who she has to hurt to attain it. She's been ruling here since before

Torgore and I arrived. She created the Skycloaks. All these guards work for her."

"Who's the guard that pushed me in?" Kari used the subject of the guards to carefully broach the topic of her father. "Quintis, I think his name was? What's he like?"

"The gatekeeper? He's alright. I reckon he knows us pit fighters are all on borrowed time, so he treats us with respect; far better than the other gatekeepers. They all work in shifts, manning the gates around the coliseum.

"That's enough talk for one day, though. You look tired. Get some sleep," Seraiah encouraged Kari. "I just came in to meet you. Interesting stories are the only thing that makes life worth living." Nudging Torgore, the friendly Elf and the silent ogre headed out of the cell.

Unable to leave without adding more to the conversation, Seraiah turned back and told the Halfling, "I noticed that dagger strapped to your thigh. I don't know how you got it past the gatekeeper, but don't use it down here. It's an unwritten rule that this dungeon is sacred ground. We do enough killing out there, so we don't kill down here. And don't even think about becoming a Skycloak. Even if it's offered to you, say no. If you live with us, you die with us. Everyone else is our enemy."

With Seraiah's encapsulation of the pit fighters Code of Honor made known, Kari closed her one, unswollen eye, tried her best to ignore the throbbing pains and soreness all over her body and took a much-needed nap.

Chapter 122

She just killed Dart, Grizz couldn't believe his eyes. Enraged at the death of his sixteen-year-old apprentice, he encased the bulky head of his weapon in rock and charged forward, heading straight for the woman pulling her bloody spear out of Dart's body. Smashing Skullcrusher into the barbarian's back, the many layers of her leather and fur coats did nothing to stop the blow from snapping her spine and instantly paralyzing her. Grizz then moved to the other barbarians, but could only activate his element right before swinging it since having the extra weight any longer caused the ice underneath him to crack.

Instead of fighting against the three remaining barbarians alongside his Dwarven friend, Willis returned to the ones Grizz had saved him from. Among this group lay the barbarian shaman, who was still alive, writhing on the ground from a broken leg.

"Stop!" the warrior Elf yelled to both Grizz and the enemies Grizz battled. The power in the young man's voice commanded their attention as they turned to find the twenty-two-year-old holding the shaman with his sword to his throat.

"There's been enough bloodshed. Let's go our separate ways."

"Your direfox killed one of our younglings," one of the barbarians retorted. "He must die."

"You can't have him," Willis declared. He placed his hand on the orange-furred beast covered in blood as Copper came up beside him, panting heavily from killing the direwolf he battled.

Seeing that Copper was alive, Grizz breathed a sigh of relief, followed by a second one upon noticing Krause pull Nash from the frigid waters. The commander took off his cloak, wrapped it around the shivering eight-year-old, and led him to the shore on the far bank of the river.

"Reparations need to be paid. We're desperate for food," the shaman spoke from where he lay on the ice. His thin cheekbones, similar to the rest of the barbarians, showed he wasn't lying. "Give us your dogs, sleds, and all the provisions on them," he pointed from the canines and the sled Willis had been riding to Krause's sled and the two surviving huskies in the distance.

"You can have it all, but we're taking one of the sleds," Willis compromised, knowing they'd need something to transport Dart's body for a proper burial.

Once the barbarians agreed, Grizz sheathed Skullcleaver across his back and picked up Dart's lifeless body. Three barbarians held spears at his, Willis's, and Copper's backs as they followed them to the crash site. There, the enemies took the two dogs and all the provisions off Krause's sled. One of the men even reached into the frigid waters and grabbed Nash's two crutches and a wooden chest from Grizz's sunken sled that had floated to surface. Every object had value to them.

"Hey, I need those for my son," Grizz told the barbarian who tucked the crutches under his armpit and headed back to the shaman with the other barbarians.

"He can crawl for all I care," the thin-framed man called back without an ounce of care in his voice.

Grizz swore at the men under his breath and laid Dart's body on Krause's empty sled. The only remaining item was a thin blanket, with which Grizz covered the teenager's body. With Willis and Copper walking alongside him and Grizz pulling the sled, the three headed to the far shore.

"Do you think-" Grizz began to ask Willis as they walked, but the Elf sharply cut him off, his face red with anger. "You couldn't have handled that any worse! The last thing I want to do right now is talk to you."

In silence and solemnity, they reached the bank and rejoined Nash and Krause, the latter of whom stood soaking wet and shivering cold.

"Thank you for saving my boy," Grizz told the commander, quickly shedding his outer layers and covering the commander with them. He buttoned the fur cloak closed for Krause since the Human's frozen fingers disallowed him from grasping the small clasps. As the Dwarf stepped away to engulf his son in a hug and check him over for injuries, Copper replaced him. The direfox sensed Krause's chills and curled up next to where the commander sat down in the snow, trying to use its body heat to warm him and prevent hypothermia.

"Is Dart dead, like mom and Liam?" Nash asked his father.

Grizz nodded, soberly. "The barbarians killed him."

"They killed him because of you!" Willis's pent-up anger exploded as he yelled at Grizz from where he stood next to Dart's body on the sled. The Elven warrior's face burned even brighter than it had minutes prior. He trudged through the snow and stood face to face with the Dwarf. "We should've bargained from the beginning, not run away! You saw how skinny they were! They were starving! They would've taken our food and that would've been the end of it."

"You don't know that," Grizz rose from where he kneeled with Nash to glare at the Human. "If you would've listened to me, we wouldn't have lost valuable time which could've helped us escape."

"A couple of seconds wouldn't have made a difference! How dare you try to pass the blame onto me when you're at fault! If we would've followed Krause's plan, Dart might be alive. He should be leading us, not you!"

"Krause forfeited his right to lead when he abandoned Serendale!" Grizz yelled, caring more about winning the argument with Willis than censoring his words so he wouldn't hurt the feelings of the Human who sat no more than twenty feet away. Grizz pointed to the veteran warrior to drive his point home even further. "Do you think I care if the title of commander comes before his name? That label doesn't signify intelligence, yet whenever a warrior leader speaks, you esteem them as if they're words from Alazar himself. You did it in Hunters Den with Griegan, in Misengard with Ortega, and you constantly do it with Krause. Just because someone's in a position of power doesn't mean everything they do is correct. Learn to think for yourself!"

"Think for myself? I'm the one who negotiated our escape!" Willis shouted. "You wanted to kill them all!"

The conversation between the two grew even more heated and turned into an angry exchange of personal attacks, where every other word that came out of their mouth was a cuss word. Things grew more chaotic when Krause tried to break it up, but got involved in the arguing himself. Copper grew annoyed and barked at them all, while Nash cried, bothered by all the shouting.

"I'm done with this!" Willis finally roared, his voice echoing off the trees of the Frostlands Forest behind them. He angrily stormed off, disappearing beyond the trees to collect firewood for the night.

With everyone in irritable moods at the death of the sixteen-year-old, they realized the best way to prevent arguments was to avoid each other. Wordlessly, they built a campfire. Even though there were a few hours of daylight left and they could've made progress on their route to Bogmire, everyone seemed content with holding off on further travel as they sat around and stared into the flames. All their food had been taken by the barbarians, but no one had an appetite because Dart's death had made them sick to their stomachs.

Grizz sat quietly, using the sharp blade of a dagger to shave the stubble growing on his scalp. He did this monthly, preferring to remain completely bald and have only his tattoos showing.

Once done, after sitting for a long while, he broke the silence by standing and telling the group, "I'm going to kill them all. I don't want anyone to come with me."

"The barbarians? You can't!" Willis stood up and clenched his fists, preparing to fight the Dwarf. "I made a deal with them so no more blood would be shed."

Nash echoed Willis's disapproval and began crying again as he clung to his father's leg. "Please, dad, I don't want you to go."

Ignoring his son, Grizz countered Willis' opposition. "*You* agreed to leave them in peace. *I* never promised anything."

Leaving before any rebuttal could be made, Grizz set off across the ice, back from the direction they came. He walked alone until Copper bounded after him and trotted along by his side. Grizz welcomed the Animal Monster's company, knowing how savage the direfox could be in battle.

"Get ready to tear them apart, boy. We're going to make them wish they never crossed us."

Chapter 123

Steve awoke to find himself shirtless, with Aurelia and his armor piled in the corner of the room he lay in.

Immediately panicking, his heart raced, remembering a similar situation in Celestial, where he regained consciousness and the minotaur, Ironmaul, tortured him.

Despite being in a comfortable feather bed, Steve couldn't shake his bout of post-traumatic stress. The body-wide soreness and pulsing pains from his sunburned face, arms, and legs only increased his anxiety.

Hearing the loud thuds of footsteps coming down the hallway towards his room, Steve grabbed his plate of armor and held it in front of him as if it were a shield. *Ironmaul is going to burst through this door and attack me*, he fully believed.

Without knocking, a heavily-garbed woman, dark of hair, eyes, and skin, entered the room and found the terrified Human. Rather than coaxing him or trying to help ease his mind, she said with little care, "I thought I heard you stir. It's about time you woke up. You've been asleep nearly a full day."

"What's happening?" Steve asked, still confused as he came to his senses.

"I found you in Deletion, coming back from selling my wares in a small village. You were passed out, baking in the sun, so I brought you back here to Stonegate. What were you doing out there all alone?"

"Stonegate?" At first, Steve was too preoccupied picturing the map of Element in his head to answer the merchant's question. When he finally realized the area he must've been found in, he responded, "I was headed to Holders Keep."

"You must have passed it somehow." The woman rolled her eyes as if having to explain his whereabouts was an inconvenience. "You weren't anywhere near the prison."

I can't believe I missed it, Steve was dismayed, realizing he'd probably been close. *This is perfect, though. Stonegate is one of the two cities Kari and I were going to travel to after Holders Keep. I can wait for her here.*

Thinking of the woman he loved, Steve hoped for a word on his girlfriend's well-being when he asked, "Did you find a half-Elf, half-Human out there? She was probably in the same area you found me."

"No," the woman stated, then totally disregarding the warrior's worry, repeated her question more slowly, insulting his intelligence. "I'll ask you again. What were you doing out there in the middle of nowhere?"

Knowing any reply he gave would only receive another curt response from the merchant who made it clear she no longer wanted the burden of caring for him, Steve declined to answer as he asked, "Can you point me in the direction of the Warrior Barracks? I need to speak with the commander here."

"In Stonegate, we go by the term general, not commander. You would think if you were seeking someone you would know their proper title."

"Sorry, it's just that I'm from Celestial and there we're used to calling-"

"I don't care," the woman stated flatly, interrupting Steve's excuse. "You're in no condition to walk the twenty minutes it takes to get there. You're severely dehydrated. Drink some water first." The woman got up, grabbed a pitcher of water off a side table, but tripped on the rug next to Steve's bed, spilling half the pitcher all over the warrior.

Gasping in shock at the unexpected chill, Steve combed his fingers through his wet, displaced hair, setting the strands back to how they were. *She tripped and spilled the water on me on purpose*, he knew. Rather than calling her out on it or responding harshly to her incessant hostility, Steve realized, *there must be a reason she's acting this way.*

Using humor to ease the tension and open communication, he smiled and joked, "Although my sunburn makes me look like I'm on fire, I can assure you, I am not. But I don't blame you for trying to put me out."

The merchant didn't smile. Instead, she rudely tossed Steve a nearby towel and inquired, "I take it by the fact that golden sword is in your possession and you wear red armor that you're Stephen Brightflame. Word has come to this city about how you led the defense of Casanovia. Is it true that you are related to Oliver Zoran?"

"Yes, he was my grandfather."

The woman shook her head at the idea of Steve's lineage. "I couldn't stand that man. He was a pompous jerk. Only someone who's self-centered would build his own city and declare it the capital. You're probably going to be just like he was. I get that same arrogant vibe from you."

"Well, you're welcome to pour the rest of that pitcher on me if it makes you feel any better."

Suddenly, as if she hadn't been callous towards Steve at all, let alone blatantly insulting of him and his ancestors, the woman's grimace disappeared and she finally smiled.

Steve cocked an eyebrow as her teeth shone brightly against her dark skin. "You've only been pretending to be hostile this whole time. Is this some sort of joke?"

"Forgive me, your majesty," the woman apologized, bending down to one knee and bowing her head to the floor.

"Please, rise," Steve politely ushered her up. "Until my coronation, there is no need to bow. Formality is the least of my worries in this time of war. Right now, all I care about is knowing what this charade is about."

"It wasn't me, but my warriors who found you in Deletion. My name is A'ryn Elesora," the woman announced, removing her gray and brown headdress to reveal close-cropped, curly hair. Each of the frizzy locks bounced with her every movement. "You don't need to look any further than me to find the General you seek. I'm sorry I lied about being a merchant and acting this way, but I wanted to see how you treated who you believed was an average, everyday citizen."

A'ryn took the wet towel from Steve's hand and handed him a fresh one to continue drying himself off. "Some men in positions of authority wrongfully believe they're better than the working class, women especially, and treat them as inferior. I needed to know if you, as our future king, were like that or not, especially when antagonized."

Ahh, Steve nodded, finally understanding. *I can't blame her for her deception. Her methods were unique, but if I were under new leadership, I'd also want to know if the person I was following was someone worthy of serving under.*

"Well, did I pass your test, General?"

"So far," A'ryn teased him about the ongoing evaluation. "And please, call me A'ryn when it's just the two of us speaking, and Elesora when it's related to my position as warrior leader. In the Desert provinces, we take pride in where we're from and distinguish that through our names. Anyone whose name starts with a singular letter followed by an apostrophe means they came from either Al Kabar or Stonegate."

"So it's like how those from the Seacoast Cities hyphenate their first names."

"Yes, just like Elmwood and Oceanside," A'ryn nodded. Knowing she was appealing to the future king, she promoted the southern hemisphere's Primary Cities by saying, "Our cultures make us unique. We want what's best for our people and we want to keep our identity. That's why we cherish our traditions."

"Want what's best for them," Steve repeated A'ryn's words to himself while thinking back to one of the things she had seemed hostile about. "Is there a part of you that wasn't fully acting when you said King Zoran was self-centered for making Celestial the capital?"

The general cocked her head to the side and took time to contemplate the question before responding, "Well, I certainly always held a grudge against him for that, being a Stonegate citizen my whole life."

"What do you mean?"

"For centuries, people argued whether the capital of the kingdom should be Misengard or Stonegate. Misengard was the capital from reigns centuries ago, but here in Stonegate we'd grown to become one of the most populous cities. Zoran decided on neither. He created

Celestial, a place that embraced the future. I don't blame him for ending the trivial matter the way he did. I would've done the same thing, but I can't help but imagine how great it would've been had Stonegate become the capital. So many people could've experienced our culture."

A'ryn sighed and poured Steve a glass of water from what little remained in the pitcher she held. "I don't envy the position you'll inherit. This is the stuff you'll have to deal with as king. And there will always be people who question you and are unhappy with your decisions, even if you make the right ones."

"I know if I become king, I won't be able to please everyone," Steve agreed with her assertion and took a moment to quench his parched throat, "but by listening to citizens from throughout the kingdom, it will inform me of what needs to be done. In most cases, I'll likely do what's best for the majority."

"I heard that was how you handled Casanovia. You knew defeating Silas's forces would save tens of thousands of lives in the north, so you risked sacrificing Casanovia's people to prevent that. You're lucky Silas split his army and Almiria came to your aid. If those things hadn't happened, there's no way you would've won."

"I realize that, and by Alazar's grace, we found victory, but I wouldn't change what I did, even if I could go back. Many others stood with me and were willing to die to help give the kingdom a fighting chance."

The general stroked her chin between her thumb and index finger, ruminating. "I guess whatever saves the most lives is the right choice. Sometimes sacrifices have to be made to create a better future long-term."

She opened a nearby dresser drawer and pulled out a fresh tunic and sandals which she tossed to Steve. "Put these on. I want to show you something."

Steve slipped on the unique attire he could tell was exclusive to people of the desert provinces. The sandals were a sturdy leather he could tell wouldn't fall apart even after years of usage, and the tunic featured a high collar which he could only assume was to help protect the back of his neck against sunburn.

After fastening his swordbelt around his waist, he followed General Elesora outside. The many buildings they passed were various shades of brown and tan, matching the desert floor they walked upon. However, the dull palate of the city came alive from the vibrant, colorful paintings on the walls of the architecture all around them.

It's different here than in Celestial and most of the other cities in the northern hemisphere, Steve thought, taking in the scenery. A'ryn led him through a market where each vendor had a load-carrying camel and a tent to help keep themselves and their wares out of the scorching sun.

People are trading their handcrafted goods rather than reaching for their coinpurses and spending money. Look at all these beautiful items, Steve wished the general would slow down so he could inspect the unique pottery, woven baskets, attire, and abstract art being exchanged between vendors and shoppers.

"Follow me into the fortress," A'ryn beckoned, leading Steve into what was the Desert province's equivalent of a castle. The giant building was crafted out of clay, sand, straw, and water, and was impressive in both size and structure.

At the top of one of the fortress's many towers, A'ryn gestured for Steve to look down over the parapet. Below, he found a vast, open courtyard where male and female warriors trained with various weapons.

"Until you told me you were in charge here, I forgot Stonegate was one of the few cities that allowed women warriors in their ranks," Steve admitted.

"Elmwood is the other. It's a decision left to each province individually, but I'd like to see a kingdom-wide mandate passed that makes every city in the kingdom allow women to join Warrior Training if they so desire. I've never understood the controversy of why they aren't able to."

"Neither have I," Steve agreed. "The last time they took a vote on the matter in Celestial, the twelve commanders couldn't reach a majority decision and the motion to enact change failed to pass. I think if a woman can meet the requirements of Boot Camp and pass the classes and exams of Warrior Training like everyone else, then, by all means, she's earned the right to serve. It's not like they're incapable because of their gender."

"I'm glad you see it that way," A'ryn smiled, happy Steve agreed with her opinion. "I think you'll be pleased by the quality of warriors Stonegate has to offer you. Over a half under my command volunteered their services once I told them about the plans to take back Celestial. Hundreds of civilians are taking up arms as well."

"We need every man and woman we can get. I hope all the other Primary Cities are taking this as seriously as Stonegate is. The last thing we can afford is to underestimate the challenge the Hooded Phantom's army poses for us."

"Showing you warriors training isn't the only reason I brought you up here," A'ryn directed Steve's attention to the horizon. There, a giant mountain sat ominously, dwarfing all others around it. Not even its peak could be seen, as it was lost somewhere above the many layers of clouds. "That's Mount Divinian. There's no higher point of elevation on Element. All throughout history, kings climbed it as a rite of passage so they could see the different lands of their kingdom. Many have made the trek to the summit. Even King Zoran. I think you should follow in their footsteps."

"Are you serious?" Steve couldn't tell if the general was kidding. "There are far more important things to do. I need to gather all the volunteers and head to Triland so we can all journey together to Almiria. That's where our army is gathering."

"You don't need to worry about that. I'll have everyone ready to go by the time you return."

Noticing Steve's apprehension, Elesora tried to convince him.

"I can't imagine what it's like to find out your royalty and that you're the only remaining heir to the throne. And you must be dealing with the pressure and responsibility that comes with assuming the role of king, but why wouldn't you make the ascent? Some traditions need to be kept alive."

Steve glanced down at Aurelia. *I'm not going to tell her I don't find it worth my time when this prophecy speaks of my death. It's hard to envision myself taking the throne when I know I won't survive this war.* Then, altering his mindset, he thought, *I guess if I'm going to give my life to save the kingdom, then seeing its land from its highest peak would be a fitting experience.*

A'ryn continued trying to persuade Steve as he stood staring off at the distant mountain, deep in thought.

"From my experience and what I've heard others say, the top of Divinian can be an ethereal moment. The mountain often provides insight and clarity, especially because it allows you to get away from the busyness of life and all its distractions. Not only should you make the hike because it's a tradition of your grandfather and kings of ages past, you should go to work through whatever you're dealing with."

As Steve began to state that everything was fine, Stonegate's warrior leader called him out on playing down her assertion.

"Please, Stephen," A'ryn argued, "Even a person who is blind could see you've got things heavily weighing on your mind. Your anxiety is written on your face. It's in the very way you carry yourself. At least take some time to think about it. If you decide to go, I can put a team together that will take you up the secret trail that leads up to the summit. I hope you'll be up for it. The beautiful sights of this world aren't meant to go unseen."

Chapter 124

Exhausted from fighting the skeletons, Ty and Shana sat with their backs against the stones of an old building, sore, dirty, and sweaty. "I don't have the energy to stand up," Ty exerted, each word fading more than the last.

"Me neither," Shana agreed. "Using our elements to that extent requires so much of our energy." She rested her head on her boyfriend's shoulder. "I just want to sit here forever. I'm starving, but I'm too tired to get up and find something to eat."

"Shana Latimer and Tyrus Canard?" a middle-aged woman carrying a torch in one hand and a picnic basket in the other came up to the couple. "I knew I'd find you here."

Who is this lady? How did she find us by this building in the middle of the night and how does she know our names? Shana wondered.

"Your presence has been requested by the person who sent me," the seemingly clairvoyant woman explained. "They want to meet you, and they're someone I think you'd like to meet."

"Who is it?" Ty asked.

"Well, that takes the fun out of it. Come on, follow me, and you'll see," the woman beckoned, turning and setting off in the direction she'd come from. When Ty and

Shana remained sitting, she walked back to pique their interest to the point they couldn't say no.

"Tyrus Canard," she spoke confidentially, as if she'd memorized everything about him, "son of Caesar and Sarah Canard. Brother of Darren. You have a nephew named Lucan and a sister-in-law named Cassandra."

"Hey!" Ty finally stood up, uncomfortable with the amount of personal information this lady knew.

Turning to Shana, who was also pulling herself up, the woman said, "Shana Latimer, the night you met Tyrus, you sat in Casanovia's Applewood Inn and ordered cheesecake with strawberries on top. And you, Tyrus, ordered tiramisu," she looked back to the Elf.

"How do you know all this? Were you there?"

"No. The person who wants to meet you told me all this," the woman explained. "She also told me that before I approached you two, you would be talking about how tired and hungry you were. Here," she reached into her basket, and grabbed the two desserts she had just mentioned, strawberry-topped cheesecake and tiramisu.

"Do I have your attention now?" The woman asked with a knowing smile. "My name is Ca-talia. Let's get going."

Unable to suppress their curiosity, Ty and Shana followed the mysterious woman as they each ate their desserts. A portly lady of a light-brown complexion, Ca-talia led them towards the section of Oceanside that sat on the water. They took countless sharp turns on dozens and dozens of piers and docks until they came to a small, unassuming houseboat in need of major repair.

"I can see why you didn't give us directions here," Ty tried to crack a joke to break the tension of who they were about to meet now that they made it through the maze of close-quartered houseboats and fishing vessels.

"I'm sorry our establishment isn't as prestigious as others, but I hope you'll find it welcoming," Ca-talia apologized. Pulling a key deep from the folds of her skirt, she unlocked the boat's door and motioned for the Elf and Human to follow her inside.

In a small living room full of potted plants, an elderly woman sat by a fireplace on a wooden rocking chair. She wore a colorful afghan over her lap despite being so close to the house's hearth.

"Tyrus and Shana, this is my mother, Olvi Espirito," Ca-talia introduced them to the woman in her eighties, whose ear-to-ear smile added dozens of extra wrinkles to her already wrinkled face. She had the same light-brown skin as her daughter, but instead of being large in size, Olvi was small and frail.

"I've been waiting to meet you both for many years," Olvi grabbed a nearby cane and tried to stand, but after two failed attempts, she gave up and resorted to extending her trembling hand to both her guests. After pointing to a couch where the two could sit, she shared, "First, I want to thank you for helping save Oceanside. If it wasn't for you, I would've had to take my cane and fight the skeletons myself."

Imagining the elderly woman taking on the entire skeleton army, Shana smiled and stated, "Olvi, that's a lovely name. It's not hyphenated like your daughter's. Are you not from either of the Seacoast provinces?"

"This isn't where I was born, but it's where I settled down. I like it here," Olvi smiled, baring stained teeth, a few of which were missing. She closed her eyes and listened to the gentle breeze rustle windchimes somewhere on the back of their houseboat.

"Can I offer you some tea?" Ca-talia asked.

While Shana smiled and politely nodded her head, Ty declined, caring more about finding out who this woman was than small-talk or refreshments.

"How do you know us, Olvi?"

"Be patient!" Shana whispered to Ty after elbowing him for being impolite.

Too curious to wait, Ty repeated his question even louder, making sure Olvi could hear. He noticed Ca-talia peek her head out from the around the corner where she'd gone to prepare tea. She had a slight smile on her face as she stared at Ty and Shana, excitedly expecting their reaction to her mother's revelation.

Olvi responded by pointing her cane at Ty. "Before King Zoran, I was the one who controlled the element you have."

"You were one of Alazar's elect?" Ty's mouth dropped. He used his pinky finger to pick at his ear, as if he'd incorrectly heard the elderly woman.

Again, Olvi didn't answer Ty's question directly and rather asked one of her own. "I heard King Zoran was killed. Tell me, do you know who the other elect are or is it only you two?"

"No, we know them..." Shana began to say, but Ca-talia interrupted her from where she emerged from the back and leaned against the frame of an arched door.

"You'll have to speak up," she reminded Shana. "My mother's hard of hearing."

"There's five of us," Shana heightened her volume. "And we're all friends. They're in other cities right now."

"That's nice. I didn't know the other elect too well in my time. We were all together only briefly, during the Second Great War."

The Second Great War! Ty thought as he listened. *That's when Draviakhan defeated Alazar's elect.*

Before the attack on Celestial and everything that's happened in the past few months, that was one of the most catastrophic times. It wasn't until King Zoran killed Draviakhan that the kingdom could begin to be restored. I wonder how Olvi survived.

"What was I saying?" Olvi stopped to think, losing her train of thought. She sat there for a full minute, her wrinkled face looking as if she was sucking on a sour lemon as she tried to refocus.

"You were talking about meeting the other elect," Catalia reminded her. She turned to Ty and Shana. "Sorry, her mind isn't what it used to be. She's very forgetful."

"I am not!" Olvi yelled at her daughter with a bite of harshness in her voice. Pretending like she suffered no memory lapse, she continued, "I was about to say that the other elect discussed the visions they saw that accompanied their elements. You know what it's like," she looked to her two guests, "one second it's a normal day, the next, everything turns white and you get to watch a moment from another time and place. It was fun hearing about what the others saw. It was like someone explaining their dreams, but it was more real than that."

Ty and Shana nodded, and both thought, *That was exactly the same effect our visions had on us.*

"Tell me, what did you see?" Olvi asked, leaning forward in her rocking chair, eager to hear the story.

"You go first, Ty," Shana encouraged him, since Ty's vision came first chronologically.

"Mine was the murder of my parents by a man named Malorek. He is now called the Hooded Phantom, the one who attacked Celestial. He's the reason the Accursed came here. He wants control of the kingdom."

"And in mine, I found out that Malorek is my biological father," Shana explained. "We all saw each other's visions when they happened."

"Interesting!" Olvi was enthusiastic. "That didn't happen for us. But the elect in the generations before me had collective visions. After I gave up my element, I sought as much information as possible on the subject. The details were hard to find, but I found a couple accounts in an old tome. Throughout time, the visions are something special Alazar gives his elect. He shows people the past, present, or a possible future. They can be individual or collective."

Olvi entered a fit of coughing, prompting her daughter to bring her a glass of water.

While the elderly woman took a while to drink and get her breathing back under control, Ca-talia spoke in her place.

"My mom has told me a lot about what she researched back in the day. She said visions usually occur at the onset of an element. Sometimes people get a bonus vision at the end, like she did, but they always occur at the moment Alazar knows is best for the person receiving it. The visions are meant to inform them or inspire them."

Or sometimes he uses them to reveal information the recipient doesn't know, Ty thought, thinking about how his vision of the past showed him the identity of the man who murdered his parents.

"It makes sense you all saw yours collectively," Olvi rejoined the conversation, finally catching her breath. "You all have a common enemy who has personally affected your lives. Now, you know his story and each other's and it's brought you closer since you're all a team."

After a brief pause, Ty and Shana could tell that only seconds after she'd rejoined the conversation, Olvi's thought process faltered again. She fumbled over her words, trying to remember what the next thing she wanted to say was. Everyone remained quiet and gave her time to figure it out, but she quickly grew frustrated. She groaned in anger and backhanded her mug of water off the tray in front of her, sending it crashing to the floor and spilling onto the rug.

"I'm sorry," Ca-talia apologized, moving to clean up the mess, but Ty beat her to it, getting up to collect the broken pieces, and taking a nearby towel to soak up the water. *I feel so sorry for her,* he thought, knowing her short-term memory and angry outbursts resulted from a disease ravaging her brain in her old age.

"Mom, why don't you tell Tyrus and Shana about what you saw in your vision? I think they'll be interested to hear it."

Taking a moment to collect herself, Olvi shared, "My second vision wasn't about the past like yours was. It was about the future. It was about my daughter meeting you two and you all coming to meet me."

"She told me what she had seen so often while growing up, I memorized it," Ca-talia shared. "It's how I knew what to say to you to get you to come and see my mom."

"It was over fifty years ago when I received my second vision," Olvi recollected. "It was during a battle against Draviakhan's army. Warriors died all around me, including the elect. It was so disheartening knowing we failed." Olvi began crying, thinking back on the unpleasant memory, but continued speaking. "When I wanted to give up and stop fighting, I saw my vision. I saw you two and knew the elements would be passed on to future generations. I saw I'd live to an old age with my daughter and knew I had a purpose awaiting me in the future. When the call came to retreat, I followed. And although I loved my element, I prayed Alazar would take it away from me, and he did."

Taking a sip of water, Olvi gave an admonishment to the Elf and Human. "Enjoy your powers while they last, because for most, there comes a time where you don't want them anymore, or Alazar decides you've served your purpose with them and takes them from you. And once they're gone, you can never get them back."

Ty noticed Olvi was crying harder now, tears streaming over the age-spots on her cheeks. His heart broke to see the elderly woman so emotional.

Either she's forgotten again and is mad at herself, or she's exhausted from having to relive such a dreadful experience. I wouldn't be surprised if she's battled Survivor's Guilt all these years after what happened. I hope that the fulfillment of her vision will bring her joy.

"Come on, mom, why don't I take you into the bedroom so you can lie down? You've been through a lot."

As Ca-talia grabbed under her mother's arm, helped her stand, and led her out of the small living room, Olvi stopped and turned around so she could say one last thing to her two guests.

"I'm glad my vision came true and that I got to meet you both," she sniffed and wiped her nose. "I see in your eyes a passion to end this tyrant's regime. I fought with that same desire in my day. But just remember, if you fail, as we did, know that not everything is lost. Oliver Zoran succeeded where we couldn't." Then, looking directly at Ty, she said, "Even when your war reaches the darkest of times, don't give up hope."

"She's sleeping now," Ca-talia came back a few minutes later, closing the door behind her. "She seems at peace."

"It's easy to tell that she's been through a lot."

"She has, but she's always been someone who stayed positive and looked forward to seeing how her life would unfold, rather than allowing herself to be haunted by her past. I think her faith in Alazar helped her with that."

"I don't get how she saw the future," Shana questioned. "I know I wasn't raised in a religious home, so I don't know all these things, but how did Alazar give her an accurate vision of something that hadn't happened yet?"

"The way I've heard it explained is to think about the branches on a tree," Ca-talia gestured to a small, potted birch she was growing indoors. "Imagine every little branch is a timeline. Every time any person faces a decision in their life, no matter how inconsequential, each potential choice creates a new branch off of the existing one.

"With all your potential choices," Ca-talia pointed to Ty, "interacting with all of yours," she turned to Shana, "and all of those choices dependent on everyone else's in the world, there are an endless number of branches. Even though only one of the branches is what can truly happen, all of them are timelines that could have occurred had different choices been made."

"Alazar showing your mom a vision of you meeting us before it happened means that Alazar can see all the possible branches that will ever exist?" Shana gathered, but posed the statement in a question to ensure she understood correctly.

"Not all, but many. He can see all the possible choices of his creations, but not of Zebulon's creations," Ca-talia noted. "And because of free will, he doesn't know what his creations will decide or what exactly will come to pass. Anytime he shows a vision of the future, it's usually because it's one that he sees happening across so many timelines, it has a very high probability of occurring."

Upon hearing Ca-talia's explanation, Ty's face turned ashen. "We're in trouble then."

"Why is that?" Shana asked.

"Because if Alazar can see every timeline branch, that means Zebulon can too, and he told Malorek that in every version of the future, those who try to take back Celestial will be defeated."

Chapter 125

Only the moonlight and a starry sky lit Grizz and Copper's path across the frozen river. Under the cover of darkness, they traveled side by side through the chilly night. Heavy snowflakes fluttered down from high above, piling up on Grizz's wool cloak and Copper's orange fur, but the two pressed on, heading deep into the Frostlands Forest in search of the barbarian camp.

"Up ahead," Grizz whispered to the direfox, spotting firelight from afar off. Taking cautious steps, he carefully treaded through the snow, towards the clearing in the forest, checking for any traps that might expose their arrival.

They don't have much, he realized as he took cover in the brush on a hilltop above their circular camp. Between the illumination provided by the giant bonfire in the center of camp and his vantage point, Grizz could see everything in the small space enclosed by a wall of spiked wooden logs.

Copper saw everything as well and emitted a low, guttural growl at two direwolves, both of whom attacked and devoured one of the sled dogs that got loose and tried escaping from the pen it'd been placed in with the rest of the canines.

Shhh, Grizz put his finger to his mouth, praying that the direfox would follow his command. When the beast quieted, Grizz tapped his finger into the snow, encouraging Copper to crouch down next to him.

Taking his cloak off and preparing for the fight to come, Grizz scanned the barbarian camp and counted thirteen small huts. Each was thatched with straw, water reeds, and animal pelts, and seemed barely strong enough to support the snow falling down atop them.

There can't be more than fifty people who live here. There are only two watchtowers, but they're nothing more than crudely-made tree stands built into the sides of the only two pines in the encampment, Grizz shook his head at the primitive nature of the settlement.

A woman came out from one of the huts along with her two toddlers and made her way towards the nearest watchtower. She and her kids carried food that Grizz recognized had come from the sleds taken from his group. The woman placed the meal in a basket and used a pulley-system to hoist it up to the sentry who was nearly at the same high elevation as Grizz and Copper.

That must be his wife and kids, Grizz could tell, watching on as the toddlers waved and the woman blew a kiss to her husband in the tree stand. After the three left, the man closed his eyes, prayed aloud to All-Mother, and devoured the meal within minutes.

Their shaman wasn't lying, their camp needed food. What am I doing here? Grizz shook his head. *These people aren't hurting anyone. They're just trying to survive, and I'm here for revenge, which I doubt Dart would even want. I went through the same thing with the Python. I built it up in my head so much thinking killing that monster would bring me peace, but while it was a relief to rid the world of a beast capable of such evil, I was left just as hollow as I was before I slayed it. Causing the deaths of enemies doesn't restore the lives of those we've lost.*

"Come on, Copper," Grizz patted his orange-furred companion, "let's return to the others."

"Don't move!" a voice belonging to a woman shouted from behind where he crouched. It was followed by the creaking of a bowstring being pulled back.

In a three-move process, Grizz covered his armor in rock, commanded Copper to stay, and turned to face the barbarian who'd found him.

"I said don't move!" the woman repeated, this time more stern. Like the barbarians he'd fought earlier, this one was also dressed in white, a perfect camouflage for the Frostlands they lived in.

Showing he meant no harm, Grizz extended his open-palmed hands outward from his body. He dared a quick glance down towards the camp, happy to see neither the sentry, direwolves, or anyone else had been alerted to his trespassing.

"I just want to leave," he uttered. "It was wrong of me to come here. If you lower your bow, my direfox and I will walk away."

The barbarian shook her head, atop which rested an ornate crown. It featured neither diamonds nor gemstones like typical crowns and tiaras, but was a unique-looking silver diadem with a golden wreath design.

"I can't let you leave. Your direfox killed one of our children, you paralyzed one of our women, and broke our Shaman's leg. My people told me what happened," she explained.

"You're the chieftain of this tribe?" Grizz asked, surprised at the woman's level of status. *She looks to be only about twenty-eight, the same number of namedays*

176

as me. And she's also like me in that I can tell she's weathered in a way, as if harsh experiences in life has aged her beyond her years.

"Yes, my name is Cloverleaf, and I've earned my position by defending this village against monsters, the Breathless, and people from the kingdom. My tribe and the other seven across the Frostlands are tired of these kinds of attacks. Countless times we've had to defend ourselves from enemies like you."

"I'm not your enemy. I don't want to fight, but I have a son and I will stop at nothing to make it back to him. If you loose that arrow or alert the rest of your tribe, I'll kill everyone that refuses to surrender."

Grizz noticed the woman tense her muscles and pull her bowstring back even further, psyching herself up for what was to come. *She knows she can shoot me and be attacked by the direfox, or shoot Copper and be attacked by me.*

Copper growled again, sensing Cloverleaf stressing over her ultimatum, so Grizz stepped in front of his monster companion and tried one last time to defuse the situation.

"I know we have our differences between our cultures, beliefs, and faith, and that's why you left the kingdom, but can we for once have an instance where there isn't bloodshed?"

"Your history is wrong," the chieftain argued. "We didn't leave the kingdom of our own volition. Those in power banished us to the wilderness. They sent us to live like monsters simply because we believed in All-Mother as our god instead of Alazar. And despite unprovoked attacks against our tribes by those who feel our excommunication wasn't enough of a consequence, we're surviving."

177

"You barely look like you're holding on," Grizz countered. "Your people are struggling. Your shaman said you were starving."

Coming to a realization of a possible truce, Grizz explained, "My party and I are traveling to Bogmire before heading south. If you let me go, I'll bring you food and supplies for you and your people when we come back through this way."

Immediately, the chieftain considered the offer. The shock of the proposition caused Cloverleaf to lose her focus on the Halfman and direfox in front of her and lower her weapon, but after a moment, she raised it again.

"I won't trust you. I can't."

"You can," Grizz calmly disagreed, trying to help the woman make the best decision for herself and her tribe. With rock still employed atop his brown, metal suit of armor, he mentally willed each piece to pull apart from the rest. Once the plate, spaulders, and gauntlets had all separated and were off his body, Grizz used his abilities to hover them through the air and drop them in front of the chieftain. He then did the same with Skullcrusher, willing it over to join the armor pieces.

"I forged this armor and that halfaxe, halfhammer by myself, for myself. It's important to me. Take it as collateral. You keep my armor and weapon and I'll keep my word that I'll return to you with food. All I ask is that you bring me the gray chest with our belongings and the pair of crutches that should be with them. That's the deal. You can shoot me if you don't like it," he offered, pointing down to his torso, armored only by a cloth tunic.

Instead of releasing her arrow, Cloverleaf lowered her bow, this time for good.

"Wait here," she ordered. Turning on her heels, she disappeared into the forest. In the meantime, Grizz grabbed his wool coat and put it back on, already feeling the effects of the cold and snow of the Frostlands. At the bottom of the hill, Cloverleaf appeared before the gates of her camp and gave a distinct whistle, signaling the gatekeeper to let her in.

Grizz and Copper stayed together, watching the camp, only to hear a shouting match once Cloverleaf entered the largest hut. Eventually, everything went quiet, and the chieftain came out with a man and woman who each held one of the ends of the chest and followed their leader out of the encampment and up the hill.

"Moonbeam, Eaglebeak," Cloverleaf directed the two barbarians with nature-inspired names, "place the chest in front of the Dwarf and take the armor and weapon."

Even though they stayed a safe distance away from Grizz to deliver the goods, Copper growled the entire time, recognizing the two from the battle on the frozen river. The barbarians, in turn, eyed the direfox and Halfman suspiciously, expecting some sort of attack.

I'm not going to hurt you, Grizz wanted to say, as he once again rested his hand on Copper's back. *Let's just complete this exchange without anyone letting their emotions turn this into something worse.*

"The chest is yours for the taking, Dwarf," Cloverleaf told Grizz once the two barbarians had taken the armor and Skullcrusher. "I had to order my men to put back some of what they'd taken out of it, but you'll find that they did. Your items are still inside."

"Stay," Grizz ordered Copper. As he walked forward to the chest, countless distrustful thoughts of how he could be betrayed ran through his mind. *They could be having their people take positions in the forest around here, ready to fire their arrows into me while my focus is stolen by this exchange. Maybe they filled this chest with blackpowder and rigged it to explode upon opening. Ugh,* Grizz hated the feeling of being on edge, but knew the three All-Mother-worshiping barbarians likely had the same concerns for their safety. *They probably think Krause and Willis are hiding near here, ready to ambush them.*

Upon slowly lifting the lid of the chest, he found everything inside, plus enough dried venison to last them a day. *They even left in here the valuable gold ingot General Graynor gave me.* "I thought you might've kept this for yourself," Grizz pulled the bar of solid gold out of its box.

"Gold doesn't have much value among our tribes. We trade necessities, not unnecessaries. The kingdom's reliance on gold, silver, and bronze as currency makes money a commodity that enhances greed."

The last item Grizz pulled out to inspect was Nash's two crutches.

"Can I ask why you requested those specifically?" Cloverleaf asked.

Instead of Grizz answering, the other barbarian women, who Grizz could only assume had been given the more feminine-name of Moonbeam, whispered in the Chieftain's ear.

"Is it true you need the crutches because your son struggles to walk?" Cloverleaf rephrased her question, given the details Moonbeam shared from what she saw during the attack.

Grizz nodded, but chose not to elaborate.

"If you bring him back with you when you fulfill your end of the bargain, we may be able to help him. Our holistic medicine practices are decades ahead of your clerics' abilities. In certain areas we can do what they can't. I hope that's extra incentive to return to us with the food you've promised."

"My word was incentive enough, but if you can say you can help him, I'll bring him."

"Just the two of you," the chieftain ordered. "We can't have others knowing of our encampment's location."

"Just the two of us," Grizz agreed, picking up the chest and leaving with Copper.

Chapter 126

Kari awoke in the morning to commotion coming from the front of the dungeon. Footsteps, shouting, and clanging metal armor came down the hallway.

"Not here," she heard a voice call out.

"Not here, either," called another, closer than before.

They're checking all the cells, Kari could tell as she rubbed her swollen eye.

After a minute, a Skycloak rounded the corner with a spear in hand to ward off any prisoner attacks. He checked over the four prisoners in the cell before his eyes came to a rest on Kari. "I've found her! The Halfbreed in blue armor is in here!" he called over his shoulder.

Within seconds, three other spear-toting Skycloaks appeared in the doorway.

"We're commanded to bring you to Councilor Kexian," one of the men informed Kari, roughly grabbing her off the ground, and escorting her up towards the spiraling staircase leading up and out of the dungeon.

Whereas before none of the prisoners in the overcrowded dungeon paid much attention to her, now everyone watched the rare occurrence of the Skycloaks coming down into the dungeon to take away a specific prisoner.

"I'll take her from here," Quintis said, sorting through his ring of keys to find the one that unlocked the gate leading out to the coliseum floor. He took Kari by the arm and headed towards the opposite exit of the other Skycloaks. Once they were out of sight, Quintis breathed a sigh of relief, sorted through his keychain again, and unlocked a small room under the lower bowl of the arena. Glancing around to make sure no one spotted them, he pushed Kari in, entered behind her, and closed the door.

Upon seeing they were in a storage room full of boxes and other supplies used in the coliseum's violent events, Kari knew Kexian did not want to see her. *The meeting was a ploy my father used so he could reunite with me in privacy.*

"Kari," Quintis uttered, so choked up he couldn't accurately pronounce the two-syllable name of his daughter.

"Dad!" Kari hugged her father. The last time they shared such an embrace, she was four years old, only a few days from her fifth nameday.

"I'm so sorry I couldn't say anything last night. I knew you'd be safer if no one knew who you were." He cupped his hands on her face. "My daughter," he cried. "Look at how you've grown!"

"I've missed you so much," Kari began crying herself. "Deep down, I knew you were alive. I never gave up hope."

"What brought you to Holders Keep, though?" Quintis wiped his eyes. "Everyone's been talking about how a Halfling voluntarily entered the prison and how you must want to kill someone who wronged you. That's usually the only reason people come here. This place is dangerous."

"I'm not worried about that," Kari answered with an aura of confidence that forced her dad to stop looking at her as if she were still a four-year-old. "The kingdom is just as scary of a place right now. Celestial has been taken over by a man we call the Hooded Phantom. Monsters call him the Faceless, but to you his name is Malorek."

Quintis clenched his fists so hard his knuckles turned white. The former warrior archer's face went ghostly pale, so Kari ushered him to sit down on a nearby crate.

"Malorek," Quintis breathed out the name as if it were a curse. "He's still alive? When I heard Princess Kyra and Queen Evalyn had been murdered but not King Zoran, I assumed Zoran killed him."

"As far as we know, Zoran thought he did, but somehow Malorek survived."

Quintis punched a nearby crate and shook his head. "Malorek! He's the reason I'm in here!"

"What exactly happened?" Kari took a seat across from her dad in the close confines of the storehouse, longing to learn the answers to the questions she'd spent nearly all her life trying to solve.

"I was sent with a team of warriors on a mission to retrieve a target alive at a house in Celestial. We were told the man had eloped with Princess Kyra against King Zoran's wishes and was abusive towards her. I didn't know it was Malorek until I saw him. He killed all the warriors with me, and then knocked me unconscious. When I came to, Malorek set the house on fire and told me about his plan for framing me.

"Then, he went out and found a warrior and told him I was responsible for the murders. That warrior came into that house and saw my arrows sticking out of everyone on the mission. One of the men on our team was his father. Even though Malorek caused his death, the son

184

blamed me because I appeared guilty. He wanted to kill me, but couldn't bring himself to do it, so he forced me onto a transport headed to Holders Keep that night. He figured I'd be good as dead if I was sent here, and he was right. I've been here for seventeen years."

"Eighteen," Kari corrected him.

"Eighteen," Quintis shook his head. "I've grown so bitter. I never got a fair trial or anything. Every day I hoped someone would figure it out so I could be saved from this terrible place. Every day I longed to see you and your mother, and it broke my heart not being able to do so. You look so much like her," Quintis grabbed Kari's face for a second time, using a thumb to wipe away a tear falling down her cheek.

"Dad, mom died shortly after you left."

"I know," Quintis said quietly, and then was silent for a minute.

Kari grabbed her dad's knee, gently squeezing it to let him know she was there to support him. With her other hand, she removed the locket she wore around her neck and placed it into her father's palm.

Quintis began crying, recognizing the jewelry as the one his wife wore. When he opened the locket, he found the small portrait of his wife Kari had put it in it and began weeping at the sight of his beloved.

"Thank you, Kari," he squeaked out, appreciating that she was willing to give him the jewelry. "She was the love of my life. I can't believe she's gone."

After wiping some snot from his nose with the back of his hand, he explained, "There was a lady from our district who I knew that was sent here a few years after me. She told me that my wife died. She also mentioned she heard rumors that I was behind the murders and that I had an affair with the princess."

"I couldn't believe it, but I understood. Since Kyra and Evalyn were killed the same night as the warriors and a couple bystanders saw me being led away in binds, it was easy for them to jump to the conclusion I was responsible, especially since that was the last day anyone saw me. I figured rumors would spread, so I prayed and prayed you and your mom would not hear them and have your view of me tarnished."

"I don't think mom heard them, but she was heartbroken you were gone so unexpectedly," Kari admitted. "I only found out about the gossip recently, and I'm sorry to say that it made me doubt what I knew to be true." She shook her head in disgust at herself, embarrassed she had even considered her father was capable of cheating on her mother and abandoning her.

"Don't beat yourself up about that," Quintis rubbed his daughter's hand, seeing the regret in her eyes. "The spread of false information can lead to so many rumors and conspiracies that the actual truth is lost forever. It's dangerous when people accept what they're told at face value without researching all the facts for themselves."

Or worse, crafting stories based on rumors that got the details both wrong and out of order, Kari clenched her fists, thinking about the irreparable damage caused because of people conflating her dad's actions with Malorek's. Although she was angry at the wasted years, Kari tried to focus on the fact they were finally reunited.

"Alazar showed me you were innocent and that Malorek was to blame. He gave me and four others a series of visions that are playing out the story of his life and what led to him becoming the Hooded Phantom." Kari placed her hand on her chest and coated her plate of armor in ice. "He chose me to be the bearer of the element of water," she confessed.

186

A smile crept over Quintis's face, proud of his daughter, but it was immediately replaced with a frown, knowing of the tragic endings of many of Alazar's Elect. Still, he told Kari, "I'm sure you're well-deserving of the power he's imbued you with. You might need your abilities tonight. Kexian's got some sort of monster she's going to have a bunch of the fighters battle. She does crazy stuff like this from time to time. I'm convinced she has a secret tunnel leading down Mount Anomaly and out into the desert and she has her most trusted Skycloaks bring up monsters from Deletion. The earth-dragon that guards this place helps corral them for her."

"So, she could escape if she wants to?"

"I don't believe she has any reason to. She's achieved more here than anywhere else in the kingdom. She barely has to work for it because she makes it off the hard-working backs of everyone in this prison."

"Why are you in her service?" Kari nodded to Quintis's sky-blue cape.

"I choose to be. Ever since she staged a mutiny and took command with those loyal to her, she's gotten progressively crazier. One minute she's the nicest person to be around, and the next minute she's terrifying. People fear her. One wrong look and she'll throw you in with the pit fighters or have you tortured. I've spent a long time trying to earn her trust, doing terrible things in the process, so I can be promoted from Skycloak to her inner circle. Once I become her trusted confidant, I can take her out and end the oppression. It's dangerous having one person in so much control and power. That's why each Primary City institutes a leader among the clerics, lawmakers, and warriors. They all balance each other out. It's not like that here."

Taking her out may be the way I can earn the respect of the people in this prison, Kari thought. With a plan forming in her head, she stated, "Whatever this monster is, I'm going to take it on and show off the power I have with my element. I'll announce to everyone in the coliseum my offer for freedom and that we'll leave when help arrives from the outside. If Kexian sends her guards to stop me, the pit fighters will be more than willing to fight alongside me to end their horrible treatment. Will you be able to unlock the gates so we can all stand against the Skycloaks?"

"I can," Quintis nodded, "but I'm apprehensive about letting these people out into the kingdom. This prison isn't a reformative one like others. These convicts are put here to keep them away from society because of the damage and destruction they'll cause."

"Their freedom is a risk we have to take. Our primary goal is to take back Celestial no matter what. We'll deal with whatever fallout there is after that."

"Okay," Quintis agreed, trusting his daughter. "I'll make sure the prisoners can get through the gates and can join you in the revolt. I'll be by your side too. We need to get you back to the cells, though. The match is scheduled to be held tonight."

Kari nodded, standing up, also knowing she needed to return to her designated dwelling. *I have to rally everyone,* she told herself. *This plan won't work if the pit fighters aren't willing to risk their lives for a better one.*

As Quintis led her back to the dungeon, she asked him, "Do you know if I can trust Seraiah and the Gladiator they call Torgore? What did they do to get in here?"

"The ogre was sent here from Triland. Primary Cities sometimes put monsters in their transports if they captured one, but don't want to kill it. He'll be helpful to your cause. He can harness the power of lightning. I've seen him use it to his advantage against opponents time and time again. He's so brutal, I turn my head so I don't have to watch.

"For Seraiah, it wasn't just one thing she did. She was put in here because of the Three Strikes Rule. Three criminal offenses, the last of which involved a kidnapping. She was addicted to some sort of narcotic and told she wasn't allowed to see her child. So she broke into the father's house and took the child, but ended up getting caught days later. Remember though, you can't fully trust anyone here, except me, of course," Quintis said as he unlocked the gate leading to the armory, and then the one leading down to the cells. "I'll try to keep you alive, no matter what. Good luck," he whispered as she descended the stairs into the dark dungeon.

"You want to do what?" Seraiah asked minutes later, incredulous at the idea of Kari's proposed plan.

"I need your help rallying everyone down here," Kari repeated herself, looking to Torgore and Seraiah for aid. "We don't have much time."

Torgore smiled and punched his fist into his palm. He may not have been able to speak, but his excitement for the thrill of a battle against the Skycloaks was clear.

Seraiah was not as eager. "No!" she argued, spitting on the ground through one of the gaps in her teeth. "This is a terrible idea! No one will join your cause. Every few months, someone comes in here, sees the conditions we live in, and asserts themselves as the champion that'll kill Kexian and set everything right. You're not the first, and you won't be the last. We're tired of getting our hopes up only to fail!"

"I'm not like the others. All they need to do is break through the iron door and enter the armory. From there, they can watch me through the fifty-foot gate looking over the floor of the arena as I defeat this monster single-handedly. They'll see that I have the power to lead them against the Skycloaks," Kari stated, still keeping the fact she had an elemental power a secret.

"And you convinced the gatekeeper to let us all out?"

"Yes, he wants in on the revolt." Kari also kept secret that Quintis was her father, but Seraiah's eyes narrowed, skeptical of the Halfling's claim.

"You're not telling us everything. Do you know him or something?"

Kari remained silent, causing Seraiah to grow angry. "Trust goes both ways. You can't ask us to risk our lives for you if you're not willing to keep us fully informed."

"Quintis is my father," Kari divulged, knowing the risk in doing so, but that she needed to gain the trust of Seraiah and Torgore to have any hope of a successful rebellion.

Only the ogre seemed on board, who, although unable to speak, let out a noise from deep in his throat to gain Seraiah's attention and nodded to her with passion in his eyes.

"Come on!" Kari encouraged the Elf, trying to convince her a revolt would work. "I know what it's like to struggle and not have much. No longer will everyone down here have to be tired, uncomfortable, and starving. We can change that! We can end the oppression of the pit fighters and everyone in this prison not wearing a cloak."

"Alright!" Seraiah threw up her hands up. "Let's split up and start getting everyone prepared."

"Good," Kari clapped her hands. After Seraiah left, but before the ogre followed, Kari told Torgore, "Tonight you'll be dining at Kexian's table."

Again, Torgore slammed his hand into his palm. Soon, the very ones that fed him endless protein, forced him to train relentlessly, and turned him to the behemoth he was, would be the ones to suffer his wrath.

That night, Kari stood by the inner door. She repeatedly smashed her ice dagger into the rusty hinges, getting them to the point where they'd break with one big heave. A host of pit fighters stood behind her. So many had come and were chomping at the bit to fight, some had to be sent back to their cells so the Skycloaks wouldn't suspect an uprising.

As she waited for the Gamemaster to come through the armory and to the entrance to the cells to select the participants who would face off against his monster in the night's event, she went through the steps of the rebellion in her head.

I'll volunteer to fight alone and use my element to defeat whatever threat Kexian puts before me. Meanwhile, Torgore will pull this door off its hinges to let all the pit fighters into the armory so they can watch and know they finally have power on their side. I'll declare a revolt and Quintis will open the gate leading out to the arena. Then, every pit fighter who wants to fight can rush out as we battle any Skycloaks that stand in our way.

Even with the plans in place, Kari felt a churning in her stomach. *I'm nervous*, she realized, a feeling that only increased the louder the roaring chatter of the crowd grew. More and more prisoners filed into the stands by the second.

I've been so busy convincing pit fighters to join me after I defeat this monster, I haven't even considered what I'll be facing. There are rare monsters exclusive to certain environments all across Element. Some only exist in the sea, forests, swamps, and tropical forests. There's no telling what they've pulled from out this deep in the desert. I don't even know if I will be victorious, even with my element.

Doubt crept in through the cracks in her confidence as Kari worried even more. She rubbed her black eye and thought, *I'm still bruised and sore, I don't have my bow, and so many of the pit fighters seemed skeptical of our success in overthrowing the Skycloaks.*

As she waited, the crowd went silent and a singular voice shouted out to everyone who'd come to witness whatever blood-bath spectacle Kexian had ordered in the cylindrically-tall arena.

It's the Gamemaster, introducing the night's events and building up the suspense. After an eruption of cheers, Dejana, E'liad, and a few other spear-toting Skycloaks emerged through the front gate and made their way through the armory.

She still has my bow, Kari glared at Dejana, *but it will be in my hands before the end of this night.*

"This is the one I told you about," Dejana turned to a middle-aged Skycloak and pointed out the Halfling before them in blue armor. "She's the one who voluntarily entered the keep." Then speaking to Kari, she asked, "Giving up already? Hoping you'll get picked so you can be put out of your misery?"

Instead of replying to Dejana, Kari stared unblinkingly into the eyes of the man she could only assume was the Gamemaster. "I'm offering to take on whatever you have out there by myself. Let the pit fighters have this night off."

"Okay," he agreed, taking no time to consider her decision or counter it.

It's as if he knew this is exactly what I was going to do, Kari grew concerned at his lack of contemplation.

The door was unlocked and Dejana roughly pulled Kari into the armory while the Gamemaster quickly closed and locked it again.

"Where's the gatekeeper?" Kari asked, realizing the Gamemaster was carrying Quintis's ring of keys. "I thought he was in charge of all the doors in the Coliseum."

"Hurry and pick the weapons you'll use," the Gamemaster refused to answer her, gesturing around to the tables and walls for her to choose from the vast assortment.

Finding a bronze sword, Kari buckled a sheath to her waist and slid the weapon in. She then found a wooden bow and stuffed as many metal-tipped arrows as she could into three different quivers.

I'll grab another bow in case mine breaks, she thought, noticing it was well-worn and fragile, unlike her father's steel bow she'd used her whole life.

Lastly, she put on a bronze helm for added protection.

"I'm ready," she declared, at which point she was led out to the coliseum floor. Kari ignored the cheering crowd of nearly a thousand people and frantically searched for her dad.

Where is he? she wanted to cry. *We need him to unlock the door into the armory so all the pit fighters can come out and join me once we start the revolt. Our entire plan revolves around him.*

Kari continued searching, growing more and more desperate with each passing second.

Quintis was nowhere to be found.

Chapter 127

Long after nightfall, Grizz and Copper returned to the campsite. From his hands, Grizz dropped the chest full of provisions into the snow that Cloverleaf gave him.

"Nash is sleeping over there," Krause pointed from where he sat next to the fire. The commander was in the same spot he'd been hours earlier. "He was crying pretty hard after you left. I tried talking to him, but he was inconsolable."

Saying nothing to the Human, Grizz headed over to his son and went to pull the blankets back over Nash's shoulders, but Nash wasn't sleeping at all. The boy sat up the moment he felt his father's touch, but instead of greeting his dad or being overjoyed at his return, he uttered, "I don't like that you left me. You didn't tell us when you'd be back. I was scared."

"I had to make sure no one else would be after us tonight," Grizz explained.

"You're lying!" Nash called him out. "You wanted to kill everyone who killed Dart. Just like how for months you wanted to kill the Python and all the monsters who murdered mom and Liam. It was all you talked about." Nash's voice grew louder and angrier the more he spoke. "I know you wanted revenge again tonight, but I asked you to stay with me. If you got hurt, it would've been my fault."

"Why do you think that?" Grizz asked, trying to understand why his son was so upset.

"You went after the barbarians because they killed Dart, but Dart is dead because of me."

"That's not true."

"Yes it is!" Nash cut his father off. "If it wasn't for me not being able to swim, you and Mr. Krause could've saved him in time. I slow everyone down, all because Alazar messed up when he made me!"

Working himself up to the point where he was now hyperventilating, Nash spoke through ragged breaths. "I hate that I have a hard time walking. I was always a disappointment to you and mom. The last time I talked to her, I told her I'd walked all the way to school on my crutches, but I lied. Liam had to help me. I just wanted to make her proud, but now I hate that that's one of the last memories I have of her." Nash stopped for a moment to wipe his tears.

"Why didn't you tell me this before if it's been bothering you so much?" Grizz sat down next to his son to console him. Nash cozied up under Grizz's armpit with his blanket, needing comfort more than to continue being angry with his dad.

"I didn't want you to be mad at me. If I didn't have you to talk to, I wouldn't have anyone."

"Nash," Grizz grabbed his son's chin and turned his face so he was forced to take in what he was about to say, "nothing you can do can make me love you any less."

"You're just saying that to make me feel better, but I know what I am. I'm a burden. You probably wish I died instead of Liam so you could have a son who's more useful."

"That's not true!" Grizz repeated for the second time in their conversation, trying to drill the idea into his son's mind that what he believed was false. "Let me tell you something. And I don't want you to ever forget this," Grizz spoke sternly so his point was made clear. "We're not measured by our limitations, but what we accomplish despite them. I am so proud of you, and so was your mom. You worked hard and we saw you progress, not just physically, but in who you are as a person. That's more important than anything else."

Grizz sat back, and pulled Nash tighter against him as he looked up to the starry night above. "We all go through our own trials. I suffered through some when I was younger, but those tough times made me who I am. I hope someday you'll realize your trials can be blessings. Now, it's time to get you back under these covers so you can get some sleep. Tomorrow's a new day."

Once Nash fell asleep, Grizz quietly left his son's side, no longer needing to comfort him. Heading to sit next the sleepless Serendale commander, he looked to where Dart's body lie and knew that although it'd be tough to forgive himself, he'd have to try.

"Willis is out in the Forest on watch," Krause said, his voice hollow and his shoulders slumped. He sat staring into the fire, his eyes never shifting from the orange flames. Copper laid beside the commander, exhausted from fighting the barbarians.

"That's too bad. I need to apologize for blaming him for Dart's death. I made the wrong call to run instead of bargain, but instead of accepting my mistake, I took my anger out on him," Grizz sighed. "I'm failing at leading our small group. I have no idea how you led an entire city."

"I wasn't a leader at all. The guilt of abandoning Serendale grows heavier upon me every day. I can't even sleep at night anymore."

"You'd be making another mistake if you let that moment define you," Grizz tried to help the Human who clearly struggled from depression. "Dwelling on bad moments of the past doesn't help you move forward."

When Krause offered no response, Grizz changed his approach to giving advice. "Sometimes you have to focus on the positives, whatever they are. Think about how you faced your fears and challenged yourself to battle monsters in Casanovia and Misengard."

"I only fight because I refuse to let my cowardice hurt more people than it already has."

Grizz smiled, happy he received a reply, but shrugged all the same, not caring what reasoning the commander had come to that got him to fight. "Regret or revenge, it doesn't matter what makes you lift your sword, just as long as you do."

"No part of me enjoys it though." Krause shook his head. "I should've never become a warrior. I should've stood up to my father and told him his plan for me was not what I wanted for my life. He wanted me to serve, get married, and have children. But all the stories he told me growing up of killing monsters and taking down criminals; they terrified me instead of inspired me. And I wasn't interested in finding a wife and settling down. Men were my preference, not women." Krause stopped momentarily and chuckled to himself.

As Grizz watched the commander in his melancholic state, the man's back straightened and his shoulders no longer slumped. It was as if the moment Krause revealed his close-kept secret, a heavy burden lifted off him. "If my father could see me now, he'd be so disappointed in what

I've become. I'm everything he despised in a man. You're probably the type of person who thinks the same."

"That used to be my mindset, but not anymore," Grizz stated flatly. "Ever since my wife led me to Alazar, I try to follow his teachings. I know he's clear in his Holy Books on his design for marriage, but even more than that, he calls us to love everyone. It's not easy for me to be loving since only a handful of people have showed me true love in my life, but it's their examples I strive to emulate."

Krause scoffed, not at Grizz, but at the idea of love. "Try loving yourself when the culture you grow up in is based solely on virility and your father mocks you for not conforming to his ideals. I never asked to be attracted to men or to hate the idea of fighting monsters, but he made me feel ashamed and worthless because I did. I think that carried over into how I performed as commander, which I only became because my father died. Even then, I still felt trapped, forced to remain a warrior to uphold his honor."

I don't want to be a father that treats his son like that. I want Nash to know that who he is and what he's capable of isn't defined by his orientation. Neither is it defined by his race, skin color, gender, or disability. Grizz glanced over to where his son lay sleeping and wished he could tell him his thoughts in person. *I want him to know that what defines us, both in this life and the next, is if we believe in Alazar and if we follow his edicts of loving everyone and treating everyone with respect, no matter what differences we have.*

"I'm sorry you've spent your life with this on your mind. That's a long time to feel trapped," Grizz couldn't imagine what Krause had gone through. "But know that you're not worthless. You telling me this takes a level of courage I don't even know if I would have the strength to reveal. I'm honored to have you at my side."

Krause nodded and held the bridge of his nose between his fingers.

He's trying to hold back his emotions, and he's able to do it well, Grizz could tell. *I'm sure his stoicism stems from the idea of toxic masculinity his father instilled in him since his childhood years.*

Even though he didn't cry, Krause sought to escape the heavy conversation by standing up, stretching, and whistling to get Copper's attention. "Come on, boy. Let's go relieve Willis."

"Actually, I'll take watch for the rest of the night," Grizz rose himself. "I should apologize to Willis about earlier. Plus, you all deserve as much sleep as you can get."

As Krause sat back down, Grizz walked past him and momentarily stopped beside him to place his hand on the commander's shoulder. It was a wordless, simple gesture, but one that signified the fostering of a deep respect between the two men.

In the morning, once Grizz returned and everyone was awake, the Dwarven blacksmith called everyone together. Spotting a scenic view overlooking the river from the shade of two trees, he led the group to it as he pulled the sleigh across the snow that carried the sheet-covered body of Dart. Through the powers of his element, Grizz easily created a six-foot hole in the ground that he gently laid the corpse down into and then covered.

The three men, the boy, and the direfox shared their silent goodbyes and returned to the campsite.

Knowing everyone was hungry and needed sustenance, Grizz went to pull a bag of dried venison from the small bundle of cargo he'd retrieved from the barbarians, but his hand bumped against a sackcloth tucked in the pile. Pulling it out, as well as the venison, he looked inside. "I almost forgot about this," he said aloud to himself, smiling as he weighed the bag in his hand.

"What've you got in there?" Nash asked.

"Oh, it's just something to eat," Grizz purposely teased him, trying to lighten the mood after the funeral. He dropped the bag in question and held only the provisions.

"No. No. The sack you just put back. You smiled at it," Nash pointed.

"I don't know," Grizz began searching through the cargo, pretending like he couldn't find it. As he did, the corners of his mouth behind his long, black beard curled upwards even higher.

"Tell me!" Nash requested with childlike wonder.

"Well," Grizz drawled out his words to create suspense, and explained, "I wasn't going to mention this until later, but I have a special project I was thinking you and I could work together on. I've had it with me since we left Casanovia." Pulling out the sack and setting it in Nash's lap, Grizz allowed him to open it. As he did, he leaned forward and whispered what it was in his son's ear.

"And then we'll mix it with this," Grizz continued, grabbing a latched box which he opened, revealing the gold ingot inside.

"I can't wait! This will be fun!" Nash exclaimed, overjoyed at his father's project.

"We can talk about it more later. Let's keep it a secret for now," Grizz cautioned, hearing Willis and Krause's voices approaching from behind.

"I think we're ready to go," Willis spoke for both himself and the commander. "We can head to Casanovia to rent horses to take to Bogmire. That's the fastest option we have."

Grizz lifted Nash, placed him on Copper, and set out with his party. Their travelling, however, wasn't as enjoyable as their journey to Twin Peaks. Despite the few moments of banter or Grizz drumming up excitement in Nash about their secret project, no one could deny morale was low in the days after the death of Dart. Even arriving in Casanovia and hearing from Captain Nereus and Commander Artazair about the vast number of warriors and civilians volunteering to head to Almiria did nothing to lift the spirits of the Serendale crew. Nonetheless, they pressed on to Bogmire, knowing that in time, the pain of their fallen comrade would lessen.

Chapter 128

Instead of finding Quintis waiting by the gate so that he could let out the pit fighters to overthrow Councilor Kexian's regime, Kari found her father bound and gagged on the second deck of the Coliseum. He stood on a luxurious balcony, not in his armor and sky-blue cloak, but in a blood-stained tunic. Even though he was far away, she could see he had cuts and bruises on his face and a black eye that matched her own.

Once Kari saw who was standing next to him, she understood how their plans had failed.

Amidst the padded couches, tables of food, and countless bottles of mead, Seraiah stared down at Kari with an evil smirk across her face. No longer did she wear the tattered clothes she had on in the cells. Now, she stood adorned in silver armor and a sky-blue cape of her own.

Seraiah! Kari wanted to wrap her hands around the throat of the woman. *She betrayed us! She must've revealed our plans so that she could elevate her position from pit fighter to Skycloak.*

While her knuckles turned white as she gripped her bow in anger, Kari's eyes were drawn from the Elf who betrayed her to a bald woman with gauges in her ears and a golden collar around her neck.

That must be Councilor Alexis Kexian.

With a single nod down to the Gamemaster, who then nodded to Dejana and the other Skycloaks waiting at the far side of the coliseum, Dejana and her group pulled on ropes to open a large gate.

Kari held her breath in anticipation of what she'd be facing. Out from the darkness came a monster scorpion as tall as the second-story apartment she used to live in in Celestial. It had sharp pincers and a terrifying barbed tail that lashed about violently. Scared from the riotous crowd which grew even louder at the sight of the beast, the Animal Monster used its element to cover its exoskeleton in a layer of rock.

Kari responded by employing her own element, giving her blue armor a layer of protective ice, although she didn't know how effective it would be against a beast so large.

The monster used its six legs to scurry across the sand floor of the Coliseum, crushing the various bones and skeletons as it made its way towards its enemy. The Gamemaster and Skycloaks immediately used the diversion to take cover behind the gate, leaving the Halfling alone in the fight.

Kari fired two ice-tipped arrows. The first, rather than hitting the charging beast, flew into the wall underneath the lower bowl because of her unfamiliarity with the bow combined with her only being able to see out of one eye. Her second shot harmlessly bounced off the scorpion's stone-covered surface.

With no time to dodge to either side, Kari rolled under the belly of the scorpion while drawing her sword and trying to plunge it into the monster's underbelly. This, too, was impenetrable. Now positioned behind the beast, Kari was forced to evade the scorpion blindly jabbing its barbed tail down, hoping for a critical strike. The attacks were so fast, Kari barely had time to avoid them, but she managed to back away and create separation between herself and the beast.

Using the opportunity to again go on the offensive, Kari aimed her sword below the scorpion and sent a plume of frost beneath its legs, hoping it would make it slip and fall, but the sweltering heat of the desert prevented ice from forming. The scorpion turned, lowered its head, and plowed into Kari, knocking her down and trampling her as it ran over her.

As she struggled to pull herself up, Kari saw through the kick-up of sand that the Gladiator and many other pit fighters had broken their way through the inner dungeon gate and were in the armory. Torgore tried pulling open the locked gate leading out to where she was on the coliseum floor, but it was much larger and sturdier than the rusty gate he'd ripped off its hinges.

They haven't given up, so neither should I. The passion of those willing to die to free themselves from oppression can never be underestimated. I need to free them.

Sprinting to them, Kari yelled to the armed pit fighters, "Take cover along the walls!"

Remaining in front of the gate, she baited the scorpion, allowing it to charge her once more. Lunging out of the way at the last second, the rock-covered, thousand-plus-pound beast slammed into the wall, not only denting it, but collapsing the stonework all around the gate.

Dazed, the monster took time to recover by using its element of earth to burrow into the deep pit of sand that served as the base of the Coliseum. Although Kari knew it'd be impervious to her metal tipped arrows, she notched another one and tried to focus her Half-Elven ears on any noise that might give off the scorpion's location.

I have no idea where it will come up and attack. Realizing how crazy she must look, panickedly checking the sand all around her, Kari knew, *It's playing with me, building up my fear before it strikes. And it's working,* she admitted to herself as she felt her heart racing. *I don't know what to do. The monster has the advantage.*

Hearing tunneling underneath her, Kari didn't have enough time to roll out of the way before the scorpion burst through the desert surface in an explosion of sand and launched her into the air. Just as quickly as she went up, she came plummeting down, crashing into a pile of bones, landing awkwardly, nearly dislocating her shoulder.

If I can't defeat it from damaging it on the outside, I'll have to kill it from the inside. Grabbing the thickest, sturdiest bone she could find, Kari dodged a barb strike and batted away one of the giant gnashing pincers with her sword while working her way towards the monster. When it screeched at its prey for annoyingly evading its attacks, Kari jabbed the bone into the scorpion's maw. Drawing an arrow as fast as she could, she fired it upwards, sending it through the roof of the beast's mouth and piercing into its brain, killing it instantly. The scorpion fell at Kari's feet, twitching for a few seconds even though it was dead.

Collapsing in exhaustion, losing her element the moment she hit the ground, Kari took a minute to catch her breath. Around her, the crowd cheered at the monster's defeat. With the Coliseum a small circle of four bowls stacked on top of each other, it was significantly louder than Celestial's oval, two deck arena.

Kari scanned the Councilor's balcony, trying to find her father, but neither Quintis, Seraiah, Kexian, nor any of Kexian's personal guards were there.

Accompanied by a chorus of boos from the stands, the bald-headed woman and her guardian Skycloaks emerged on the coliseum floor from one of its entrances. The Gamemaster, Dejana, and others entered through a different gate and joined alongside Kexian in a show of force.

At the middle of the arena, Kexian held a bound and gagged Quintis Quinn as a shield in front of her. To the Celestial warrior's throat, she pressed a golden half sword which matched the collar around her neck and many bangles on her arms.

"Let him go!" Kari yelled, notching an ice-tipped arrow, and aiming it at the self-asserted Councilor of Holders Keep. Behind her, all the pit fighters from the dungeon squeezed through the busted gate and came forward to stand to support their blue-armored, element-wielding, scorpion-killing leader.

Kexian refused to acknowledge the Halfling's demand and instead pointed Kari's attention to Seraiah. "A few hours ago, this lowly pit fighter got Dejana to free her from the cells so she could come and share some news with me. She had a feeling that you were connected to Quintis. First, you asked specifically about him and no other Skycloak, and then he took you away to talk to you. Seraiah confirmed her suspicions when you told her he was your father and you planned on leading a revolt against me and my Skycloaks. I can't let that happen."

Speaking loud enough for the crowd to hear, who were already quiet, listening in on the exchange, Kexian shouted, "The woman you cheer wants to lead you to your death! She's offering you freedom from prison so she can put you on the front lines in a war for the kingdom.

"I won't let them leave," her voice grew softer as she stared directly at Kari. "You've forfeited your life by standing against me. Now drop your weapons and call off your fighters. I'll let your father live, but I'll give you an easy death."

Even though Kari knew Kexian was lying about both proclamations, she pretended to struggle with her ultimatum, grimacing at the helplessness of her predicament. All the while, she thought, *I've longed for my father my whole life. I will not let this woman kill him just because we're threatening to collapse the luxurious way of life she's built for herself here.*

Faking acquiescence of Kexian's desires, Kari moved her notched ice arrow away from where it was aimed at the Quintis-shielded councilor and fired it off into the distance.

Tossing her bow to her side, followed by her sword, Kari saw Kexian smile in victory. Knowing she'd gotten the villain to ease up, Kari, who still controlled the arrow's trajectory, looped it around in the sky, sending it back towards her enemy. The arrow pierced through the back of Kexian's bald skull and came out her eye, killing her instantly.

A collective gasp came from the crowd upon witnessing the brutal kill of the Holders Keep leader. As Kexian's body fell to the ground, Quintis broke away from her lifeless grasp on him and ran towards his daughter. Kari immediately picked up her bow and shot two archers aiming to take down her dad.

"Kill them all!" the Gamemaster yelled to those around him, heading straight for the former Skycloak gatekeeper who'd betrayed them all. Quickly picking her sword up out of the sand and cutting her father's binds, Kari handed Quintis the weapon, which he used to plunge into the Gamemaster's stomach.

Before the rest of the Skycloaks converged upon the Halfling and the Human, the pit fighters ran forward, eager to kill those who served the woman that forced them to live in such terrible conditions.

The Skycloaks had just as much fervor behind the swinging of their blades. Each realized if they took control and ended the revolt, they'd become the new councilor, and acquire all the perks that came with the position.

The crowd encircling the violent battle in the stands above sat neither silent nor cheered. Most stood in awe and murmured about how the events of the night would change the culture and operations of Holders Keep. A few members of the crowd jumped down, picked up the weapon of a fallen combatant and killed a Skycloak, likely one that had oppressed him or her.

Feeling an arrow bounce off her ice-coated armor, Kari turned to find she'd been shot at by Dejana. *That's my bow, you're shooting me with*, Kari seethed.

She drew an arrow and shot Dejana through the leg, immobilizing her. Walking up to the Skycloak, the woman handed the blue bow back. Clutching her injured leg, she pleaded, "Please don't kill me!"

"You're theirs to kill, not mine," Kari uttered. She stepped back, away from the chaos of the brawl and watched as one pit fighter ran their spear through Dejana while another bashed her in the head with a morning star.

All over, the dungeon dwellers gained the upper hand against the unsurrendering enemy. Kari watched Torgore reach his hand into the mouth of a Skycloak, grab the man's tongue, and forcefully rip it out.

That must've been the one who did the same to him, Kari thought, turning away from the violence.

After he killed the man, Torgore picked up a double-bladed sword. The unique weapon featured two blades coming out from the same hilt and had a gap down the middle of it. The ogre tore his way through the battlefield with the weapon, blasting his element of lighting at anyone who came near him. He headed to where a group of pit fighters cornered Seraiah. They ripped off her armor and cloak before punching and kicking her until she no longer moved. Torgore, intent on delivering the final blow to the woman he thought was his friend, stepped on her back to keep her down. He then grabbed her hair and yanked, snapping her neck as if he were breaking a stick in half to build a campfire.

After he dropped her corpse down to the sand, he shook his head over her dead body, disappointed at her betrayal.

With the remaining Skycloaks quickly defeated, the pit fighters, invigorated with an energy Kari didn't know they had, ran around cheering and hollering.

Once they settled down, Kari met her father at the center of the arena and looked to the crowd around them, most of whom were still in shock, processing the change in power.

"The rumors are true," Kari spoke as loud as she could so even those in the top bowl could hear her. "I'm here to grant you freedom if you join me in the fight to reclaim Celestial. This world wants you to stay here and rot. They want you dead because they view you as worthless, but you're not! Your lives still have value and the potential to do good. Make the right decision and join our cause. A new beginning awaits each of you. It's yours for the taking.

"All I ask is that in addition to your fealty, there be no more bloodshed among the Skycloaks throughout this Keep. We've already ended their regime, so spare the lives of those who remain. The imbalance between you exists no more! Get ready to leave this prison tomorrow afternoon, but tonight, celebrate your liberation."

Quintis came to stand next to his daughter and scanned the crowd who seemed unsure if Kari's too-good-to-be-true offer was legitimate. Encapsulating her address in an upbeat tone he called out, "What are you all waiting for? Kexian's storehouse has enough food and wine for you all!"

In the biggest elicitation of cheers that night, the crowd quickly dispersed, everyone exiting as fast as they could to get their hands on the food, drinks, and comfort Kexian kept exclusive to only herself and her Skycloaks.

Kari smiled and hugged her father. She pulled back and winced as she checked over his cuts and bruises. "I'm sorry. It's my fault you got hurt," she apologized.

Quintis waved off her concern and stressed the injuries weren't serious. "Nothing you did is to blame. Even though Seraiah betrayed us, telling her and the ogre was needed so the pit fighters would join in on the revolt."

Kari nodded and handed her father the sapphire-embedded bow he used to become one of the best warrior archers in Celestial. "It's long past due this is returned to your possession."

Quintis took the weapon and brushed his fingers over the blue-painted metal. "The memories I made when I carried this were the happiest ones of my life." He gave the bow back to Kari and closed her hands around it. "I hope you can say the same of your time with it someday. It's yours now."

211

Chapter 129

After Ca-talia allowed Ty and Shana to spend the night in their spare room, the elemental couple sat together and shared breakfast on a double-decker vessel. Their second-story dining patio provided a scenic view of the Darien Sea, but also showcased the destruction of the city from the skeleton attack.

Killing time before an afternoon meeting they'd scheduled with Oceanside's commander, the Elf and Human ate slowly as they talked, dissecting the many bits of conversation they'd had with Alazar's former lightning wielder.

"Even though it was painful, I'm glad I received a vision of my past for what it revealed," Shana divulged, "but, can you imagine seeing a vision of something from the future like Olvi did? That would've been cool too."

"I know. It's weird to think about alternate timelines existing where things turned out different from what we know," Ty theorized between mouthfuls of scrambled eggs. "What if King Zoran never defeated Draviakhan? What if my parents were never murdered? What if I died when Celestial was overtaken?"

What would've happened if my mom never went to the tavern the night Malorek was there? Shana thought to herself.

"I didn't even know seeing visions of the future was possible," Ty admitted. "The only thing associated to that idea is Alazar's Book of the Future, but I've never read that much of it. Few people have actually. It's the least-read of the three Holy Books he gave to his four races, because no one can make sense of it. The Book of the Past explains creation and history, the one about the present explains how to live our lives, but the Book of the Future is full of a bunch of prophetic poems that are so generic, they're rarely understood until they've already been fulfilled."

"I know throughout history, there are always groups of fanatics that arise because they become obsessed with believing a certain prophecy from that book." Shana recalled her own experience with zealots and explained, "We had a few of them in Casanovia a couple years ago, but their interpretation of the prophecy must've been wrong because what they told everyone would happen never transpired. That's part of the reason I never got into religion. I didn't want to be like those kinds of people."

Ty nodded, thinking about his own encounters with extremists. "Some people become so obsessed trying to figure out the hidden meanings they drive themselves crazy."

"And everyone they try to proselytize to," Shana noted, rolling her eyes.

Ty nodded in agreement. "I get that some people don't follow any gods, some have varying levels of commitment, and some are fully devoted, but when you're manipulating and controlling people to follow your beliefs, that's when it must be stopped."

He sighed and got off the tangent of cults and reverted the conversation back to what they'd learned from Olvi. "I never considered how Alazar acquired each of the prophecies in the book, but it makes sense based on what Olvi and Ca-talia told us. He must've looked at a bunch of future timelines and wrote hints about what he observed in the form of poems. There are prophecies like the one about the Self-Proclaimed King or the one about the First Great War, which were fulfilled in history exactly as they were written, but there's still many that have yet to come to pass."

"Like the one on Steve's sword."

"Yeah, Aurelia," Ty thought of the inscription on the golden blade. "Someone years ago must've created that sword and etched the prophecy on it. Funny how the sword is now in the hands of the person who's going to fulfill it."

"It's called the Prophecy of the Twins," Shana explained. "I helped Kari research it this winter in Misengard's library. She desperately wanted to find some loophole to prove it wasn't Steve who'd fulfill it. We didn't find what we wanted, but we learned a lot about prophecies we'd never encountered before. There's a prophecy about people trying to resurrect loved ones after they die, but it discusses how it's impossible. Once they're dead, they're gone forever. There's no way to bring them back, no matter how badly you desire it.

"I'm sure that one has been fulfilled many times and will continue to be since people have a hard time accepting death. I heard after Zoran's wife and daughter were killed, he struggled so much he scoured through ancient texts, trying to see if there was some way to manipulate time or travel to another timeline, but Alazar clearly says that that is just as impossible as reviving the dead. What's done is done. The past can't be changed."

"Talking about death leads me to something I've been wanting to discuss," Shana timidly brought up the subject. She paused. "We need to talk about how you fought last night. You've been reckless ever since I met you, but it's getting worse and worse, especially when we fought the Accursed. You were nearly killed when you let them swarm you like that.

"At first, I thought it might've been that you were emotional seeing your great-grandfather as the Skeleton King or that you wanted to defeat as many of the Accursed as possible so there'd be less in Celestial, but the more I thought about it, I realized this wasn't an isolated incident. You're constantly taking these kinds of unnecessary risks. I know you're a happy-go-lucky person and you like to live life to its fullest, but it's another thing to push life to its limits. I'm scared your arrogance it's going to lead to your downfall."

"I'm not going to die. I already told you how I survived a fall on my gryphon in Celestial, I wasn't killed when the Spider Queen's lair collapsed on me, and I made it through the past three battles we've been in. If Alazar can see all the future timelines, he wouldn't have given me the ability to control lightning if he knew my life would end soon."

"Did you not hear what Olvi told us?" Shana's raised her voice, annoyed at Ty's stubbornness. "We're not invincible! Before Zoran, Draviakhan killed most of the elect!" Shana grabbed at the roots of her pink hair, swore under her breath and stated, "I don't know if your belief you won't die is feeding your arrogance or your arrogance is feeding your belief you won't die!"

"I'm not worried about death," Ty reiterated, more angrily this time. He spoke to Shana with annoyance, as if she should know the reasoning behind his actions. "My focus is on honoring my forefathers and leaving a great legacy like theirs."

"You already have your legacy! Out of everyone on Element, Alazar made you one of his elect. Why isn't that good enough? It seems like you just want attention and to be known as the next hero of legend. You're trying so hard to leave a legacy for yourself, it's going to be the very reason you lose it altogether."

"We're going in circles," Ty spat, hearing Shana cycle back to her claim he wasn't invincible. Making it clear what his objectives were, he stated, "All I care about is living up to my family name and having children who can carry the Canard name on to future generations. Is that so wrong?"

"No, but..."

"Then why are you giving me such a hard time about this?" Ty cut her off before she could even finish.

Rather than answering, Shana asked her own question in a calm, composed, and collected manner, directly contrasting Ty's. "Tell me, Ty, where do I fit into your precious legacy? Am I just a means for you to obtain the children you want?"

When Ty began to answer, Shana cut him off, showing him the same lack of respect he'd shown her. "No, now you listen to me. I've given up so much to be in this relationship with you. I had a chance to run for councilor of Casanovia, to fulfill *my* dream, *my* legacy. But I came here with you and risked that position being filled by someone else. I wanted to see if what we had was real, but it's clear to me now you only think about yourself and what you can get out of me. My worth isn't based on the value you assign."

Shana got up from the table and began walking away, but Ty grabbed her arm, trying to hold her back.

"Let go! How dare you grab me like that!" Shana slapped him across the face.

She briskly walked away once Ty released the tight grip around her arm and shook off the unpleasantness of their first fight. With distance between them, she made her boundaries clear by stifling her tears, pushing her hair behind her ears, and announcing, "I'm going to Andonia. I don't want to talk until I'm ready. If that means I haven't found you by tonight, then you can sleep somewhere other than the ship."

Chapter 130

In the morning, Kari recruited a handful of people who hadn't drunk themselves into a stupor to help her collect all the weapons and armor they could find in Holders Keep. The team spent most of their time on the coliseum floor, taking as much as they could from the bodies of both Skycloaks and pit fighters killed in the revolt.

I've seen so many corpses in the past four months, it barely even bothers me anymore. Being exposed to such depravity makes you numb to it, Kari thought, feeling bad she didn't care as much as she used to as she ripped an unpunctured piece of armor off a Skycloak.

She tossed the spaulder into one of many nearby chests they'd gathered to help store and transport their collection. The armor and weapon-filled trunks would be carried by prisoners to Almiria for the coming battle for Celestial. Kari ordered only chests with padlocks be used, with two reasons behind her demand: "For safety, I don't want any prisoners to have a weapon until they reach the capital," she told her team. "I also don't want anyone staying behind in Holders Keep to use them against each other. From here on out, there will be no more coliseum battles. They're inhumane and they end today."

"How's it going?" Quintis found his daughter after spending the night trying to prevent the pit fighters from getting too out of control.

"We're almost done," Kari gestured to the seven chests with no less than thirty articles of weapons and/or armor in each. "We'll be able to divide this up once we get to Almiria. Every bit helps."

"I just wanted to let you know people are already gathering around the gate, getting ready to head out, but I also came to tell you two dragons came down to the farming section of the prison. They asked for you specifically."

Kari rolled her eyes. *Glaciara and Boulderdash. They threatened to kill anyone who tried to leave,* she remembered. *This is going to be a problem.*

"Do you want me to come with you?" Quintis asked as Kari headed off.

"No, I'll be fine."

Upon arriving at the front of Holders Keep, Kari expected to find the blue-scaled dragon and the male brown one. She found Glaciara, but instead of being accompanied by Boulderdash, the female monster was standing with a red-scaled dragon Kari knew well and was ecstatic to see.

"Crimson! You're alive!"

"I am," he smiled at Kari, thrilled to see his Halfling friend. "I escaped Nightstrike in the storm, although not unharmed," he uncurled his wing to show where his skin had been torn. "I found a traveling caravan of people. One of them stitched me up, and once I could fly, I made my way here, knowing it was where you and Steve were headed."

"Steve's not here," Kari grew nervous. "We got separated. You didn't come across him in the desert?"

"No," Crimson said, "But I'm sure he's fine," he tried to quell the Halfling's fears, seeing the worry in her eyes.

"We need to hurry," Glaciara added urgency to their reunion by telling Kari, "Boulderdash is sleeping, He doesn't know about the revolt, nor that Crimson's here."

"I thought you were against the prisoners leaving?" Kari couldn't understand the female dragon's change of heart.

"I was, but now that Crimson explained more of what's at stake, I'm willing to break my oath if it means what's best for the kingdom. Boulderdash though, he sees things in absolutes. I don't think he'll allow the escape to happen if he finds out."

It took no more than an hour for the hundreds of eager prisoners to file out onto Mount Anomaly's plateau, officially exiting the confines of Holders Keep. From halfway up the volcano-ravaged mountain, the men and women stared at the open world around them. For those who'd been imprisoned for many years, surrounded only by the high mountain walls, it was disorienting to view expanse of the desert and again see what the horizon looked like.

Although she was nervous about the ramifications of unleashing so many of the worst criminals back into the kingdom, Kari couldn't help but smile at the infectious joy on the faces of the freed captives. None brought her more delight than the last prisoner to leave, Quintis Quinn, who made sure everyone got out that wanted to. From afar off, Kari watched her dad, after eighteen years, take his first step of freedom back into the world that had so ruthlessly shut him away.

Standing between Crimson Singe and Glaciara, it pained Kari to know what she was about to ask, for it meant leaving the father she'd only so recently connected with.

"Crimson, could you fly me to Al Kabar? That was the next city Steve and I were supposed to recruit in. Maybe he's there."

"It depends," the dragon turned to Glaciara. "Do you need help escorting the prisoners to Almiria?"

"No, I'll be fine," Glaciara answered. Kari noticed the blue-scaled dragon looked downcast that Crimson wouldn't be accompanying her, but Glaciara didn't show the emotion for long, and continued speaking by making her rationalization known. "The least I can do after breaking my oath is escort them to Almiria and make sure none attempt to escape."

Kari headed to tell her dad of her plans, but as she crossed the landing, Boulderdash rose from the side of Mount Anomaly.

"What is this?" he roared upon seeing the host of prisoners. He landed behind the other two dragons and covered himself in his element, showing his willingness to fight. "Glaciara, did this dragon convince you to break your oath?" Snarling at Crimson, he pushed past the red-scaled dragon to confront the fellow guardian.

"The kingdom needs the help of the prisoners," Glaciara explained, not taking her eyes off Boulderdash as he circled around her.

The stone dragon shook his head at the argument. "No! We've discussed this. We're required to ensure they remain locked away. I will kill every last one of them and any dragon that aids them in their escape," he stopped in front of Crimson, driving home his last point.

"Then you'll have to kill me," Glaciara took back the dragon's attention. "I refuse to be a slave to an oath when I know what's right."

221

"So be it." Although Boulderdash took a second to consider the weight of his next decision, he remained resolute in his stance. He blasted a tornado of wind out of his mouth at Glaciara, but Crimson jumped in front of it, taking the full brunt of the attack on his shoulder.

Flapping his giant wings, Crimson rose into the sky and would've breathed his 1000-plus degree flames down on Boulderdash if it wasn't for the nearby people also on the landing. His reluctance to attack allowed Boulderdash to sprint forward using his element of wind and lunge into Crimson's underbelly with his body weight weighing at least ten-tons from his stony scales.

Boulderdash continued to command the wind to propel him, even as he was airborne, driving Crimson back and back, all the way to the top of Mount Anomaly. With the rock wall thinner at the ridge, Crimson was tackled through a section of the sheer mountaintop. Since his injured wing was still gaining strength, he couldn't gain control and prevent himself from spiraling down into the buildings of the prison far below.

Instead of the broken pieces of mountain falling down on top of him, Boulderdash used his element to mentally control as many of them as he could. Five large, jagged pieces hovered in the air around his body as he stared at the red dragon from the blue sky. Then, flying down, parallel to the vertical rock wall, he sent each piece one-by-one down at Crimson. Crimson dodged the first two, but was hit by the remaining three. Each one slammed him down to the ground. The second he pulled himself back up, he'd get drilled again.

"He's injured. Can't you help him!?" Kari cried out to Glaciara.

"I don't want to kill Boulderdash. He's my friend."

"You care for Crimson too, don't you? I can see the way you are around him. I know you don't want him to die either!"

Torn on what to do, Glaciara flew to where the two dragons fought. Before Boulderdash could land a killing blow, Glaciara tackled him just as he'd tackled Crimson by using her wind element to give speed and velocity to her elementally-empowered body.

The brown and blue dragons tumbled over and over each other before coming to a rest. Getting up, one covered in stone and the other in ice, they began headbutting each other. At first, Boulderdash used it as a basic attack, but it turned into a match where both dragons were willing to bet their entire life that their element was sturdier than the other.

Glaciara slammed her ice-scaled head into Boulderdash, who again headbutted her with his skull protected by the element of earth. Back and forth, they battled in a feat of strength. Ultimately, it was Glaciara who gained the upper hand. With a single strike, she knocked out Boulderdash, who fell to the ground and immediately lost the defense his element provided.

Glaciara, presuming the fight over, allowed her body to revert to its regular scales. Behind her, Boulderdash awakened. Angry that he'd been defeated by a female dragon, he blasted another powerful tornado at Glaciara. Normally, the strike could immediately incapacitate a monster, but Glaciara was lucky enough to have missed taking the full brunt of it.

As she turned in disgust at the dragon's dirty tactics, Crimson came forward. With Boulderdash's focus solely on Glaciara and his stone armor still not employed, Crimson breathed his hottest fire onto the dragon. Boulderdash cried out in pain and tried to use his wind element to push the torturing flames away, but the fire was too powerful for anything to break through Crimson's attack. The red dragon didn't let up until he knew there was no way his enemy had survived.

"You okay?" Kari asked the two dragons after they came back down to the landing. Both were unsteady in their flight and breathing heavy from the battle.

In no mood to talk after the death of the friend she'd served with to protect Holders Keep, Glaciara simply muttered, "I'll see to it the prisoners make it to the intended destination."

"Is your wing damaged?" Kari asked Crimson, who came up behind the ice dragon and was flexing it back and forth.

"Still recovering. I should've known I'm not at full fighting capacity."

"You and me both." Kari rubbed some of the aching bruises she'd suffered from her battle with the scorpion and the ensuing revolt.

Finding Kari with the red dragon, Quintis emerged from the crowd of people, having just broken up a fight between a group of prisoners.

He's displeased with their actions. His underlying apprehensions are rising again, Kari could tell from the scowl on her father's face.

"Dad, I have to go to Al Kabar and continue to recruit. If you come with me, you wouldn't have to deal with them anymore."

"Someone has to keep them in line," Quintis bowed his head, accepting the responsibility. "I'd love nothing more than to spend time with you and catch up, and I feel like a terrible father saying no, but I still consider myself a warrior, so I need to do what's best for the kingdom. That is leading these prisoners to Almiria with Glaciara."

"I understand. I'll miss you until I see you again."

"May the days be swift until then," Quintis said, hugging his daughter goodbye.

Kari watched as her father headed to the front of the throng of people and led them down the steep mountain stairs, down to the desert far below to begin their trek. She climbed up onto Crimson after giving him a few minutes to catch his breath, and then the two took to the skies high above Deletion on their way to Al Kabar.

Chapter 131

After spending a couple of days drinking more water than ever before, Steve felt replenished.

Although he was still sore from the countless miles he'd wandered through the desert, he was well-rested enough to explore Stonegate and meet with many of the locals to explain how much their help was needed for what they'd be up against. Eventually, while cutting through the courtyard of the fortress, he ran into A'ryn, who walked hand-in-hand with a woman considered a Human, but stood even taller than Steve. If her hair had been in bouffant form like the general's, her height would've been even more considerable, but it was pulled back into tight dreadlocks.

"Stephen, I'd like to introduce you to my girlfriend, L'ayla," Elesora gestured to her partner. "L'ayla, this is who I was telling you my warriors found in the desert."

"Ah, yes, Zoran's grandson, our future king! It's nice to meet you" L'ayla shook Steve's hand while looking him over. Her dark brown eyes went from Steve's black hair to his fair (albeit, sunburned) complexion, his blue eyes, and his red armor.

She's sizing me up, Steve could tell. *This is how most people who know I'm part of the royal bloodline seem to look at me when they meet me. They want to see if they can envision me as king.*

As he attempted to read L'ayla's reaction to gain insight into her first impression, Steve was surprised she seemed neither impressed nor unimpressed. She simply smiled and asked, "What do you think of Stonegate?"

This is how I wish every interaction would go. L'ayla isn't judging me based on my appearance. She understands a person's potential is based on their character and actions, not what they look like.

"I like it here," Steve told the fellow Human. "I can see the pride the citizens have in their city. What do you do for a living?"

"I help run the sewage and composting here," L'ayla beamed.

Steve nodded, happy L'ayla wasn't embarrassed to share the fact that she worked with waste when many cities looked down on those who worked in sanitation.

"That's an essential profession," he commended her. "I always appreciate the people who work behind the scenes that help keep normalcy for so many. Those types of jobs and the people in them never get the attention they deserve."

A'ryn put her arm around her girlfriend's waist. "L'ayla does more than manage Stonegate. She's in charge of sanitation for not just here, but all the towns and villages in the province. She's always modest, and that's why I love her."

The general kissed L'ayla's cheek, prompting a passerby in the courtyard who witnessed the moment of affection shout out, "Next time you clean the cesspools, throw yourself in it. We don't need people like you in Stonegate!"

"Let him be," A'ryn commanded Steve, seeing that he looked ready to march after the man and confront him.

"Does that happen often?" Steve sighed, angrily staring down the offender as the man slunk away.

"Far too often. Since I'm the warrior leader of this city, most people know about my relationship, but despite my position, they apparently still need to say demeaning things."

"Can't you do anything about it?"

"People like that, nothing we say could change their mind. I'd love to have laws that outlaw hateful speech and give consequences for it, but the mayor of this city has yet to enact anything regarding that. I can only hope it happens soon."

Adding her input, L'ayla shared, "The progress made here in garnering respect for women and allowing them to serve in the warriors is encouraging, but it seems like in other ways we're moving in the opposite direction."

"I'm sorry you two have to put up with those kinds of people," Steve looked from General Elesora to L'ayla. "The love you two share is no less real than the love in a relationship of opposite genders. No person deserves to be treated harshly, especially by strangers like that."

"Do you have someone you love?" A'ryn asked, then turned to L'ayla and winked. "A person you can't imagine losing? Someone you want to run to and tell the funny things that happened to you during the day or the great accomplishments you achieved?"

"Yes," Steve smiled, picturing Kari's face. In his mind's eye he imagined her pale skin, dark hair, blue eyes, and slightly pointed ears. He thought of how her eyes lit up when she smiled - her teeth not exactly perfect, but they were perfect to him. "Her name is Kari."

"Oh, yes, that's the Halfling you asked about when we first met," Elesora recalled. "You kept muttering her name in your sleep along with the words 'lost' and 'desert,' so I sent out additional searches to look for her. I'm sorry to say we found nothing."

Steve sighed, wishing for news of Kari's safety, but could only hope she'd made it out of Deletion alive. "The sooner I can continue my travels, the more likely I can find her," he told the women he stood with. "Her and I were supposed to go to Triland, so maybe she'll be there."

"We can give you an escort there."

"Actually, before I head there, I'd like to take you up on your offer of putting me in touch with the guides who can lead me to Mount Divinian's summit."

"What made you decide?" A'ryn smiled, knowing it was what was best for the future king.

"You were right about my anxieties and burdens. You wouldn't believe the amount of things constantly weighing on my mind," Steve admitted, glancing down at Aurelia. "If time and relaxation are proven to be an important part in healing physical injuries, then mental health deserves no less attention. I hope the hike will allow me to take my focus off the things bothering me. Even if it's only a temporary reprieve, it'll be beneficial."

"I think it will be," Elesora agreed, and then with a shrug, added, "At the very least, you'll get to say you stood at the highest elevation on all of Element. If you're ready now, I'll just need to go and saddle my horse and find some of my warriors to join us for your protection. It's a day's ride to the small village at the base of the mountain. The guides who know the mountain live there."

"Don't you need to stay here and keep order?"

"Nah," the general waved her hand as if she were flicking a bug. "I have captains who step in when needed. Besides, it's my job to check in on all the villages and towns in our province, so that often takes me outside Stonegate's walls." She nodded to her girlfriend. "That's how the two of us met. I can make my rounds while you head up the summit. If that sounds good, follow me to the stables and we'll get you a horse."

"Works for me!"

"Looks like I'll be gone for a couple days," A'ryn kissed L'ayla goodbye. "I'll see you when I return."

Steve enjoyed his ride with A'ryn and the seven warriors she insisted accompany them, but he grew anxious the closer they got to Mount Divinian. *I've seen it from afar, but up close, this mountain is even more massive than I realized! Sometimes when I look over the Darien Sea, the sheer size of it is intimidating, especially with so much water taking up the horizon. That's how it is with Divinian, except this stretches up into the skies farther than I can see.*

When they all arrived at the small village at the mountain's base, A'ryn took Steve to a small log cabin home and introduced him to J'leem, the lead guide who often scaled the mountain.

The burly man's four kids crawled all over him, unsuccessful as they all attempted to wrestle him to the ground. J'leem playfully tickled them while explaining to Steve about climbing Divinian.

"There's four of us who were planning on heading up the mountain to collect rare herbs to send to the cleric schools in Bogmire. They only grow on Divinian this time of year. We were scheduled to make the trek a few days from now, but it's no big deal if we leave tomorrow and head to the summit," J'leem explained. "It'll take three days to get to the top, weather-permitting. One day's ride, two days climb if we leave at first light."

"I'll leave a couple of my men in the village to be here when you come back down Divinian," General Elesora told Steve. "As far as your expedition, you'll be safe in the hands of J'leem and the other guides. They're reliable, trustworthy men. Once we rejoin each other, we can head to Triland together."

With no inns in the village, J'leem offered the floor by his fireplace as a place Steve and the two warriors could bunk for the night.

Early the following morning, Steve watched J'leem kiss his wife and children goodbye as he bundled up the provisions provided to him. Steve tied down his pack of food, a bedroll, spiked boots, and a walking stick to the mule he'd be traveling on. He saddled his mount and followed the four guides through a low-lying layer of fog to a stone archway that marked the start of the mountain trails.

"Do you usually have trouble up there?" Steve asked, eying swords the guides carried on their waists.

"Rarely," J'leem answered, "but my father always told me the day you don't come prepared is the day you'll wish you were."

Stronger than donkeys, but slower than horses, the five mountaineers used their mules to plod up the steep Mount Divinian. With each step, it got colder and colder. *Last week I was in the desert and was so hot and dehydrated I would've given anything to be in this climate. Now, all I want is to return to Deletion's warmth because I've never felt temperatures more frigid than this. My face feels so frozen I don't think I could even smile if I wanted to.*

In the distance, the group of men watched a wild storm with fierce high winds and lightning. A deep rumbling came from a ridge many miles from their vantage point, followed by an incredible avalanche down the mountain slope.

"The storms and snowfall constantly change the landscape of the mountain," one of the guides shared. "That's why we travel up this side. Its terrain makes it the easiest to climb and the safest against the weather because the wind comes from the other direction."

Continuing on, after stopping to watch the magnificent event of nature, Steve felt his ears pop once they crossed a certain threshold. With the sun beginning to set after their long day, J'leem held up his hand, stopping the group near a frozen waterfall, still thawing out from winter.

"We'll camp here for the night." Turning and speaking specifically to Steve, the only one who hadn't made the trek before, he explained, "This is also the point where we leave our mules behind. The terrain from here on out is too steep for them to handle."

After an uncomfortable sleep in which he shivered the entire night, Steve tiredly awoke and followed the guides' lead in taking his bundle off his mule's back and strapping it to his own. Most of what Steve did was copying what the guides did. They were men of few words. The only times they spoke were about food, finding shelter, and the weather. Anytime Steve tried striking up a conversation, they responded with one-word answers.

These men live a simple life that I'm not accustomed to, Steve thought after receiving a negatory response when he asked them if there were any economic or social issues in the province they'd like to see changed.

Kingdom-wide, I'm sure there are many people like them that find contentment in the small-town type of atmosphere. That's why it's so important we stop the Hooded Phantom and prevent his army's reach from extending to even the most remote places.

While he appreciated the men's work ethic and drive, Steve couldn't deny that the travel was too much for him physically.

On their second day up the mountain, the rocky terrain was coated with a blanket of snow that grew deeper and deeper the higher they went. *My leg hurts so much,* Steve rubbed his thigh under his many layers which did little to protect him from the unrelenting cold.

I don't know if it's the temperature, this elevation, or if I'm weary from trudging through snow this deep, but I'm in a lot of pain.

Trying to bite his tongue and hold in his complaints, Steve pushed on, but his noticeable limp forced the guides to slow down to compensate for the warrior's improperly-healed injury.

These men may not talk much, but at least they're encouraging, Steve thought, empowered by their constant remarks of positivity both to him and each other. The four constantly shouted out maxims and adages whenever weariness set in. Each one resonated with Steve as he heard them.

"You'll regret it forever if we quit now."

"Despite the difficulty, the end result will be worth it."

"You have the opportunity to do what few men before us have done."

"If you can do this, there's nothing you can't accomplish."

We must be close, Steve could tell after many hours of travel. Looking up, there wasn't much more between the mountain and the bright blue sky above. Reaching a plateau, the lead guide took Steve to the edge of a giant cliff.

"See that?" he pointed to a mountain far in the distance. Instead of a peak, a jagged rim marked its summit. "That's Mount Valpyrio."

The volcano where my grandfather battled and killed Draviakhan, Steve knew.

"My father knew him," the guide revealed, somehow knowing Steve was thinking about King Zoran and Mount Valpyrio's significance as the location of such a monumental event in history. "He was the guide that led your grandfather up here many years ago. Now I have the honor of doing the same. I respect any man who's able to make it this far. May your commitment to this kingdom match the resolve you had in climbing Divinian."

"This path will lead you right up to the summit," the guide escorted Steve a few steps over to where a windy, snow-covered trail twisted up around large sheets of rock. "It's yours to take alone. We'll wait here for you in there," he pointed to an overhang that created a small cave. "You only have a few minutes once you reach the top. There's not enough oxygen in the atmosphere to survive longer than that."

"Thank you," Steve nodded to the guide and then to the three others already in the cave, seeking refuge within its walls from the chilling wind.

Turning from them, Steve began his ascent up the final section of Mount Divinian.

His heart beat faster with every step he took, but he didn't know if it was because he struggled to breathe or it was because of sheer excitement.

My grandfather and the kings of the past made this very climb. I'm following in the steps of the famous men Thatcher read to me about from storybooks.

In the last quarter mile, Steve felt his chest tightening more than ever before. *The air is getting thin,* he told himself. *I can't panic and hurry, making myself require more oxygen and I can't go too slow and take more time than I should.* Continuing at a comfortable pace, he turned a corner around a giant rock and found dozens of flags adorning the trail before him. All were the many colors of the Primary Cities. With their strings fastened to the surrounding rocks, the decorations were strewn both along the sides of the path and hung overhead, across it. At the top of the steep incline, a metal pole stood, planted in the snow with a white and gold flag attached.

There it is, the peak! Steve wanted to run to the destination he'd been envisioning for their three days of taxing travel. Heading upwards, the deep snow evened out, allowing him to comfortably walk under all the flags flapping in the wind.

At the top of the summit, Steve used his gloved hands to grab the pole marking the highest point of Mount Divinian, and thus, the highest point on all of Element. Finding a level place for his feet, he inhaled the deepest breath he could and cast his gaze out over the world.

This is amazing, he took in the white, gray, brown, green, and blue hues of the lands below. With the sky clear of clouds, nothing blocked his view of the wide array of colors belonging to the various unique landscapes.

The north featured mountains and forests, the east held the expanse of Deletion, the south contained the rolling hills of the Savannah, and to the west he could make out the outskirts of the Darien Sea. Following the massive body of water to where it met land, Steve knew what city lied there. "Celestial," he said out loud to himself.

Holding the hilt of the sword sheathed at his side, Steve prayed, "Alazar, I love this world you had a hand in creating. The fate of everything I look upon depends on the results of what happens in Celestial in the coming weeks. I don't want to lose this war. For nearly five months I've journeyed through this kingdom and seen it up close. I've seen a woman and her family willing to give up all her money and resources to help others, I've seen new life born, sacrifices for the greater good, friendships being made, relationships developed, and children with more bravery I could ever hope to have."

Due to the lack of oxygen and the difficulty in speaking his words aloud, Steve finished his prayer in his head, thinking, *This is already a great kingdom, but it's not perfect. I've also seen poor leadership, people taking advantage of others, corruption in warriors, the horrors of war, children in orphanages in need of loving families, races prejudiced against each other, and people considered inferior because of their skin color, gender, race, orientation, or abilities.*

I don't know if this prophecy is about me or not, but if I survive this war and become king, let me be a ruler that builds upon what my grandfather started. Help me uphold the values already in place in this kingdom while eliminating the many evils of society that hurt so many. Help me keep growing as a person. To always be pursuing love, friendship, and harmony and to emulate what it means to be loyal, honorable, and courageous. Let me be a man worthy of leading this kingdom.

As Steve finished his prayer, seeing nothing except the darkness behind his closed eyelids, everything suddenly turned white. It was at that moment Steve received his vision.

Chapter 132

After King Zoran ordered a couple of his Guardian Knights to gather some of the best warriors to capture Malorek alive, he sent Kyra to a secure location, high in one of the castle's towers. An on-staff cleric tended to the princess's twins in the castle's infirmary before visiting Kyra to put ointments and bandages on her injuries. Malorek's physical abuse throughout their marriage had continually escalated. No beating had been worse than when Kyra announced her intention to divorce her vile husband.

Oliver and Evalyn stayed near their daughter, always keeping her in sight. While the queen sat with Kyra on the bed, holding her hand, Oliver angrily paced back and forth, blaming himself for his daughter's condition. Seeing his daughter in such a state of physical and emotional suffering broke his heart. His rage only grew, despite his wife's efforts to calm him.

"I knew he couldn't be trusted!" the king shouted.

"I'm sorry!" Kyra cried, thinking her dad was mad at her.

"Honey, this isn't your fault," Oliver clarified, feeling sorry his demeanor made her think he was mad at her when she was the victim. Putting the blame on himself, he said, "I sensed something was off the moment I met him. I should've done more to find out about his past."

"Don't worry, we're going to make sure he never hurts you or the twins again," Evalyn promised as she stroked Kyra's hair, who'd buried her head in her lap.

"I'm going to go see if any reports have come in," Oliver whispered to Evalyn a short while after Kyra fell asleep. "I'll send Sir Harris in to stand guard. Another knight will be posted at the door. I love you," he whispered to his peacefully-sleeping daughter, kissing her on the head. "I love you both," he corrected, squeezing his wife's hand before quietly stepping out of the room.

Chapter 133

In the middle of the night, Evalyn, who had fallen asleep holding Kyra, awoke with a start when Sir Harris, muttered to himself, "There's something moving out there." As he squinted, an arrow flew through the rainy darkness outside and pierced through his skull. Kyra woke up just in time to see the knight fall to the ground, dead. She, along with her mother, let out an audible shriek when, seconds later, Malorek emerged through the window, holding his bow at the ready. The warrior posted outside the room burst in, only for Malorek to kill him too.

Wasting no time, the enraged villain drew his sword, moved to the bed and ripped Kyra from her mother's clutches. The princess awkwardly fell to the ground, so Malorek reached down and wrapped her hair around his hand over and over again, then forcefully picked her up by it.

Holding his blade at her throat, he ordered the queen, "Take me to your husband. If you scream or try to run away, your daughter dies."

Despite bleeding from various wounds, especially where he'd been shot with an arrow in his shoulder and foot, it was easy for Malorek to keep control of Kyra. Any time her feet faltered, he tugged her hair, jerking her head backwards. He kept her in front of him with his blade at her neck as he followed Evalyn down the tower stairs. Warriors posted throughout the building were helpless. Any attack on Malorek would cause the princess's death and possibly the queen's.

"The king is in the throne room," one of the guards revealed after Malorek drew blood from Kyra, showing the legitimacy of his threat.

Instead of entering the majestic, glass-ceiling throne room from the main, double set of doors, Malorek told Evalyn to lead him in through the less conspicuous side entrance. Together, he and his two captives came out on the platform at the front of the room. They stood next to the golden throne, behind which was an oversized, circular stained-glass window featuring the five elemental colors.

Standing fully-armored with his knights, Oliver's jaw dropped at the sight of his wife and daughter held hostage by the man he assumed would be brought to him in chains.

"Leave me alone with him!" Malorek yelled to the men conferencing with the king.

Nodding to those accompanying him, Zoran commanded his knights to leave so he could handle the situation on his own and prevent anyone from escalating the already dire situation.

"Let them go," he told Malorek in the calmest voice he could muster once everyone left. Oliver didn't know what the unstable warrior before him was willing to do, so he tried his best to keep the man calm. "Whatever you want, I'll give you. Just please let them go."

"Draw that golden sword of yours and impale yourself," Malorek sneered. "The only way they live is if you die."

"Dad, don't!" Kyra cried, seeing her father considering the sacrifice.

For her outburst, Malorek pulled her hair, snapping her head back once again.

Quenching his furiousness at the situation, Oliver took deep breaths, trying to think of any possible scenario that would give him leverage and free the two hostages he loved so dearly.

"You've done nothing to earn my trust. I could kill myself and then you could kill them. Let them leave this castle and you have my word I'll do what you want."

As Malorek considered the offer, Zoran watched Evalyn reach into the waistband of her dress and pull out a hidden dagger. A quick shake of his head was not enough to deter his wife. Evalyn lunged at Malorek to kill him, but the warrior easily stepped out of the way and drove his sword through her stomach. At the same moment, Kyra tried to flee, but Malorek's grasp of her hair kept her from escaping. He pulled his sword out of Evalyn and plunged it through the heart of the princess. Both the queen and Kyra fell to the ground simultaneously, each lying on opposite sides of Malorek. They died within seconds, their blood spilling down the steps of the platform the throne sat upon.

"No!" Oliver cried, running forward to the bodies of his dying wife and daughter. Forgetting Malorek was even there, Oliver's sole purpose was comforting his loved ones as they took their final breaths, but when he bent down to hold them, they were already dead.

Capitalizing on the king's grief, Malorek stepped forward to kill the man he despised.

This is it. The final step to fulfill my plan and take the throne is Zoran's death, Malorek thought to himself as he raised his sword and brought it down.

Instead of driving the blade through the king, Zoran blocked the steel with one of his elemental powers as his golden-armored gauntlet became covered in stone. With tears streaming down his face, Oliver stood and ripped the weapon out of Malorek's grasp. He threw the villain's sword away from them, and drew Aurelia. Malorek stood no chance unarmed against a man with all five elements.

The king grabbed Malorek's plate of armor with his left hand, paralyzing him with a jolt of electricity. Leaving just enough life in the man so that he could deliver one final attack, Zoran raised Aurelia and commanded the hottest flames he could muster to burn on the blade of his sword.

Too broken-hearted and emotional to vocalize any words to the man who took the lives of his family, Oliver sent an inferno of fire straight into his wife and daughter's murderer.

Believing his enemy to be dead, but his anger not yet quenched, Oliver used a powerful pulse of wind to send the still-burning body flying backwards through the stain-glass window behind the throne.

Dropping his sword and returning to the bodies behind him, Zoran fell to his knees and yelled out a lament of such dismay, it echoed throughout the castle. Warriors, knights, and aides entered the throne room to find their princess and queen dead and their king mourning over their bodies. Each person wept for the losses of the two women. The attendants had spent their lives serving the royal family. Many had watched Princess Kyra grow up before their very eyes.

Once he was done weeping, Oliver stood up, climbed up the stairs onto the stage and walked to the window Malorek had been blasted through. Even though it was the middle of night, he looked down at the jagged rocks and the fast-flowing Fluorite River that served as the castle's moat. He knew Malorek's body had been swept away, never to be seen again.

Distinguishable in a crowd by a severely crooked nose, a man named Arios, who served as Oliver's top-aide, cautiously approached the king and asked, "Do you want me to have the body found, sir?"

"No, he's dead. And he's the last person on this planet that deserves a proper funeral. I never want to hear his name mentioned. As far as the people of the kingdom are concerned, all they need to know is that the person responsible for Evalyn and Kyra's deaths will never hurt anyone again. That's the only statement I care to make."

"Yes, sir. And, your majesty, I know you're grieving, and I urge you to take all the time you need, but there is the issue of Princess Kyra's twins we need to address. We have many options. They can be sent to an orphanage, raised in the castle, or put up for adoption. Or we can find other alternatives for their upbringing."

"Are they still in the infirmary?"

"Yes, your highness," Arios was perfectly polite every time he addressed the king. "Both of your grandsons have been checked over by the head cleric and are healthy. One of the twins had a gash on his neck that needed to be stitched up, but he's fine. They're available for you to visit whenever you'd like."

"Take me to them now," Zoran demanded, while wiping his eyes. "I'll decide what needs to be done." He squeezed the brow of his nose between his fingers as if he was pinching off an oncoming migraine. Even though all he wanted was to go to his chambers and be alone, he knew the fate of the twins needed to be resolved before he grieved.

At the castle's infirmary, looking down on the two cribs, one holding the brown-eyed baby named Silas, and the other holding the blue-eyed baby named Cyrus, Oliver shared his theory and intentions with Arios. "The prophecy inscribed on the sword I carry speaks of twin boys. One will serve Alazar and the other will serve Zebulon. Both eventually die, but whichever survives longer will end up sacrificing his life to achieve a defining victory for the kingdom. I think these are the twins the prophecy references because they meet all the conditions.

"Chances are one of them will inherit Kyra's personality and the other will inherit their father's. We only need one to be my successor, someone whom I can raise here in the castle, who will hopefully have children of their own before their sacrificial death. The kingdom could use an heir as a hope for the future to get their minds off of what happened here tonight."

"How will you know which one to pick?" Arios asked, looking down at the pair of nine-month-old babies, unable to tell which one was birthed first.

"This one," Oliver gently picked Silas out of his crib. "He has the same brown eyes as his mother. He'll be the heir I bring up myself, the one to carry on the memory of Kyra."

"Are you sure, sir?" Arios sought confirmation as he stood over the baby Oliver had already turned his back to. The aide noticed Zoran didn't seem fully convinced he was making the right choice and that he was hurrying in his decision so he could return to grieving.

"Yes, the other one has a wound on its neck by the hand of its father. It'll forever be scarred."

"What shall be done with Cyrus, your majesty?"

"I don't care," Oliver shrugged his shoulders. "The prophecy says he's going to die at some point. I don't know if it'll be when he's little or grown, but it doesn't matter. The Prophecy of the Twins will still come true. Whatever you decide, I don't want him in this castle, and I don't want him to know of his past. Get rid of him and make sure you change its name to something else."

"Yes, sir," Arios nodded, prepared to carry out the order.

Before he left the infirmary, Oliver called out, "Arios, You and I can be the only ones who know of this." When the attendant nodded, understanding and promising to abide by the plan, Zoran added, "You've always been loyal to me. I fully trust that you'll keep the secret."

Even though it was still night, Arios knew the Warriors' Watchtowers never closed. The young aide rode through Celestial, holding Cyrus tightly in the nook of his arm. Disguised as much as he could be in case anyone recognized him as King Zoran's attendant, he went to two watchtowers and couldn't find a single warrior interested in adopting the baby. All he was told was, "try an orphanage."

Upon reaching the arena district, Arios decided to try one last watchtower in an attempt to find someone to take in Cyrus before dropping him off at an orphanage.

"Hi, I'm Titus Thatcher," Arios was greeted by the warrior on gate duty as he tied his horse to a hitching post outside the watchtower. "How can I help you?"

Putting on the most convincing act he could of a distraught father, Arios directed Titus's attention to his sleeping baby, and lied, "I'm looking for someone to adopt my son. The boy's mother, my girlfriend, is unstable and tried to take the boy's life tonight." He pulled back the folds of the blanket Cyrus was wrapped in to reveal the freshly-stitched wound on the baby's neck. "This isn't the first time she's endangered him, but I'm making sure it'll be the last. For the child's safety, I can't have him around her anymore. I had to sneak out in the middle of the night just so she wouldn't find out I'm giving up her baby."

"I'm sorry to hear that. I can't imagine what you're going through," Titus empathized with the man who looked to be around twenty-three, the same age he was. "Have you tried to get her help?"

"I have, but we don't have much money."

"What do you do for a living?"

"We both work as blacksmiths here in Celestial. We run a shop together, a struggling shop," Arios noted, adding whatever details he could think of to make his story as legitimate as possible.

"Have you looked into assistance? There are organizations and initiatives that might provide enough support to get your girlfriend the care she needs and help your business get back on track. They'd allow you to keep your son."

"I've already accepted money from both those programs," Arios answered, summoning tears to well up in his eyes.

Sighing, wishing there was something he could do to allow the man to keep his son, Thatcher broached the subject of adoption by asking, "Can I see him?" to which Arios handed him the baby, finding it hard to believe the warrior seemed genuinely interested. "What are you looking for in the adopting family?"

"I'd like for the family who takes him in to be involved with the warriors, like you are, sir. I'd like to know my boy will be safe and protected."

"If he didn't grow up having a mother, is that something that would concern you?" Titus asked. He began tapping his foot, nervous that the answer he received would exempt him from being able to help the man and the child.

"I'd be okay if he grew up in a single-parent home. I believe a family is most effective with two parents, but I'd never discredit the impact even one adult can have in a child's life."

Being open and honest, Thatcher shared the trauma that'd recently befallen him. "Three days ago, my firstborn baby died in childbirth. My wife died too. Natural causes." Trying not to become too emotional, he continued, "We buried them yesterday, but I came right back to work."

"I'm sorry to hear that." Arios couldn't believe the man was holding it together. "Why didn't you take time off, though?"

"For me, I knew what was best for me was getting back to a sense of normalcy. Plus, I have two other boys, Darren and Ty, who I'm raising at home. Their parents were murdered and I was the kids' godparent, so it's up to me to support them now."

"If you were selected godfather, you were chosen for a reason. Their parents must've seen something special in you."

"I hope I can live up to the father they thought I could be," Titus expressed. "I think my wife would be pleased if I took in one last child in memory of her. We always wanted three kids."

"Titus, I'd be honored if you adopted my son for me," Arios said.

Taking a deep breath, accepting the responsibility he was about to assume, Titus nodded and asked, "What's your name, sir? I'm sure the boy will ask me someday."

"I'd prefer not to give it. I think it's best for me to cut ties with him completely."

"Okay," Thatcher understood, knowing that some people's way of handling grief was to bury it completely. "What's his name, though?" the warrior called out as Arios turned and slowly walked away.

"Whatever you want it to be, he's yours now."

Titus looked down into the blue eyes of the now-awake baby he swaddled in his arms and whispered softly to the boy. "I'll give you the name my wife wanted for our son; Stephen."

Chapter 134

Malorek awoke to the sounds of crashing waves on the shore. Before even opening his eyes, he screamed out in pain and clutched his face. *My jaw and nose are broken,* he could tell immediately, cursing at the pain. Tenderly moving his fingers to check other spots of agony, he knew he could add broken teeth, and severe burns to his list of injuries. *I'm also blind in one eye,* he grew dismayed the more he rubbed it and tried to open it, but found that he could see nothing.

I'm on Celestial's beach along the Darien Sea, Malorek could tell from the sounds and smells. It was the darkest hours of night, equally far from both the sunrise and sunset. Crying out, the injured warrior crawled through the sand and made his way towards the water, only to be horrified by his reflection made possible by the bright yellow and green moons. His entire face was grossly disfigured. The sight of himself caused Malorek to vomit, which only added to the throbbing pains. Alone in the dark, he laid on his back and tried to focus on controlling his breathing, but each inhale caused excruciating pain.

The last thing I remember was seeing a flash of orange hit me in the face and then being hit by a burst of wind. I vaguely recall falling, but then I blacked out. I must've landed in the castle's moat and been carried along by the

Fluorite. Then I was dumped into the Darien Sea only to wash up on shore outside Celestial. I can't believe I'm still alive.

"You've got a lot of fight in you," a deep, raspy, slithering voice came from out of nowhere. The presence of another person startled Malorek, especially because no one had been on the beach just seconds ago.

Forcing himself up and out of the wet sand, Malorek expected to see King Zoran or one of the Guardian Knights standing behind him on the beach, ready to kill him. But what Malorek found when he turned around resembled nothing close to a man. An unnerving assemblage of dark, swirling clouds hovered nearby. Malorek could feel darkness and evil emanating from the ominous, unnatural form. Even though he'd never met him in person, he knew who stood before him.

"I am who you think I am," the disturbing voice again came from the void, able to read Malorek's thought process.

"Zebulon," Malorek stated, surprised he could utter a word since he felt paralyzed by a unique fear he'd never experienced in his life. In his shocked state, he forced a second word out of his pained jaw. "How?"

"Both Alazar and I have the ability to change our appearance and come to and from Element as we please," the dark god answered. "There are only two limitations we are bound by: We can't cause death and we can't look like any creation dead or alive."

As Malorek stood there, Zebulon's cloudy, smoke-like visage disappeared and in its place stood an average-looking minotaur. The darkness reappeared, only to disappear again and reveal a massive direwolf. After a third switch, Zebulon stood in the shape similar to a four-limbed Human in a suit of armor.

He's showcasing the abilities he speaks of, Malorek knew. *These are some of the forms he can come to Element as.*

Zebulon gestured to himself and spoke no longer in his chilling tone, but in the normal-sounding voice of a Human, comfortably matching the figure he employed. "Twenty-four years ago, it was in a decrepit form similar to this that I came to Element to procreate the leader I envisioned. I figured if I could put my power in the form of one of Alazar's creations, they could succeed where Draviakhan failed. I found a fifteen-year-old girl in Misengard and forced myself on her. She became pregnant with you."

Taken aback at the revelation of his parentage, Malorek closed his only seeing eye to collect himself, but Zebulon had no desire to wait around for his offspring to process the information.

"You have my blood flowing through your veins," Zebulon continued speaking while switching out of Human form and back into his cloud-covered appearance. "It's how you can control the elements. Anyone who shares my bloodline has access to the five elemental powers. The more you do to serve me, the deeper your connection is to me, and the more elements you'll be able to wield."

Either this is too much to take in, or my body is shutting down because of my injuries, Malorek thought as he went paler than he already was and began seeing tunnel-vision. *I feel like I'm going to faint.*

"Stay with me," Zebulon ordered. Somehow, through the power and command of the voice alone, Malorek felt emboldened and shook off his dizziness.

"You became everything I hoped you would be. You were abandoned, bullied, beaten, and betrayed, all at the hands of Alazar's creations. They treated you like they've treated my creations for so many years. You experienced the struggle and suffering monsters endure because of the actions of the four races. That's why there's no one better than you to set things right in this world. I want you to lead my forces in war. You can be as strong in the elements as the king you despise. Strong enough to defeat him, take the throne for yourself, and enslave Alazar's people."

Seeing his chance to exact his revenge by killing King Zoran with powers he always dreamed of, Malorek craved the opportunity before him. *I've always wanted to be king of the four races, but being the king of monsters would make me ruler of all.*

"I want that power," Malorek told the dark god. "If Alazar's creations were forced to serve monsters instead of themselves, their overconsumption of natural resources would end. By spreading around the wealth this world provides, I could eliminate the oppressive world your creations suffer in. Those who've known suffering will know prosperity and those who've known prosperity will know suffering. I can enact the change that's needed. I want this," Malorek repeated the same words he began his argument with.

Immediately, he felt imbued with the powers of the elements. He tested one out by turning the damaged plate of armor he was wearing into fire. The shifting light of the orange flames highlighted Malorek's sinister smile as he relished his newfound abilities.

"You're going to do great things," Zebulon said, pleased at the potential he saw in the alliance with his son. "Now, ask me the questions I know are on your mind."

Knowing the dark god could tell what he was thinking, Malorek felt free to ask, "You're saying anyone who has your blood in them and serves you can harness elemental powers? There are three of us then? Myself and my twin sons?"

"Yes. They and any of their offspring. But there are two more you didn't mention presently living on Element. The woman you forced yourself upon last year bore a daughter who she named Shana. She, too, has my bloodline. And there is a final person, but I do not foresee them ever serving me."

"Why don't you impregnate hundreds of women here? If they all have kids and those kids have children, you'd eventually have hundreds of people with your bloodline."

"I no longer can do that," Zebulon explained. "There is a third limitation Alazar and I are bound by. When we come to Element, we are mortal. The Human I impregnated so she could give birth to you thrust a dagger between my legs, making it impossible for me to procreate again." Zebulon's fury could be seen through the pulsing shroud of darkness as he explained the event. "But I don't need more people of my bloodline to achieve success. In every upcoming future, you end up on the throne in Celestial. It is your destiny to lead my forces to victory and nothing can prevent that."

"How do I begin?"

"Tend to your wounds. Survive this day. Then, begin building an army. One that outrivals Draviakhan's during his reign. There is an abandoned castle in the side of Mount Valpyrio. You can centralize your recruiting efforts in the very place where Draviakhan was defeated.

"I'll aid you by giving you control of the Accursed, as I've done a few times throughout history for people who the future shows will use the undead for my cause. The Skeleton King will be yours to command, and he'll carry out your orders with those in his army.

"It may take many years to obtain the numbers you seek, but once you do, attack the capital when they least expect it. Murder the king and take his throne. City after city, kill anyone that stands in your way until the world is under your authority. Your son can help you in your efforts once he's old enough."

"Which one?" Malorek asked.

"The one named Silas. The king kept him to raise him in the castle as his successor, but in most futures Silas won't turn out how he wants. Like you, he'll grow up rebellious and angry. He'll want to lead your army throughout the kingdom so he can attain elemental powers and become king. Let him have his desires. He's a strong candidate to fulfill the Prophecy of the Twins."

The Prophecy of the Twins, Malorek recalled a few of the words from reading it in the Book of the Future in his youth. "That ends with the death of both twins, so you're saying to appease Silas because he's going to die, anyway?"

"Exactly. It will either be him who fulfills the prophecy or Draviakhan's most powerful son, Nightstrike. You can use both of them in your efforts to overtake Celestial. And be assured that in every future across all timelines, you or your son will stop every attempted rebellion after you take Celestial. You will never know defeat."

"But what of when it's all over for me?" Malorek dared to ask a final question. "What becomes of me when sickness or old age kills me off?"

In a tone that suggested the answer was something Malorek should've already known, Zebulon answered,

"Alazar and I each have our own paradises. You will reside with me in mine, and in that life you will once again have power over all others because of the work you do for me here on Element. It is not until then that you will see me again. Conquer all in my name."

Chapter 135

As quickly as Steve's vision started, it ended, at least in terms of time passed on Element.

Now I know how my mother and grandmother were killed, he shook his head at Kyra and Evalyn's tragic murders. *And I can confirm that I am the rightful heir to the throne. What's more, there's a man named Arios who can attest to my lineage. If Arios survived the attack on Celestial, he can confirm that I am the son of Princess Kyra.*

Not only that, the dark god said Nightstrike can also fulfill the Prophecy of the Twins. That means he was born from the same egg as another dragon. There's only one I know of with similar power who could be a son of Draviakhan. Crimson Singe. Crimson killed his father to end the Second Great War, and now I have to do the same to end the Third.

Running the prophecy through his head, Steve confirmed that Crimson met all its requirements as a candidate to fulfill it. He smiled, relieved to no longer be alone in bearing the weight of its words as its sole fulfiller. But as quick as his smile appeared, it vanished. *If it's not me who makes the sacrifice of my life to claim victory, how can I be happy if it's the legendary dragon I call friend?*

Does Crimson know of his lineage? Steve wondered. *Something was bothering him the night I found him awake in Deletion. Does he know the prophecy and was thinking about his potential death, just like I was?*

Steve disregarded the questions he knew he couldn't learn the answers to until he reconnected with the red dragon. *I don't even know if I'll get the chance to ask him. I don't know if he survived his desert battle against Nightstrike.*

As he worried about the aerial monster, Steve looked down to see flames coming through the heavy-layered articles of clothing he was wearing to combat the snow and cold.

He took off his gloves, unbuttoned his wool cloak, and touched his fire armor underneath. Like his clothes, his skin didn't burn. *My element doesn't harm me or the attire I'm wearing unless I will it too,* Steve realized. *It's like how an Animal Monster's fur or feathers aren't affected by their element.*

Removing Aurelia, burning in its sheath, he swung his golden fire sword through the air, but his fascination and enjoyment of his newfound powers was short-lived. As Steve reflected on the vision that preceded the acquisition of his element, he grew angrier by the minute.

Celestial's downfall, the implications that he might still be the fulfiller of the prophecy, and the challenge they faced in defeating the Hooded Phantom all weighed heavily on his mind. More than anything, though, Steve was infuriated by his vision's most disturbing revelation.

Inside me, the blood of Zebulon runs through my veins. Any children I have could grow up and set themselves against everything we're trying to achieve in taking back the kingdom. They could acquire all the same elemental powers the Hooded Phantom has. Even if we defeat Malorek, this curse will remain through mine and Shana's bloodlines unless we decide not to procreate.

The nineteen-year-old struck a rock with his fire sword. In his anger, his thoughts turned to a verbal expression of rage as he yelled to the heavens, "For months I've been dealing with the idea that I'm going to die in our attempt to take back Celestial, but now I know that even if I survive, I have to sacrifice my future, my offspring. Obtaining the peace we're fighting for requires everything of me!"

Exerting too much energy from his combined outburst with his elemental energy use, Steve tried to catch his breath, but struggled due to the limited oxygen from his high point of elevation. Quenching the fire on his armor and Aurelia, he put his sword in its scabbard, closed his eyes, and focused on controlling his breathing. Knowing that talking to Alazar was a helpful technique in calming him down, he prayed as he often did in times both good and bad.

Out of everyone in the world, you selected me to be one of the few to wield your divinely given powers. There's a history of iconic and influential people that have been your elect and used their abilities to serve your cause. I want to continue their work. I don't know what's in store for me, but help me to make the sacrifices to achieve peace, no matter what it takes.

Finishing his prayer, Steve opened his eyes and took in the majestic sight from the mountaintop one last time. *Please give safety to my friends as we finish our missions and make our way to Almiria. Let us go on from there to take back the capital and eliminate all the evil that seeks to cause your creation's suffering. Amen.*

Using the same impressions he left in the snow on his way to the summit, Steve descended Mount Divinian's peak. His breathing slowly returned to normal as the oxygen level in the atmosphere increased.

Passing through blizzard-like conditions because of wind blowing snow across the trail, Steve used his element to cover himself in flames. He did the same with Aurelia, holding up his sword before him as if it were a torch. The intense heat evaporated the snow in his vicinity, helping with visibility, but he still struggled to see more than five feet in front of him.

As the only stationary fixture around him, Steve placed his free hand on the mountain wall and ran his fingers along it as he walked. He moved cautiously forward, knowing any misstep could cause him to fall off the side of the mountain's dangerously narrow trails.

The guides must be right around here, he knew, calling out for their help. Instead of the response he expected, he heard the clanging of their swords and the three men shouting at something. Then, everything went quiet, the high-winds stopped, and the bright blue sky reappeared.

Those winds were not a natural occurrence. A monster used their element to create them.

Steve readied Aurelia and took his metal shield off his back, summoning fire to ignite them both. Rounding the corner, he found the four guides all lying at the mouth of the cave they'd taken shelter in. Pools of blood stained the snow underneath their unmoving bodies.

Near them, a fifth figure stood alone, concealed by the darkness of the cave. With weapons in both hands, long hair, a small-frame, and pointed ears, Steve could've sworn the silhouette belonged to Ty, but he realized it was something else entirely as it stepped forward into the daylight.

It's a drow, Steve muttered to himself upon seeing the Elf-sized figure revealed. "Drop your weapons!" he commanded the monster with stark white hair and skin as blue as the sky.

"Why, so you can attack me too?" the drow shouted back, unceasing in its leaden pursuit forward, coming straight for the warrior.

"Are you an assassin sent for me?" Steve asked.

"No. I don't know you. I have no issue with you unless you keep your sword drawn."

"I won't sheath it," Steve held his ground. He gestured to the bodies of the guides. "You murdered these men. I can't let you leave."

"Then I'll kill you too," the drow claimed, almost with an air of disappointment. Yet, all the same, it covered its shortsword in orange flames and controlled the wind with its green-glowing, single-handed axe. With its elements employed, the monster ran forward to attack the fire-armored warrior.

Before allowing the drow to get anywhere close to him, Steve sent a giant inferno coursing out of Aurelia towards his enemy. The plume was so large; the drow was completely lost in the flames.

Suddenly, the monster appeared at the top of Steve's vision, coming down from a tremendous leap as it powerfully swung its axe and sword down onto its Human attacker. Steve threw up his shield, preventing his skull from being split open, but the drow mentally controlled the high-altitude winds and sent a concentrated blast downwards. Steve flew backwards, landing in a snowbank which instantly melted from the heat of his armor.

"Don't you know drow skin is impervious to all temperatures?" the monster teased Steve for his futile attack. It ran forward again with ice-covered weapons, reaching Steve the second the warrior pulled himself up. The two battled in back-and-forth close-quarters combat on the open plateau.

With both man and monster immune to the effects of fire, the drow held the advantage, using its wind element to keep Steve on the defensive.

In order to gain an upper hand, Steve used his shield and sword to block the array of blows raining down upon him. During one brutal attack, he caught the drow's axe and shortsword on Aurelia's hilt.

Seeing the five gemstones and diamond embedded in the weapon's handle, the drow stumbled backwards. With its focus disturbed, it stopped attacking, but remained in fighting stance with its weapons held at the ready. "Where did you get that sword?" it asked, its eyes evident of its bewilderment.

"It belonged to King Oliver Zoran and now to me," Steve answered, wondering what connection the monster had to Aurelia.

"King?" the drow struggled to grasp the information being revealed to him. With his white eyebrows furled and his black eyes turned to slits, he asked, "Where is he?"

"King Zoran?" Steve asked, unsure of what the drow wanted with his grandfather. "He's dead."

"By your hand?"

"No, by my enemy's".

"He was mine to kill!" The drow growled to itself, but loud enough that Steve heard its utterance. Looking up in frustration, the monster noticed the bright moon. Although it was daytime, the red moon shone brightly at such a high elevation. "It should be green." The drow muttered, again to itself. "Tell me warrior, how long has it been?" Rephrasing the question, it asked, "What year is it?"

"We're less than a year until the new millennium. It's 999."

"Nearly fifty years," the drow shook its head in astonishment, turning its back to Steve and walking to the edge of the mountain to look over its side.

Considering attacking the murderer since it'd let its guard down in its shock, Steve instead sought to empathize with the monster coming to grips with reality. "If I put my sword and shield down, will you drop your weapons?"

Before it could respond, a great trembling came from a ridge high above.

An avalanche! Steve watched the white-covered terrain shift and slide down Divinian's mountainside. "Head inside!" he directed the drow to the cave entrance behind where it stood, knowing it was their only avenue of escape.

The drow easily made it into the protective den because of its close proximity to it, but Steve knew there was no way he'd make it in time. Sending all the fire he could muster out of his sword towards the snow already piling up in front of the entrance, he hoped to buy himself enough seconds to make it into the cave, but he wasn't even close.

The avalanche hit him with such force, it knocked him down and nearly covered him completely. It was only because of another element he survived being buried alive and suffocating to death.

Coming out from under the shelter of the den, the drow blasted its wind element above Steve's head, creating a barrier between Steve and the avalanche. The high-speed, horizontal tornado churned away all the snow that would've engulfed the young warrior, allowing Steve to free himself and run into the safety of the mountainside cave.

Entering after the warrior, the drow made it back inside as the entrance was covered behind him. With both man and monster standing in fire armor, they illuminated the dark surroundings of the small conclave they stood in. There was no exit.

"Does your offer still stand?" the drow asked.

In response, Steve tossed his sword and shield into the space between them. Both lost their flames the moment they left his hand, but his fire armor remained.

In similar fashion, the drow tossed its own weapons forward.

I know he has a secret dagger hidden under his cloak, Steve could see the bulge near the drow's hip. *I'm not going to call him out on it, though. I'm sure he knows I have a hidden dagger of my own strapped to my leg.*

"My name is Stephen," Steve introduced himself. "What are you called?"

"Cryonic to some. Wayfayer to others."

"Why'd you save me? You could've left me to die. You even had the chance to kill me, but you didn't."

"If you were dead, you wouldn't be able to tell me how you came by that blade."

"I've got questions for you, too," Steve assured the monster.

"What do you want to know?" Cryonic asked, attempting to defuse the tension between them by ceding the conversation to the warrior.

"I don't know where to begin," Steve's thoughts poured out in a disorganized mess. "You're a drow, yet somehow you were outside in the sun, unharmed. What were you doing near the peak of Mount Divinian? And why were you confused about the year?"

Cryonic smiled at the bumbling warrior, baring a set of pure white teeth, the cuspids of which hung downwards in sharp points. "I have a rare condition called melanism. Instead of being confined to the dark like most drow, my disorder allows me to roam free.

"I guess I have Zebulon to thank," the Wayfarer mused. "He spent little time on his monsters at creation. His uncaring approach caused both cosmetic and internal abnormalities, such as Draviakhan's five heads, or my melanism."

"Alazar's people have similar issues," Steve said, being purposeful not to sound like he was arguing when he was genuinely interested in understanding the conditions some people lived with. "I've known people with mental illness, epilepsy, and blindness. There are even disabilities that haven't received names yet. There's a Dwarf I traveled with who has a son who struggles to walk. And my half-sister is missing the pinky fingers on both her hands."

"Unlike Zebulon, those aren't instances of Alazar botching his creations, though," Cryonic explained. "From my understanding, any problems in the four races stem from the effect of evil that Zebulon installed into the nature of this world. If it wasn't for the dark god's influence, Element would be like Alazar's heaven. No one would suffer from maladies or know pain."

This isn't any average drow I'm stuck in this cave with, Steve thought. He considered the wayfarer's intelligence, showcased not only by Cryonic's critical thinking, but his ability to articulate. *He hasn't squandered his unique ability of being able to travel through this world. He's educated himself in the ways of it.*

Steve listened intently as the drow followed up his comments by saying, "Unfortunately, suffering and pain are all many of us know," Cryonic mused, looking off into the distance as if he was deep in thought.

"That's the reason I came up to Mount Divinian, to get away from it all. But Oliver Zoran sought to kill me. He didn't want me to pass on my genes and create a whole race of drow not only impervious to being burned or frostbitten, but also able to roam freely in the world in the daylight."

"What happened?" Steve asked, eager to hear the drow's account, but not yet eager enough to reveal his relation to Cryonic's enemy.

"We fought. I cut his eye, blinding him permanently, but he ended up freezing me alive in a lake on this mountain. I was brought to life when an avalanche on the far side of the mountain set me free."

"So the last thing you remember is battling Oliver Zoran?" Steve asked.

"Pretty much. My body was preserved and all my memories remain. It's everything else around me that's apparently changed," he looked to where Aurelia lay and then to its new wielder. "You said Oliver became king?"

"Yes," Steve admitted, before explaining everything from Zoran's defeat of Draviakhan, to the Hooded Phantom's murder of the king, to Alazar's new elect.

"You should know," Steve cautioned, "the reason I carry Aurelia is because I took it from my twin brother, Silas Zoran, King Zoran's grandson."

"You're a grandson of Oliver?" Cryonic picked up on Steve's indirect way of revealing his lineage. He shook his head in disappointment.

"I'm sorry he tried to kill you," Steve apologized as he nodded. "I understand how you must've felt. I too, have a defect my grandfather would've likely wanted eradicated. Like you, it's one caused by Zebulon, but I firmly believe that it's wrong to end someone's life for something they don't have control over."

Cryonic appreciated Steve's viewpoint, especially since the warrior didn't intend to carry out his grandfather's vendetta. He glanced towards the covered entrance to the cave, where the four men he killed laid somewhere at the bottom of the avalanche-covered plateau. "I only take a life for two reasons. To protect my own or to save the lives of innocents."

"Did the guides fall into one of those categories?" Steve asked with a sense of disdain, still upset at their deaths.

"I told you, they attacked me. They saw what I was and assumed I was evil. The only way I could ensure my safety while being outnumbered was to create a windstorm and attack with stealth. Unfortunately, I think it's what caused this avalanche."

"It's not a total loss, though," Steve opined. "We might've killed each other otherwise." He took a deep breath, sizing up Cryonic. "You said you're willing to kill to protect the innocent. Does that extend to Alazar's creations?"

"Not exclusively. The reasons for wars are never as black and white as either side makes them out to be. I've seen members of the four races do things in the name of Alazar, but brought nothing but dishonor to their god. And I've seen Zebulon's creations ban together for noble causes. Rather than picking sides indefinitely, I prefer to fight for whatever causes I deem just. I don't care which god's creations I side with. Sometimes that's against Alazar's people, sometimes I'm alongside them."

"Would you be interested in fighting alongside us? We're rallying against the Hooded Phantom and his forces. Our cause is a righteous one. We seek to liberate the capital and end the lives of those who are forcing Alazar's creations to suffer."

"Righteous causes are often subjective," the drow stated, once again showing his level of intelligence was at a higher level than what Steve believed monsters were capable of. "Have you taken the time to consider Malorek's intentions? Are you sure there's not more of a reason why he's doing all this?"

Taken aback by the question, Steve's only response was, "He finds joy in causing suffering. He's evil incarnate."

"That may be true, but like I said, it's seldom that simple. You view him and his army as evil, but he probably thinks the same of you and your followers. Before I commit to a side and fight, I must know what I'm doing is justified." After sighing deeply, Cryonic replied in a non-committal way, "I'll come with you for now. But I'll give it time before I decide whether I'll fight with you or draw blades against you."

"Once you've seen what I've seen, you'll be alongside me," Steve said confidently, and then changed the inflection in his voice, "But if you decide you're my enemy, at least give me a heads up first if you're going to try and kill me."

Cryonic laughed. "Alright, that much I can promise."

Feeling comfortable that a level of trust had been established with the drow, Steve proposed, "Now what do you say we both use our fire elements to melt the snow blocking our escape so we can descend this mountain?"

Chapter 136

"Ty, is everything okay?" Min-Ye met the fellow Elf on Andonia's main deck after seeing him jogging down the dock. "Shana came onto the ship crying. She went straight to the cabin and refuses to talk to anyone."

"Everything's fine," Ty grumbled and kept hurrying, not wanting to explain their argument.

I know Shana told me to leave her alone, but I have to see if she's okay after witnessing Steve's vision. I can't imagine what she must be thinking about, coming to terms with the knowledge she and Steve come from the bloodline of Zebulon.

"Shana, it's Ty," he called out while knocking on the cabin door. His heart beat fast, anxious to see his girlfriend after their heated argument.

"I don't want to talk right now," she immediately cut him off.

I can tell she's crying by the sound of her voice, Ty knew. *And frustrated.* Nonetheless, he persisted. "I saw Steve's vision. Are you sure you're okay?"

"I told you, I don't want to talk until I initiate it!" Shana's anger cut through the door separating them. "I don't need you to comfort me or check in on me. I'll be fine on my own."

Hurt by her lack of need, but also trying to be respectful of the distance she desired, Ty softly shared, "Whenever you're ready, even if it's the middle of the night, I'll be right here." He pulled a crate over and sat a few feet from the cabin, willing to wait as long as needed.

Hours passed, during which time Jun-Lei and Kyoko ventured into Oceanside to speak with the leadership on Ty and Shana's behalf. Jun-Lei went to the clerics while Kyoko went to the warriors, and both mother and daughter managed to successfully clarify the need for help, to which they were promised a strong number of volunteers.

Meanwhile, Ty never left his spot on the crate outside the forecastle cabin, where he worried about Shana's well-being and if he'd lose the woman he felt closer to than any before her.

"Shana!" he was caught by surprise when he heard the creaking of floorboards followed by her opening the door. He immediately delivered the apology he'd spent hours rehearsing in his mind, but Shana walked right past him with no greeting or physical contact.

"Come, follow me," she simply said, heading across the forecastle deck to lean on the railing at the mast of the ship. "We'll talk over here."

Her eyes are dry, and she looks well-put-together, as if she's made up her mind, Ty analyzed every part of her, trying to get an idea of her emotional state.

Shana took a moment to feel the breeze of the sea on her face and breathe in the fresh air. "I'm sorry it took me a while to sort through things."

"Don't apologize. You should never apologize for prioritizing your mental and emotional health. I'm sorry for coming to see you earlier," Ty moved the blame to himself, "I was just really worried about you after Steve's vision."

"It hurt me to see it," Shana admitted. "It was enough when I learned from my vision that I was Malorek's daughter, but finding out I stem from Zebulon's bloodline...that was tough news to digest. I'm thankful for it though, because that revelation helped me to determine what to do about our relationship."

Shana took a deep breath and struggled to make eye contact with Ty as she explained, "Dating you for the past two months has been the happiest ones of my life, but in learning recently how important your legacy is to you, and how future children you want are a part of that, it's made my decision easier.

"I'm not the type of person who can stay at home, cooking, cleaning, raising toddlers, waiting for you to come home from work each day. That's fine and respectable for some people, but it's not for me. All I ever wanted was to work in politics, but having a family would make that career nearly impossible."

"Don't do this. Please, don't say what you're going to say," Ty's voice broke and tears welled in his eyes, knowing where Shana was taking the conversation. "Your mom could help us. You don't have to give up on your dreams."

Despite his pleas, Shana continued, saying, "It's not just that, though. Knowing I could further Zebulon's bloodline and create people who harm others like how my mother was hurt makes me not want to have children. I know *you* want kids, though, and you'll be a great father someday. I've seen how much fun you have interacting with Nash and others we've met in our travels, but I can't give you what you seek. It hurts me so much to do this, because you're my best friend, but the best thing to do is to end the relationship between us."

"You're breaking up with me?" he asked after a silent moment. "Just like that?"

"It's for the best," Shana repeated herself. "I know it hurts, but it's better to end this now rather than drag it out longer than it needs to be. I know someday you'll realize you're happier with someone else than you ever could've been with me."

"You don't have to do this," Ty shook his head and stuttered through his reasons why the end of their relationship could be avoided. "I...I would give up my job as a warrior if you wanted to work as a politician. With you and me together, we can raise them right and not worry about Zebulon's connection to them."

"I can't," Shana shook her head. "The dark god can take any child tainted by his blood and empower them with elements if they carry out his will. Think about it: If we had two kids who served Zebulon, and they each had two kids that served Zebulon, in a few hundred years you'd have thousands with elements serving him while Alazar only has his five elect. We've already seen what one person can do with that type of power."

"Are you saying you refuse to have kids?" Ty pointedly and succinctly asked. Their entire conversation was a blur to him and now he needed a definitive answer to a simple question to help him process everything.

"Yes," Shana stated boldly and confidently. "And we're lucky I haven't gotten pregnant yet, now that we know the risks."

She sighed, seeing Ty struggling to come to terms with the ending of their relationship. Knowing he was looking for any excuse to stay together, she added, "It wouldn't be fair for me to stay in a relationship where I couldn't give you something I know you want so badly. Deep down, you'd always resent me for it." Then, trying to let the heartbroken Elf down easily, she claimed, "A part of me will always love you and the time we shared. But, since I know it'll be too painful to be in each other's company for the foreseeable future, I've decided to leave."

"What!? When?" Ty was once again taken aback by the onslaught of change Shana was throwing at him.

"I'm hoping tonight. I'm going to meet the aerial captain here and find some guys who will fly me to Almiria so we can begin getting everything organized for our army gathering there. I know you'll probably be heading to Triland soon since you're due to rendezvous with Steve and Kari. I'll send a dove to let the three of you know I made it safely. When you arrive in Almiria, I'll understand if you don't want to talk or interact with me, but I'm hoping you will."

With that, Shana stepped forward to the rattled warrior and kissed his forehead. Without another word, she collected her belongings, said goodbye to Jun-Lei and the Andonia crew, and headed off into Oceanside to find the aerial warriors' barracks.

Chapter 137

"Have either of you ever been to Bogmire before?" Krause asked his fellow Serendale men as they slowly trudged through a muddy trail in the swamplands. When neither the Elf nor Dwarf answered, the commander shared, "It's an fascinating city. It's just like this," he pointed to the green and brown murky water and dead trees on either side of where they rode, "except the entire city is built into the treetops. It's all connected through man-made platforms and bridges."

"What's that?" Nash asked, spotting a sign crudely nailed into the bark of a redwood up ahead.

"No Giants Allowed," Willis read as the words became more visible.

"Oh, yes, I should also mention many people in the Swamplands still aren't over what happened in the year 917," Krause explained.

"Was that the Race Wars?" Nash asked, reminded of when Grizz mentioned the conflict in Twin Peaks.

"No, the bulk of those occurred centuries prior, but this was an extension of them – a war between Giants and Humans."

"917 was over eighty years ago," Willis did the math. "Humans here are still bitter about what happened?"

"Can you blame them?" Krause asked. "Giants around these parts believed Humans were inferior to them, so they started putting limitations on them in society and the Humans started an uprising because of it. Eighty years isn't that long ago," he corrected Willis. "There's still people around who suffered and lost loved ones from all that hate."

"People hated each other because they were a different race?" Nash turned and whispered to his father, who he rode alongside, exchanging a nervous glance at the men riding in front of them because they weren't fellow Dwarves.

"Yes, and it's found all throughout history," Grizz explained, speaking loudly so Nash knew they were among trusted company. "People are constantly treated poorly because of their race or gender, or a variety of other things. Even if there's a movement to change that mindset, strains of it always remain in society. Wars never truly end until the underlying issue that started them is resolved."

"Don't you remember how Ivan Griegan said mean things about you? His father taught him that people that weren't the same race as him weren't as good."

"Why did his dad think that, though?" Nash was persistent in his questions, like a typical eight-year-old struggling to understand the complexities of the world.

"He, like all of us, was born into a world tainted by evil. You know the god of darkness, right?"

"Zebulon." Nash confirmed.

"Right, without him, Element would be a perfect place. There would be no death or sadness. It would be paradise. But since Zebulon exists and helped create this planet, there's evil in its framework that infects all creations physically, spiritually, and mentally. One of the dark god's goals is to make Alazar's creations suffer. Sometimes that happens through the destruction and mayhem caused by people or monsters, but other times it's accomplished by the twisting of our ideals and morals."

"I'm guilty of that," Krause admitted, and was honest with Nash. "I grew up in a home where I was taught anyone who had a different skin color than me was inferior. I treated your dad wrong the minute he set foot in Serendale, and said terrible things about your mom when she married him simply because I thought it was wrong they had different pigmentation. But in traveling with you and your dad, you both have changed my mind. I realized that the way I was led to think about people based on their appearance was wrong."

"That's the most important thing," Grizz explained. "We have to get to know people different from us. Zebulon wants nothing more than to make you hate others because then you're becoming like him. And even more than that, he would love to get you to hate yourself, to make you feel like a failure or that your life is worthless. But no matter how down you may get, you always have to tell yourself the truth: that you are important, you are loved, and that your life has meaning and purpose."

"I'm not going to let him trick me," Nash was resolute. In his innocent, optimistic view, he asked, "If everyone has evil in them then they must have good too, right?"

"That's why some monsters, like the very one you're riding, are our friends," Willis nodded to Copper. "He, like all of us, has free will and isn't forced to embody the dispositions of the god that created him. All of us exist on a spectrum between good and evil. Where we are on that spectrum is determined by how we were raised, our experiences, and the current circumstances we find ourselves in; those among many other things. The more we can get both people and monsters to abandon the way Zebulon would have us live and adopt Alazar's way of peace, the better this world will become."

"We're almost there," Grizz called to the three riders behind him. "Same deal as before, we'll talk to the warrior leaders here and try to get them to lend us as many volunteers as possible. The mayor can address the citizens, and then we'll lead everyone to Casanovia. From there, we'll head to Almiria with all the Casanovia and Bogmire recruits."

Our journey is almost complete, Grizz thought. *It won't be long before we're standing at the gates of Celestial, ready to take on the Hooded Phantom's Army.*

Chapter 138

"Wait here," Steve told Cryonic after the Human and drow had spent two days together traveling down Mount Divinian. "The family of the guides live in this village. It's best if you stay here. It wouldn't be considerate to have you by my side when I tell them what happened. I'll come back later with food and then, if you still want to accompany me, we can ride to Triland."

"Like I told you before, I'll stick by your side until I can determine if your cause is just," Cryonic looked around and shrugged his shoulders. "It's not like I have anywhere else to go."

"Where were you from before you were frozen?" Steve asked, implying it may be a place the drow could return to.

"It's easier to ask where I haven't been," the Wayfayer answered. "I've spent time in Evernight, Underdeep, and Deletion's Abyss. I have no doubt each one holds enemies seeking my death if I set one foot there. At this point, I've learned home is wherever I find myself."

Steve nodded, reminded of hearing about Evernight, Underdeep, and Deletion's Abyss in Warrior Training. *They're all huge, subterranean realms where drow and dusk trolls live. The caverns go miles deep below the surface.*

Not pressing the issue to learn more, Steve handed Cryonic two of the mules' reins for their future travel and hopped up onto another. Then, he took the reins of the remaining ones to lead them down into the village.

"Sit tight, and I'll see you soon," Steve nodded goodbye as he headed away from the drow.

Once he rounded a bend in the mountain pass and the village came into focus, he began sweating despite the chilly weather.

Why do I keep having to be the bearer of bad news? Steve asked himself, envisioning how he'd spend the next few hours as he rode down the last of the winding mountain path. He gulped down a lump in his throat that reminded him of when he told Emma that her husband Cyrus was killed in the attack on Celestial. *I'm always willing to console someone who needs it, but it's emotionally taxing, and each time I feel guilty in a way. So much death seems to surround Alazar's elect, especially me. I know these men might've run into Cryonic regardless of if I was there, but I still feel responsible.*

After speaking with the men's widows, and worse, seeing that another one of them had young children, Steve solemnly walked away from the last house he visited. Drained from sharing the devastating news to the brokenhearted families, he headed to the village's one and only tavern and ate a breakfast that didn't bring him the same cheer it usually did.

"Someone told me you were here in the tavern," General Elesora slid into the seat across the table from Steve a long while after he'd arrived. "I just got back to the village and came straight here once I heard what happened. If I thought there was even a remote possibility you'd come under attack, I wouldn't have recommended you go up there. I'm sorry you had to go through that."

Steve continued staring down at his plate, using his fork to play with the half-eaten eggs and ham that had gone cold over an hour ago.

"Some of those men had wives and children!" he finally looked up. Tears welled in his eyes and his cheeks flushed as he lamented, "What did they die for, so I could catch a scenic view?"

"They died in service to you and this kingdom so that you could follow in your grandfather's footsteps and other kings of ages past who also made the climb to the summit. I told you before that many who trod that path felt the weight of the challenge of ruling and knew at that moment whether or not they were the right man for the job. Did you learn where you stand?"

"I did, and I learned much more than just that," Steve confessed, hinting at his vision.

"I know the loss of men is difficult, but it's going to happen all the time during your reign. Especially when we all unite to take back Celestial. People will make sacrifices for the common good. Some will die. Maybe even ones you love. But we can prevent their deaths from being in vain by finding the positives of what came out of their lives and making the most of their sacrifices."

"What were the positives of losing men up on Divinian?" Steve glared out the window at the mountain.

"Aside from you finding out if you want to take over as king? Maybe it's this, right here," A'ryn gestured to the space between them. "Without what occurred, I wouldn't have had the chance to give you the advice I'm giving you now. Whether it's helpful or not, I don't know, but just know everyone goes through hardships like this, but trials better prepare us for what's to come. Whatever the positives may be, we have to believe they exist and try our best to find them in memory of those who give their lives. They deserve no less than that."

Steve nodded, trying to take the general's words to heart even though it was tough amidst his discouragement. "The drow that the guides attacked traveled down Divinian with me," he revealed. "He's with two of our mules at the base. I didn't want to bring him into the village of which he killed the fathers of four of the families."

"You didn't kill him?" A'ryn stood, reaching for her sword and looking in the direction of the mountain pass.

Steve beckoned her to sit down. "He doesn't deserve to die. The guides attacked because they felt threatened. Cryonic simply defended himself. He's not against us," Steve sternly invoked, seeing by Elesora's expression that his explanation wasn't sufficient. "I'm going to travel throughout Triland's province to some of the smaller towns and villages to continue recruiting for our army. I want you to head back to Stonegate, gather your own warriors and anyone willing to join you, and come to Triland. By the time you arrive, we should be there. With both cities together, we can have everyone use Triland's ships to sail to Almiria. That'll be the fastest way."

"I can't allow you as the future king to travel that far west with only a drow accompanying you," Elesora countered, still skeptical of the idea. "A lot could happen on that two-day ride."

"If he wanted to kill me, he would've already. Besides," Steve raised his fork and engulfed it in flames, "I'll be fine. I received my element on Divinian's peak, so I can protect myself. And Cryonic has two elements of his own."

A'ryn shook her head, uneasy with the decision, but accepted it nonetheless. "Alright, but only because you wield the most devastating weapon on all of Element," she forced a smile, nodding to Steve's tiny fire fork. "You better stab that thing deep into the Hooded Phantom and end all this misery."

"Oh, I have something much larger for that," Steve said, patting Aurelia in its sheath at his side.

Elesora stood and shook Steve's hand. "Till Triland, then."

Steve nodded. "Till Triland."

Once he paid for a large basket of non-perishables and fastened it to his mule, Steve rode back to Cryonic to give the drow half the food. The Anthropomorphic Monster used his long nails to tear through it, devouring it within minutes.

"The rest is for our trip. I was told it'll take two days to get to Triland on these mules," Steve explained.

"Good, then we'll have a lot of time for training," Cryonic declared, grabbing his axe and his sword. One glowed orange with flames and the other green with wind. "Come on, Brightflame, draw that golden scimitar of yours and let's have at it!"

"I'm not in a mood jovial enough for fighting," Steve declined. *Even after talking to Elesora, I think it'll take time to get over the deaths of the four guides and being with Cryonic doesn't make it any easier.*

"I'm not taking 'no' for an answer. Monsters in Celestial won't care about how you feel, and if the best you can do is what you showed me on Divinian, you're not going to stand a chance against their leader with his five elements."

Giving no warning, Cryonic sent a plume of ice from his sword that Steve had no choice but to cover his red armor in flames to defend himself.

"Good!" Cryonic exclaimed when Steve struck back by swinging the flaming blade of Aurelia into his axe.

The two went back and forth, defending blow after blow. Every few minutes, Cryonic would chime in with advice.

"Remember to consider how much energy your enemy might have, what elements they're employing, and the weapons they're utilizing. It's a mind game as much as its physical," Cryonic warned, covering his sword in fire, his axe in ice, and his armor in wind. As he rained down an assault of blows that sent Steve backing up against his will, the drow instructed, "Not only do you have to react quickly, defending yourself from every strike, you have to counter each element as best you can while planning your next move."

"I yield, I yield!" Steve cried out through ragged breaths. He stuck Aurelia's sharp tip in the ground and rested on its hilt. "Let's break for water," he proposed, disappointed in knowing that if the fighting had been real, Cryonic would've landed three fatal strikes in the last twenty seconds alone.

As Cryonic drank from his own canister, Steve looked at the black-eyed drow's ice element and asked, "How'd my grandfather freeze you if you control water?"

"My battle against him was fierce. We were both winded, but he outlasted me. I couldn't summon my elements even if I wanted. We fell through a frozen lake high up on Divinian and before I drowned, Zoran attacked me underwater with his frost. My skin may be impervious to the cold, but I was encased in ice and couldn't move. Then everything went dark and I awoke after the avalanche pushed me up and out of the bottom of the lake and onto dry land, only to find those four guides shortly thereafter."

Steve nodded, imagining what it'd be like to be unconscious for five decades, only to wake up and realize how much time had passed.

"Draw your sword. Let's go again," Cryonic ordered after they'd rehydrated. "I know you're tired and exhausted, but you learn best when you're at your worst.

"This time, consider how like all element wielders, you only have so much energy to manifest your element. You can use a few large attacks or many small attacks. Or, you can cover your armor in your element so you don't get burned. Try to find a healthy balance between attacking and defending with your powers."

Okay, Steve wished they could get on their way, but he knew it was no use saying no. *I'm sure the other elect are also training whenever they have the chance. We all know what we're up against in Celestial, so we need to push ourselves to prepare, even when we're not in the mood to.*

For another half hour, the monster and man battled, and it wasn't until their third bout that Steve countered the drow's attack and created an opening that would've landed a killing blow.

"Not bad!" Cryonic sheathed his sword and axe.

"There's still room for improvement, though," Steve replied, being his usual, perfectionist self. "But I'm thankful for how far I've come. Even though I was proficient in swordfighting after Warrior Training, the peace the kingdom was experiencing made me go a while without needing to use what I'd learned, so I lost my skills. When Celestial was attacked, every battle I was in I barely escaped with my life. My confidence was shaken, but I'm finally feeling like I'm getting back into the natural rhythm I'd learned but forgot."

"You'll get there," Cryonic encouraged the warrior. "And I bet having an element doesn't hurt at all in helping get your confidence back," Cryonic bore his sharp cuspids in a smile, seeing how Steve loved every time he could employ his fire abilities in battle.

Steve smiled back, "No, it doesn't hurt at all."

As Steve walked to the brush at the side of the trail to relieve himself, Cryonic grew serious and said, "It's not your skills that worry me, it's your injury."

"What injury?" Steve spoke over his shoulder as his back was turned to the drow.

"Your leg," Cryonic was more specific. "You've been limping. I noticed it earlier, and it's only getting worse."

"Oh," Steve shrugged. "I guess I'm used to it by now."

Buttoning the front of his pants and turning around, he explained, "My brother, Prince Silas Zoran, broke my leg when we fought against each other in Casanovia. It aches whenever I do too much, you know, like hiking up the tallest mountain in the world," Steve pointed over to the fork in the mountain pass where it led up to the higher levels of Divinian. "There's not much I can do about it," he shrugged again, knowing little could be done about the affliction he'd face for the rest of his life.

"There may be some salves that could at least provide cooling relief, but you'll have to learn how to fight through that pain."

Together, the monster and man ended their training, mounted their mules and headed west. They spent a few days traveling throughout the province, where Steve recruited civilians from some towns in the area that were large, although not populated enough to technically be considered cities.

All throughout their journeying around the shadow of the mountain, Steve and Cryonic conversed and continued to get to know each other, just as they did on their descent down Divinian.

From discussing kingdom history to hearing Cryonic recount some of his most epic battles, the two travelers were never short on conversation. Perhaps nothing was more interesting to Steve than listening to the drow explain social issues and conflicts between the four races and monsters in the past, as well as debating how things had and hadn't changed since Oliver Zoran's reign.

I enjoy his company, Steve realized. *Not only is he helping prepare me for battle, it's healthy to talk to someone with viewpoints and perspectives that I could never understand unless I went through those experiences myself. I'm willing to listen and learn to expand my knowledge, just as he is from me. These are the friendships this world needs more of.*

Chapter 139

After Holder's Keep, Kari flew alone to Al Kabar on Crimson Singe and spent a while recruiting as many people as possible. Her time was uneventful, but the half-Human, half-Elf appreciated the reprieve from action after all the violence that'd occurred between Nightstrike's attack in the desert and what happened in the prison atop Mount Anomaly.

Leaving the care of all the volunteers she'd rounded up in the hands of Al Kabar's warrior leaders, she told them to head to Almiria, where the army was gathering and making preparations for the final battle of the war.

"Shall we travel with them?" Crimson asked Kari as she sat in the saddle on his back. With his wings spread wide, the two hovered over the caravan of over a thousand men and women exiting the desert city.

They have a long trek to make through canyons, mountain trails, forests and the prairie before arriving in Almiria, Kari knew, looking to the northeast. *Although I'd love to head there to see my father, I miss Steve more than anything.*

"I think I'd like to head to Triland. That's the rendezvous point where Steve, Ty, Shana, and the Andonia crew were all supposed to meet up. I've been nervous about what happened to Steve after Nightstrike

287

attacked us, so it'd give me some peace of mind to know if he's there."

"You're in love," Crimson teased.

Kari smirked and spoke to the dragon from the blind spot on his back. "You can't tell me you've never felt this way too! I saw the way you and Glaciara gazed at each other back in Holders Keep. I know there's some sort of past there."

"I assure you I don't know what you're speaking of," Crimson said in a way that was all-too-obvious he was lying. Quickly changing the subject, he powerfully flapped his wings, flying up to a jetstream that he could use to soar west.

Crimson Singe pushed himself to his limits, attempting to reach their destination within two days. On the first night, they stopped in Stonegate for a brief rest. Kari hoped to find Steve, knowing she and him were originally due to visit the Primary City, but in speaking with A'ryn Elesora, the general told her, "Steve and a drow he's with are currently traveling throughout Triland's province. I just returned from speaking with him in a village near Mount Divinian. If you fly to Triland, he'll probably be arriving there in a matter of days."

Thank Alazar, he's alive! Kari thought once she heard the good news. *It was encouraging enough to know he got his vision, but now I have official confirmation he's alive.*

"There's Andonia!" Kari exclaimed in the late evening following her early morning departure from Stonegate.

Even though the sun was setting, it was easy to make out the old, three-masted ship, where it sat docked among many other vessels on the Etherwell River. *Ty, Shana, Ryland, and the others must be here already!*

"I'll set you down on the bank, and then head to a nearby field or somewhere more open," Crimson announced. "With the Primary Cities all on high alert, I'm sure the aerial warriors have already spotted me as an unfamiliar monster and will come to interrogate me any minute now."

"I'll reconnect with you tomorrow," Kari decided. "Once they come closer and discover who you are, they'll likely let you sleep in their stables instead of out in the wilderness."

"And hopefully give me a meal or two," Crimson nodded. His growling stomach rumbled up through the Halfling's legs as he slowly descended near Andonia.

"See you tomorrow then," Kari unstrapped her saddle and slid down a few of Crimson's scales once she reached a point she could safely jump down to the ground.

"Kari Quinn!" Jun-Lei and Kyoko came to the rail of their main deck and called down to the Halfling. They'd seen the giant red dragon make its descent and drop her off.

"How are you and the crew?" Kari ran up the gangway to greet the shipmaster and her daughter. Before Jun-Lei or Kyoko could answer, she peppered them with additional questions in her excitement at seeing familiar faces. "Did you run into any trouble during your travels? Are Ty or Shana around? What about Haruto and Min-ye?"

The shipmaster and her daughter could only smile at the thrilled Halfling. "Almost everyone is here."

"Almost? Is everyone okay?"

"Oh, of course," Jun-Lei answered, apologizing for even briefly making Kari worry. "Everyone's fine as far as we know. Shana and Ryland left early to head to Almiria so only the crew and Ty are here."

"Ty's here?!" Kari beamed, excited to see one of her best friends.

"Yes, but he's been a little down lately. He and Shana broke up. He's barely eaten, drank, or spoken in a few days."

Kari's heart sank at the news that Ty and Shana were no longer a couple, but she was even more bothered at hearing about Ty's depression. "What happened? Their relationship seemed to be going so well."

"We don't know," Jun-Lei explained. "Ty hasn't talked about it. All he does is sleep. You should go talk to him. He's in the forecastle cabin. Maybe you'll get farther than any of us did."

"When you're done, come chat with us!" Kyoko added. "We can't wait to catch up and hear about your travels!"

"Ty?" Kari headed up to the forecastle deck and knocked on the cabin door, entering only after hearing a mumbled response. Inside, she found her Elven friend lying in the dark on one of the cots. His hair was unkempt, and his usually clean-shaven face had blonde stubble.

"Kari?" Ty pulled himself up. Although he immediately went pale and stumbled forward, he found his way into the Halfling's embrace.

"You're light-headed. Come on, let's go down to the hull and scrounge up whatever food we can find."

"I don't need to eat anything," he muttered.

"Yes, you do. I'm either dragging you down there with me or I'm bringing something up."

"Alright," Ty unwillingly conceded, putting his arm over Kari's shoulders so he could use her as a crutch.

Once they stepped outside, he closed his eyes and threw his hands up to block out the last rays of the sun. Even though it was dusk, the change from spending so much time in the dark cabin to the outdoors was jarring.

In Andonia's hull, Ty slumped into a seat by the table while Kari rummaged through various cupboards.

"Talk to me," Kari requested, trying to keep Ty engaged and socializing. *The best way to lift the spirits of someone who's depressed is to show them they have something I want to hear. And that something can't be related to why he's sad.* "Tell me some of the exciting moments from your journey."

"Well," Ty thought, "Malorek sent the Accursed to Oceanside and I confirmed the rumors I heard a couple years ago; that my great-grandfather is their leader. I wouldn't say that was exciting to find out, but what happened afterwards was. Shana-" Ty stopped for a second at the mention of his ex-girlfriend's name. "Shana and I met the woman who was Alazar's lightning elect before King Zoran. She's an elderly woman now with memory problems, but she told us so much. She revealed we can give up our element voluntarily, but also that Alazar sometimes ends his elect's time with the elements before they want it to end. Her daughter shared the most interesting idea though: the concept of timelines, which I'd heard of before, but never really knew anything about."

"I only know a little about it from what I read in the Holy Books," Kari shared, tossing Ty an apple. "The only other time I heard them mentioned was in Steve's vision that we saw. Zebulon mentioned in all the timelines that either Silas or Malorek will defeat any uprising."

"I know, it's disconcerting. Steve and I discussed it back in the Evergreen Forest and we realized we can't let ourselves give up hope, even if the dark god himself is saying we don't stand a chance. What about your journey, though? Steve's not with you?"

"No, Nightstrike attacked us in Deletion and we got separated, but I spoke with the general in Stonegate last night and she said he's in the province and should be here soon."

"Good!" Ty smiled, the first time Kari had seen him do so. "You must look forward to seeing him!"

You have no idea, Kari thought, wanting to answer the Elf out loud, but she was hyper-analytical of her responses and didn't want to show her enjoyment over her relationship when Ty had just lost his. Instead, she replied, "Yeah, it'll be nice when we're all together again."

Grabbing some salted crackers and a half block of cheese, she took a seat across the table from Ty, sliced the cheese, and handed the Elf a stack to eat with the crackers. Together, the two friends enjoyed their platonic relationship as they sat, chatted, and munched on their snacks.

After Kari told Ty of her travels, Ty responded, "I was so happy to learn your dad was alive. I only found out this morning," Ty reached into his pocket and pulled out a letter with a broken wax seal and handed it to Kari. "Shana sent this from Almira. A dove delivered it to the city today, so Jun-Lei brought it to me."

"Sent in care of Tyrus Canard," Kari read the outside of the envelope, but upon opening it, saw the actual greeting was addressed to all of Alazar's elect.

Dear Elect,
Ryland, the Oceanside aerial warriors, and myself have arrived safely at the predestined rendezvous point. You'll

be proud of what's been accomplished here so far. I got to meet Darren and his family. Ty was correct in assuming the initials on the letter from Celestial were penned by him. Darren and one of the capital's watchtower commanders, Commander Ostravaski, used a secret passageway to escape the city, but I'll let them tell you their story in person.

Kari, your dad arrived with a dragon named Glaciara and all of Holders Keep and we've got them settled in just fine.

Grizz sent word that he and Bogmire's forces are heading to Casanovia where they'll collect the volunteers and all head to Almiria. He said they even managed to recruit hundreds of clerics who had either passed through or were in training at the various schools in Bogmire.

Large groups of people are coming in every few days. There's still a lot to prepare, but I wanted you to know that everyone here is optimistic, and that we're all waiting to see you and everyone you bring with you.

Good luck and safe travels,
Shana Latimer

"I'm glad everyone's okay and that Shana made it to Almiria safely," Kari folded the letter, placed it back in its envelope, and handed it to Ty. Taking the opportunity to finally bring up Ty's relationship with Shana, she asked, "I heard you and Shana broke up. Is that true?"

Immediately, Ty bowed his head and Kari noticed he looked her in the eyes. It was as if the person she'd been talking to for the past twenty minutes changed at the very mention of Alazar's wind elect.

"Yeah, it's true."

Ty went silent, so Kari fumbled over her words, trying to think of something positive to keep the conversation going. "Jun-Lei says she's barely been able to get you to talk. They just want to help, you know. They care about you."

"I know, but I haven't been in the mood. Seeing you and knowing you and Steve are okay are the first things in days that've pepped me up."

"You're allowed to be sad. I hope you know you won't always feel this way."

Ty shook his head in disgust at himself. "This all could've been avoided, though. It's my fault. I grew arrogant, thinking my element made me invincible. And with that power, all I cared about was myself and the legacy I could leave behind. I wrongfully considered the children Shana and I could have as part of that legacy and didn't consider Zebulon's bloodline or her opinions on the matter. I got so obsessed it led to the downfall of the first relationship I had that actually meant something to me."

Ty took a break to compose his rising anger at himself before finishing his rant by noting, "The worst thing is Jun-Lei had warned me too!" Ty noted. "A few days before we broke up, she said power sometimes changes people, that for some it amplifies their deepest desires and they are never content. She was right."

"I'm sorry, Ty. Life is full of these types of trials where we fail and make mistakes, but the most important thing is we don't let them destroy us more than they have to. We can learn from what went wrong and improve ourselves in spite of it. I wouldn't give up on Shana just yet. You should tell her what you just told me. I don't know if she'll change her mind, but it's worth talking to her and finding out definitively. Everyone knows how much you care for her."

"I think I'll do that once we get to Almiria," Ty nodded. Kari could tell he was nervous, but was already psyching himself up for the eventual conversation.

"Are you feeling better now?"

"A bit, but I know this is something that I can't just snap out of. It's easy to fall into self-hatred and feel like I screwed up something special, but I have to keep telling myself what's true; what you said: as long as we accept our flaws and mistakes and try to better ourselves, things will get better even if they seem like they won't in the moment."

Kari nodded, appreciative of the honest answer. *Poor Ty,* she thought, sad for what he was dealing with. *Sometimes the funniest people are the ones most prone to depression.*

Before her, Ty appeared much livelier than when she'd found him in the forecastle cabin. Openly venting about his struggle helped change his mood and perk him up. The Elf looked at the walls of the hull around them and laughed self-deprecatingly, "I don't know what it is with Andonia, me, and negativity. First my bout with seasickness, then learning the details of my parent's murder, then Shana breaking up with me." He picked up a cracker and slice of cheese, shoved them in his mouth, and kept talking while he chewed. "You know, Kari, I don't know what we'd do without you. Sometimes I think you're the one that's holding everything together. What do you say we go into the city and get a full meal?"

"That sounds more like the Ty we all know and love!" Kari smiled and jumped up from her seat, knowing some authentic food was what would be best for Ty, especially since he hadn't been eating.

Standing up to join the Halfling, Ty put his fist on his waist, creating a triangular opening that Kari could slide her arm into like thread through a needle.

Locked together, arm in arm, the Halfling and Elf ventured into Triland where they could find a tavern to dine in and both enjoy what they had in each other: true friendship.

Chapter 140

"Triland!" Steve smiled, coming over a hill in the countryside in the late morning after another day where he and Cryonic had vigorously trained. In the valley the two looked down upon a mass of buildings stood which they knew could only be the location of the province's Primary City.

"How do you think they'll receive me here?" Cryonic asked.

"I'm not sure," Steve answered, feeling bad for the drow because of the anxiousness he sensed in the monster's voice. In a couple of the towns they'd visited, people refused to offer Cryonic food, lodging, or acknowledge his existence. "Everyone has a different level of aversion to friendly monsters. It could be none, it could be a little, or it could be extreme. Most have only ever seen Animal Monsters in their city, like the aerial monsters we use. I'm not sure what the reaction will be to an Anthropomorphic like you, but as long as you're by my side, I'll make sure you're protected. And even if I couldn't, I think you could fend for yourself," Steve laughed.

The tiniest sliver of a smile appeared under Cryonic's dark black eyes. The drow kicked his heels into his mule, taking off down a hill towards the Primary City known for being in the middle of where plains, woods, and mountains converged together to form a scenic landscape.

Once in the bustling city, bystanders gawked and pointed in their direction, surprised by the blue-skinned drow wearing armor, carrying weapons, and walking freely.

The farther they made it into the denser, more populated sections, the more people stared.

Cryonic has a hood that he could put up that would cover his long, white hair and help hide his identity, but he's not using it, Steve noticed. *For someone nervous about his acceptance, he's brave in showing he doesn't care that people see him for what he is. I respect that.*

After asking for directions to the warriors' barracks, Steve and Cryonic headed through a busy market. Banners featuring Triland's colors of purple and green hung everywhere as civilians shopped among various vendors in the white cobblestone plaza.

This city has a diverse population, Steve could tell, noticing Humans, Giants, Elves, and Dwarves of every skin color perusing the wares and goods. It was the face of one particular half-Human, half-Elf, however, that stood out to him on the far side of the plaza.

No way! Steve thought, hurrying through the crowd, forcing Cryonic to slip through the narrow spaces between people just to keep up. "Kari!" Steve called out, seeing her slightly pointed ears, dark hair in a braid, and blue bow strapped across her back. He ran up and engulfed his Halfling girlfriend in the tightest hug he'd ever shared with anyone.

"Steve!" Kari teared up. She grabbed his shoulders and held him at arm's length to look him over, as if double-checking to make sure it was actually him there in person. "When'd you get here?"

"We just arrived. If I had known you were already here, I would've come and found you first thing!" Steve hugged Kari again and told her, "I've missed you so much! I was so worried not knowing if you survived the desert." Not deterred by the people in the crowded market, many of whom had turned to see why he'd run through it, he grabbed the back of Kari's head and kissed her deeply, a kiss that Kari returned even more passionately.

"Get a room, you two!" Ty said, coming up to them with his typical teasing humor.

"Ty!" Steve pulled away from Kari and hugged his brother. He then embraced Jun-Lei, who was with Ty, and patted Kyoko's shoulder since she was carrying a crate of goods she and her mother had bought from market vendors. "I'm so glad to see all of you. We have so much to catch up on."

"You and Kari should spend some time together first," Ty recommended.

"Clearly," Kyoko smirked, having seen their kiss.

Jun-Lei nudged her daughter with her elbow, almost making her drop her crate. "There's an arboretum just a few blocks over," she pointed in its direction. "It's open to the public to walk through. Might be quieter than here."

Kari looked to Steve and nodded, receptive to the idea of leaving the noisy market. She intertwined her fingers with his, and said, "We can come to Andonia when we're done. Ty, I'm sure you want to tell Steve about your adventures, too."

"Yeah, but you two take all the time you need first," Ty stated, knowing the couple needed to have a conversation about the implications of Steve's vision. "But first, Steve, show us all your newfound abilities."

Steve shook his head and smirked, hating that the Elf purposely made him the center of attention, but he obliged and showcased the element of fire by covering his red armor in flames.

"You, me, and Kari aren't the only ones here with elemental abilities," Steve turned to the blue-skinned drow behind him. "This is my friend Cryonic. We've been spending a lot of time training together. Jun-Lei, do you think you can take him with you to Andonia?"

"Sure!" the Elf welcomed the monster, not letting his long white hair, fangs, or black eyes affect her hospitality. It was a direct contrast to the many civilians in the market who pointed at the drow and whispered among themselves. One man even ran to fetch the nearest warrior on patrol. "We were just about to head back there anyway. Glad to have you come aboard!"

"Shall we?" Steve raised Kari's hand and brought it up to kiss the back of it once the group headed away.

"First things first, I need to return this to you," Kari countered, untying Steve's blue sash from around her waist and handing it to the warrior.

"Wow, you kept this?" Steve asked, holding it up to inspect it like a fine jewel. "I figured it got blown away in the sandstorm in the desert after I gave it to you."

"No, it helped save me! And I could never get rid of it knowing how much you loved it as part of your jousting attire for the Tournament. I had Haruto stich up the holes and then I cleaned it as best I could."

"It looks great, thank you!" Steve took the fabric and wrapped it around his waist as they headed to the arboretum. The whole way there, he and Kari couldn't contain their smiles, happy to be in each other's presence.

Once in the fancy, manicured garden, they found a secluded spot near a cluster of sixteen-foot-tall arborvitae trees that helped block out the bright, springtime sun. For nearly an hour they sat on a bench in the shade, recapping the events that'd occurred since being unwillingly separated in Deletion. Kari showed Steve the mark of Holders Keep permanently seared on her shoulder, explained her time in the notorious prison, finding her father, and reuniting with Crimson Singe.

"Speaking of Crimson, your sash is not the only thing I have for you," Kari smiled, excited to share her news with her boyfriend. "Crimson never lost the bundles we strapped to the back of his saddle. When I was in Al Kabar, I searched through them and found King Zoran's golden crown inside. Your crown," she corrected herself. "It's safely locked away in a chest on Andonia."

Steve breathed a sigh of relief. *I was worried it was lost forever. The King's Crown is sought after because it's worth a lot with its five gemstones and diamond. I'm glad it didn't fall into the wrong hands. Plus, it means a lot to me since it was my grandfather's, and it'll be what I wear at my coronation.*

After thanking Kari for telling him about the crown's safekeeping, Steve shared his journey, bringing up meeting General Elesora from Stonegate and everything that happened on Mount Divinian, including obtaining his element and vision.

"I'm nervous to talk about what Zebulon revealed to Malorek in my vision," he admitted, staring down at his feet. "I haven't been able to stop thinking about how I have the blood of Zebulon inside of me. If our relationship continues on into marriage, which I would love for it to, then it's going to affect us. I'm torn about what to do and I'm worried whatever way I decide, you'll disagree with it."

As Kari sat with Steve, she noticed his conflicted emotions, evidenced by his neck becoming blotchy, a sign of his rising anxiety. *It's nice he's bringing up marriage for the first time,* she tried to pull a positive aspect out of his monologue. *I'd love nothing more than to have him as my husband, but I can't daydream about that right now. I need to help him work through the deliberations I can tell he's stressing over.*

"Zebulon's bloodline was an issue for your brother and Shana," Kari shared, taking both Steve's hands in her own to help calm him. "Shana broke up with Ty and headed to Almiria early, partly due to them disagreeing over if they should have children and continue the bloodline, but that's not going to happen to us."

Steve kept his head bowed in disappointment over the news of the couple, but Kari said, "Look at me," making sure he wouldn't miss what she was about to say.

"Just know, no matter what you decide, I'm sticking with you. I know you'll make the right choice. You always care about doing what's right more than anything else, and that's why I love you. Our relationship has made it through every hard thing so far and we'll make it through this too."

"Okay," Steve breathed a sigh of relief and felt free to share his thoughts. "Like I said, I'm torn because we can eliminate a huge part of Zebulon's power on Element by cutting off his bloodline by not procreating. I so badly want to say no to having children to protect the kingdom, but I've always wanted a family, especially because I grew up not knowing mine. Deep down though, I know I have to do what's in the best interest of everyone else in this world, not just me.

"Kari," Steve got her attention, gripping her hands tighter as his eyes filled with tears. "As much as it pains me to say it, given the circumstances, I think the right thing to do is to not have any children."

Whereas before Kari could tell Steve was stressed due to the difficult conversation, now she saw his face twist in anguish at the verbalization of the choice she knew he would make from the moment his vision ended.

Even with that foreknowledge, the impact of officially learning she wouldn't bear any children with him if they got married wasn't any less emotional. Like Steve, Kari always dreamed of raising a family of her own.

"I feel sorry for you," Steve spoke softly, biting his lip to keep himself from crying too hard. "I'm hurting the happiness of our future because of my bloodline. This is my fault."

"None of this is your fault," Kari assured him. "I can't be mad at you for something you don't have control over. I'm just disappointed with the situation. It shouldn't be predetermined before birth that you can't have the freedom to live your life to the fullest, but that's how it is. And I'm sorry it's something you never asked for, especially because you've told me before how you wanted to die surrounded by love, by your sons, daughters, and grandchildren, peacefully and happy. Zebulon took that from you the moment he came to this planet and sought to procreate. That's why no matter what sacrifices we have to make, it'll feel great to thwart his plan.

"Don't worry about me," Kari added. "Even knowing of a future without children, I still want to be with you. The sadness I have from not being able to raise a family with you is nothing compared to the sadness I'd have from not being with you at all."

Steve kissed Kari on the forehead. *How lucky I am to have someone like her,* he thought to himself. *She's so supportive and caring. I can't imagine going through this with anyone else.*

Gently grabbing the sides of Kari's face, he kissed her on the lips, even more passionately than the one they'd shared in the market square.

"I didn't know how much I loved you until I thought I lost you," he whispered.

"Same here," Kari agreed, cozying up to Steve and laying her head on his shoulder.

The two sat together for a long time until Steve asked, "You said you flew here on Crimson Singe?" When Kari nodded, he stated, "I need to talk to him about another aspect of my vision."

"About him being the twin of Nightstrike?

"Yeah."

I can tell Steve's torn, Kari thought, *just as I am. I'm happy it might not be Steve the Prophecy of the Twins speaks of, but I'm sad it could be the dragon we've befriended.*

Looking up to the skies, Kari saw the sun had fully set and the stars were out, bright and twinkling. "I'd check the aerial warriors' stables for him. Do you want me to come with you?"

"I always love when you're with me, but for this conversation, I think it should just be him and I."

"Okay," Kari said, trusting Steve's determination. "I'll head to Andonia and get to sleep."

"I'll walk you there before I find Crimson," Steve stood up, helping Kari to her feet. "After hearing Shana was poisoned, we need to be extra careful. Someone is conspiring to kill us elect."

"Especially after you and I were attacked by Nightstrike," Kari agreed. "The dark dragon definitely knew our travel route, so I can only assume it's someone that was with us in our meetings."

It makes me sick to my stomach, Steve thought. *We're all trusting someone close to us we shouldn't be, and it's only a matter of time before they try to strike again.*

When they arrived hand-in-hand at Andonia, Kari kissed Steve goodbye at the docks and said, "If I'm not up after you get back, I'll see you in the morning."

Chapter 141

Steve found Crimson Singe in the large, open part of the stable. The red dragon sat talking to a brown-feathered phoenix and a gryphon whose colors signified its water and wind elements.

The rest of the aerial warriors' monsters are sleeping in individual stalls, but these three are awake and having a good time talking to each other, Steve could tell as he walked up to the group.

"I'm glad to see you alive, young Brightflame!" Crimson nodded his head in greeting as Steve approached them.

"I hope I'm not interrupting."

"Not at all," the phoenix answered. "Crimson was just telling us about a time in his youth he battled a green gryphon that he could barely see it was so fast."

"I'd love to hear it sometime," Steve admitted. Turning to the monster he'd come to speak to, he stuck his pointer finger up to the night-time sky and asked, "Mind if we go talk somewhere?"

"Not at all. Would you like to put a saddle on me?"

"No, I don't think we'll be going far."

"Climb on up, then," the dragon kneeled, lowered himself to the ground, and then pushed off his legs, propelling himself up to the skies once Steve was seated. "Where would you like to go?"

"How about over there?" Steve spotted an old, abandoned sawmill on a hillside. The land had been cleared and leveled to build the structure, but nature was reclaiming the area.

As they headed towards it, Steve noticed the jagged scar on Crimson's wingskin. "Did you injure your wing when Nightstrike attacked us?" he called ahead to the dragon.

"Nothing that couldn't be fixed," Crimson straightened out his wing, showing its flexibility still worked fine. "I searched for you and Kari in the desert, but couldn't find either of you."

"There could've been ten of you searching and I don't know if you would've found us," Steve assured the dragon it wasn't a big deal as he descended to the ruins. Underneath, as the dragon's massive body blocked out the moonlight, forest critters residing in the area scurried off into the nearby forest.

"What did you want to talk about?" Crimson asked once Steve had disembarked him. When the warrior fumbled over his answer, failing to communicate the issue, Crimson extended his neck and brought his face close to Steve's, cocking his head to look at the nineteen-year-old as close as possible. "Something's bothering you, isn't it?"

Getting straight to his point by forgoing his attempts to be tactful, Steve explained, "I received my vision from Alazar and in it I saw Zebulon appear to Malorek. He told Malorek that Silas would likely be the one to fulfill the prophecy on this sword." Steve reached down to his side, grabbed the hilt of Aurelia, and pulled out the golden weapon. "But Zebulon said if it wasn't Silas, it would be

Nightstrike, which means Nightstrike has a twin brother. That dragon is you isn't it?"

For a long moment Crimson didn't say a word, but then he nodded, validating Steve's theory.

"Nightstrike and I hatched out of the same egg, both sons of Draviakhan, but thanks to Oliver, I didn't align with their views on the world. It didn't matter though, back then, people were so mad at Draviakhan for the damage he caused, they wanted to eliminate his entire lineage because we were extra powerful in the elements and they didn't feel they could trust any of us."

So the fact Nightstrike sought Crimson's death for killing their father is not the only reason Crimson went into hiding, Steve realized. *He was also hiding from the very people he helped save from Draviakhan.*

"You spent a lot of time with my grandfather. Didn't you know what the prophecy inscribed on this blade said?" Steve gestured to Aurelia again. "Why haven't you said anything before now? Believing I was the only one capable of fulfilling it has given me so much anxiety!"

"I knew. Of course, I knew," Crimson admitted. "Oliver read me the prophecy once he realized Nightstrike and I met the criteria to fulfill it. I was prepared to sacrifice my life to bring it to pass when the time came, but then you and Silas were born. Zoran and I met in secret throughout all these years and when Kyra gave birth to you twins, he told me he believed one of you would fulfill the prophecy. Although, he thought it'd be Silas who'd carry it out, not you.

"I'm sorry, Stephen," Crimson looked away from the nineteen-year-old, unable to face him, knowing he could've helped prevent Steve's anxiety. "I wanted to tell you earlier. In fact, I almost told you when you and I talked that night in the canyons. But I knew first you needed to get your vision and learn the full story of your past. Meanwhile, I was waiting to see if you were worthy of being king. I wanted to see how you responded to the belief that your life would be the price that had to be paid to achieve victory. By pressing forward with the plans to reclaim Celestial, you've proven you're willing to make that sacrifice for this kingdom and its people."

With a pained smiled, Crimson finished, "Knowing the grandson of my best friend is worthy enough to carry on in his place, I'm content to die. I'm going to fulfill the prophecy so that you don't have to."

"Crimson... I," Steve wanted to counter the dragon's intentions, but one glance from Crimson told him the dragon already made his decision.

"It's going to be okay. I'm at peace with it."

Steve shook his head, hating the idea of losing the legendary monster. Knowing the sacrifice would be made so that the kingdom could have a king, he asked, "Do you think I can be as great a ruler as he was?"

Crimson smiled again. "Oliver wondered the same thing when he was on his adventure. I'll tell you what I told him: it seems to me like you've won over every person you've met. And I wouldn't be surprised if you continue to. You're an honorable, loyal leader, and you stand up for what's right. You're exactly what this kingdom needs. You'll carry on what your grandfather started and your children will grow to be good men and women like you. For many generations, I can see your line changing this kingdom for the better. That's what I'm willing to die for."

Steve bowed his head. *I don't want to tell Crimson of the decision Kari and I just made. After I die or decide to end my reign, with no children, the kingdom will need to elect a new king. It won't be my offspring that takes the throne.*

"I know I told you that due to being a prime target of the enemy, I wanted no one to ride me into battle for their own safety," Crimson mentioned, "but if the situation calls for it, it'd be fitting to work with a Human one last time, especially to help take down Nightstrike and end my twin brother's negative influence on this world."

"I'd be more than happy to help you in that endeavor," Steve nodded. "There's nothing I want more than to see Nightstrike fall."

Following their conversation, Crimson flew Steve to Andonia.

"Who's the drow?" the dragon asked as he circled around in the sky before landing. The blue-skinned monster stood in the crow's nest of the ship's main mast. His stark white hair blew in the breeze as he stared at Triland's nighttime lights.

"I met him on Mount Divinian," Steve answered, seeing Cryonic settle in for the night. *I know he's kind of a loner, but I wish he didn't feel like he had to sleep in the crow's nest.*

Upon touching down late in the night, Crimson spoke softly so his loud voice didn't wake anyone. "I'm going to be leaving for a while. I know of some dragons and other aerial monsters who may help our cause. I asked Glaciara to accompany me. We'll bring all the recruits to Almiria once we're done."

The more, the better, Steve thought, before telling Crimson, "Stay safe."

Entering the forecastle cabin, Steve found Ty and Kari in their cots, already asleep. He kissed Kari's forehead where she lay in the top cot, and then took the bottom cot on the other side of the aisle, underneath where Ty slept.

It's good to be back in the company of my friends, Steve thought before fluffing his pillow and laying his head down for the night.

Chapter 142

In the morning, Steve and Kari met Ty at a quaint little bakery in Triland's commerce section to share breakfast. Since the Human and Halfling couple had already caught up, Ty brought Steve up to speed on everything he'd endured since leaving Misengard.

"After Shana left, I was too depressed to do anything," Ty explained. "Jun-Lei and Kyoko stepped up and spoke to Oceanside and Triland's leadership on our behalf. Oceanside is already on their way to Almiria, but they couldn't spare that many because they're recovering from the attack by the Accursed. Meanwhile, Triland plans to offer everyone they can spare."

Adding further details, Ty shared, "I ran into one of the sentries before you two got here and he said they spotted a large caravan from Stonegate heading this way. They'll all be in the city within the next hour."

"That's great," Steve dabbed at the corners of his mouth with his cloth napkin. "Once General Elesora gets here, we can all head out together. We can sail west on the Etherwell River, across the Darien Sea and north to Almiria."

With so many hands already hard at work, it took no longer than three hours to finish getting every ship packed with supplies, warriors, and civilians who all volunteered to head to join the army's ranks. While the packing went quickly, the travel itself took longer. The five, fully loaded vessels and six smaller civilian boats took five days to sail to Almiria.

The city slowly came into view as the fleet rounded Lake Azure's coast. Twice the size of Casanovia, Almiria sat on a plateau populated with giant hills. The terrain gradually sloped downwards towards Whitebark Woods, which allowed the aqueduct that carried water to Celestial to work so efficiently.

Andonia led the Triland and Stonegate fleet, sailing into Almiria's main port, which already held ships from Elmwood, Twin Peaks, and Misengard.

Steve followed Kyoko down to the main deck and helped her tie the dock lines to the cleats. Then, he disembarked Andonia with Ty, Kari, General Elesora, her girlfriend, Cryonic, and the group of forty-five other people they'd traveled with. Even though they were at sea level, they emerged into a valley with dozens of hills all around them. Colorful mansions populated each, a direct contrast to the many run-down homes with muted colors that sat at the base of each hill.

Kari studied each mansion as they passed by them. *These must be the houses Mr. Sep told us about when we were in Hunters' Den. He said the acres and acres of trees cut down in the Evergreen Forest were used to supply the wood for the fancy homes in Almiria.*

Look at all this! she stared in disbelief at all the intricate details. *Decorative corbels, stone balconies looking out over the lake, ornate columns, and rain chains used to direct water into landscaped flowerbeds. I didn't have any of these in my one-bedroom apartment in Celestial. I can't imagine how much these houses must've cost.*

Their infrastructure is like Celestial's, Steve thought, gazing across the plateau Almiria sat upon. *Back home, the cheaper architecture was farthest away from the castle, nearest the city's inner wall. Here, it seems more vertical where the higher up people live, the nicer the homes and buildings are.*

"I can see where Almiria's warriors tried to make a stand against Silas and his monsters," he pointed, drawing Ty and Kari's attention to a section of the city where many of the smaller houses had collapsed or burned down. "When Commander Artazair arrived in Casanovia with all the Almirians that'd evacuated, he told me some warriors stayed behind to give all the ships a chance to escape. That must be where the battle occurred."

"No way!" Ty exclaimed, but his reaction wasn't in response to the damaged section of the city Steve was pointing at. He ran towards a group of people coming towards them, heading for one specifically.

"Darren!" he cried, engulfing his brother in a hug. "I'm so glad you're alive. I thought you died in Celestial!"

"It'll take more than a collapsed watchtower to keep me down," Darren embraced Ty just as tightly. "Steve! Good to see you," he moved from his blood brother to his foster brother.

Behind the twenty-three-year-old Elf with short, blonde hair, the exact opposite of his brother Ty's, the three other people Darren had been with came to greet the travelers: Shana Latimer, Celestial's Commander Ostravaski, and Misengard's Captain Ortega.

After his moment of elation at seeing his brother for the first time since the weekend of the Warriors' Tournaments, Ty immediately tensed up upon seeing Shana. Although he tried to avoid her, scared that

314

interacting with her would lead to the same heartbreak as before, Shana took the opposite approach and came directly up to him.

"How have you been?" she asked, neither hugging Ty nor shaking his hand.

"I've been well," Ty lied. Seeing Shana staring into his eyes, almost as if she was searching them for the truth, he took the focus off himself by saying, "I see you changed your hair to a new Fluorite Color."

"Yeah, blue this time," Shana twirled a strand around her finger. Intent on addressing the tension between them instead of hiding behind generic talk, she grabbed Ty's hand, squeezed it, and said, "I feel bad about how we left each other. Maybe we can talk sometime soon."

For a moment, Ty was taken aback, not sure how he should respond. Forging a spiteful response, wanting to say, "no" and hurt her the way she'd hurt him by leaving, he told Shana what he honestly felt. "I'd like that."

Their brief moment together was interrupted when Darren asked Ostravaski, "Commander, do you remember my brothers, Tyrus and Stephen from training them in Boot Camp?"

As the Giant stepped forward to greet the warriors, Steve thought about how he'd seen the commander in Malorek's vision during Boot Camp, how he remembered Ostravaski from going through Boot Camp himself, and how he appeared now, with a full beard that didn't look like it'd been shaved in any of that time. *This man has spent thirty years, almost half his life, leading Warrior Boot Camp in Celestial before finally being given a watchtower to command for his final years of service. He's a veteran warrior if there ever was one,* Steve thought, looking at the red and blue pieces of armor

Ostravaski had earned over the years. The Giant's commander's badge punctuated his outfit.

Since he'd worked with so many trainees, Steve was surprised to hear the Giant reply, "Of course, Stephen Brightflame, I remember you because of your strange last name and the fact you were a perfectionist who graduated early, and you, Canard, you were always pulling pranks. I trained your father Caesar when he was becoming a warrior."

"Steve and Ty are two of Alazar's elect, like me," Shana told Ostravaski. She gestured to the only other female elect, and said, "And this is another friend, Kari Quinn."

"Ahh, you must be Quintis's daughter! He's told me a lot about you."

"Do you know where I can find him?" Kari asked the group at large. *I can't wait to see him.*

"He's taken it upon himself to watch over everyone from Holders' Keep," Shana answered. She tapped her foot as she watched the hundreds of people coming in off the ships from Stonegate and Triland. "Once everyone's divided up and knows where they're staying, I'll send someone to tell him you're here.

"Captain Ortega, can you help me lead everyone to the sections of the city we have prepared for them? Darren, you and the commander can show Steve, Ty, and Kari where they'll be staying."

Since she was splitting off from her elemental friends, Shana mouthed the words to Ty, "I'll find you later," before heading off to direct the groups of incoming people.

"What happened in Celestial?" Ty asked Ostravaski and Darren immediately after Shana left. "Shana told us in a letter you escaped through a secret passage?"

"Yeah, in my watchtower they destroyed," the Giant commander spit a wad of tobacco he'd been chewing into the dirt path and pressed and twisted his massive boot into it. He pointed to an aqueduct that ran through the heart of Almiria, southwest, as far as the eye could see. "That aqueduct runs all the way down to Celestial and was built into the architecture of two of the twelve watchtowers there, one of which was the one I commanded. When Sir Lambert helped design the city, he placed a secret passage in each of these towers that led down into the sewers. I was evacuating warriors and civilians under the watchtower when it collapsed."

"Many people didn't make it down in time, but we did," Darren bowed his head. "We lived down there until winter, sending people up to get food, and rescuing as many as we could from the city."

"What about Lucan and Cassandra?" Ty interrupted.

"They're fine," Darren reassured him. "I found them and brought them down into the sewers with us, but it took longer than I wanted since I had to wait for my broken leg to heal first."

Hope it healed better than mine did, Steve thought to himself. Even at the mention of the phrase "broken leg" his mind flashed back to the snapping sound when Silas kicked it the opposite way of how it was supposed to go.

Darren finished recapping their escape from Celestial by explaining, "When the first blizzard hit, we all snuck out and crossed the farmlands unseen. The snow kept coming down and covered our footprints. A hundred of us made it out and came straight to Almiria. Once there, I used my initials and a secret code in the letter I sent to the Primary Cities. I knew if the Hooded Phantom or any of the leaders of his army found out who I was or where we were, that would put us in danger."

"Hey! Speaking of Cassandra and Lucan," Steve pointed the two out to Ty since he noticed them coming their way.

"Uncle Ty! Uncle Steve!" Lucan wrapped his arms around their legs since the brothers were standing next to each other.

Greeting his nephew as he usually did, Ty picked up the boy and spun him around so fast it made Lucan's legs fly up and spin horizontally to the ground. After Ty set Lucan down, Steve ruffled his nephew's messy blonde hair. "You've gotten so big!"

"He's not the only one," Cassandra came up to the group, holding her enlarged stomach with two hands as she walked. She was much slower than her son, but just as happy to see her two brothers-in-law were alive.

"You're pregnant? I'm going to have another nephew or niece?" Ty nearly jumped up and down in excitement.

"It was a surprise for both of us," Darren smiled. "We think she's almost six months along."

"So you had this baby in you before the attack even began?"

"Yes, and thankfully everything feels right so the stress from the attack and trying to survive day-after-day in Celestial didn't affect the pregnancy."

"How is it in Celestial?" Steve asked. "Darren says it was a while before he could rescue you out of there?"

At the very mention of Steve's question, the countenance of Darren, Cassandra, Lucan, and Ostravaski fell.

No one could bring themselves to answer, except for Ostravaski. All the Giant responded with was, "Maybe after you settle in, we'll let you know the state of the capital. Not today, though. It's a lot to take in."

"Why don't we show you where you'll be staying?" Darren changed the subject. He gestured back towards Lake Azure, towards a section of bluffs higher even than the ones they'd passed by. As they walked, he explained, "So far, Ostravaski, Ryland, Quintis, and I have led the organizational efforts. But none of us would be anywhere without Shana. Ever since she arrived, she's taken charge and made sure everything is running efficiently. She's even employed Ryland's artistic skills to help draw a bunch of color-coded maps that divide all the Primary Cities into different areas of Almiria. I'll make sure you guys each get a copy of it so you can know where each encampment is."

Darren led them past one of two blackpowder and pitch depots, where the substances were being collected and stored in barrels for use in the upcoming battle. Following the depot, they moved through a section where builders worked on siege towers, iron ladders, and other weapons that could help to either scale or demolish Celestial's thick, stone inner wall.

Next, they traversed through a maze of tents where everyone who'd come from Twin Peaks was stationed. At the far end, they arrived at the base of the tallest hill in all of Almiria, a cliff rising high above the waters of Lake Azure.

"This is where mom, dad, me, and others have been staying, preparing it for you all," Lucan excitedly told his uncles and Kari, pointing to the top of the hill where a tall, white stone castle with a built-in lighthouse sat.

"Apparently, the current owners weren't able to hide or make it to the ships to escape Almiria when it was attacked," Cassandra solemnly shared. "Like much of the city, it was in disarray when we arrived, but we got the castle back to its esteemed state while other Celestial escapees readied the rest of Almiria."

"We can't stay here!" Kari gasped at the lavish structure.

Even though the castle was only one-tenth the size of the Royal Castle in Celestial, Steve sided with his girlfriend, staring in awe at the grand building. "She's right, it's far too extravagant."

"It's not negotiable," Ostravaski stated, putting an end to any arguments. "Shana told us about how she was poisoned and that there is likely a betrayer in our midst. This castle is the most secure place in the city. As Alazar's Elect, you need to be kept as safe as possible. You'll have guards all day and night stationed at every entrance, and we'll have only the most trusted cooks preparing your food. Each one will be kept under close watch as they work."

"Listen," Darren could tell the thoughts behind Steve's scrunched face. "I know you're skeptical of all these accommodations, but if you're going to lead this army and eventually become the king, then people need to start seeing you as such."

Unable to think of any reasonable counters, Steve and the rest of the group followed Darren up a steep hill to the castle, past warriors who stood on guard. Inside, they found the castle had its own inner courtyard full of fresh flowers, well-maintained shrubbery, and a fully stocked stable of horses.

"You'll find a bedchamber for each of you here," Ostravaski gestured, pointing to a hallway where each room had already been prepared with fresh clothing, beds, and other provisions.

Instead of separating, however, the three companions all entered Steve's chamber, the largest one of all. Steve lied down on the bed, Ty admired the decorative awnings and furnishings, and Kari went out onto a balcony overlooking Lake Azure.

"Look at the view from up here!" she called out, letting the slight breeze rustle through her dark hair. *It's so peaceful. The moon is bright, the sky is cloudless, and Andonia and all the other ships look like floating lanterns down on the calm water.*

"If you need anything, we'll have a warrior posted in the hallway and he can have someone fetch it for you," Ostravaski explained and headed for the door. "I've got to go find Captain Ortega since we were developing a list of provisions we'll need for battle, but I'll see you all in the morning."

"Come on, Lucan, we should go too," Cassandra took her son's hand. "It's getting late. You need to get to bed."

"But mom-"

Darren interrupted his five-year-old son. "No complaining. We already let you stay up later than usual so you could see Uncle Ty and Uncle Steve. Besides, it's hard work for your mom carrying around your future brother or sister," Darren pointed to his wife's pregnant belly. "Since you're a man of the house, you need to make it as easy as possible on her. Now say goodnight and come with us to bed."

It wasn't long after the family of Elves left that a Human with a longbow slung across his back stepped through the doorframe.

"Dad!" Kari ran to her father and wrapped her arms around him.

"Quite the climb to this castle," he patted Kari's back, letting her know he needed a chance to catch his breath.

"Steve, Ty," Kari looked to her boyfriend and friend as they walked forward to meet the man they'd only seen in their visions, "I'd like to introduce you to my father. Dad, this is Stephen Brightflame and Tyrus Canard. They're the ones I've told you all about."

"Ah, yes, I've heard so much about the two of you," Quintis stated, shaking each of their hands. "I'm so thankful my daughter had the both of you to keep her safe."

"I think it's Kari who's protected us," Ty corrected Quintis. "She's saved us more times than I can count."

Steve nodded. "We wouldn't be alive without her. You have an incredible daughter, sir."

Quintis beamed at the compliment, put his arm around Kari, and spoke sentimentally to her, not caring about the two warriors in the room with him and his daughter.

"Ever since you were born, your mother and I knew you would do great things. Little did we know you'd be one of Alazar's Elect. She'd be just as proud of you as I am."

Turning to the Elf standing before him, Quintis told Ty, "You know, Tyrus, I already told Darren this, but your parents would've been proud of you, too. Caesar and Sarah were good friends of my wife and I. I held you just a few days after you were born," Quintis cupped his hands, reenacting the moment. "Even as a baby, you had that same mischievous smirk you have now.

"And Stephen, Malorek may be your father, but Titus raised you. From what Kari's told me, you sound so much like him. Every dad wants their daughter to date a man of honor and character like that."

"Who would've ever thought it?" Quintis shared his thoughts out loud, "That the next generation – the children of a small group of friends in Celestial's Warrior Training would be three of the five Alazar handpicked to give his elemental powers to." He pointed to Steve and Ty. "I look forward to getting to know the both of you better, especially you, Steve, not only as the future king, but as the man dating my daughter. And speaking of dating, I hiked up here with Shana. Ty, she told me to tell you she's waiting for you in your room and wants to discuss your relationship."

"Good luck!" Kari told Ty as he headed for the door.

Steve shared his well-wishes. "I know you left on bad terms in Oceanside, but I'm praying that whether she decides to rekindle the relationship or end it for good, that whatever happens it'll be what's best for both of you."

Once Ty left, Steve sat back down on his bed and rubbed both his eyes with the palms of his hands. "I'm tired. I think I'll head to bed."

"I'll give you two a moment to say goodnight," Quintis offered, stepping out of the room.

"He seems like a nice guy," Steve told Kari, who took a seat next to him on the feather-stuffed mattress.

"I think you'll both get along."

"I think so too," Steve agreed. He leaned over, kissed Kari, then escorted her to the door. There, he handed her off to Quintis, who waited for his daughter in the hallway.

"Are you going to stay up here in the castle for the night?" Kari asked her dad.

"I wish I could, but I'm staying with everyone from Holders Keep. They've got all of us in a run-down section of the city. I just wanted to come say hello since I heard you arrived."

"I'm glad you did. Tomorrow we can spend more time together. I'd like to come down and see Torgore."

Quintis smiled at the mention of the ogre. "He's been invaluable in helping keep order. He's nervous everyone will be marched back to Mount Anomaly if they get too out of control. He may not speak, but no one dares stand up to him. I'm sure he'd love to see you."

"Tomorrow then!" Kari hugged her dad goodnight and kissed him on the cheek.

As Quintis walked away, Kari, intent on getting his opinion of her friends, asked, "By the way, what do you think of Steve and Ty?"

"I meant what I said. They seem like good guys and I'm thankful for the friendship you have with them. I can see what you have with Steve is real."

Quintis's chin quivered and his eyes welled up as he shared, "Make sure you hold onto that bond and enjoy your time together. There's no worse feeling than not being able to be with the ones you love."

With that, he walked away, leaving Kari heartbroken that her father's words came from an unfortunate experience.

He knows that even though he's free, he'll never get back the life torn from him by Malorek, Kari thought, clenching her fists. *I may not be able to right that wrong, but I'll make sure the Hooded Phantom doesn't do that to anyone else.*

Chapter 143

Gulping down the nervousness from the butterflies in his stomach that seemed to fly all the way up into his throat, Ty took a moment to himself in the hallway before he entered his room.

I don't know if Shana will change her mind about us or if she'll stick with her decision, but at the very least, we need to have an amicable friendship since we'll be around each other. I want to be a couple, but I'm nervous she won't feel the same, and I definitely don't want this conversation to lead to another fight like the one we had on Andonia.

Entering through the open door of his room, Ty found Shana sitting at a hutch next to a fireplace she'd just lit. Her blue hair glowed in the flickering firelight from the crackling logs as she sorted through dozens of papers.

"Hi, Ty!" she smiled upon seeing him and extended her arms to the spacious bedroom. "What do you think of this castle? Pretty nice, huh?"

"It's the nicest place I've ever stayed, that's for sure," he responded, taken aback by Shana's positivity. *This is the exact opposite of the last time it was just her and me. I hope that's a good sign.*

"I learned the history of this place from an elderly man who hid during the attack instead of evacuating with the rest of Almiria," Shana explained as Ty leaned against the wall to listen. "He said that many generations ago, a rich man built this castle for his family and claimed all the surrounding land. The man employed guards who protected the area from monsters and even designed a secret passageway in the castle in case he needed to evacuate. People began moving here and building houses of their own since it was such a safe place. All they had to do was pay fealty to the man who wanted to be called lord."

"So it was like a mini-kingdom in a way?"

"Yes, he lived in this castle on this highest hill. The higher elevation you lived, the wealthier you were. The more impoverished sections of the city are at the bases of the hills. It's been that way even up to this decade, but even though the man and his family made Almiria what it is, no one remembers their name. That's why when I heard the story, I decided to start this," Shana held up the papers she was working on.

"We're about to engage in one of the greatest battles in history. I want its participants to be remembered, so I'm documenting the name of every person who comes to Almiria to aid our cause. We'll be able to supply accurate information for future generations who want to look back on this time."

Shana shifted in her seat and explained an additional reason she was creating a roster.

"I also thought that considering Steve's and my bloodline, if either of us have children, they should be tracked to determine who could have elemental powers through Zebulon."

"I thought you were opposed to having children?"

"I still think it'd be wisest not to, but I've been thinking for any relationship to work, compromises need to be made. I was unflinching when it came to the idea of kids. My main focus is to become a political leader who can make positive change while yours is to get married and have a family, but I realized those don't have to be mutually exclusive. We can work together to attain what we desire. A big part of life is about pursuing dreams, and it's made even more special when you have someone alongside, encouraging you and supporting you and, in turn, you can support and encourage them. I can't imagine doing that with anyone but you. You're my best friend. I just don't know if I've screwed things up so badly that we can't get back what we had.

"Our breaking up was my fault, not yours," Ty stepped forward, closer to where Shana sat. "I was the one that first drove a wedge between us when I let my power get to my head. You were right about what you told me in Oceanside: I allowed it to make me think I was invincible, and that made me arrogant and no fun to be around. I'm sorry you had to deal with me when I was like that, but I'm not going to be that way anymore."

"I trust you won't be," Shana stated. "What do you say we forgive each other and move forward from this?"

"So are we officially back together?!"

"There's only one thing we need to discuss," Shana shuffled her feet and cleared her throat. "If I'm going to be a councilor, the chances of it being in Celestial are slim. Personally, I've always wanted it to be Casanovia, but I need to know if you're willing to move from the capital to live where I work."

Ty sighed, not having considered the possibility of moving after the war was over.

During his silence, Shana shared her worries that Ty wouldn't be willing to make the adjustment. "I know Steve will reign in Celestial as king and your brother, sister-in-law, and nephew will be there too. And I know it's where you grew up, so I've been nervous you're partial to staying there."

"I'm not," Ty assured her, resolute in his decision. "I don't care if you're councilor to a group of seagulls on some remote island. Nothing matters more to me than being by your side. I'm sure Steve, Darren, and Lucan will be sad if I leave, but being an aerial warrior means I can always fly to Celestial if needed. And I know they wants what's best for me, even if that means moving away." Summing up his stance, Ty stated, "I'll follow you wherever you go. I care about you more than anything else in this world and I'll support you to the ends of it.

"So, tell me," Ty asked again. "Are we back together?!"

Shana answered his question by leaning forward and kissing Ty deeply. The kiss led to many more, each one more intoxicating than the last, made extra special by not having been in each other's company for so many days.

Since Ty was standing, Shana jumped up, wrapped her legs around his waist, and crossed her arms around the back of his neck.

Clung together as tightly as possible, they continued kissing as he carried her over to the bed and laid her down on it.

"I've never wanted you as badly as I want you now," Ty whispered.

"Stop talking," Shana commanded him. Her breathing becoming increasingly heavy the more she became aroused. Unclasping Ty's armor, she pulled the metal pieces off of him, tossing them to the floor.

Ty helped Shana ease her armor off of her, and then they both removed each other's tunics so they felt only the warmth of each other's skin as their bodies pressed against each other.

Shana grabbed a handful of Ty's blonde hair, pulling it to jerk his head back so she could kiss his neck. After she'd left multiple marks that would undoubtedly turn into tiny bruises, Ty ran his hands through her hair, massaging her scalp with his fingertips as he pressed his lips into hers. Shana's gentle moans only served to excite him further, increasing Ty's desire to pleasure her even more. Together, the Elf and Human took turns making each other feel good until they were both fully satisfied.

With the logs of the fireplace reduced to embers, Ty used his pointer finger to draw on Shana's arm, outlining her tattoos as she lay asleep on his chest. He felt her soft inhales and exhales on his skin as he drifted off himself. *I'm going to marry this woman,* he knew, closing his heavy eyelids and giving into the comfort of the bed. *I've never known love like this.*

Chapter 144

With his head nestled into the pillow just right and his blankets providing the perfect warmth, Steve was completely comfortable and didn't want to move a muscle out of his relaxed position when someone knocked outside his bedroom. Pulling himself out of bed, but not without an annoyed groan, he opened the wooden door with decorative iron grilles, only to find a fair-skinned Dwarf, the only one Steve knew that tied his hair in a top-knot.

"Ryland!" Steve embraced the forty-one-year-old Halfman even though he hadn't put on a shirt on after waking up, was barefoot, and had hair sticking up every which way.

The Casanovian warrior carefully balanced a tray with two plates as he returned the hug and patted Steve's back with his free hand.

"I heard you arrived last night, but I wanted to let you settle in, so I thought I'd bring your breakfast this morning and bend your ear for a few minutes if that's okay."

"Sure, come on in," Steve gestured to a table where Ryland could set the food down. The plate of eggs, sausage, biscuits, and fruit smelled incredible, but Steve knew he couldn't partake of it. "I appreciate the favor,

Ryland, especially because breakfast is my favorite meal of the day, but I've been ordered not to eat anything unless it's directly from the cooks."

"This is from them. I just came from there," Ryland responded, sitting at the table and picking up a fork to dig into his own plate.

"I know, but I've got to follow these orders strictly, especially after hearing about how Shana was poisoned. No offense to you."

"None taken," Ryland threw up his hands. As Steve made his way to the chest of clothes at the end of his bed and began dressing himself, the Halfman solemnly explained, "Shana's poisoning is actually why I wanted to speak to you. I was on Andonia with her and Ty. I watched her suffer firsthand. When she told me she was flying to Almiria early, I accompanied her so I could start an investigation and determine who tried to poison her and the other elect. I had a couple of false leads, but last night I found out who the traitor is."

"What?" Steve asked in disbelief that Ryland had solved a riddle he had spent hours racking his mind over. The idea of a betrayer had bothered him from the moment he saw Nightstrike coming after them in the desert, when he knew someone had sent their recruiting plans to the Hooded Phantom. Hearing about Shana's poisoning had only furthered Steve's anxieties that someone was out to get them, but no longer would the mystery matter. "You know who betrayed us?"

"Yes," Ryland nodded. "But it's not just one person. It's a group of people. And they're forming a plan to kill you, specifically."

Chapter 145

"Please, sit," Ryland gestured to the open seat at the table where he'd set Steve's breakfast. "This information will be a lot to take in."

Once Steve sat down, the sentry warrior explained, "Since Shana was poisoned in Misengard, I spent a lot of time spying on Misengard's warriors and last night I overheard some disturbing things from a group of them talking in secret. I don't know if it'll happen before, during, or after the Battle for Celestial, but they're planning a coup where they'll murder you and instate Ortega as king. And it doesn't matter what happens in the capital because if The Hooded Phantom is defeated, they'll take over the whole kingdom but if he isn't, they'll retreat, give up all the land in the southern hemisphere, and start their own kingdom in the north."

Steve took a moment to process Ryland's revelation. "Captain Ortega? I fought alongside him against the Python's forces in the Frostlands. You were there too. He bears no ill will toward me."

"I wouldn't be so sure. Sometimes people act a certain way to gain your trust, and once they spot an opportunity to get what they want, they'll stab you in the back. Don't forget Ortega's story. He's been strung along with the promise of a promotion for so long, he now sees an

332

opportunity for advancement to the highest degree. He's learned he needs to take what he wants for himself and not rely on others."

Steve sat quietly for a moment and contemplated, during which he glanced over to the locked chest in his room which held the King's Crown that was finally back in his possession. "We need undisputable evidence before we can confront them. Would you recognize the Misengard warriors if you saw them in daylight?"

Ryland shook his head. "I couldn't make them out in the dark."

Letting out a long sigh, Steve leaned back in his chair and interlocked his fingers behind his head. He looked up at the tall, buttressed ceiling and closed his eyes as he rocked back and forth, deep in thought. Unable to focus, Steve stood and began pacing back and forth.

This stress is mentally draining, he thought to himself, considering how to respond to Ryland's accusations. *I have enough to worry about for the upcoming battle without dealing with an insurrection.*

"Have you told anyone this other than me?"

"Only you, sir."

"Keep it that way. If they know we know, it'll only accelerate their plans. Meanwhile, try to figure out exactly which warriors are a part of this and if Ortega is in on it or not. Until I hear from you, we'll increase the guard around this castle."

"I'm willing to test all your food if you need me too," Ryland pointed his fork at the plate in front of him. I'm certain they were trying to poison you in Misengard, but Shana got your drink instead. Please, it's better that someone like me dies rather than you."

"Don't discount yourself," Steve spoke sternly to the warrior more than twice his age, hating to see him assigning a low value to himself. You've been one of our closest companions. You were the only sentry who stuck with us in Casanovia. You've drawn maps for Shana to help organize this city, and now you've alerted me to watch out for an assassination. Your actions have changed the course of many lives. I don't want to be presumptuous in assuming I'll survive this war and become king, and I know I can't officially offer you this position until after my coronation, but if everything works in our favor, I'd like you to be one of my Guardian Knights."

"Sir," Ryland stepped out of his chair and knelt on the floor before Steve. "There would be no greater honor."

Steve nodded and beckoned Ryland up. As he told the Dwarf to stay alert and keep him updated, Shana barraged into the room with a smile that stretched from ear to ear.

"I'm sorry to interrupt," she apologized upon seeing Ryland and Steve talking, "but there's a huge armada entering the port. Friendly," she tacked on the last word, assuring the two men they didn't need to fret.

"Who is it?" Steve asked, rushing to put on his armor so he could greet the incoming allies.

"Casanovia and Bogmire. Plus, I spotted ships with blue and white flags.

Almiria, Steve knew the city by its colors. *The ships that evacuated to Casanovia are returning home!*

"Are Ty and Kari up?" Steve asked. "Grizz is likely on one of those ships since he was recruiting in Bogmire. They're going to want to see him."

"Ty's already waiting on the beach. We were walking along the shore with Lucan, Cassandra, and Darren first thing this morning when we spotted them sailing in, so I used my wind element to hurry here and tell you the good news."

"I'll wake Kari and we'll make our way down there," Steve fastened his belt around his waist and secured his sword sheath.

"I can accompany you for safety," Ryland offered.

"We'll be fine. Getting started on your reconnaissance is priority. If we don't find out who this traitor is, it's only a matter of time before he carries out his mission of hurting one of us elect."

After Ryland nodded and left, Steve went to Kari's bedroom and used a gentle voice and caring touch to wake her. Shana headed to the stables to ready horses for each of them. In fewer than fifteen minutes, the two Humans and Halfling found themselves standing on the beach alongside Ty, Commander Ostravaski, Darren and his family, and a bunch of other people who'd come to see the spectacle of the dozens of massive ships sail into the harbor.

Above the fleet, friendly aerial monsters with warrior mounts hovered above, providing an escort. One of them, a blue-feathered phoenix, broke away from the pack and landed near the group. Lucan watched and jumped up and down in excitement as the large monster landed near them.

Clad in the bright colors of yellow and sky blue, a Elven warrior climbed down his phoenix, set foot in the sand, and made his way towards the throng of onlookers.

Captain Nereus, Steve rolled his eyes at the highest-ranking warrior leader from the city northeast of Almiria. *He and I never saw eye to eye in Casanovia. I still can't believe he threatened me by pushing me up against a wall and holding a knife to my throat. After the battle for the city, he did his best to avoid me,* Steve recalled as the dark-skinned Elven captain acknowledged Ty, Shana, and then brushed right by him to introduce himself to the commanders, captains, and warriors in the crowd.

"He's still not speaking to you?" Ty nudged Steve, noticing the lack of interaction.

"Not a word since the group he left Casanovia with returned to the city."

"Nor me by association of being your girlfriend," Kari looked to Steve and shrugged.

"I thought you guys didn't get along with him after you punched him in that tavern brawl, and you spoke out against him in front of everyone after the aerial attack on Casanovia?" Steve turned from Ty to Shana.

"We patched things up before we left there," Shana explained. "He told me he'd never met a woman that impressed him like I did, and that I'd earned his respect because I cared as much about Casanovia as he did."

"Does he think I don't care?" Steve couldn't understand why Nereus had an issue specifically with him when he'd already proven he was willing to risk his life for the city.

"Maybe he doesn't believe your claim to the throne," Kari opined. "After all, he was one of the few that refused to bow after hearing you were king."

Who knows, Steve considered the reasons behind the captain's disdain while the first groups of people began arriving on small, wooden lifeboats sent from the large ships in the harbor to shore.

"Darren, Commander Ostravaski, you two know the areas we've set aside for the recruits from Bogmire and Casanovia," Shana stated. "Would you be able to lead the incoming people there? We'll let those from Almiria return to their homes, no matter where they are in the city."

She wants to stay here and see if her mom made the trip, Ty could tell the reason behind Shana asking the favor of his brother and the Celestial commander. *She keeps casting glances out to the lifeboats, searching the faces of all the people.*

Knowing how close Shana was to her mother, Ty made a visor with his hand, blocking out the sun to scan the incoming vessels, hoping to spot Leiana Latimer. Instead, he smiled at a different familiar face. It had orange fur with white under its chin, a black nose, whiskers, and two pointy ears.

With his neck stuck out, trying to keep his head above water, Copper forwent a lifeboat and used his four paws to paddle to shore. Once there, he juddered his soaking fur coat, sending water spraying over everyone nearby. The friendly direfox proceeded to lick Kari, jump up on Ty, and rub against Steve's legs since all three came over to greet their monster companion.

"I remember in Hunters Den when you were all too timid to even pet him!" a deep voice called out from a lifeboat that broke the water's surface and came to a rest in the sand.

"Grizz!" The Human, Elf, and Halfling all exclaimed, running over to the burly Dwarf.

Hugs were plentiful as Grizz, Nash, and Willis greeted the friends they so dearly missed.

"Nash, you're walking without crutches!" Ty couldn't believe his eyes as he bent down to his knees to engulf the eight-year-old in an embrace.

"Yeah! My Dad and I split off from the group on the way here to visit some barbarians he promised he'd bring food to. Their shaman gave us the ingredients to a potion I can drink that helps me walk!"

"It's some concoction of lavender, turmeric, chamomile, and some other herbs that temporarily strengthen the parts of his brain that affect his muscles," Grizz explained more in depth and rubbed Nash's hair. "I'm so happy we found something to help him. And we even made it back to the convoy in time to set sail across Lake Azure."

"With Bogmire, Casanovia, and Almiria, no less!" Steve still couldn't believe the hundreds and hundreds of people quickly filling up the beach and heading into the city.

"We recruited plenty of warriors and civilians," Nash beamed at their success.

"Not to mention clerics," Willis added. "When we went to Bogmire, we learned the high cleric was there visiting, since the city has one of the top institutes for cleric training. Knowing the battle to take back Celestial will be epic in scale and there will be many in our army that'll need medical attention, we asked her for the service of the school and to send requests to anyone she could. She obliged with overwhelming support and gave incentives to any clerics at the institute willing to join. Many of them may be inexperienced, but we'll take all the help we can get."

"Where's Krause and Dart?" Kari asked, looking around for the two Humans.

"Krause is on that ship," Grizz pointed to a four-masted carrack with green horizontal stripes painted across its hull. "He met a man in Bogmire he's become close with. They wanted to sail together here." Grizz smiled for a moment, happy for the commander, but then bowed his head, not wanting to address what happened to Dart. Willis answered in his stead, but supplied succinct details. "We were attacked. Dart was killed fighting honorably."

Steve, Kari, Ty, and Shana, all groaned at the death of the sixteen-year-old and stood silent for a moment until childish laughter lifted their spirits. Nash giggled endlessly, running up and down the beach, playing with Copper. The small Dwarf used his newfound mobility to chase after the direfox. Copper, panting with his tongue hanging out, would stand still, baiting Nash, and then sprint away the moment the boy came close to him.

"Can I go play with them?" Ty overheard Lucan nearby, asking his mom if he could join in on the fun.

Noticing Cassandra's skepticism of letting her five-year-old play with a monster, Ty advocated on his nephew's behalf. "He'll be fine. Copper's friendly and he's great with kids."

"Alright, but be safe," Cassandra cautioned.

"I'll go with him," Ty tried to make his sister-in-law more comfortable by taking Lucan's hand and leading him over to where the direfox and Dwarf played. Ty joined in on the chase and, just like the two boys, laughed with childish glee as they all worked together to catch Copper.

After they had their fun, the Serendale crew headed into the city with Cassandra and Lucan, leaving only Steve, Ty, Kari, and Shana watching the lifeboats head back to the ships to gather the last of the waiting travelers.

On one of them, Almiria's one-armed Naval Commander Ishaan Artazair returned to the city he'd led the evacuation from. With him stood Shana's fifty-eight-year-old mother, Leiana Latimer.

"Mom!" With tears welling in her eyes, she took Ty's hand and led him to the woman who raised her and who she had such a close bond with. "When we received word

Casanovia was on their way, I was hoping you'd make the trip!"

"I don't know much about war or what I can do to help, but I do know justice was never served after what Malorek did to me, so I'm willing to help take him down, however I can," Leiana stated, then twisted a strand of her daughter's hair around her finger. "I like the new color!"

"That's not all that's new," Shana lifted her sleeve to expose a new tattoo on her arm.

"Always find what's positive," Leiana read the cursive font out loud.

Shana nodded and smiled, studying the tattoo herself. *The excitement at seeing the new art on my body never subsides until long after the ink dries. Anytime I look at the tattoos on my ongoing sleeve, I'm happy. Each one has significance to me.*

Explaining the meaning behind the four new words, she told her mom, "This was something you mentioned to me after the attack in Casanovia and it's been stuck in my head ever since. When I overheard a recruit telling someone she had inking experience, I asked her to scrawl your words out for me."

"It looks great," Leiana encouraged her daughter, as she did no matter what tattoo Shana got.

While Shana and Ty caught up with Leiana, Steve and Kari made their way to Commander Artazair.

"Ishaan!" Steve approached the warrior leader, shaking the only available hand of the one-armed Human. He was excited to reconnect with the man he remembered could always make him laugh.

"Ah, Stephen! I'm surprised you remember an insignificant warrior like me now that you're the royal, majestic, blue-eyed king!"

"No one calls me that."

"Oh right, they call you the royal, majestic, *courageous,* blue-eyed king! Forgive me for leaving out such an important adjective!"

"You're eccentric as always, commander." Steve grinned, "but your lack of speed troubles me. This is the second time you've led a convoy to the city I'm in and again you're the last one to shore!"

Artazair smiled, knowing Steve purposely lobbied up the comment because he wanted to hear the self-deprecating humor Ishaan loved to employ. The commander always appreciated when people understood his comedic style and played into it.

"I prefer to let everyone else tread through the water and scare any sharks away. Can't lose my other hand! What a sad, unpleasurable life that would be."

"Especially because it doesn't look like you can afford a prostitute," Kari chimed in the second Ishaan had finished speaking while pointing to a hole in his tunic.

Artazair snorted while Steve cocked an eyebrow at his girlfriend, surprised because he'd never heard her make a crass joke.

Kari shrugged and smiled smugly at her boyfriend, as if he should've known what she was capable of.

"I like this one! You've got a good one here!" Artazair pointed from Steve to Kari.

"My name is Kari Quinn," Kari officially introduced herself to the commander. "I don't think we ever met in Casanovia because I was laid up in the infirmary until only a couple days before Silas's army arrived."

"We haven't. Artazair took her hand and kissed the back of it. "I would've remembered a face as beautiful as yours, my lady."

341

"Commander, good to see you!" Shana exclaimed, coming over with Ty and Leiana to greet the warrior leader. She looked to Steve and Kari to make sure it was okay she borrowed their horses, and then told Ishaan, "Let's ride into the city so I can explain how we've set things up. It'd be nice to get your input since you're from here. Plus, since all shipmasters and warrior naval leaders keep a log of their passengers, I'm hoping we can transcribe those rosters for our records."

"Shouldn't be a problem," Artazair obliged and climbed up onto one of the stallions. "After you, my dear."

Shana blew Ty a quick kiss, said goodbye to Steve and Kari, and then beckoned her mom to mount the remaining horse and follow her, "Mom, you can come with me and I'll take you up to the castle where you'll be staying with me and the other elect."

While the three headed for the city, Steve motioned for Ty and Kari to follow him up a nearby bluff, one of the tallest in Almiria, let alone the entire province. As they climbed, they overheard Ishaan's peppy voice as he cantered his horse in between the two Human women and sat up straight as if he were a royal prince returning to his kingdom. "You know, when I arrived with the fleet in Casanovia, you all threw quite the feast in the mess hall there. Any chance there are similar plans for my grand return?"

Shana giggled at the middle-aged man who shared many of the same mannerisms and comedic timing as Ty. "Yes, your excellency! Many hands are working hard, preparing a banquet of turkey, leek soup, and potatoes."

"Seems like quite the personality!" Kari continued listening to Artazair jest with Shana and Leiana until they were out of earshot.

"It may seem like he takes nothing seriously, but there are little ways you can tell Ishaan cares more than he lets on," Ty admitted, understanding the commander's character because it was so similar to his own. "Both in Casanovia and here, I noticed he was the last one to set foot on land. He makes sure everyone is safe before himself. I'm glad we have a person like that on our side."

"None of us would even be here if it wasn't for him," Steve agreed. "If he hadn't had the foresight to sail the Almiria evacuees along the coast instead of directly to Casanovia, they would've been attacked by the Hooded Phantom's aerial monsters. Him, Ryland, Jun-Lei, Darren and Ostravaski– there's so many people where if you remove them from the story of how we got to this point, our chances in this war completely collapse."

Arriving at the top of the cliff, Steve, Ty, and Kari felt the breeze of the sea at their backs as they gazed out over Almiria. Before them, they could see the people from the ships splitting off into the different sections of the city Shana had pre-arranged for them to stay in. In the already populated parts of the city, people moved about the streets, carrying out whatever wartime efforts they were attending to. The smoke from forges rose high into the sky as tireless blacksmiths churned out armor and weapons.

"This is our army," Steve stated, staring across the landscape. "It's incredible what we've accomplished here with the efforts of so many people from all twelve provinces."

"There are more volunteers than we originally expected," Kari stood equally impressed at the sight before her. "Good thing Shana ordered people to make as many tents as possible. We'll need them not only for all these recruits, but for when our army rests out on the prairie after our march to Celestial."

"I hope we have enough people that we can win decisively without too many causalities," Steve noted. "There were so many monsters in the attack on Celestial. I know we defeated a fourth of their army led by Silas in Casanovia and another fourth with the Python's remnant in the Frostlands, but even with half of their army left, it must be close to what our numbers are."

"I'm sure with Shana's roster she'll have the total amount in our ranks sometime tomorrow. Plus, we still have stragglers coming in who didn't arrive with their city's convoy. Not to mention the aerial monsters Crimson Singe is gathering. We're going to be formidable by the time we're set to march."

Steve wrung his hands together, thinking about how close they were to the reclamation of Celestial, an event six months in the making.

Everything has been leading to this, he knew. *The future of the kingdom depends on all these people before us, and I will be honored to lead them into battle.*

Little did Steve know, he would draw Aurelia that very night, for the Hooded Phantom knew of their gathered army and was sending his strongest riders to Almiria to kill as many people as possible.

Chapter 146

In Almiria's main temple, the large banquet hall could only hold six-hundred people at a time. The capacity was woefully short of their collected army's numbers, but Shana's organized logistics allowed each section of the city to dine in shifts throughout the late afternoon and night.

"We're being called down to the temple to eat," Cassandra came in to get Steve, Ty, and Darren once word had come that those in the castle would dine together with the survivors from Celestial.

The three brothers arose, ending the hour together where they allowed themselves to relax from war-preparations and reminisced about some of their favorite stories from being raised by Titus Thatcher.

Closer to the temple, Steve met with Kari, who'd been helping Shana alert each Primary City's group when it was their turn to head to the banquet hall. Three trusted warriors accompanied her for protection everywhere she went in case an attempt was made on her life. Likewise, each of the four elect had their own teams assigned to never leave their side whenever they traveled throughout the city.

"That's him, the one those warriors are guarding," Steve overheard a child's voice whisper from a line of

345

people exiting the temple as he waited outside for his turn to enter. "He's got red armor, a blue sash, and black hair!"

Looking in the direction, Steve spotted a young boy pointing at him and telling his sister, "People say he's going to be the new king."

"Does that mean Crimson Singe is here?" the girl asked her brother, craning her neck, searching the skies for the legendary dragon. "Supposedly he helped fight in Casanovia."

Steve nodded to the two kids, who each gasped at the fact he acknowledged them, and then followed his group into the banquet hall where Shana ushered them in. She held a book and a quill in her hand that she feverishly scribbled in.

"You're the last ones," she spoke to those who gathered to eat. "I'm sorry it's so late, but there's more than enough for everyone and we've made sure none of the food has been tampered with," she spoke her last words specifically to Steve, Ty, Grizz, and Kari.

"Have you eaten?" Ty stepped out from the line of guards surrounding him to check on Shana. "I'm worried you're so busy keeping order you haven't taken the time to focus on yourself."

"Yes, I had some food earlier," Shana reassured him with a smile. "I ate with my mom when she was in here with Casanovia's group earlier." For a moment, Ty frowned, and Shana knew he was disappointed they'd barely spent time together. "Don't worry, I'm still planning on sitting with you while you eat. Let me just escort everyone in first."

The companions joined the survivors who'd escaped Celestial in a single-file line, and each accepted a plate of food before finding an open table Quintis Quinn had saved for them. Like Shana, the warrior archer had eaten earlier in the day, but he stuck around so he could see Kari as he split time between his daughter and those from Holders Keep.

The amount of food was bountiful, and the company was pleasant as everyone chatted while eating. Ty challenged Grizz to an arm-wrestling contest that Ty decisively lost. Ostravaski puffed on the mouthpiece of his pipe, inhaling vanilla-scented tobacco as he sat with Quintis and shared stories of their craziest experiences from serving in Celestial. Kari and Shana discussed the timelines and where they might be now had different points of their journey gone differently. Darren and Willis entered a friendly debate about which two elemental powers would be the strongest to have. Even the two youngest at the table, Lucan and Nash, enjoyed their time holding in their laughter as they worked in tandem to sneak Copper food under the table.

It's nice to sit with family and friends and eat an enjoyable meal, Steve thought as he watched everyone smiling and laughing. *It seems as if the war is the last thing on anyone's minds. This reprieve is exactly what we need.*

Kari noticed Steve taking in the relaxed atmosphere and squeezed his hand. "You know, I have a surprise for you for tomorrow."

"You do?!" Steve smiled at the idea Kari had taken the time to plan something special for him. "What is it?"

"I can't tell you!"

"Not even a hint?"

"A hint and nothing more," Kari compromised, temporarily pausing to build up suspense. "I ran into a person from your past."

Steve sat in silence, trying to think of who would be in Almiria that he already didn't know about, but someone who Kari also knew. As he deliberated long and hard, nearly everyone but him and those at his table trickled out of the banquet hall into the night that was now dark with steady rainfall, lightning, and thunder.

Darren stood from the table and made his way towards Steve, bending down to speak softly into his brother's ear, "I'm sorry to break up such a happy time of reunion, but with a lot of people already here that haven't been brought up to speed on Celestial's status, now might be a good time for Commander Ostravaski and I to explain the state of the capital."

It's going to be painful to hear about Celestial, Steve knew, *but it'll be good to know what to expect when we get to the city.* He nodded in the affirmative, then announced to everyone, "We're going to have a meeting before we call it a night." Beckoning a guard over, he asked. "Could you have some warriors find General Elesora of Stonegate, Commander Artazair of Almiria, and the drow, Cryonic? I'd like them all here."

While they waited, for the second night in a row, Darren declared, "Lucan, it's time to say goodnight and head to bed."

"Nash, it's time for you to get to sleep too," Grizz turned to his son.

"Can I sleep in Lucan's room?" Nash asked, not wanting to leave the side of his new friend who he had so much fun being around.

Grizz looked to Darren, who shrugged and nodded, not taking issue with the inquiry.

"I can take them both to the castle," Cassandra offered.

"Thank you," Grizz appreciated the help. He got up from his seat on the long bench of the eighty-foot table they sat at and crouched down to say goodbye to Nash.

"Make sure you listen to Mrs. Canard and behave yourself. No sneaking out or anything, okay? I don't want to hear of any problems in the morning when I come pick you up."

After Nash promised to behave, Grizz whispered in the eight-year-old's ear, "Tomorrow, you and I will finish up the project we've been working on. All that's left is the final touches." He winked at his son to keep the secret that only the two of them knew about, and then kissed his forehead. "I love you. Have a good night."

"Love you too," Nash buried his face into Grizz's long beard and wrapped his arms around his dad's neck.

Copper got up from where he was lying on the floor to follow the two boys and Cassandra to the castle, but Grizz noticed the direfox acting strangely. Copper paced back and forth between those staying behind and Nash, Lucan, and Cassandra, who were leaving.

"What's wrong, boy?" Grizz scratched the monster behind his orange ears. "Why don't you head with the boys and keep them safe tonight?"

The direfox yipped a higher-pitched guttural sound than the usual bark he made when agreeing to something. With no further utterances, he trotted alongside the Dwarven and Elven boys as they followed Cassandra home.

"Shana, Quintis," Steve turned to the two Humans, "Darren and Commander Ostravaski are going to fill us in on Celestial. I know you two already heard everything we're about to hear, so I understand if you don't want to stay."

"I'll stay," Quintis repositioned himself on the bench, scooching closer to Kari, taking her hand, and looking into her eyes.

I figure what we'll be told is difficult to imagine, but is it really that bad my dad feels he needs to stay here and comfort me? Kari questioned. Her heart raced as she wondered if she'd underestimated the state of Celestial.

"Once was enough for me," Shana stood, taking the opposite approach of the archer. "I can't bear to hear those details again. I've got a few more things to take care of tonight anyway." Ty got up with Shana and walked her to the temple exit to make sure there were warriors that could escort her.

"Can we meet up after I'm done here?" he asked.

"Yes, of course," Shana grabbed Ty's yellow armor and pulled him in for a kiss. "I just need to head to the library and drop off the roster I made to the scribemaster, but first I'm headed to the castle to visit my mom. She said she wanted to talk to me when I had a chance. It seemed like something was bothering her."

"What do you think it could be?"

Shana shrugged. "I don't know, but I'll find you after I'm done with my errands." With another quick kiss, she pulled the cloak of her tunic over her head and ventured out into the stormy night with three warriors at her side.

High on the rooftops, the traitor that'd been actively planning against Alazar's Elect watched Shana leave the temple. In each of his hands, he gripped the hilts of blood-covered halfswords and across his back rested a nearly empty quiver. The weapons had just been used to kill the sentries keeping post at various entry points around Almiria. Employing the same strategy Prince Silas and his eleven warriors had used to clear the way for the

Hooded Phantom's army to arrive at Celestial undetected would now allow Almiria to be similarly attacked. The dark night and heavy rain would only further mask the approaching riders on their way to cause death and destruction.

As Silas's twelfth warrior, purposely stationed in the north to infiltrate and sabotage the Primary Cities, the betrayer's long-term machinations were finally about to come to fruition. The veteran warrior had spent months gaining the trust of Alazar's Elect, and now it was finally time to upend everything they'd worked for.

Chapter 147

"So we're just waiting on General Elesora and Commander Artazair," Steve declared after Cryonic walked in and took a seat alone at the table next to where everyone sat.

It seems like Steve is inviting the people who arrived in Almiria either yesterday or this morning and haven't yet heard the firsthand account of what's happening in Celestial, Grizz realized. *He's being strategic about it, though,* the Dwarf could tell, scanning the room and noticing that the few in attendance were all warrior leaders the nineteen-year-old had personal experiences with and trusted. *He's using this as an opportunity to collect his closest confidants and form his inner circle, the ones he knows he doesn't have to worry about betraying him. It wouldn't surprise me to hear that some of these warriors are the ones he's considering for his Guardian Knight positions.*

Willis, who also seemed to realize Steve's precise, hand-picked selection of people, asked, "What about Captain Ortega?"

Giving no indication of his distrust of the Misengard warrior based on Ryland's trepidations, Steve simply answered, "Ortega will not be apart of this meeting."

"Would you consider inviting Twin Peaks' former General Graynor?" Grizz piped up. "He's an honorable man whose years of experience would be a valuable addition to our army."

Ostravaski nodded. "I've known General Graynor for many years and can confirm what Grizz says. The man's a giant in both stature and character."

Steve thought for a moment, and, trusting in both Grizz and Ostravaski's judgment, called another warrior over to go and fetch the experienced veteran. Once Graynor, A'ryn, and Ishaan arrived, they found a seat along with everyone else. Graynor, however, sat at the table with the lone drow, seeing Cryonic alone.

"What the commander and I have to share won't be easy for you to hear," Darren stood with Ostravaski and addressed the collected group of people. "A darkness fell upon Celestial the day it was attacked, and that veil hasn't been lifted since. The capital's citizens are living in misery as they're being forced to serve monsters. They're being tortured, worked to death, and made to entertain the monsters in the most violent ways. I watched the chaos happening firsthand while rescuing survivors and bringing them down into the sewers."

"It's bad," Commander Ostravaski agreed. "The Hooded Phantom gave each race of monsters a section of the city and control over the people in that section. He wants to make it clear that what the citizens are enduring is a consequence for creating the survival of the fittest world monsters have had to live in for so long.

"First, they killed all nineteen-year-old boys in the city by order of Silas due to some prophecy."

"The Prophecy of the Twins," Steve interjected, grabbing his sword and pulling it halfway out of its sheath, revealing some of the inscribed letters and explaining, "Silas wanted to eliminate the chance of his twin fulfilling the prophecy."

"It was terrible to hear about the executions," Darren lamented. "We could hear the cries of the people mourning those lost from underneath the city. After that day, they split families apart, often killing the youngest and forcing the rest to watch. Even pets were put to death or given to direwolves to eat. They tried to lower the civilians' morale to such a low point that no one had the will to fight back.

"After separating families, they categorized everyone based on their trade. Blacksmiths, farmers, carpenters, tailors, and bakers were all considered valuable and kept alive, but librarians, bankers, merchants, teachers, and others were deemed unworthy. They made examples of people in those professions, or used them as leverage against those deemed valuable.

"Monsters took the idea of the Tournaments and brutalized it. They made those they decreed expendable fight in one-on-one combat or a Battle Royale with actual weapons instead of blunted ones. They had archery tournaments where people were the targets. Anyone who didn't fulfill the role given to them as a slave was put in cages in the streets and left to rot, burned at the stake, or given over to the Skeleton King to add to his army."

Darren shook his head, and Steve, Ty, Kari, and Grizz could tell he was thinking back to the awful things he'd either witnessed himself or heard about second-hand.

In the momentary silence, Cryonic looked to Steve from where he sat with Graynor and said, "Steve, I know I told you I had yet to decide if I would fight for your army, but after hearing these things, I'll take up arms alongside you. You have my blades."

Steve nodded to the drow, thankful for the help of a monster so powerful, and then listened to Kari ask, "Hasn't anyone banded together to lead a revolt?"

"There have been attempts," Ostravaski shared. "But the citizens are kept weak because they're overworked and starved."

"They're not all starved," Darren argued.

"Oh right," the commander rolled his eyes at the memory. "Sometimes, instead of withholding food and water, monsters force people to keep eating and drinking until they die. I think the monsters are figuring, 'if you're going to take this much food from the environment, then you better be willing to eat it all yourself.'

"Anyways," Ostravaski refocused himself and got back to Kari's question. "The Hooded Phantom always seems to squash revolts before they become a threat. Even altercations within his own army he handles thoroughly. A faction of orcs fought against ogres, so Malorek ordered their leaders to be beheaded. They resolved the issue that day. The monsters fear the one they call The Faceless, but they're willing to follow him because he's given them what they've always struggled to attain for themselves: food, bountiful land, a safe home, power, and slaves."

"We have to save them," Darren resounded Steve's plea. "The population of everyone in Celestial has been reduced by fifty percent, if not more."

"Fifty percent!" Steve blurted out the number in disbelief. He shook his head, struggling to comprehend the sheer number already killed. Thinking of half the people he interacted with on his daily patrol simply vanishing, never to be seen again, made him sick to his stomach.

"Yeah, between the initial attack, all the deaths since then, the nineteen-year-old males Silas put to death, and those given over to the Accursed, fifty percent is what we estimate."

Ostravaski solemnly nodded, knowing the number was shocking, but likely accurate. "There's been as many civilian deaths over the past five months as there were during the entirety of Draviakhan's reign."

"Then we'll have to make sure this war ends just like the last one," Steve told everyone. "Oliver Zoran ended the life of the five-headed dragon and we're going to do the same to Malorek. We need to end this for all who are suffering with no way to fight back for themselves."

Chapter 148

The butt-end of Shana's spear hit the dirt with every other one of her steps as she walked the path up to the clifftop castle. The wind and rain increased in their veracity, and flashes of lightning became more prominent with each passing minute, ominously illuminating the old white-stone structure ahead.

I wish I could go back in time and see what this city looked like when the lord of this castle ruled over these lands, Shana thought, spotting an ornate column, part of which had been chipped off and never replaced. *It's always fun to imagine a place at the height of its splendor.*

Inside, she asked the three guards accompanying her to wait outside her room as she entered. There, she found her mom relaxing, nearly drifting off to sleep since she'd spent most of the morning and afternoon helping prepare food in the banquet hall. The moment Leiana saw Shana, however, she perked up.

"You look so regal walking in here," Leiana stated.

"What do you mean?" the comment made Shana snicker as she made her way over to the cellarette and grabbed a vessel of red wine to pour out into two flagons.

"There's just this aura of confidence you have ever since you left Casanovia. Maybe it's your wind powers or maybe you've embodied the leadership role you've taken on here, but you've never looked more grown up to me than you do now."

Not knowing what to say, Shana handed her mom one of the flagons, sat down with her, and listened to her continue, "Captain Nereus seems to notice something in you, too. Back home, people wanted to hold an election to fill the positions of the fallen commanders and Mayor Hughley, but Nereus told them it's best to wait until the war is over. I think he was trying to get them to hold off so you can be there in person to run for mayor since he believes you'd do a good job."

"Ever since I was a girl, it's been my dream to campaign for that position. I'd be honored if the people thought I'd make a wise councilor and elected me," Shana smiled at the idea. "Ty's even willing to move to Casanovia or wherever I can find a mayoral job."

"I've noticed you two seem closer than ever. Do you think he's the one?"

Shana grinned even wider and blushed at the idea of Ty becoming her husband. Before she could answer, Leiana exclaimed, "You don't need to say it. I can tell by your smile!"

Sharing her daughter's joy, Leiana added her support at the thought of Shana's potential spouse. "I like him. You two are fitting for each other."

"What was it you wanted to talk to me about?" Shana asked, changing the subject because she didn't want to be too presumptuous about her future with Ty.

Immediately, Leiana lost her smile, took a deep breath, and revealed, "There's something I have to tell you, Shana. You have two half-brothers."

"I know. Silas and Steve," Shana's brow wrinkled, confused why her mom was stating information she'd already learned.

"No, not them. From the first time I was assaulted, years before the incident with Malorek," Leiana began hyperventilating as she could still feel the utter darkness and presence of evil from the event decades prior. The horrific memory and emotions it brought on caused her to erratically pause between every few words as she revealed, "I'm sorry, but I lied to you when you asked if I got pregnant from it. The truth is I had twin boys that time too, but I abandoned them."

"It's okay, mom," Shana took Leiana's flagon and set it on a nearby table since her mom's hand was shaking so badly. "You don't have to apologize to me. It was wrong of me to even ask that question in the first place."

Leiana nodded, dabbing her tears from her eyes and controlling her breathing. "It's hard for me to talk about. I was only fifteen when it happened, still a year until I came of age. When I told my parents, they didn't believe me. They told me I got what I deserved being so promiscuous and said I lied about being assaulted. They kicked me out and I had no choice but to get rid of the babies when they were born. That's why all your life I wanted to be to you what my parents weren't to me: a good parent who trusts you, helps you, and loves you."

"I couldn't ask for a better mom," Shana set her own flagon down so she could hug Leiana. "You've made me into who I am and I'll always be thankful we're so close. We don't need to talk about it ever again unless you feel you need to," she wiped her mother's tears with her thumbs and walked over to a nearby desk in the room they shared. Pulling out a stack of papers, she said, "Do you want to come with me to the library and drop these off to the scribemaster? He's going to make copies of them and it might be helpful to clear your mind."

"A walk would be nice, even in this weather," Leiana stood and grabbed her cloak upon seeing the torrential downpour outside. "Sometimes it's fun to walk outside in a storm, but you better protect those papers from the rain. I know how hard you've worked on that roster."

Shana found a tunic to wrap the papers in, carefully placed them in her bag, and rested its strap on her shoulder. Opening the bedroom door, she requested the guards escort them back down to the city. The men happily obliged, so the mother and daughter held hands all the way down the hill and into the heart of Almiria.

It was there the chaos began with a far off scream.

"Did you hear that?" Leiana asked. Her heart sunk, her eyes widened, and her voice quivered with each word of her question.

"Yes," Shana nodded, tightening her grip on her spear as more screams and shouts came from the other side of the city. "Mom, we need to get you to safety. Almiria is under attack!"

Chapter 149

"What was that?" Kari interrupted Darren and Ostravaski while they shared more details about the state of Celestial. She and her father had been the only ones to hear the sound of distress from far off. It was quickly followed by the clanging of steel on steel, and the warcries of men and women engaging in battle.

"Was there a training drill scheduled for tonight?" Steve breathlessly asked Ostravaski while standing and drawing Aurelia. Every other person at the table did the same, rising from their seats and readying their weapons as their heartbeats multiplied exponentially when the commander answered, "No."

Outside the banquet hall in the pouring rain, the sounds of battle now seemed to come from all directions. A warrior on horseback galloped up to the group, announcing, "We're under attack. All sorts of Animal Monsters and their mounts are wreaking havoc on the east side of the city and heading this way."

"I have to go protect Nash!" Grizz took off, not wasting any time.

"I'm coming with you!" Darren ran after him, knowing Cassandra and Lucan were with the Dwarf's son.

"So am I!" Ty joined his brother, remembering Shana had been heading to the castle as well. He turned back to

Steve and Kari to apologize for leaving them, but Steve shooed him away. "Go! Make sure she's safe."

"Is it only riders attacking?" Kari turned to the warrior who alerted them. She looked to the dark skies, exploding with flashes of lightning, fearing a devastating attack similar to Celestial and Casanovia, but found no aerial monsters among the dark clouds.

Before the warrior could answer, a second warrior came towards them, shouting, "The enemy has made it past the sentries posted in the west. They're led by a large, black minotaur."

Ironmaul, Steve knew. *That means the Hooded Phantom knows we're here. We tried to keep our army's location secret, but I'm guessing the traitors in our midst are working with Malorek and told him about us.*

"The monsters are attacking similarly to how they did in Celestial," Steve told the surrounding group, using his gauntleted forearm to wipe the rain pouring from his hair down into his eyes. "They're coming in groups from different points around Almiria. Each of you head to your section of the city! Try to get everyone huddled together in the same place. That way, you can minimize the confusion and chaos and fight off monsters as a group."

"We can't leave the side of our future king!" A'ryn argued.

"He won't be alone. I'll protect him," Cryonic promised.

"I'll stay too," Ostravaski stood alongside the drow. "The rest of you need to go."

"I love you, Kari," Quintis squeezed his daughter's arm before notching an arrow in his bow and heading to where everyone from Holders' Keep was stationed. Elesora, Graynor, and Artazair ran off as well, leaving only

Steve, Kari, Ty, Ostravaski, Cryonic, Willis, and ten warriors behind.

"We'll be safest in open space," Ostravaski pointed to a two-acre park adjacent to the temple they'd just come out of. The sprawling grounds sat in the heart of Almiria and featured a three-layer fountain in its center. Shana had refused to populate it with tents and required it to be one of the few locations throughout the city left as a place people could escape from all things related to war.

"We'll be able to see whatever's coming for us from any direction," Steve nodded, surveying the landscape. He turned to the warriors closest to him. "You four search this area and tell anyone armed to come to the fountain. Tell everyone else to go into hiding."

Only minutes after their group reached the fountain, overflowing from the heavy rain, fifty warriors joined them. Together, they all stood with weapons ready, waiting to defend themselves against the incoming monsters.

"The enemy's closing in on our location!" Willis warned the group, hearing the sounds of battle growing closer. No sooner did he speak, the ground beneath their feet rumbled and nine horses, five direwolves, and four direboars stampeded into the park.

Kari and ten other archers fired arrows at the Anthropomorphic Monsters atop the mounts, but only seven of the arrows found their mark. Out of the seven, only three dropped the rider to the ground.

At the front of the horde, the monsters mounted on horses plowed through the huddled group and swung their weapons viciously at anyone in range. With everyone staggered, the direwolves came in behind and savagely attacked, as did the direboars, who rammed their sharp tusks straight through the shields and armor meant to ward them off.

Kari's ice armor protected her from being impaled and she would've lost her head had she not ducked under the swing of a fiery scimitar meant to cleave through her neck. The onslaught of attacks took all of her focus to avoid. She turned and fired an arrow covered in the hottest water she could muster into the back of an orc riding a massive direboar. A second arrow, this one of ice, tore the rider from its saddle, where Commander Ostravaski used his giant foot to stomp on its head.

Standing back-to-back, Steve and Cryonic turned both their weapons and armor into fire and readied themselves against the direwolves before them. The flames emitting from their metal were so hot the rain evaporated before it ever touched the blade. The shifting orange firelight didn't scare the beasts, who lunged with their claws, only to be sliced by Aurelia and impaled by Cryonic's axe and sword.

"Watch out for the ones on horses! They're wheeling around to plow through us again!" Willis shouted. The Serendale warrior noticed Kari's back turned to the horde, so he tackled her over the ledge of the fountain and into the lowest bowl to save her from being trampled. The decorative stone barrier protected them both, as did the wall of water Kari raised and froze to ice when she saw two riders turn in their saddles and fire arrows at her and the red-haired Human.

"Thanks!" the two told each other, both grateful to have someone looking out for them.

"Stephen," Ostravaski breathlessly came up to the warrior shrouded in flames. "I overheard one monster say, 'Go tell Ironmaul we've found two of their elementals. They're with a drow.' It seems like they're

364

targeting the elect and other powerful members of our army." Even as the commander spoke, two of the monsters blew into horns, alerting other monsters to their location. "Let's head to the castle before they converge upon this place. With Grizz, Ty, and Darren already there, we can make an organized stand. If that fails, there's a secret passageway leading to safety if we need to escape."

"I will not abandon these men, not while I can help them in this battle!" Steve argued, running forward to help up a fallen comrade.

"These men already face enough of a challenge." Ostravaski came up behind him, refusing to drop the issue. "By leaving, you'll save them from certain doom, but we need to go now!"

"I can't follow you!" Steve shouted, gesturing to the carnage all around them. "Our sentries didn't alert us, so I know they were killed before the attack, just like in Celestial! I don't know who I can trust right now!"

"You're questioning my loyalty?" the Giant reeled back as if a dagger had been thrust into his chest.

"I'm questioning everyone!" Steve yelled.

The commander took a deep breath, trying to understand Steve's perspective, and urgently shouted above the noises of the chaotic battle around them. "Listen to me! I know we've been betrayed and there's nothing I could say or do right now to make you trust me, but we need to get you out of here!"

"He's telling the truth!" Willis fought his way over to Steve, carrying the reins of one of the enemy's stallions in his hand with Kari at his side. The Serendale warrior spotted Steve glancing between the street leading up to the castle and everyone fighting in the park and knew he was debating leaving. "I watched a rider gallop off to find

Ironmaul and bring him here. Take this horse and leave this area. I'll stay and fight."

Ostravaski is right, Steve's mind raced through what was the best plan of approach to the news he was a prime target. *My presence here brings more danger to this group than they're already in.*

"Kari, we're heading to the castle," Steve announced, reluctant to leave the unfinished battle in case they needed his help. He grabbed the horse's reins from Willis and told the warrior, "You and Cryonic help finish these riders and go aid another section of the city as soon as you're done. I don't want anyone to be in this area when the enemy focuses their attack here."

"You two! Grab those horses and come with us!" Ostravaski randomly selected two warriors standing near where a group of three riders had been torn down from their mounts and killed. The men gave the commander one horse and each took one for themselves while Steve mounted the remaining stallion and pulled Kari up to sit behind him.

"Speed, strength, and safety to you," Willis called up to his Human and Halfling friends.

"And to you, friend," Steve saluted the red-headed warrior. With a shout, he lashed the reins of his steed, taking the horse from a canter to a gallop as he rode to the castle. He kept the fire on his armor employed, thankful it only affected what he willed it to, so he didn't burn Kari behind him or the horse underneath him.

If these monsters are here for me, then let them see me. We'll draw them to the castle and show them how powerful Alazar's five elect are when we fight together!

Chapter 150

Ty, Grizz, and Darren ran on foot towards the castle, passing through the dozens and dozens of tents in a section of fields Shana had designated for everyone from Twin Peaks. At the far end, nearest the hill the castle sat atop, monsters rode around using either their elements or torches to set fire to everything they could. Even the heavy rain wasn't enough to put out the tent fires once they were aflame. Half the warriors tried rescuing their belongings, while the others attacked the enemy in disorganized groups led by General Dvorak.

"Help us!" the warrior leader called to Grizz once he spotted the fellow Dwarf coming through the area in his suit of rock armor and with his double-headed weapon in hand.

First the drow underneath Twin Peaks, now this, Grizz shook his head. *Dvorak's ranks are in chaos when order is needed the most. He should have never usurped Graynor's position.*

"They're your men to lead!" Grizz shouted to the general, swinging Skullcleaver into a nearby direboar, but otherwise not stopping from his mission of sprinting to Nash to keep him safe.

Ty and Darren followed the Dwarf's lead, saving what lives were in imminent danger, but remained primarily focused on making it to the castle.

What little guilt they felt for leaving the unprepared and uncoordinated Twin Peaks warriors to fend for themselves was alleviated by a few friendly aerial monsters landing throughout the area to both ward off the enemy and prevent the tent fires from spreading throughout the entire section of the camp.

They have our aerial monsters at a disadvantage, Ty knew the struggle the dragons, gryphons, and phoenixes faced. *These riders came into Almiria so quickly and without warning, by clashing with our army, they've made it impossible to attack from above. Our monsters won't take the chance of killing members of our own army.*

While two of the aerial monsters were successful in helping curtail the enemy, Ty watched in horror as an ogre took a pike and ran it through the gryphon he flew in the Battle for Casanovia. The monster who delivered the blow with the long, spear-tipped shaft turned around and steered its direboar straight for the fallen aerial monster, impaling its mount's horns into the gryphon's neck. More Animal Monsters came in and joined in on the assault, assuring the death of the powerful beast.

"Keep up, Ty!" Grizz yelled behind him to the Elf who'd slowed down, preoccupied with the carnage all around them. "If the enemy's made it this far, some likely already went to the castle."

Grizz's assumption was correct, as the three men came to the hill the castle rested atop and found the bodies of both warriors and monsters strewn about. Beyond them, the ornate doors in the entryway to the castle lie broken off their hinges.

"It looks like the enemy forced their way in," Darren gathered, sprinting up the steep hill.

He's right. The guards here would've done anything in their power to keep those doors closed, Ty knew, following close behind.

Halfway up the hill, two orcs emerged from the castle, one of whom had a blade covered in blood.

"Whose blood is that?" Grizz shouted as he ran. The question was rhetorical since Grizz sought to find the answer for himself. The two monsters standing in his way only served to delay him in finding if his son was alive.

Caring only to dispatch the orcs as quickly as possible, Grizz paid no heed to the fact that they both had the element of lightning as he continued running forward. Even while they blasted his armor, he continued charging forward, and swung Skullcrusher around and around his head, slamming it into the nearest orc once he was close enough. Transferring the wound up momentum of the attack, he targeted the second orc and hit it too, crumpling its armor as if it were paper. With the monsters critically injured, Darren and Ty plunged their swords into them and followed Grizz into the castle.

Darren cut to the front of the group, leading Grizz to the room Cassandra, Lucan, and he had been staying in.

Meanwhile, Ty broke off from them and headed for Shana and Leiana's room down a separate corridor, but found neither woman present in it.

They must have already left, he thought, turning to head back to where his brother went. As he ran, he heard Darren scream, "Noooo!" and cry out the name of Alazar, pleading to the god of light, "Don't let it be this way!"

Ty's heart sank at the sound of Darren's wail of lament. *I've never heard him groan in agony like that. That's the sound someone makes when they've come across one of their loved ones dead,* Ty knew, wondering if it was Cassandra, Lucan, or both.

Ty ran as fast as he could to be by his brother's side, but when he came to the doorway, Grizz moved to stand in the way, preventing Ty from entering.

The Dwarf placed his hand on the Elf's shoulder. Not only was it an act of condolence, it was Grizz's attempt to slow Ty down to prepare him for what he was about to behold.

"I'm sorry for your loss," the Halfman stated. He shook his head back and forth as he gritted his teeth.

Stepping out of the way, Grizz allowed Ty to enter the room, where the Elf found Darren on his hands and knees, lying by Cassandra. Ty turned his head away immediately, unable to gaze upon the sight of his sister-in-law's mutilated body. It looked as if the orcs they'd just encountered outside had taunted her, tearing apart the top half of her outfit until she was naked, before killing her by stabbing her in her pregnant stomach.

Ty crouched on the ground and put his arms around his brother, holding him as Darren mourned the death of his wife.

The wails of the weeping warrior echoed down the hallway, following Grizz during his frantic search for Nash and Lucan.

They weren't in that room, so they must be hiding somewhere in the castle. Please don't let their fate be the same as Cassandra's, Grizz prayed as he flung open door after door, only finding empty rooms.

From the end of one hallway near one of the castle's towers, Grizz heard the barks of Copper, so he ran to the door, only to find it locked from the inside.

Wasting no time, Grizz turned his suit of armor into heavy rock, warned, "Stand back!" and charged through the door shoulder-first.

"Nash?" he called out before even scanning the room.

As Copper came up to Grizz, brushing against him and wagging his tail, Grizz watched as Nash and Lucan, both unharmed, crawled out from under the room's bed.

"Dad!" Nash cried, running into his father's arms, who'd fallen to his knees.

The grown Dwarf engulfed his eight-year-old, grabbing the back of his head and holding it against his chest.

"Thank you, Alazar! And thank you, Copper," Grizz rubbed the direfox's head.

"Mrs. Canard gave us a key and told us to run here with Copper and lock the door from inside while she went and got help," Nash explained. "What's going on out there?"

Nash wasn't the only one in the room with questions. Before Grizz answered Nash, the blonde-haired five-year-old asked, "Did you see my mom, Mr. Grindstone?"

What do I say to Lucan? Grizz thought long and hard about how to respond. *Should I take him to be with his dad, where he'll see his mother's body, or should I spare him the sight since he's so young?*

With a deep sigh, reflecting on his own mother's murder when he was a boy, Grizz sheathed Skullcrusher behind his back and took Lucan's hand in one of his hands and Nash's in the other. Copper trotted along, following behind as Grizz led the boys and placed them in the room next to where Darren mourned.

"Lucan and Nash are safe next door," Grizz quietly entered and told the Elven brothers. "Copper's safe too," he gestured to the direfox, who walked up to Darren and licked the warrior's hand.

He barely even knows Darren, but as he does with everyone, Copper can sense the pain someone's in and wants to help, Ty got up and pet the monster.

"Ty, go find Shana," Darren stood, wiping his watery eyes and running nose. "I know she can fend for herself, but I also know you'll feel much more comfortable being by her side to help protect her."

"There should be horses in the castle's stables you can take," Grizz also encouraged Ty to go find his girlfriend. "I'll stay here and guard the castle from any more monsters."

"Alright," Ty nodded, hugging Darren one more time, who grabbed a quilt and placed it over Cassandra so that he could bring Lucan in to say goodbye to his mother.

Grizz stepped out of the doorway again, this time letting Ty out of the room instead of in. The two clasped each other's shoulders, wordlessly wishing each other safety before Ty took off running to grab a horse and head down into the city.

Chapter 151

"The library's near here," Shana took her mom's hand and spoke urgently. "It has an underground section that'll be the safest place for you to hide while I fight."

She led Leiana down streets towards the building, but when she came to a plaza on the way there, three orcs atop Animal Monsters were rounding up civilians like dogs herding sheep. A few warriors among the group attempted to fight back, but the mounted assailants slayed them.

"I have to save them," Shana told her mom, staring in horror as the orcs returned to the group and began killing people who were kneeling and had their hands over their heads.

"They've surrendered!" she sprinted forward, pointing her spear at the closest orc. She fired a pulse of wind from the weapon, which ripped the monster from the saddle of the direwolf it rode upon. Its body crashed through the window of a nearby building and remained out of sight.

The direwolf charged Shana, who stood her ground, but angrily thought to herself, *I wish I had my shield with me. I grew complacent, thinking we were safe here and I didn't need it.*

Staying where she was, Shana flung throwing daggers at the gray beast, but when they didn't slow it, she planted her spear on the ground. Angling the weapon a second before the monster pounced allowed its sharp, metal tip to impale the direwolf through its gut.

Shana pulled the spear out and had the opportunity to kill the beast, but was hesitant, unsure if she should deliver the fatal blow when she knew it was already going to die.

The direwolf capitalized on her indecisiveness and as its last act, jumped up and swung its massive paw at its Human enemy, slicing through her armor and gashing her between two rib bones. Shana winced, but was undeterred as she fired a powerful, concentrated blast of wind, sending the beast through the air where it crashed to the ground and died.

Instead of continuing to murder the collected citizens who'd surrendered, the two remaining riders charged at Shana, but a bright flash of orange in the distance blinded them both. Shana turned to see what produced such an explosion, and in that same moment, noticed its shockwave careen through the area they were in. Before it reached her, Shana focused on the blast and used her element to prevent herself from being hit. It was almost as if she was in a protective bubble as all around her the ground shook and every glass window nearby shattered.

"Mom! Are you okay?" Shana asked, running to Leiana's side. She, the orcs, and many of the people who'd been trapped and rounded up by the monsters had been knocked down from the explosion's shockwave.

"I'm fine," Leiana stood, wiping broken pieces of glass off her body. "What was that?"

"I think monsters ignited and destroyed one of our two blackpowder depots," she nearly cried, knowing the amount of time and resources that went into collecting the materials. Then, hearing the growls of the two remaining direwolves, Shana told her mom, "I'll take care of these monsters, you get these people to the library or whatever other shelter you can find."

Leiana refused to leave her daughter's side, so she stayed nearby and pointed in the direction of safety for another woman to lead everyone to. Shana gladly took advantage of the space she had to attack without restraint.

Direwolves don't have elemental powers, and neither of these orcs have green skin. That means I have total control over all the air in my vicinity. They can't stop what I'm about to do.

Summoning the wind to glide along the ground towards herself, she used it to levitate all the pieces of broken glass. Adding to her attack's power, she pointed the tip of her spear to the sky and shot a continuous stream of wind out of it, then mentally controlling both the natural and summoned wind, she created a vortex that spun vertically around her.

With the hundreds of pieces of broken glass as part of her tornado, not to mention the rain caught up in her summoning, Shana pointed her spear at the helpless orcs who'd climbed back atop their mounts. In an impressive blast, she sent all the wind and sharp debris at them. Their deaths were quick, painless, and inevitable due to the severity of the attack.

The extensive power required used up so much of Shana's energy, she nearly collapsed, but her mom caught her before she fell.

The first orc Shana had sent through a window arose, grabbed its horn, and blew into its mouthpiece, alerting all nearby monsters to its location. Either the expelling of the air from its lungs was too much for it to handle, or it had been injured from Shana's attack, because it fell over halfway through its attempted contact for reinforcements.

"We have to get out of here!" Leiana told her daughter, urging her to follow to the safety of the library.

"It's too far. I can't make it," Shana held her side. Blood poured from her wound. She managed to take a few steps before stumbling and putting all her weight on her spear to hold herself up.

"Come on, it's only a short distance, only a few streets away!" Leiana pleaded. She nervously glanced at the roads leading into the plaza, knowing monster reinforcements would arrive at any moment, and her daughter was in no condition to fight them.

Chapter 152

Steve, Kari, and Commander Ostravaski rode through Twin Peaks' tented section of Almiria. First, they passed Graynor, who used his giant figure and voice to rally men to himself and efficiently lead them against the monsters. Then, minutes later, the group came upon where Dvorak and his warriors battled. Ty, Grizz, and Darren had already run through this area and seen the struggling general, but he struggled even more now. The Dwarven warrior leader had failed to capitalize on the support the aerial monsters provided. In the chaos, monsters atop their mounts slayed the disorganized warriors left and right as tents continued to burn all around them.

"General Dvorak," Steve called out as he galloped past the warrior leader, "gather as many horses and men as possible and ride with us to the castle. We're drawing the enemy there!"

All the way down the main path he raced upon, Steve repeatedly yelled to the warriors, "Follow me!" while swinging the flaming Aurelian Sword through any enemies that dared to approach his growing assembly of horse-mounted warriors. Kari sat behind him and shot ice-tipped arrows, while more and more men took up the call and followed the fire-armored Stephen Brightflame.

"Ty!" Steve called to his brother, who was coming down the castle's hill as Steve made his way up it.

"Woah! Woah!" the Elf pulled up on the reins, slowing his mount.

With the three of Alazar's Elect stopping to meet, Ostravaski led the group of nearly one-hundred warriors to the top of the hill where he began organizing their ranks. General Dvorak argued he should be in charge, but in six words, half of which were vulgar, Ostravaski shot down the Dwarf's assertation.

Taking a deep breath, heartbroken to have to deliver the news of their sister-in-law's death, Ty spoke loudly enough so Steve and Kari could hear him over the battalion moving past them, "Monsters got to the castle before we made it there. Darren and Lucan are alive, but they killed Cassandra."

No! Steve's eyes filled with tears at the thought that Darren lost the love of his life. His mind immediately moved to Lucan, and how terrible it was for a child to lose their mother.

"How are they?" Steve asked, wondering about the state of his older brother and nephew.

Ty couldn't form a verbal answer, so he just shook his head.

"What about Shana, Copper, and Grizz's son?" Kari asked, eager to know the fate of their friends.

"Grizz is with Copper and Nash, but Shana must've left before the attack. I think she went to the westside of the city to the library. I'm headed there now to find her."

"Go that way," Kari pointed to a narrow access road leading down the side of the hill. "There'll be fewer monsters. We're trying to lead them here, away from the rest of the city."

"I'll come back with Shana as soon as I can," Ty promised, combing back the wet strands of his hair, and taking off.

Steve and Kari joined up with Commander Ostravaski, General Dvorak, and all the gray-and-black-armored Twin Peaks warriors who survived the attack and regrouped with them.

Out of the hundred collected in the courtyard in front of the castle, fifty were on horses, lined up in nearly perfect columns and rows, while the other fifty had no mounts.

At the bottom of the hill, monsters atop their mounts also gathered. A brown minotaur with a broken horn rode back and forth before them, barking orders to those under his command.

"That's not Ironmaul," Steve stated aloud.

"No, his name is Taurusen," Ostravaski knew the monster's identity. "He serves directly under Ironmaul, but he's nearly as strong, so don't underestimate him. He's killed many warriors I've known with his lightning element." As the commander spoke, some of their enemies in the growing crowd of monsters below blew their horns, again alerting others they had found Alazar's Elect.

"Ironmaul and more of their forces will be here soon," Dvorak announced. "We should attack now."

When Steve looked to Ostravaski, the commander didn't oppose the idea, and for the first time found himself in agreement with Twin Peaks' general.

"You may have led Casanovia, Almiria, and Misengard in battles, but there are many in your army who you have yet to gain their trust on the battlefield. These are your men now to lead, Brightflame."

Steve nodded and accepted the responsibility without issue. "If we're going to retreat once Ironmaul and others converge here, let's at least take out one of their army's highest-ranking officials first."

"I'm more effective with ranged attacks, so I'm going back with the men on foot," Kari leaned forward and kissed Steve's cheek before hopping off their horse.

"Promise you'll survive and come back to me," she looked up to where he sat tall on his mount.

"I promise," Steve nodded, grinning at how Kari asking him to make such a declaration before battles showed how much she valued him and their relationship.

Once Ostravaski ordered a warrior to hand their shield and helm over to Steve to give him extra protection, Steve took a deep breath, preparing himself for battle. He trotted his horse out to the frontline so all the gathered warriors could see him, much like what the minotaur Taurusen was doing below. Brightening the fire upon him to an even higher degree, Steve gained his men's attention and, wasting no time, yelled, "Ready your weapons! We attack now! Fight with me and let us drive the enemy out of this city!"

Spurring on his horse with a warcry that was carried up by the men behind him, Steve charged forward. Heading downhill allowed him to pick up speed, much faster than Taurusen and the monsters pushing up the inclined slope.

Steve headed straight for the minotaur, blocking his enemy's blast of lightning on his shield. He swung Aurelia once he was in proximity, but the minotaur deflected the blow with its sword.

With his momentum not slowing, Steve continued forward, chopping off the arm of an orc and sending a plume of fire out of his shield towards another enemy before his horse collided with another. Both steeds kept their balance, neither able to fall over because of the tight confines of those engaged in battle all around them.

As soon as Steve unwillingly slowed and couldn't move anywhere due to the congestion, his head snapped back as the riders who'd been charging behind him crashed into his horse. The momentum of other warriors carried them farther ahead into the enemy lines until they too, had no room to advance. The warriors who'd been on foot filled in whatever spaces they could, while Kari and anyone who preferred a bow over a sword stood back in a line and picked off monsters as best they could.

With the army mixed in with monsters all around him, the battle quickly became a mad free-for-all. An orc whose mount had been killed reached up, grabbed Steve, and ripped him down from his saddle. The monster went to slam its hammer down onto Steve, but Ostravaski sliced its back open before it could. Steve returned the favor by impaling an orc who fired a blast of wind at the commander, trying to knock the Giant from his mount.

Instead of squeezing forward, Steve allowed Ostravaski to lead that charge while he headed back the way he'd come. Avoiding the vicious bites of direwolves, stingers of spiders, tusks of direboars, and the blades of the monsters who rode atop them, he pushed his way to Taurusen.

The brown-furred minotaur had an arrow in his shoulder and multiple gashes across his body, but pain only intensified his attack as he cut through the leg of a horse, killed its rider, and killed three more warriors around him before Steve could make it close enough to stop him.

With his lightning sword, Taurusen swung wildly at Steve, who avoided the attacks by ducking out of the way or batting the minotaur's sword with his shield.

When Steve went on the offensive, instead of dodging or deflecting, Taurusen fought to stop Steve at the point of his attack, closing the space between them and catching Steve's sword arm in his hand before Steve could follow through. The minotaur drove his knee upwards into Steve's stomach with so much power it lifted Steve's feet off the ground.

Since Taurusen held his grip around Steve's wrist, Steve made the fire on his gauntlets even hotter, burning the minotaur's hand and forcing him to let go. Once he did, Steve resumed his offensive attack, but failed to land a mortal wound to the skilled minotaur.

The minotaur's and Human's one-on-one battle remained evenly matched until an orc snuck up behind the preoccupied Steve to drive its lance through the fire-armored Human. Luckily, Taurusen noticed the dishonorable attacker and sent a blast of lightning through the rain, killing the orc before it could impale the red-armored warrior he enjoyed fighting.

Similarly to the orc, a Twin Peaks warrior capitalized on the minotaur being distracted and ran in to attack Taurusen.

I can't kill one of our own men, Steve shook his head, unwilling to send a plume of fire out of Aurelia or his shield to save Taurusen. Instead, he alerted the minotaur by calling out, "Behind you!"

Taurusen turned, deflected the incoming blade, and kicked the warrior, sending him somersaulting backwards across the ground. Instead of resuming his battle against Steve, he headed straight for the gray and brown-armored man, seeking to end the warrior's life.

"Brightflame!" Ostravaski rode up to where Steve rested his hands on his knees, trying to catch his breath. "It's time to retreat! We need to get you to an escape passage in the castle. Ironmaul arrived with a bunch more monsters. He's killing everyone at the frontlines."

"Ironmaul," Steve seethed, marching forward.

Ostravaski moved to block the warrior with his horse. "Listen to me, Stephen, we've lost nearly all our men in this area. General Dvorak and the warriors close to him are all dead. Some gave their lives so I could ride back here to warn you. The forces we gathered were already outnumbered, but now with our casualties, the monsters have more than triple what we have."

"I won't run and hide like a coward!" Steve argued, once again trying to press forward and attack.

Ostravaski dismounted his horse to speak to Steve face to face. "I'll knock you out and drag you to safety if I have to!" he yelled. Then, taking a moment to compose himself, seeing his emotional response only made Steve want to pull away, the commander grabbed the warrior's shoulders to prevent him from moving and looked down on the Human as he tried to reason with him. "It was admirable to lead the enemy here, away from the others. No one doubts your courage to fight, but there's too many of them. We tried to make a stand, but we failed. It's better to live to fight another day than to lose this war tonight. Please," the commander begged, an odd appeal from a man known for being gruff and stoic. "I'll even call the retreat for you."

"I can call for it," Steve finally relented. His shoulders sagged in disappointment. "I called them into battle, so it should be me who calls them out."

It took a deep breath and a willingness to forgo his pride for Steve to force himself to utter the words as loudly as he could in every direction. "Retreat! Get up to the castle!" He, Ostravaski, and the few surviving Twin Peaks warriors ran up the hill, while Kari and the other archers rapidly fired arrows, killing any enemies that dared follow them.

Eventually, the archers' success forced the monsters to stop giving chase, allowing the warriors to regroup near the castle. Before they entered, everyone turned upon hearing the horde of monsters repeatedly slam their weapons against their shields. Their Animal Monsters added their growls to the drum-like sound and together the entire portion of the riders who'd attacked the Twin Peaks section of Almiria split down the middle.

Ironmaul, Steve said to himself, watching the hulking black-furred minotaur stride down the passageway his forces had opened for him. He rode atop a menacing direwolf Steve remembered the monster had once been referred to by the name 'Ash.'

Ironmaul reached the base of the hill, hopped off his mount, and took a giant, bloodied hammer out of the sheath across his back. For any man, it would've required two hands to wield, but the minotaur had no problem swinging the heavy weapon with the might of his bulging muscles.

When Ironmaul took out a whip from a belt on his hip, his monsters stopped their deep, ominous drumming, allowing those looking down on them from the top of the hill to hear their horned leader's challenge.

"Send down the one who controls fire so I can battle him one-on-one," Ironmaul roared. "Let us have a fight to the death!"

Chapter 153

"We're too late," Leiana cried, hearing a horse quickly approaching before she and Shana could make it out of the plaza following the orc alerting others to its location.

Instead of monsters, however, it was Ty, with his blonde-hair and yellow armor, who emerged through the rain and galloped up to them. Sparks and electric voltage continuously spread across his lightning armor.

The sight of her boyfriend instantly made Shana smile despite being worn out from her high-energy attack. It was a sentiment short-lived, though, considering the carnage done to citizens on the far side of the plaza and the violence she knew was happening throughout the city.

"I'm glad you're both alive!" Ty breathed a sigh of relief, casting a glance at the dead direwolves and their riders, stuck full of glass shards. "I saw the civilians heading into the library and they pointed me in this direction. Leiana, you should head there. Shana, we need to get to the castle. Steve and Kari are trying to draw the enemy there to make a stand."

Leiana grimaced, nervous to let her injured daughter run off to continue fighting such dangerous monsters, but she nodded and quickly hugged Shana to see her off. As soon as she pulled out of the embrace, an arrow zipped through the air, piercing Shana through the center of her chest. She stumbled backwards from the powerful impact and fell to her knees in disbelief. The metal tip had impaled itself all the way through her body and came out her back.

Even if she didn't succumb to the fatal blow, a second arrow ensured she wouldn't survive, this one ripping through vital organs and embedding itself deep in her stomach.

"No!" Leiana screamed, horrified at the sight of her injured daughter clutching at the wooden shafts sticking out of her torso.

Ty cried out as well, and along with Leiana, instinctively lunged to catch Shana as she tried to stand, but fell back to her knees. A third arrow flew in the moment they both got to her, this one piercing through Leiana's neck.

Because of her punctured lung, Shana let out a breathless scream as she watched her mother's body collapse to the ground. Leiana's mouth gaped open in an unsightly way that made it clear she was already gone.

"We need to get to cover!" Ty panickedly told his girlfriend, refusing to believe she was dying. He tried pulling her towards the nearest building, but Shana was unwilling to leave her mother's body. Ty had no choice but to drag her away. As he did so, an arrow whizzed past his ear, narrowly missing him.

If I don't stop this attacker, I'm going to be struck too, he knew, glancing back for the briefest of seconds to see that it wasn't a monster, but the silhouette of a person aiming their bow at them. As Ty continued escorting Shana, he pointed his sword at the rooftops around where the figure was and blindly fired blasts of lightning in the area of the assassin.

Crashing through a door and taking cover in a room, Ty laid Shana down, pulled out the arrow shafts, and quickly removed her armor to check her wounds. He knew they were severe, but his eyes widened in horror when he saw how bad they actually were. Blood poured up and out of the gaping holes, which Ty tried pressing down upon, but even more blood oozed out, pooling in between each of his fingers.

"It hurts! It hurts!" Shana cried, tossing her head back and forth. She groaned in agony, not only because of the physical pain she was in, but also because of the emotional pain of having to watch her mother brutally murdered. She began coughing as she spoke, choking on the blood coming up her throat.

"I don't want to die!" she gurgled out. Her face grew paler with each passing second.

"Stay with me!" Ty cried. He helplessly looked around the room, trying to find fabric, clothes, or anything he could use to slow the bleeding. When he found nothing in sight, he shook his head and raised his palms upwards. "I don't know what to do!" His chin quivered and tears filled his eyes, matching the ones Shana had in hers.

Using what little energy she had left, Shana grabbed onto the Elf and pulled herself up. She tried to speak, but the words only came out in horrid, indecipherable gurgles. Knowing the last of her life was draining out of her, she hugged Ty, not wanting him to have to watch her as she died.

Ty felt Shana's body go limp as she embraced him. For a long time, he stayed holding her, since he knew pulling away would be giving into the reality she was dead. The poor Elf sat alone in the dark room, crying in disbelief and heartbreak over the death that could not be undone.

Chapter 154

As Darren took Lucan into the room Cassandra was murdered in and tried to explain death and the fact that the five-year-old's mother would no longer be around, Grizz left the father and son alone to comfort Nash. Although he could hear a battle raging outside, he cared more about being with his son rather than fighting.

Nash sat wiping his eyes, crying for his friend who he could hear sobbing in the next room over. Grizz took a seat next to where Nash sat against the wall with his knees pulled up to his chest and listened to his son vent. "I'm tired of these attacks, Dad. I'm tired of this war and all this death."

"I know. Me too," Grizz put his arm around the boy. "But always remember every minute that passes is a minute closer to peace."

For a moment, they sat alone trying to block out Lucan and Darren's cries and the fighting outside. Finally, Grizz stood to peer out the window and told Nash, "The Twin Peaks warriors are losing badly. They need me out there."

"I don't want you to go," Nash pleaded. "Every time you leave I get scared."

Through the rain, Grizz watched Steve and Kari and a few other warrior survivors make it up to the top of the castle's hill, not far from the room he looked out from. At the bottom of the hill, the monster horde amassed.

With our dwindled numbers, there's no way we can find victory unless all of our allies in Almiria come to our aid, but each section is fighting their own battles, Grizz looked out across the landscape to see smoke columns rising from various places and the flashes of color here and there as monsters used their elemental abilities.

"I have to help," he told Nash. "I have a responsibility to my friends."

"You have a responsibility to me as your son."

"I do, and it's teaching you to do what is good and right in this world. The best way I can do that is to lead by example."

Grizz's brown armor pieces rattled as he stood, marched to Darren and Lucan's room, and quietly retrieved Copper. He allowed the father and son to continue mourning, but brought the direfox to Nash and said, "Copper will protect you until I return. I need to leave now."

"Please, don't go!" Nash begged again, clutching at his father's leg.

In previous years, Grizz would've roughly pulled his son off of him and scolded him, but now he remained patient and cleared his throat, a signal Nash knew meant his actions were inappropriate. Nash released his grip and went back to sitting against the wall next to Copper.

Grizz took the chance to impart wisdom to his son, gazing down to him and sharing, "This world will only grow darker if those in power don't help those in need. I know you don't want me to go out there, but it's what I have to do, and I hope you can understand that."

He bent down and kissed his son on the top of the head, rubbed Copper's fur, and then took off towards the castle's entrance.

Pointing his hammer at Steve, Ironmaul reiterated his demand by yelling to the top of the hill, "You, red-armored warrior, come and face me!"

With one glance at Steve, Kari knew from his hair matted with rain and sweat and his heavy breathing from battling Taurusen that the chances of him defeating Ironmaul were slim. "Don't do this, Steve," she told him, seeing that he was considering accepting the challenge. "He's one of the biggest and strongest monsters the Hooded Phantom has."

Commander Ostravaski agreed with the Halfling. "I'll tell you where the castle's hidden passageway is so you two can escape. Let us remaining warriors buy you time."

Kari grabbed Steve's arm and whispered to him, trying to provide a sense of calmness to the intensity of the situation. "Our army still needs you to lead them. We've suffered losses tonight, but we aren't defeated." She jerked her head towards the castle, pleading with him to withdraw to safety.

"I'll take on the minotaur," someone came up from behind them and spoke, having emerged from inside the castle.

The group turned to find Grizz, already holding Skullcrusher in his hands with his armor suit covered in rock.

"Grizz, no!" Kari shook her head, not wanting to see the Dwarf take on such a dangerous monster alone.

"It's okay," Grizz stared into the Halfling's blue eyes with his soft brown ones. He pointed to Commander Ostravaski and the Twin Peaks warriors that remained. "If

I fall in battle, these men will hold off the enemies long enough for you two to escape with Nash and Lucan. At the very least, I'll be able to weaken this monster for them."

At first, Steve wanted to do everything in his power to prevent the Dwarf from fighting on his behalf, but one look from Grizz changed his mind.

"You can do this," Steve encouraged his friend, finally accepting that the battle against the minotaur who tortured him would not be his. "Make Ironmaul wish he never brought his forces here."

Grizz nodded, turned to the enemy waiting for him, and began walking down the hill. He picked up his walk into a jog, and then his jog into a sprint, heading directly for the minotaur.

With his dual-headed weapon encased in rock, Grizz spun its hilt over and over in his hands as he ran, leaving it to chance to determine which side of the weapon's head he would attack with first.

When it landed on the hammerside he called Skullcrusher, he raised the weapon mightily over his head and swung it down as hard as he could. Instead of aiming for the minotaur, the Dwarf hit the ground, causing the top few inches of muddy soil to explode out from the center of where his hammer landed.

The ripple lost its intensity the farther it traveled, but it did what Grizz intended, forcing the surrounding monsters and their mounts to step back and give him space in the one-on-one battle.

"No interference," he warned Ironmaul, who remained where he was, unflinched by the attack since the monster used his own earth element to force it to move around him.

The minotaur responded by grunting and rushing forward, wildly swinging his own hammer of rock, which Grizz batted away with Skullcrusher. The impact sounded exactly like one would expect if two boulders slammed into each other at high speed.

"Do you think he can win?" Kari clutched Steve's arm as they stood together and watched the heavy-hitting battle.

"I don't know, but he must believe he can. There was no fear in his eyes when he accepted the challenge."

"Everyone, stand ready," Ostravaski shouted to the surrounding warriors. "Either the Halfman defeats this minotaur and we resume the fight in driving these monsters away, or he loses and we hold them off so Steve and Kari can escape." The commander then looked to the couple he stood with and told them, "You can lift up the fourth and fifth stairs in the back tower to uncover a hatch if you need to escape."

With one look at Steve, Kari could tell retreating was the last thing he wanted to do. *Please win, Grizz. Our army's morale will never recover if we have to flee and regroup somewhere else.*

At the base of the hill, Grizz slammed Skullcrusher into Ironmaul's armored shoulder, stumbling the minotaur with the heavy blow. His follow-up attack failed to have the same success as Grizz whiffed on his powerful swing and took the brunt of his foe's hammer into his chest.

Even though rock armor typically offered vigorous defense and made it difficult to get stabbed or impaled, it did little to protect from hard-hitting attacks from the same element. It was like a warrior wearing a helm. The helm protected them from glancing blows, but a direct hit could damage the skull or even the brain inside. Likewise, Grizz and Ironmaul's bones and muscles could still be broken or bruised because of the severity of their attacks.

Their brawl lacked technique, style, and counterattacks, and was instead a straight-up match of endurance and strength, in which each of them swung their weapon into their enemy as hard as they could.

Grizz took another blow to his chest, this one more powerful than before, breaking his sternum and nearly forcing him to drop to a knee to recover. The monsters who'd formed a half-circle around him and Ironmaul whooped and hollered, elated that their leader landed a devastating blow. But the jeering and pain only enraged and empowered Grizz. He ignored the pain in his chest and retaliated with a powerful, angry, earth-shaking strike to Ironmaul's midsection. He heard a cracking sound and the minotaur snort in pain as the monster's ribs broke underneath his armor plate.

Just as pain incensed Grizz, it also infuriated Ironmaul, who held his hammer at arm's length and spun 360 degrees, using momentum to add to the power of his attack.

Instead of stepping out of the way of the aggressive attack, Grizz trusted the craftmanship of the weapon he'd forged and swung the anvil side into Ironmaul's mallet with as much strength as he could muster. The head of the minotaur's weapon broke and partially fell apart, its large, iron pieces losing their rock covering the moment they hit the ground. No longer did they touch the weapon held by Ironmaul, so no longer could he activate his element through them.

With only a section of his hammer still intact on the end of its handle, Ironmaul used one hand to wield the broken weapon while grabbing his whip with the other. Grizz swung viciously, hoping to land a critical hit, but the aggressive strike failed to find its mark, leaving him unbalanced and unwillingly turned around.

Ironmaul capitalized on the Dwarf's mistake and slammed his broken mallet into Grizz's spine. The rest of his weapon broke upon impact, but the damage was done. Grizz's legs went numb and he fell to his knees. Skullcrusher fell from his hands and bounced just out of reach in front of him.

He broke my back! Grizz knew, wincing from the severe pain. Since he couldn't use his legs, he tried crawling forward to grab his weapon, but Ironmaul lashed his whip and wrapped it around Grizz's ankle. Hand over hand, the monster pulled the Dwarf backwards through the dirt and away from Skullcrusher.

With his dark-skinned enemy beneath him, Ironmaul reached down, ripped off Grizz's armor, and threw each piece into the cheering horde. As the monsters fought over the pieces so they could have them for themselves, the minotaur began using his whip and rock-covered boots to lash, kick, and stomp the armorless Dwarf, brutally assaulting the Halfman.

"No!" Steve cried out from where he watched. He took a step forward to aid Grizz, but Ostravaski held him back. The Giant solemnly shook his head, wordlessly telling Steve there was nothing he could do to stop the violence.

"I can't watch this!" Kari buried her face in Steve's chest as he put his arm around her to comfort her the best he could.

Unlike his Halfling girlfriend, Steve watched with a furrowed brow and gritted teeth. *I know what's about to happen, and there's nothing I can do to stop it!*

While Grizz lie writhing on the ground, panting and groaning in pain, Ironmaul slowly walked over to Skullcleaver.

The minotaur picked up the half-axe, half-hammer, examining it in his hands with an impressed smile. Pointing the two-headed weapon at the red-armored warrior glaring down at him from the top of the hill, Ironmaul never let his gaze waver from Steve as he walked over to Grizz, raised the bladed axe above his head, and slammed it down deep into the Dwarf's stomach.

Chapter 155

Commander Ostravaski and all the Twin Peaks warriors bowed their heads at the fatal blow, leaving only Steve refusing to break eye contact with Ironmaul, seething as he glared at the minotaur.

The monster smirked, slid the weapon into the sheath across his back, and stared at Steve as he announced to his horde, "Our work here is done! Let the survivors know our power as they wallow in the death of their fallen."

Finally turning around, he stared down at the Dwarf writhing on the ground and kicked him again. Then, the minotaur climbed onto his direwolf and shouted to all those under his command, "Sound our victory and let our riders know we're headed back to Celestial!"

The group cheered and yelled, spurring on the beasts they rode upon, leaving Grizz behind in the cloud of dust they kicked up.

"I'm going to him!" Steve claimed, rushing to be by the Dwarf's side in his final moments. Kari followed along and the closer she got she saw the blow from the axe had been so forceful it'd nearly cut through him completely.

Grizz did a sort of half-sit-up, pressing his fingers against his gaping wound, trying to push it closed. In realizing the futility of his actions, he laid his head on the ground, and spoke to the sky, "I can't believe this is how I die."

"We're right here with you," Steve grabbed the Dwarf's hand.

"Hurry and go get Nash Grindstone!" Kari yelled up to the top of the hill. "He should be inside." Before anyone moved to carry out the order, the Dwarven boy appeared in the castle's front doorway alongside Copper. Tears already streamed from his eyes.

Oh no, Kari winced. *He witnessed the whole fight from the castle.* She noticed Nash's pale-face and labored breathing. *He's scared to see the injury up close,* Kari could tell, and although she was correct, Nash surprised her by overcoming his fears. Halfway down the hill, he turned his walk into a run, most afraid of not being with his father as he died.

"Steve," Kari alerted him since he hadn't yet noticed the eight-year-old approaching. "Let's give Nash time alone with his father."

With no objections to the suggestion, and knowing the next words he spoke to Grizz would be his last, Steve said, "It was an honor to fight alongside you and to call you friend." He pulled away to step aside with Kari, but Grizz tightened his grip on Steve's hand, preventing the warrior from leaving. He looked up into the warrior's eyes and responded, "I wish I could've survived to see you reign. You're going to make a great king, Stephen Brightflame."

Grizz let go, so Steve stood and walked over to Kari, wrapping his arm around her as Copper came to sit next to them. Together, they all watched Nash bury his head in his father's chest and sob into Grizz's beard.

"Dad! Please don't die. You're all I have left!"

"Nash, I'm sorry. This isn't what I wanted for us," Grizz teared up himself as he ran his fingers through his son's dark hair and wiped the tears falling down Nash's cheeks.

"Does it hurt?" Nash asked, keeping his eyes on his father's face because he couldn't bear to look down at his open stomach. With each inhale Grizz took, there was a sloshing sound coming from the gaping wound. It repulsed Nash, but the boy was undeterred from leaving his father's side.

"No," Grizz answered, trying his best to smile and show he wasn't in pain even though he was. "Listen to me, son," he changed the subject, knowing the importance of each of his life's waning seconds. Although it caused agony for him to talk, he ignored his discomfort and shared, "There was still so much left I wanted to teach you, but I know you'll grow to be even better than I was. I'm so proud of you and what you've overcome.

A spasm jolted through Grizz's body, and although he did his best to hide his pain from Nash, it still forced him to grit his teeth and grimace in pain.

"Just try to breathe," Nash tried to sound as soothing as possible. He could tell his father was in agony and that his time was quickly ending. "I love you, dad," he made sure to say before it was too late.

"I love you, son." It took all of Grizz's willpower to utter the four words and lean forward and kiss Nash's forehead. When he laid back down, he closed his eyes, never to open them again.

Chapter 156

"Dad? Dad?!" Nash grabbed Grizz's shoulders and tried shaking him back to life.

Steve cautiously approached him, coming up behind the boy along with Copper, who whimpered and laid down across Grizz's legs. "He's gone to be with your mom and brother," Steve shared, trying to be as sensitive and compassionate to the child who'd yet again suffered devastating loss.

"This isn't fair!" Nash shouted and buried his face in his father's chest for a second time.

"I know, but-" Steve wanted to console the eight-year-old, but Kari came over and led her boyfriend away.

"He needs time to himself," she explained, holding back her tears. "I was only a few years younger than him when my mother died, so I know what it's like. The best thing we can do for those who've suffered loss is to give them space and comfort to grieve."

The Human and Halfling made their way over to Commander Ostravaski and Graynor. The latter of the two Giants had successfully fended off the other side of Twin Peak's camp from the attackers and mournfully watched Nash crying over his father's body. Although Steve and Kari had never been told of Grizz's connection to the former Twin Peaks general, they picked up on the link when Graynor eulogized, "Grindstone didn't have an easy life, but he grew from his mistakes and became a great father to his son."

"He suffered more tragedies in his twenty-eight years than someone who's lived a full life," Kari added. "And I'm sure he hates the fact he can't be here to raise Nash, but I like to imagine he's happy to be reunited with his wife and other son. He always talked about how much he loved them."

The rain tapered off to only a light sprinkle as the four stood there, reflecting on the attack that'd caused the death of the Dwarf and so many others. In the distance, the siege towers and other wooden constructions burned fiercely, set on fire by the monsters to ensure they couldn't be used against them in Celestial.

After a while of silent mourning as they watched the storm clouds move away to reveal the starry night and the bright brown and green moons, Commander Ostravaski asserted, "We should send our aerial monsters after the riders. We know they're headed back to Celestial. They'll be easy to find in Whitebark Woods."

"No," Steve immediately shot down the idea. "Malorek would've thought ahead and considered how they'd be vulnerable on the way back. He's probably ordered his aerial monsters to stand ready in Whitebark, hoping we take the bait and follow."

"If he flew aerial monsters near Almiria, why wouldn't he have used them in the attack?" Ostravaski questioned.

Steve didn't waste any time in answering. "Because Malorek sending his forces here to defeat us wasn't his primary aim. He could've done more damage if he wanted to. Instead, I think his intent was to send a message. By attacking Almiria at dark, he's now attacked us at every phase of the day. When you look at Celestial,

Casanovia, Oceanside, and now Almiria, his army has attacked morning, afternoon, and night and has also attacked through land, sea, and air. Malorek wants us to know he can defeat us any time he desires, through any means he desires."

"Plus," Kari chimed in, supporting Steve's argument, "by not attacking with his aerial monsters or sending more of his army here, he's showing us what his army is capable of when they're not even at full strength."

"You're both over-analyzing too much. By deeming Malorek so intelligent, you're crediting him with enough foresight that you believe he's set a trap. And because of that, we're missing out on an opportunity to avenge our fallen brethren."

"He is intelligent!" Steve countered. "Us elect saw his life play out in visions. Everything the Hooded Phantom does is purposeful and has meaning. Every order he gives is planned, calculated, organized, and methodical. To say it isn't is to underestimate him. And if we do that, we'll lose this war. Look what happens when we're caught unprepared!" he gestured to the bodies of Grizz and the warriors killed by Ironmaul's riders all around them.

Ostravaski, much in his alpha-dog type personality, spoke louder, trying to get the last word in. "I understand you saw visions, but I have years of experience, and if you're going to lead our army, you have to understand warfare is just as much mental as it is physical. It can drive you crazy trying to figure out your opponent's approaches and counter approaches, debating what they may or may not be doing. Allowing the enemy to get inside your head and play mind-games is dangerous. Graynor's a former general, he'd agree with me," the commander turned to the fellow giant.

"You're not wrong," Graynor spoke calmly, the opposite of Ostravaski's rough tone and demeanor, but with all due respect to you, commander, there's a time to be aggressive and go after the riders, but it's not now. Our army has suffered massive losses. We can't risk losing more. I don't know if there are aerial monsters in Whitebark waiting for us or not, but that's beside the point. Our priority now is caring for our dead and wounded, and regaining the morale of our army.

"Commander, if you want to be productive, go find Ty, Shana, Leiana, and Quintis, and bring them all here," Steve requested. "And if you come across any of our army's leaders, bring them along too," he added listing their names; "Willis, General Elesora, Cryonic, Ryland, Jun-Lei, and Artazair. I'm close with all of them and I want to make sure they're safe."

"I don't think that's the best idea. We've been betrayed. The number of people around you needs to be kept to a minimum until we figure out who this traitor is. We still don't know who to trust."

"This is not up for debate!" Steve shouted, ending yet another disagreement with Ostravaski. "I want them brought here now!"

The Giant nodded and left, trying to be respectful of the future king's wishes despite his apprehensions.

"Graynor, could you go check on Darren and his son in the castle?" Kari asked politely. "We could use some time alone."

"Of course," Graynor bowed and headed off.

"Ostravaski was just trying to help, you know," Kari told Steve, who she could tell felt like he disrespected their mournful surroundings by lashing out. "Just because he made it harder by not agreeing with you right away doesn't mean he needs to be yelled at."

"I know, I was wrong. I'm just stressed that we've lost so many warriors and took it out on him. Look at this," he again gestured to the bodies all around. "In less than an hour they caused so much destruction." His eyes came to a rest on Grizz's lifeless body, where Nash continued to mourn. "I can't believe he's gone."

Me either, Kari thought, unhappy that their Dwarven friend's story was completed with an unpalatable ending.

She watched Copper leave Nash's side and trot over to Steve. He nudged the warrior with the top of his head, as he often did when he sensed someone in distress.

"I know you and Grizz were good friends," Steve sympathized with the direfox, bending down and scratching Copper behind the ears.

While he did so, Copper barked, alerting Steve and Kari to Ty, who came riding on his horse into the area.

"Something's wrong," Steve told Kari, noticing Ty's pale face and red eyes as he dismounted his steed. From knowing the Elf his whole life, he could tell when Ty was troubled. But instead of Ty speaking with them, the Elf spotted Grizz's body, solemnly made his was over to it, and knelt down alongside Nash. The boy and the yellow-armored warrior spoke for a long time, uninterrupted. Following a long, tight hug, Ty grabbed his horse's reins and led the stallion over to his brother and Kari.

"I'm sorry you had to see Grizz like that," Steve apologized. "I wish we could've broken the news to you so it wasn't such a shock."

"Nash told me it was a black-furred minotaur that killed him," Ty spoke slowly and softly, uncharacteristic of his usual boisterous inflections.

"Ironmaul," Steve confirmed.

Ty sighed, heartbroken as he imagined the formidable monster felling the Dwarf that'd become a close friend.

"Grizz wasn't the only one we lost," he inhaled a deep breath and pinched the bridge of his nose with his thumb and pointer finger, trying not to cry. The technique proved useless. As his breathing became labored, his chest trembled and tears streamed from his eyes the longer he kept in the news he knew he had to share.

"Shana's dead too!" he uttered, collapsing to his knees as if the words that spilled from his mouth came back and punched him in the gut. On all fours, he wept. Kari ran to him, fell to the ground alongside him, and embraced him in a caring hug. Copper picked up on their emotions, whined, and laid down on the other side of Ty while Steve stood silent at the revelation of his half-sister's death.

It was a long minute before he began crying himself, overcome by the loss of their companions. "Ty, I'm so sorry."

"Leiana's gone too," Ty choked out. "I saw the person who did it from afar. It wasn't a monster."

One of the traitors, Steve knew, clenching his fists. *Everything we've done, everything we've accomplished, how can we have lost so much of it so quickly? Maybe Ryland was right, maybe Captain Ortega and his captains are sabotaging us, but now we know they're working with the Hooded Phantom. They informed Malorek of our position in Almiria so he could send his riders to come and weaken our army.*

For over an hour, longer than even the length of the attack, Steve, Ty, and Kari stayed where they were, too shocked and despaired to get up and move. Warriors moved back and forth around them, cleaning up the damage and destruction. Many salvaged what they could from the burned tents, some of which reignited on their own and needed to be extinguished by aerial monsters now that the rain had let up. A few of the warriors tasked themselves with collecting the bodies of the fallen. Using wooden boards, they carried each body individually to an open field where civilians that'd survived the attack dug graves. Nash accompanied Grizz's body, refusing to leave his father's side.

Eventually, Commander Ostravaski rode up to Steve, Ty, and Kari. His face was solemn and grim, forewarning of the bad news he was about to share.

"Is my dad alive?" Kari asked, holding her breath.

"Yes, Quintis led those from Holders Keep well. They all worked together to take out many riders," the Giant reassured her while dismounting his steed. He then turned to Steve to speak, but before he could, Steve said,

"Commander, I need to apologize for earlier-"

"Don't bother," Ostravaski interrupted him, "we were both irritable over what happened. Besides, you might still be angry with me."

"What do you mean?"

"I confirmed those you asked me to retrieve were safe, but I couldn't follow your order and risk bringing them to you knowing we've been betrayed. You don't know how valuable your life is, and I'll protect it even if I have to disobey your commands."

Steve thought for a moment, and then shrugged, not allowing himself to get upset at the circumstances of the insubordination. "In this instance, it's fine since I mainly cared about learning they survived. Can you tell me what you found?"

In a solemn voice, far different from his booming, assertive tone, the commander shared, "What happened here in the Twin Peaks section occurred all throughout Almiria. Every camp suffered massive casualties from the unexpected attack. Some more than others, but all more than they should have. The numbers will undoubtedly rise, but as it is now, we've counted 474 dead and 510 wounded with such severe injuries they won't be any use to us going forward. Altogether, it's a percentage of our army we really needed."

This hurts our chances of winning, Steve knew, casting his gaze downward. *Even with half of Malorek's army defeated in Casanovia and the Frostlands, we're still vastly outnumbered. I'll never forget the sheer amount of monsters that attacked Celestial.*

There are more deaths you should know about, Ostravaski told Steve, Ty, and Kari. "Brightflame, Kari," he pointed to the couple, "You were with me when we saw General Dvorak fall, but Twin Peaks wasn't the only Primary City that suffered a high number of casualties. Misengard did as well. Captain Ortega survived, but the riders killed most of his warriors."

"Ortega's men?" Steve shook his head in confusion. "They were fighting?"

"Yes, the monsters they battled were the last to leave. Ortega ordered his men to block their escape. They killed many, but the price was high.'"

Ortega and his captains can't be the traitors, then. Ryland was mistaken, or he knowingly lied to me, Steve realized. He closed his eyes and pondered deeply, considering if Ryland was the traitor. *It can't be him either, though. He's helped us so much in the fight against the Hooded Phantom.*

With the mystery of the saboteur now more perplexing than even before, Steve asked Ostravaski, "Can you have a tail put on Ryland Artisan? I need his every move to be watched without him knowing. Steve gestured to his Elf and Halfling companions, and said, "Once we're ready, Kari, Ty, and I will sit down and discuss who else in our ranks we want to have followed. We need to find out who this traitor is before they cause more harm to our efforts."

"I'll put my most trusted sentries on whoever you come up with," Ostravaski nodded. He then returned to his somber tone and mentioned, "There's one more death I'm sorry I have to inform you of. All three of you were close to this person," he looked from Steve, to Ty, to Kari. "A handful of the enemy riders went to the harbor and attacked there. They killed the shipmaster of Andonia. Jun-Lei."

Taken aback at the revelation, Steve uttered, "No!" and shook his head in disbelief. He stared up at the stars and sighed. *Jun-Lei was the heart and soul of Andonia. Kyoko must be crushed, not to mention Haruto and Min-Ye.*

Running through the deaths in his mind, he pictured the faces of each of those lost that pained him deeply. *Jun-Lei, Leiana, Cassandra, Cassandra's unborn baby, Grizz, Shana.*

Next to him, Ty and Kari's eyes welled, also imagining those that died.

"Who caused this?" Ty drawled out through gritted teeth. His anger increased in every word he pronounced as he spat each one. "They alerted the Hooded Phantom to Almiria, killed the sentries so the riders could go undetected, and killed so many people we loved."

"I don't know, but we'll find out. Whoever it is will be put to death," Steve promised. "Until then, we'll continue with our plans. Our attack on Celestial will commence."

As Steve spoke, his sword turned to rock, his armor turned green, and the wind began circling around him. He closed his eyes, accepting the fact that the elements of his fallen comrades now belonged to him. When he opened them, he announced with renewed ambition, "The Hooded Phantom, Nightstrike, IronMaul, this betrayer; they're going to pay for what they've done. We're going to free our people and reclaim our home. It's time to end this war once and for all!"

The *Story of Evil* will conclude in...

THE
STORY OF EVIL

Volume V: Battle for the Kingdom

After the companions split up and traveled throughout the kingdom to recruit fighters to their cause, they were betrayed and attacked in Almiria. Now, Stephen Brightflame leads his army's depleted forces against the Hooded Phantom and his monsters in an attempt to take back the capital and end the war. *Battle for the Kingdom* culminates in a battle of epic scale the whole series has been building towards. Experience the heart-racing final chapters in *The Story of Evil*.

Tony Johnson

Thank you for reading The Story of Evil - Volume IV: The Cursed King. **If you liked this novel, please consider rating and reviewing on www.amazon.com.** I appreciate any feedback, whether positive or negative, because it helps me grow as a writer. Thank you for your support!

Now, here's a special preview from a
chapter in the final volume in Tony
Johnson's *The Story of Evil...*

Chapter 157

The overcast sky matched the gloomy moods of the
people underneath it. Across Almiria, the warriors and
citizens who'd traveled from the kingdom's twelve
provinces to join the army mourned their losses. None
more so than those in the makeshift graveyard visiting
the burial sites of loved ones. It was the first afternoon
people could come and pay their respects now that
everybody had been buried and a stone had been placed,
bearing the name of who lied underneath it.

"It should be just up ahead," Ty softly told Nash as he
escorted the eight-year-old. Copper followed closely
behind. Both the direfox and the Elf had barely left the
boy's side in the three days since the attack by Ironmaul
and his riders.

In solemnity, the three headed past where Andonia's
crew members sat huddled together at Jun-Lei's grave,
grieving the loss of their shipmaster.

*She was a great mother to Kyoko and aunt to Haruto
and Min-Ye,* Ty eulogized. *Ever since we met Jun-Lei in
Port Meris, we noticed the close bond she shared with her
family and how incredible of a person she was. The world
is a darker place without her wisdom and teachings.*

"Here we are," Ty told Nash a few minutes later,
stopping at a fresh mound of dirt. A small rock with the
name "Grizz Grindstone" painted in white letters sat atop

the soil. Five-hundred similar burial sites surrounded them in the field where they stood. "It's not permanent," Ty promised. "After this war ends, we'll get his body moved to Serendale so we can bury him next to your mother and brother."

Instead of responding, Nash remained silent. Ty could see the boy intently staring at Grizz's grave with furrowed eyebrows and a pronounced jaw from gritting his teeth.

"It's okay to be angry, you know," Ty calmly told him. "I was mad too when my parents died. For many years. You work so hard to build a relationship, but then the one you love is ripped away. No warning, no chance to give a proper goodbye. It's so unfair. You lose someone you made memories with, have inside jokes with, and shared your innermost thoughts with-" Ty paused, realizing he was speaking more about losing Shana than Malorek's murder of his parents when he was two years old.

"Are you angry too?" Nash asked, his first words in hours. "Are you mad that Shana and Ms. Latimer are gone?"

Ty glanced down at Nash, touched that Nash cared about his mental state amid mourning his father's death. *Grizz raised you right,* the Elf thought to himself, blinking repeatedly to fight off the tears welling in his eyes.

"Yes, I'm furious," Ty admitted after a moment, refusing to expand on his answer. He didn't want to tell Nash the more bitter details of his grief, agony, and heartache; of the nights he stayed up, replaying the events is his mind to see what he could've done differently to save Shana and Leiana; of how he constantly imagined torturing the traitor that shot them once he figured out who it was. There were even darker thoughts of self-harm Ty tried to keep at bay. He didn't want to mention that he took Nash under his wing not only to help Nash through his grief, but because he knew caring for the eight-year-old would occupy his mind. The busyness allowed Ty to put up a wall, blocking him from dealing with his emotions surrounding Shana's death until the time was right.

"It's important not to direct your anger towards your dad, Alazar, or even yourself," Ty explained. "The only one to blame is Zebulon and those who serve him." He gestured to the many people around them, similarly mourning at the gravesides of their loved ones. "If it wasn't for the dark god's evil influence in this world, you, me, and all these people wouldn't be hurting like we are. War and death exist because of him. Your dad knew eliminating evil brings peace, and he gave his life for that cause."

"I know he did, and I'm not mad at him, I'm mad at whoever betrayed us. I want to know who did this."

So do I, Ty agreed. "Hey, why don't I give you some time alone to talk to your dad?" he suggested.

"What am I supposed to say?"

"I don't know, but I'm sure he's desperate to hear what's been going on, how you've been feeling, everything you're thinking. Thatcher, the man that raised me, often took me to my parents' graves and told me to have a conversation as if they were standing right there in front of me. I always found it therapeutic." Ty stopped and explained the four-syllable word he'd just used in simpler terms, so it'd better make sense to the eight-year-old. "I always found that talking helped me feel better. I hope it does for you too."

Ty left Nash alone and patted the orange-furred direfox on the head as he left the monster behind to protect the boy. He wandered to the far side of the field of graves, to the section where those from Casanovia were buried. There, after searching through name after name, he found Leiana and Shana's graves.

Immediately, Ty began hyperventilating. He dropped to his knees, trying to catch his breath, but no matter how much he gasped for air, none seemed to enter his lungs. Thinking about the fact that Shana's body was beneath him, barely six feet under the ground, created a pit in his stomach that made it even more difficult to breathe.

"I wish you were here with me, Shana," he verbalized his emotions through a shaking, pitchy voice. "We spent so much time in each other's company. You were my best friend, and now I feel so alone."

Ty stayed kneeled for a long while, bereaved at the grave of the woman he loved. He paid no attention to his surroundings or the gray clouds above that sent down occasional sprinkles of rain. It wasn't until he looked up and saw Darren and Lucan afar off that he finally stood.

His brother and nephew stopped a warrior to ask for directions to where Celestial's burials were, but Ty made it to them in time to lead them himself.

"Hi, Uncle Ty," Lucan gave a monotone salutation, the opposite of his usual attitude when he encountered his uncle.

Darren was equally despondent, acknowledging Ty with a simple, "Hey."

Instead of greeting them in the same melancholic state, Ty hugged them each, knowing they needed the embrace as much as he did. "I can take you to Cassandra's grave," he offered. "I passed the area it's in earlier."

Together, the three blonde-haired Elves headed to the plot holding the pregnant woman who they knew as a loving wife, mother, and sister-in-law.

"It's so wrong," Darren broke down the minute they came to the grave. "She was innocent. It should've been us warriors who died, not our wives, not the mothers of children."

"Soon enough, these monsters won't be able to hurt anyone again," Ty choked back the tears that sprung up from seeing both Darren and Lucan so emotional. "We'll put an end to each one involved in the attacks on Celestial, Almiria and all the other cities."

While the three continued mourning, Willis Wheeler stumbled through the field of graves with a wineskin of mead in his hand. Spotting Darren, the red-headed Elf headed directly for the Celestial warrior.

"I know it was you!" he slurred his words, pointing to the elder of the two Canard brothers.

Sensing an unfortunate altercation, Ty grabbed Lucan and placed the five-year-old behind him at the same time Willis chucked the alcohol at Darren, who easily dodged the errant throw.

Ty quickly stepped between the two men and grabbed Willis's shoulder spaulders. He knew he could send electricity through Willis's armor to temporarily paralyze the Serendale warrior, but instead he tried to talk him down.

"Willis, you need to relax. You're intoxicated. This is not the time nor place for whatever issue you have with Darren."

"It is the time and place!" Willis argued, pushing Ty out of the way. "He's the traitor! We can't let him infiltrate us anymore!" He drew his sword and attacked, but his slow, drunken swing gave Darren enough time to draw his own sword and deflect the blade.

If those mourning around them hadn't been disrupted by the shouting, they were now from the clanging of steel on steel. Dozens of people from various spots throughout the hundreds of graves turned to watch the altercation, including Nash. The young Dwarf hopped onto Copper to head to the side of his friend, Lucan, who he noticed was dangerously near the drawn swords.

"What are you talking about?" Darren yelled, taking a defensive stance in case Willis tried to strike him again. He gestured to the grave he stood near. "My wife is dead from this attack! I had no part in it!"

Ty stormed forward and pushed Willis back, sending him falling to the ground. "How do we know it wasn't you who betrayed us?" he roared, defending the accusation against his brother. "Those who are guilty often blame someone else to get the target off their back. You didn't come with us to Port Meris, you stayed behind in Serendale. Maybe you rode off to inform Silas and Malorek."

"How dare you accuse me! I've done nothing but help you and the rest of the elect!"

Before the argument escalated further, five horses galloped up to the tense confrontation. On one side rode the Giant, Commander Ostravaski and the drow, Cryonic. On the other, Naval Commander Ishaan Artazair rode alongside one of the army's only female warrior leaders, General A'ryn Elesora of Stonegate. In the center of them all, Stephen Brightflame rode atop a white horse in his red armor with his blue sash tied around his waist. His stern gaze as he approached foreshadowed his immeasurable anger at what he was witnessing.

"What's going on here?" he shouted, his voice louder than either Darren's, Willis's, or Ty's had been in the prior minute. Noticing the disturbed looks on the faces of people who had their mourning rudely interrupted, his tone grew even angrier as he yelled from his mount down to Darren and Willis. "Sheath your swords! You're disgracing these grounds!

"Artazair," Steve ordered the one-armed Almiria commander, "Would you take these boys away?"

"Of course," Ishaan obeyed immediately. Sensing Steve's seriousness, he forwent his usual quips and wisecracks and ushered Lucan and Nash to follow alongside, away from the graveyard so they wouldn't witness the drama at hand.

"Sir, I beg you to listen to me," Willis pleaded seconds later, once the commander and Copper had led the boys out of earshot. Although he'd known Steve as a friend for months and often called him by his first name, this time Willis addressed the future king more formally since Steve's no-nonsense, ruler-like countenance called for proper etiquette. The Serendale warrior's voice was still slurred and his hand shook while sliding his sword into its sheath, but he successfully delivered his damning accusation against Steve's older brother by stating, "I have reason to believe Darren Canard is the traitor we've been looking for. It's because of his letters we all came to Almiria. We were gathered here to be attacked. We know Silas had twelve Celestial warriors working for him, but we only killed eleven in Casanovia. Darren is the twelfth, and he's been conspiring against us every step of the way."

Again, Darren argued his innocence at the absurdity of the allegations, but a sharp glance from Steve forced him to stop talking in the middle of a sentence. Steve didn't take his eyes off Darren as he spoke loudly for all around to hear. "Willis, you're correct. Some new information came to light confirming Darren's culpability. We have proof he's the one who betrayed us."

Steve ignored Ty crying out, "This can't be true!" and turned to Cryonic. "Bind Darren's hands and lead him up to the castle. Wait for my further instructions there. A'ryn, head to the amphitheater on the west side of the city and set up a beheading block. Ostravaski, I want you to round up everyone mourning in this graveyard and start spreading word to anyone else who's suffered the loss of loved ones to come to the amphitheater tonight. They deserve to know the identity of the man who's brought so much pain. We may not be able to end their grief, but we can give them some semblance of closure."

As Cryonic and the two warrior leaders headed away, Steve dismounted his horse to talk to Ty, who likewise wanted a word.

"Steve, what are you doing? Darren is our brother. This must be some sort of misunderstanding! He wouldn't do this!"

"I know. He's innocent," Steve pulled Ty into a hug to whisper in his ear. "Kari and I found out who the real traitor is this morning. This is all part of a plan to expose them. Follow Willis and me up to the castle. I'll explain everything there."

Acknowledgments

Thank you to my cover artist, Safeer Ahmed, through crowdspring.com.

Thank you to Lana Turner, Karen Cooper, and Becca Johnson, my three beta readers who helped me fine-tune my book and get it ready for publication:

More than anyone, thank you to God. Thank you for sending your son to die for me and take the penalty of my sins. Thank you for allowing me to realize that you are the true purpose and meaning of life. Help me to honor you by trying my best to obey your commands and make the right choices. This world is growing darker every day. Help me to shine with your light, that through me, people may see the beacon of hope they have in your son, Jesus Christ (John 8:12).

There is no one righteous, not even one. - Romans 3:10

Do you not know that the unrighteous will not inherit the kingdom of God? – 1 Corinthians 6:9

Jesus replied, "Very truly I tell you, no one can see the kingdom of God without being born again." – John 3:3

If you declare with your mouth, "Jesus is Lord," and believe in your heart God raised him from the dead, you will be born again. – Romans 10:9

For God so loved the world that he gave his one and only Son, that whoever believes in him should not perish, but have eternal life. – John 3:16

Made in the USA
Middletown, DE
12 December 2021

55343924R00253